Jagged Souls

Miranda Grant

BOOK OF SHADOWS

Madness Behind the Mask
Cursed to be Mine
Tethered Souls
Broken Souls
Jagged Souls

DEATHLY BELOVED

To Have and to Lose
Death Do Us Part
For Better or For Worse
To Love and To Perish

JAGGED SOULS

This is a work of fiction. All characters are products of my imagination and should not be seen as having any more credibility than fake news does. Any resemblance to organizations, locales, or persons living, dead, or stuck in purgatory is entirely coincidental.

authormirandagrant@gmail.com
mirandagrant.com
Facebook: Author Miranda Grant

Edited and published by Writing Evolution.
Cover design and interior artwork by Writing Evolution.

TRIGGER AND CONTENT WARNINGS

Rape.

For those who have been sexually assaulted, I would advise you to read the soft edition and see if you can work your way up to this one. Yes, there is rape in my other books. Yes, there is violent rape in *Madness Behind the Mask*, so you might think you can handle it in here.

But please don't underestimate this warning. The rape in this one is different. It's more real. More mentally draining and way more triggering. And it makes *Madness* read like a fairytale/palette cleanser/mild af book.

So please keep your mental health in mind.

Find the full list of triggers on my website:

https://mirandagrant.com/jagged-souls-triggers
(these are also spoilers)

To all those who one starred Madness Behind the Mask *solely because of the TW list...*

Thank you for all the sales.

But if you thought I needed therapy for writing that one... wait until you find out what's in here.

And to my lovely onions...

I hope you have a therapist on call.

For those jumping into this series here:
It would be best to start with book one in this trilogy:
Tethered Souls *(you don't need to read* Madness Behind the
Mask *or* Cursed to be Mine)*, but if you're adamant about
starting here, here is a quick intro into the world:*

WORLD KNOWLEDGE

THE THREE GANGS OF ST. AUGUSTINE

1. **Shadow Domain** – this is the gang the series follows.
   They are witches who control the portal leading to
   the other Seven Planes. Their Boss is Varius Shadow.
2. **Blood Fangs** – these are the vampires. Their males
   are being forced to breed with the Death Hunt – an
   action that kills them due to the fluids of a werewolf
   being poisonous to them. So they made a pact with
   the Shadow Domain. Their Boss is Aleric Zadar.
3. **Death Hunt** – these are the werewolves. They are
   working hard to kill the other two Families. Their
   Boss/Alpha is Antonio Garcia.

MAGIC SYSTEM

1. Every witch has an innate ability that they are born
   with. The Shadow Family is special, however, due to
   a pact they made with a djinni long ago to give them
   the ability to shift into false shadows (these shadows
   cannot move vertically up surfaces), travel the world
   of the Plane of Monsters, and open a portal to said
   plane. It is extremely rare, but a strong Shadow can
   call forth monsters from their shadows.
2. All magic causes a backwash of energy on the user.
   If the user is too weak or exhausted, that energy can
   seriously hurt them or even kill them.

3. Magic kills the weak regardless of one's age. If you cannot control it, it will turn on you, more so if it's dark magic. For this reason, many witches struggle to carry to term, so they have a saying: *vorum van del mona*, which translates to: the little shit's being fussy. Meaning: the soul of the baby doesn't like the body you're making and would like you to try again. Many believe this to be a good sign that the child will be successful once they do arrive due to them already having high standards.

4. There is 'magic' and then there is 'dark magic.' Dark magic is extremely easy to use (though not control), but requires a larger blood sacrifice than the spell's benefit. Many cases of people vanishing into thin air, such as the Roanoke settlers, can be traced back to this. Sacrifices can be taken from anywhere in the world. They do not have to be beside the witch when the spell is cast. But the witch does not get to choose who is sacrificed. Sometimes, it is loved ones, the very people they are trying to protect.

5. Witches are born with magic in their blood, but they can't cast any spells until they hit their ascension (magical puberty). They can, however, use a wand.

6. Custom wands are normally only used by witches in training. More experienced witches prefer to tattoo runic designs on their bodies to help them control their magic.

7. Premade wands can be used by those who can't use magic, as long as they have reached their ascension. Before this, they don't have enough magic in their blood to activate the wands. AKA: young kids can't use them unless they are witches. All premades are legally required to be triggered by the word, "Iactus." Black market wands don't use this word.

Blood Bond

1. This is a spell only witches can cast. They can bind with either another witch or a non-witch, but all the witches involved have to make a payment.
2. It is very rare for someone to enter a blood bond as the price required for it to work has to be something that will tear the couple apart. So for someone who is over the top jealous, possessive, they might have to allow all their brothers to fuck their girl. Or watch her come on her crush's cock while she screams their name. The payment is unique to each person and is up to the witch to decide what it is. However, if the payment is not harsh enough, then the blood bond will be rejected, and the person who started the blood bond will die unless they kill the other person first.
3. At the end of the blood bond, each person involved will be able to feel the emotions of the other person. They can erect a temporary wall to stop this.
4. They will be tied together forever, in this life and the next, reincarnating with each other.
5. Most couples who blood bond turn into archnemeses within a year due to the payment required.

Mentionable Terms

1. **Human** – all creatures that were created in the gods' images. This includes all supernatural creatures too, as long as they have the ability to take a humanoid form. This term was later taken by Earth humans to mean only them when the portals to the rest of the Seven Planes were cut off, and they forgot about the rest of the worlds out there.
2. **Hybrids** – sups that are a mix of two creatures. These are extremely rare and are victims of extreme

hate crimes. They are often cut out of the womb and then they and their mother are burned or killed in some other fashion. Most do not make it to puberty due to being hunted. Though the archangels haven't officially ruled them to be illegal, they will not stand for an army of them being made.

3. **Portals** – gateways that allow travel to the other Seven Planes. Most were destroyed during the Great Extinction in order to protect Earth humans from being killed. The only one in the U.S. is controlled by the Shadow Domain. It connects Earth to Blódyrió.

4. **Ricks** – short for 'erections'. This is the street name for the incubus drugs that change a person's dick (or gives them one or more), giving them various bells and whistles for their dick(s), such as ridges, cum sacks, the ability to knot or vibrate, etc.

5. **SCU** – Special Crimes Unit. An Earth human group that governs the supernatural world here on Earth.

6. **Sup** – supernatural creature.

7. **Vs** – street name for succubus drugs that change a person's vagina and vulva. They can vibrate, make your belly expand when you're filled with cum, help with pregnancy by storing cum inside for weeks or longer, and more.

8. **Wolf** – short for werewolf.

CHARACTERS

SHADOW BROTHERS (FROM OLDEST TO YOUNGEST)

1. **Varius** – the Boss of the Shadow Domain. His mom cursed him as a child in order to hide the fact he's a hybrid (half-vampire, half-witch). But the curse has now broken, and he's mad with bloodlust.

2. **Leno** – he controls plants in every way, able to draw

out enough poison from a single belladonna berry to kill an entire city. A werewolf blinded him when he was a kid, and now he sees through his dog Krypto. He can also feel and taste what Krypto does.

3. **Khalid** – the reaper of the Family. He's tasked with killing those who turn traitor, including friends and family. He is not really close to anyone due to this. Everyone fears him. He is devoted to his *kira.*

4. **Enoch** – a telekinetic and Ezriel's twin. He will do his best to get out of work, and if he can't, he will complain. But in truth, he's the first to take a watch, the first to sacrifice himself to save his brothers. He's engaged to Stormie Green.

5. **Ezriel** – a telekinetic and Enoch's twin. He loves gaming and would've gone pro if he wasn't devoted to the Family business.

6. **Rudy** – Varius sees him as a son as he practically raised him when their father walked out. He hates violence but is the strongest Shadow brother due to his innate ability to make one's greatest fears real. However, he does not like violence, so he has been given the role of cleaner. He was born mute due to magic hitting Sau while he was in her womb.

7. **Maddox** – the interrogator. He's a shapeshifter, able to change into any person as long as he has enough time to study their DNA. Everyone but his brothers try to avoid him due to fearing him 'taking their face' and the fact that he's a little shit. Often smells of onions.

OTHER MAIN CHARACTERS

1. **Aleric Zadar** – Boss of the Blood Fangs (vampires). He's a full-on psychopath, but gods, is he charming.

2. **Antonio Garcia** – Boss of the Death Hunt (wolves).

After his wife and three pups were murdered by Sau, he's wanting to take revenge on the Shadow Family.

3. **Micha Shadow** – Varius' wife. She's an assassin – or was before Varius purchased her for her womb. Now she's a breedmare – a Shadow term for women who are bred. They're not broodmares because, in Sau's words: "They will respect us more than they do a fucking horse."

4. **Sau Shadow** – the mother of the Shadow Brothers. She was cursed by their father before he died. If she uses any magic, it'll drain her life away. She is the strongest healer on this side of the Atlantic.

MENTIONABLE SIDE CHARACTERS

1. **Dayne Killeen-McCarthy** – Micha's best friend and ex-assassin partner.

2. **Stefaan Black** – Micha's father. Boss of the Blacks, a gang of assassins that only recently gained territory.

3. **Lou Black** – Micha's younger sister. She just turned sixteen, but she's a progeny in demon summoning.

4. **Stormie Green** – Enoch's fiance; arranged marriage, though he's had a crush on her since they were kids and she punched him in the nose for tugging on her hair.

STORYLINE

(TETHERED & BROKEN SOULS SPOILERS)

WHAT JUST HAPPENED:

1. Varius tortured Micha so severely, thinking she was the traitor, that she can no longer use her magic.

2. Antonio ripped out Micha and Varius' little girl from inside Micha's womb. He then ate half of her in front of her mother, discarding the rest of her like

unwanted leftovers.

3. Varius breaks the curse that was stopping him from accessing his magic and vampiric abilities. He now has access to all his hybrid powers.

4. Micha has been kidnapped by Antonio and has been thrown into a room to be gang raped by a bunch of werewolves.

ONE

HIM

"Where is my fucking wife!?" I lunge for Maddox, not caring that he's my brother. All I want is to see him bleed beneath my knuckles as he tells me *where she is.*

My nostrils are flaring. My heartbeat is running wild. I breathe in deep, focusing on one particular scent that is fucking everywhere. My wife's blood is sprayed liberally across the floor and walls of our family home. But I can't smell her raspberry-and-cream body wash.

I can't hear her cracked voice calling for me. Can't hear her mourning our baby, who now lies dead in the palm of my left hand. I can't hear her screaming. Can't hear her rage or pain. Or her vows to kill the fucker responsible. To kill *me* for having left her alone with only one bodyguard and my mother.

I can't sense her heartbeat anywhere in this house.

Because her blood is here. Her blood is here in fucking bucketloads. But everything that makes her *her* is gone.

"Fuck!" Maddox tries to flee, triggering a hunting instinct inside of me. It boils through my veins until my teeth ache and bloodlust fills me, coaxing me to feed, to *kill*.

To lose myself in the violence until I kill everyone in this fucking city so there's no one left to hide my wife.

Grabbing my brother by the throat with one hand, I slam him into a wall. A low growl builds in my chest as I lean in.

I know the fucker likes my wife.

I know she likes him.

If he's fucking hiding her, if her absence is nothing more than an elaborate plan to steal her from me, to get me to believe she's been kidnapped by the Boss of the Death Hunt rather than by him, I will. *Kill. Him.*

"Where is she?" I roar.

His dark-brown eyes widen. Maddox holds his hands up. "V, I'm not –"

I cut him off with a snarl, not wanting to listen to his lies. One brother has already betrayed me. I can't trust any of them.

Especially not the one in front of me. Maddox likes to play with people like they're toys. He keeps them locked up so he can break them. So he can have fun with them. He's a twisted little psycho.

"Did you have fun with Dayne and Bambi?" I growl as my fingers tighten around his throat. "Have you kidnapped my wife to have more fun with her?" I can smell his panic now, can feel the terror beating away in his pulse. His guilt is so clear across his fucking face. He grabs at my hand, trying to peel me off his neck. But my fingers only tighten. My eyes don't leave his. He should've known I would do anything to get her back.

He gasps, panic in his eyes.

His heartbeat starts to thrash just like his legs.

And still I keep squeezing.

"What the fuck, Varius?" Leno shouts from further down

the hall, having just entered the scene, alongside Krypto and Ezriel. My senses push out in half a second, clocking where the rest of my brothers are through the beat of their hearts.

Enoch is in his bed upstairs, half-dead but stable. Rudy is in a chair beside him, and Khalid isn't back yet, having left with Mother and Aleric some time ago.

But they might be back at any moment, and once they are, I'll be too greatly outnumbered. A trapped animal with no way to save my wife. I need to end this *now.*

Baring my teeth, I yank Maddox forward only to slam him back into the wall. His head *cracks.* His eyes roll.

"Fuck! Ez, get him off!" Leno shouts.

"I can't! His entire makeup has chang–"

Pivoting, I throw Maddox at Ezriel. I can't let him get a lock on me. His telekinesis can stop me in my tracks.

And I cannot stop until I find her. Save her. Apologize for having failed to protect her and our daughter, who still lies protected in my left hand. I will never leave her again.

Ezriel ducks to avoid being hit by Maddox even as Leno's vines shoot forward to catch him. Hidden by Maddox's bulk, I dart forward, then drop into a slide halfway there. Ez's eyes widen at the sight of me barreling towards him.

"Oh, shit!"

As he dodges to the side, I twist to my right to follow him. Placing all my weight on that hand, I swing my left leg up and kick him in the face. His head snaps to the side. My foot sets down beside my hip, and I kick out like a donkey with my other. He flies back with a groan.

Shifting my attention, I lunge for Leno.

He opens his mouth, words forming in their infancy, but I tackle him around the torso. My shoulder slams into his solar plexus, and all that leaves his lips is a painful gasp. The back of his head hits the ground *hard.* Maddox falls to the floor behind me as Leno loses control of his vines.

Raising a fist, I go to slam it into his face for a knock-out blow, but a large furry body barrels into me first. Teeth latch around my forearm. Krypto snarls and growls as he drags me away. He shakes his head. He bites me deeper, but I can barely feel the pain over my bloodlust.

Snarling, I yank my arm forward and headbutt Krypto in the face. The dog yelps as he releases me, but before I can backswing him in the jaw, cracking it and taking him out of the fight, a vine wraps around my right arm and yanks it across my chest.

As Leno starts to drag me away, I twist on the ground and hook my legs around Ezriel's. He was just starting to regain his feet, and as I jerk mine, he topples towards me.

He reaches out instinctively to catch himself. His hands land on both sides of my head. I twist towards the right and bite down hard on his wrist, tearing through his tendon. Blood spurts into my mouth, filling me with an explosion of magical power and ecstasy.

But with a feral growl, I refuse to swallow. Despite every part of me urging me to feed on him until he's dry, to sate the Craving setting fire to my veins, I refuse. He is not my wife, and I will not feed from anyone but her.

So as Ezriel screams, I keep rolling, forcing his arm to collapse. As he starts to fall fully on top of me, I strike out twice with my left elbow, moving with hybrid speed. The first strike to his ribs breaks a bone. The second one impales it into his lung. Fuck! It just missed his heart.

He gasps as I finish rolling him beneath me, his flesh still between my teeth, his blood still pouring down my lips. But just as I'm about to rip Ezriel's radial artery apart with my teeth, I catch the scent of an angel.

And everything fades – quieting, pinpointing until all that's left is the smell of *her.*

My wife.

Not just her blood, which already paints this hall.

But *her.*

Her raspberry-and-cream body wash.

The mix of mint ice-cream and pickles, a craving she's taken to in her pregnancy.

The particular scent of sweat that covers her pillow.

All the little smells that make up Micha fucking Shadow.

My wife is home.

Tears burning my eyes, I release Ezriel and stagger to my feet. I turn, chasing her scent, and find her stumbling into the house through a hole in the hallway wall.

There are bruises on her face and cuts on her hands and arms – defensive wounds from fighting off an attacker. Her brown eyes land on me, so bright with pain and fear and a need to be held – a weakness she rarely ever shows. Blood pours from a hole in her stomach, right where Bambi used to be, curled up and protected. Both her hands press over it as if she can still protect our little girl.

But she can't stop the blood seeping down her fingers. Can't relieve the weight in my left hand as I hold what her womb should be holding.

"He... he..." Her face twisting in pain, she stumbles to her knees, her hands still clasped protectively over her stomach.

My heart stops as I stare at her, wanting so badly to believe she's real. But my paranoia spikes, and I turn back around to find Maddox. If the little shit's turned into her –

But no.

He's there, lying on the floor, bleeding from his cracked skull.

Micha is real, and she is home.

With a choked cry, I run towards my wife. I don't care that she's most definitely a trap. I know she couldn't have escaped on her own, which means Antonio wants her here. But whatever poison he has laced her with, whatever dark spell he has had his witch cast on her, we will figure it out together. Right now I just need her in my arms.

Dropping down beside my wife, I pull her into my lap.

She cries into my shoulder. I wrap my arms around her and breathe in the scent I thought I would never smell again. I listen to her heartbeat. I feel the trembling of her body. I smell the richness of fresh blood...

Then the full force of the Craving hits me in the stomach, and I jerk forward, sinking my teeth into her throat.

TWO

HIM

My wife screams, panicked and terrified. She has just been tortured, had our baby girl ripped from her womb, and Antonio did who knows what to her before she escaped.

I know she can't suffer any more trauma. I know she'll die if she loses any more blood.

But I can't tear my new fangs out of her.

Her blood slides down my throat, an orgasmic taste that explodes on my tongue. I might have tortured her so badly she can no longer control her magic, but it still runs through her veins. Still makes it so fucking heady to consume. My senses expand until she becomes overwhelming. Her taste, her scent, the feel of her body against me blocks out all else. But it isn't enough. I pull her closer with a groan.

It isn't enough!

"Varius, stop!" she screams as she beats me with her fists, but her blows are weak, her limbs too drained of energy. Fear barrels into my chest, knocking my heart up into my throat. I know I'm killing her. I know I'm hurting her. I'm reminded of all the pain she suffered after I raped her, the last time I was lost to this madness. How she cut my mark from her skin, how she didn't want anything to do with me. I betrayed her then, and I'm betraying her now.

And it's killing me.

I want to stop.

I want to soothe her.

But my fingers dig into her skin, holding her still as she tries to pull away. I'm a slave to the bloodlust inside of me, can't control my body even as my own mind rails against its binds, begging it to listen.

"Stop! Varius... stooooop! Help me! Maddox, heeeeeelp!"

I cry out against her throat, tears falling down my cheeks as my own wife is forced to beg for the aide of another man. But Maddox is still knocked out cold. Leno is helping Ezriel. There's no one left to stop me.

And so I feed on the broken body of my little monster as she bleeds out through the hole in her stomach. As I press Bambi against her, squishing our little baby between us, I drink until my wife is dead.

With her finally drained dry, I pull back. I look down at her limp body in horror, and the full weight of what I've done rips an unholy noise from my throat.

I cradle her to me, screaming and crying and begging the gods to bring her back.

She came back to me, and I killed her.

She escaped from Antonio, only to die at home.

I climb to my feet, screaming for Sau.

For Louise Warner.

For any healer in this fucking town.

Any necromancers.

But no one comes to help me.

I spin around to face my brothers, to beg them to go get Mom, to please get somebody to save my wife, but when I turn, I find the hall full of line-dancing goats.

I scream as I backpedal, squeezing Micha tighter against me. They're dancing in sync, moving sideways, their arms lifting at the elbows, then dropping again as they advance. Their soulless, demonic eyes latch onto me as their heads cock to the side in small jerks that crack their necks. They keep twisting and twisting and twisting until their heads are upside down. Sweeping their arms out, they part the air in front of them and slide forward, their hooves scratching across the floor. Their heads shoot back upright, then lean further back so they can stare at me down their noses.

But they're not the cute goats I've conditioned myself to be afraid of for Rudy. These are half-decaying monstrosities, with matted hair and wriggling maggots. Flesh falls free, revealing rancid muscles and infected bone. One's eyeball falls out as it comes for me, but it just sticks out its tongue and catches it, pulling it into its mouth for a wet *squelch*. Blood bursts out from between its teeth, as does a half-eaten maggot, which lands in its goatee and stays there.

"Rebeccaaaaa," they sing as they creep closer, tapping their hooves on the floor. "We're comiiiiiing for yoooooou."

The fuckers have always used names that aren't mine. I fell for it when I was a kid, thinking they weren't after me, that I could just stay still, and they wouldn't get me. When they danced past me, I thought I was right, but it turned out, they just wanted to stab me in the back with their horns.

So I know better now than to stay still.

But to fight, I will have to let her go, and my heart is breaking at the thought of it. At the moment, she is still warm. When I finish killing the goats and get back to her, she might be cold.

"Fucking hel, Leno! What the fuck were you thinking?" Maddox screams, his voice ringing far in the distance.

"I thought it would calm him down!"

"It's fucking *Varius*, bruh! He's obviously going to have a bad trip!"

"Well, *sorry* for –"

"Shut up and help Micha!" I shout as I finally find the strength to lay her down on the ground. When I stand, my eyes go to my left palm, and a cry of pure agony rips its way out of my lungs. I fall to my knees as I look at my little girl.

Bambi lies squished against my fingers, so flattened that there's no identifying features left. She's just a red and black blob of lost kisses and hugs and love. And I did that to her. I lost myself to the bloodlust and destroyed the only part of her I have left.

Screaming, I stagger to my feet. I need to kill something, to make the world as destroyed as I feel. Tenderly wiping Bambi across my heart, I meet the goats head-on.

One lowers its head to impale me, but I grab hold of its left horn as I pivot out of the way. I snap my foot into the goat next in line, kicking it back. But my foot sinks into its chest, and the broken ribs cut up my leg. Gritting my teeth, I yank myself free and twist around on my other foot. I swing the goat I'm holding by the horn into the second beast.

Flecks of rotten skin with tufts of matted fur drop to the floor, followed by wriggling maggots. I set my leg down, but as soon as it takes my weight, I nearly buckle. The pain is nothing, though, compared to the horror I see crawling out of the wounds. Maggots and worms and cockroaches and centipedes. And everywhere they crawl inside me, a black disease weaves its way through my veins, visible beneath the skin.

As they start eating me alive from the inside out, I pull out one of my many knives and start hacking at my leg. If they reach my heart, I'm dead.

"Dammit, Leno, pull him the fuck out!"

"I'm trying!"

A hoof slams into my hand, cracking the little bones. I drop the knife, but I twist and grab it with my other hand. Almost as soon as I do, though, I'm throwing it on a feral scream. Four goats have run past me and are now dancing on Micha's corpse, stomping her into the ground.

My knife embeds itself into one of their shoulders, but it doesn't stop them at all. Doesn't even slow them down. I lunge in their direction, but strong hands grab me from behind, the goat who kicked me having taken advantage of my distraction.

I scream as I pull against him, my eyes on the still form of my wife as they beat her viciously. There's no more blood left in her to puddle around her. I killed her, and they're desecrating her. If they damage her enough, not even a necromancer can bring her back.

So with every sickening *crack* of her bones, with every hard stomp of a hoof, I fight against the goat holding me back. But every time I manage to rip free, I'm grabbed again by another beast.

"I'll fucking kill you!" I scream, my voice mirroring the cracks erupting across my heart. The goats are merciless as they stomp on her. They break open her head and send bits of her brain flying. "Nooooo! Nooooo! Leave her aloooone!"

A goat steps in front of me, its two demonic eyes bearing into my soul. Grabbing both sides of my head, it wrenches my gaze up to the ceiling. I can feel the insects crawling through my skin, eating their way up my leg and burrowing deeper inside of me.

"Varius! Varius, listen to me!"

The goat towers above me, larger than any of the others. The ceiling stretches to accommodate him. He stares into my eyes, sucking my soul out through his gaze. Then he opens his mouth over mine and spews forth a fountain of maggots fat with the flesh of another.

They fall onto my face, then wriggle their way inside my

nose and under my eyes. I struggle against the goat's grip, but he's holding me too tight. I gag, choking on the maggots crawling down my throat, but when I try to cough them up, more of them just fall in past my lips.

"You're okay," a voice says, soft yet firm. "It isn't real, Varius. Come back to us."

But Micha's body is calling to me. She's just there, and I need to save her.

But the bugs are suffocating me. They're eating their way through my body, wriggling inside my lungs and limbs. I can feel them everywhere, and it's only a matter of time before they make it to my heart.

"Micha needs you, Varius."

I know! I'm trying to get to her!

Desperation claws at me. My heart is beating hard and fast. I can still hear her body being crushed under dancing hooves. The maggots haven't made it to my ears yet, and I can make out every break of bone, every *pop* of an organ.

The goat spews out more insects. Centipedes, spiders, cockroaches. They all crawl across my face and through whatever holes they can find.

"Listen to me, Varius. Antonio has Micha, and we need your bond to find her. Whatever you're experiencing, it isn't real. Leno has drugged you. Now come back to us so we can find your wife."

I choke on tears and bugs, feeling their legs and hard exoskeletons as they swarm down my throat.

"Come on, Varius. You're too much of a control freak to lose to this..."

"No, I'm just too amazing with my pla–"

"Leno!" Maddox snaps.

"I'm done! I'm done. Jeez. Hold his head back. I need to pour all of this down his throat."

"Fucking hel. Can't you just puff some pollen in his face again?"

"No. Now hold him."

The goat's fingers press into my face, cracking apart my cheeks and jaws. I choke on suffocated screams as he opens me up further to his poison. The bugs crawl all inside of me. The goats dance faster on my wife.

Her intestines and brain matter spew across the floor. I reach towards her in a pathetic attempt to hold her as I die.

Then suddenly, the bugs are gone.

The goat in front of me turns into Maddox, while the goats behind me shift into Leno's vines. The pain in my leg is still sharp and prominent, but it isn't from decaying flesh being feasted on by cockroaches. It's from my attempt to dig them out, the cuts of my knife having gone deep. Blood pours from a dozen wounds, and I'm suddenly aware that I'm still starving.

My eyes drop to my brother's throat...

"How are you feel–" he starts.

"Maddox, get away from him!" Mother shouts from down the hall, having just returned with Aleric and Khalid. With them is a dark-skinned woman called Stormie, and I know she was brought in by Mother solely to control me. She's a shielder, and if she wraps me in her magic, there will be nothing I can do to escape, but she won't take Maddox too. Won't leave him with me to kill.

I lunge forward, and my youngest brother falls back, his feet rushing beneath him to keep him standing. The vines around my arms, legs, and torso all tighten. I roar as I strain against them, the bloodlust urging me to kill them all.

Khalid steps forward, a shield over his face. He told me what would happen if my curse broke and I attacked our brothers. He loves me, but he is the reaper, and it is his duty to protect this family.

But he isn't the one who gets to me first.

With a cocky smile, Aleric phases and lands directly in front of me. He grabs me by the neck. When he phases again, we appear in the sky above.

The cold air shocks me into compliance. The wind rips across my face, forcing me to narrow my eyes against the burn. I start to tumble, the g-force building.

As the vampire vanishes, I fall towards the Earth alone.

THREE
HER

"You are going to die in here, Micha," the Boss of the Death Hunt purrs. I'm standing inside an old cafeteria with fourteen men facing me while he stands behind the closed door behind me. A small open window at the top of it allows him to talk freely.

"But first I'm going to breed you. You will be raped until your body is broken and torn, until your vagina is ripped to your ass, and you are down on your knees, begging me to forgive you for being a Shadow whore."

"I will never beg," I say as I scan for a weapon. But there is nothing in here except worn, grubby tables and benches too big for me to wield. Perhaps there is something behind the glass counter at the back, but I'll never get there before the men grab me.

"Oh, you will." He chuckles. "Maybe not today... Maybe not tomorrow or the week after. Maybe not even this year or the next..."

My blood runs cold at his promise of time. I try to tell myself Varius will save me before then, that he'll burn the world down to get me back, but he can't feel the blood bond. He has no idea where I am. Antonio brought me here via a teleportation circle. We could be anywhere in the world if his witch is good enough.

"Eventually," Antonio says, "you'll scream for me to kill you. But for now... I just want to hear you scream."

On that signal, the men rush forward.

They move jerkily, their legs twisting at awkward angles. Their hips clicking in ways they are not supposed to. One moves almost sideways, his bent torso speaking of a spine that isn't right. Isn't *human*.

They leap onto the tables and scramble towards me on their hands and knees, crawling and jumping from one table to the next. They move like spiders, like centipedes, like all the creepy crawlers I was terrified of as a kid.

Realizing they've been experimented on, treated like lab rats without mercy, I take a step back in horror.

They're his own men... His own Family...

So what the hel is he going to do to me?

The one in front looks at me with the eyes of a sadist. They are nothing but dark-violet pits of promised pain, like he *needs* to hurt something to stop his own agony. And the only thing he can hurt in this prison is me.

My heart jolts, but I don't follow it. I stand my ground and curl my fists. I raise both my arms, ready to fight for my life as he barrels towards me.

Antonio's laughter increases behind me, and my stomach churns, then hardens.

Then drops like a fucking stone.

Because I know why he's laughing, and I'm trying not to let it infect me.

But the fourteen men in front of me aren't just *men*.

They're werewolves.

And I'm nothing but a witch without magic, with zero hope of fighting them all off.

"You'll want to take this," Antonio says lightheartedly. A second later, a small vial of pink liquid flies past me, tossed through the window of the locked door behind me. I don't turn my head to watch it. I don't even glance at it with my eyes. And I sure as hel don't move to catch it even though I know it will save me from so much pain because what he's tossed me is a V, a succubus drug that'll alter the size of my vagina so I can take their monster cocks without damage.

But fuck Antonio and his goals.

Fuck taking a potion that'll allow me to be bred without dying – their werewolf cocks too big to fit without killing me.

He ate my baby in front of me, and I will die before I give him another to eat.

Not that he'll let me die. Not today. Not before I'm bred.

I will merely be brutalized until I'm at death's door. Their cocks will rip apart my vagina, their thrusts will bludgeon my organs, and their weight will snap my spine as they lie on top of me while their heavy hands break my arms and legs as they pin me down.

My life will fade from internal bleeding or maybe from choking. Then I'll be healed, the potion will be forced down my throat, and I will be thrown back in here for round two.

I'm not naive enough to think my defiance will make any difference to being gang-raped, that I can change anything by fighting back, but fuck. Antonio. Up. His. Arrogant. Ass.

So I let the vial hit the vinyl floor just in front of me. It bounces, then skids under the table Sadist has just reached. The darkness in his violet eyes ignites, and he lunges for me while still in his human form.

Grabbing his arms as he reaches for me, I pull him with me. I fall backwards into a roll. Hitting the floor, I kick him hard in the chest, using the momentum to throw him over my head. He crashes into the locked door behind me, but he doesn't cry out in pain. Doesn't make any sounds at all. Jumping to my feet, I dash forward, meeting the other men head-on.

My focus sharpens on two of them: one with a dozen scars across his face and shaggy black hair, the other with white skin and blond hair cropped short. They are on the floor, and they're howling in agony, their bones snapping, their skin tearing as they shift into their werewolf forms.

This is the only time they're vulnerable.

I dart between the tables. The men are only a few yards in front of me. Scar's head snaps up on a growl as he drags himself onto his hands and knees. Agony brightens his blue eyes as black fur sprouts all over his body, but I know he can't fight back. Not while his nerves are breaking off and reconnecting, while his tendons, muscles, and ligaments are being ripped away from bone. The shift of a wolf is a brutal experience, a curse from the gods over an ancient sin.

But for me, it's a chance to grab a weapon.

A chance to possibly buy myself enough time for Varius to save me.

Jumping sideways into the air, my eyes focused on the bone sticking out of Scar's left shoulder, I kick off a nearby table. Cartwheeling over him, I wrap my fingers under the head of it and grip tight.

Crack!

His flesh rips. His tendons tear completely. And I land on the bench opposite with his bloody humerus in my hand. As he howls with venomous rage, I spin around and slam the middle of the bone onto the edge of the table. My weapon splinters in two just as a man lunges at me from across the table.

Dropping into the splits, I press my forehead to my knee. The newcomer flies over me and crashes into the howling wolf behind me. I roll beneath the table, tucking my legs to end up in a crouch, then scramble out the other side.

Another man stands a few strides away, frozen in shock. The fucker clearly isn't used to his prey fighting back. I'm up and on him before his eyes have even finished widening, stabbing both of the bones into the sides of his neck. The jagged edges cut deep. He gurgles as I rip them free. Bright red streams spray out in two high-pressured fountains, his carotid arteries severed.

I slash the bones across his neck as he drops to his knees, and his head tilts back. The flesh gapes open, the muscles no longer intact enough to hold it. I turn towards Scar and the blond man beside him, hoping to kill them before they can finish their change.

Jumping, I roll across the table I ducked under earlier, knee Scar in the face as he tries to stand, then throw one of my 'knives' like a spear at Blondie's face. He can't move out of the way, and it slices through his eye and into his brain. As he drops dead, I grab a bone sticking out of Scar's leg and yank as hard as I can.

He screams, but the bone doesn't rip free this time. A blur on my right forces me to leave it as I turn to meet my newest attacker. I dodge his wild swings but only barely, his twisted body making it hard for me to predict where his fists will land.

Another man appears in the row beside us, ready to climb over the table and help his mate. I kick the bench hard and slide the whole fucking thing into him. It does nothing to hurt him, but it trips him up and buys me enough time to deal with my first attacker.

Ducking beneath his arms, I stab him rapidly with my bone-knife. I'm not aiming for a specific spot, not trying to drop him with one nicely timed strike. I'm stabbing hard and fast, hitting anywhere I can get, and letting his blood pour out like a flipped hourglass.

A blare of warning erupts across the hairs on the back of

my neck. I can feel another attacker rushing towards me, but before I can twist around, Hourglass punches me in the face with a meaty fist. My head snaps to the left as I'm tackled forward. I stab the hairy arms wrapped around my torso, but the moment he releases me, a punch from a third man rattles my brain. I stagger into a table as I try to shake the stars free, but someone grabs me by the back of the neck, lifts me high into the air, and then slams me face-first onto the floor.

The air rushes out of my lungs. My teeth feel like they've been embedded into my skull or perhaps down my throat, choking me, and my brain feels like it's exploded behind my eyes. My weapon is wrenched out of my hand. I'm vaguely aware of being lifted, turned around, and my back slammed onto a table. My legs dangle over the edge. And then I'm gasping, my eyes shooting open wide as both my makeshift knives are plunged through both my wrists.

I clench my jaw, refusing to cry out in pain, refusing to show any weakness to these assholes. But tears burn behind my eyes, and screams rail at the cage inside my chest with the knowledge of what's about to happen. I turn my head to my left to find Sadist peering down at me, one hand on the bone he just stabbed into my arm.

My heart rate kicks up at the cruel, twisted promise in his violet eyes.

Releasing the bone, he rounds the table to my feet. I kick out at him as he approaches, but he just grabs my knees and forces my legs apart. He steps between them as the other men crowd around us.

Terror flashes through me, but I'm trying so hard to fight it, to stop it from freezing me where I lay.

"I'm not going to shift when I fuck you," Sadist says. "I'm going to drag this out for hours." He leans down and licks his way up my throat. When he gets to my cheek, I jerk my head towards him. My teeth chomp down around his tongue like it's a steak. The taste of copper explodes in my mouth as he jerks back, but I know I have only managed to bite off the tip; the piece of severed flesh is small enough for me to swallow.

He sneers down at me. A crazy smile spreads across his lips. Blood pours down his chin as he sticks his mutilated tongue out. "Good. You swallow like a whore," he says, his words only slightly slurred.

Straightening, Sadist moves his attention to my legs. He has his hands still on my knees, pinning them to the edge of the table. I can't kick out at him. Can't defend myself.

My heart rate starts going wild.

He looks at me with a smirk, imagining no doubt how he's about to have me.

My body starts to shake, and I can't stop it.

Can't stop the terror.

The disgust.

The shame.

He's going to rape me, defile me, *dirty* me.

And I can't stop him.

He trails his hands up from my knees to my hips, then down to my ass. He squeezes me as he presses his hard cock against my pussy.

I've never felt more helpless.

More afraid.

There's a difference between being raped and fighting for your life.

A knife against your skin is a clear attack, and it tells you that death is the darkest outcome. We can't fight off death, so we don't blame ourselves when it comes.

But a cock...

A cock makes you feel like you did something *wrong,* like you made the wrong choice, trusted the wrong person, walked home the wrong way.

A cock makes you feel *dirty* and dehumanized. It tells

you there is something coming that's worse than death.

A thousand thoughts ram into me – if I should've tried to stab the guy who tackled me in the face rather than in his arms, if I should've dodged left instead of right, if I should have turned the knives on myself and left them with only a corpse to rape.

Or maybe I should've made a better decision all the way back in the Shadow home. When I should've screamed for Sau. When I should've hid in the basement with my little sister and cowered with the others. Or maybe I should have run after Varius tortured me so badly I lost my magic. Or perhaps when I first learned I was to be sold to him...

How many bad decisions did I make to get here?

How many different choices could have saved me?

How many –

Don't!

I grit my teeth.

Force those thoughts down.

Pulling on my training as an assassin, I keep my mind sharp, keep it above the fear and shame wanting to drag me beneath the waves.

You are a Black, I remind myself.

And a fucking Shadow.

And if I can get them to hurt me badly enough, Antonio might step in to save my precious womb.

So I close my eyes briefly and breathe out.

He won't let me die today.

As Sadist grabs my shirt and starts ripping it in half, I snap my eyes open. Determined and prepared for the pain, I rip my right arm up as fast and as hard as I can. It shoots up a couple of inches, agony flaying all the nerves in my wrist. I slide up the bone-knife pinning me to the table, but then my flesh slams into the head of the bone, and I scream as the pain increases.

There is a brief second of resistance as my momentum

meets the weight of the embedded knife. Sadist's head snaps towards my arm, watching it move with a mixture of both shock and lust.

And then the bone is being ripped out of the table. My arm is flying free. Arcing through the air, in front of Sadist's face. He sneers down at me, but then his eyes widen as I wrap my ankles around the back of his neck and yank his head towards me. I swing my arm back the way it came, and the sharp slice of the bone still sticking out of me stabs him in the cheek.

With a wet slurp, it explodes out the other side.

He screams, and I kick him off me. I twist towards my left, hoping to get my other arm free. But the fingers on my right hand won't move, the tendons severed, and too many hands are already reaching for me, grabbing me in vice-like grips and yanking me back down.

The bone-knives are ripped from my arms and tossed aside, replaced by heavy palms I can't use as weapons. More men grab my thrashing feet, and although I get a good few kicks in, they eventually wrestle me down. They yank my legs apart, and Scar steps between them in his werewolf form, one arm hanging loose, no bone to give it shape.

But before he can touch me, he's shoved aside by Sadist as he regains his composure, the promise in his violet eyes burning bright.

My pulse skitters wildly in my throat, but I meet his gaze without cowering. His eyes drop to my exposed chest as blood pours from his mouth.

"Tourniquet her wounds," he snaps, his words escaping through the two holes in his cheeks. "We don't want her bleeding out and getting off that easy, now do we boys?"

There are harsh grunts and snarls of agreement. Then my arms are wrapped, the pressure applied, and a weight settles on my chest, making it hard to breathe.

For there is a difference in fighting for your life...

It isn't as dirty as being raped.

FOUR

HER

Sadist grabs both sides of my shirt and finishes ripping it clean away. My breasts are too small to bother wearing a bra, and he exposes me completely.

"Not even fucking worth it," the man holding my right arm spits.

"Wait until they get erect," Sadist purrs. "Then you can watch the disgust in her eyes."

He pinches both of them in between his fingers, and I jerk against his touch, praying that my body doesn't react, that it doesn't betray me like he said it would. But I can feel the goosebumps rising across my skin, the sudden sensation in my chest as the fear roils deep in my stomach.

Laughing, he releases me, then grabs the top of my pants. I twist my hips from side to side, but I'm not trying to get him off. I know that's futile. Know there's not a damn thing I can do to stop this from happening.

So the reason I'm fighting back is to turn him on even

more. I want to make his dick so fucking hard that he comes quickly inside of me.

And just that thought alone, that simple admittance that I *am* teasing him fills me with so much disgust, my stomach revolts up my throat.

I don't want this.

I don't want him touching me.

I don't want him thrusting his cock inside my pussy.

But I don't have a choice.

It's being stolen from me.

My body no longer mine but *theirs.*

Now all I can do is survive.

To hopefully reduce the time they rape me so that when they break my body, when they tear apart my vagina and leave bruises on my arms and legs from pinning me down or smacking me around, that they don't break my mind too.

A small solace in a sea of pain.

But it's all the control I have left.

So I fight back. I yank my legs, trying to free them from the iron grips holding them apart. I twist my hips to make it as difficult as possible for him to undo the button on my pants and pull down the zip. I buck when he steps out from between my thighs. I twist some more when they shove my legs together and yank down my pants. As they work to get them and my shoes off, I kick out as hard and as fast as I can. But I only manage to rip one leg free and slam my heel into one smug face before they grab me again.

Now I'm spread eagle, my shirt hanging down my sides, my chest bare, and only my underwear covering my pussy. I breathe heavily, tears hot behind my eyes, pain shooting up my arms despite the numbness of the tourniquets and the pressure of the men holding me down.

Stepping between my legs again, Sadist runs his hands up from my ankles to my thighs. Goosebumps trail in his wake, like acid burning across my skin, his touch a disease I can feel burrowing its way into my bones, into the very essence of who I am.

I was born into a family of assassins that were called to do the dirtiest of deeds. I have violence to my name and sins etched into every tattoo covering my skin.

I was beaten until I could withstand torture.

I have kept secrets I would've been all too happy to spill because I am a fighter.

Because I'm a fucking Black.

Because I'm a fucking Shadow. Wife to Varius Shadow himself.

But right now…

In this moment, in this pinpoint of time that has warped my world to fit inside its vice, all I am is a victim.

Just a *thing* for these men to use.

Not even human.

Sadist's fingers slip under the top of my underwear, and as the entirety of me wants to recoil, to sink into the table and flee from his touch of disease, he tears the cotton apart.

The rip of it resonates in my soul, terrifying and final. My last poor, pathetic defense is torn away, leaving me bare and helpless.

Reducing me to nothing but a shell of shame.

And I freeze.

Despite my want to fight back, despite convincing myself it's still a way I can take control, still the 'best option' when I know doing so won't get me killed because Antonio wants me alive…

I can't.

My limbs are frozen.

My lungs are frozen.

Every fucking atom inside of me is frozen.

So even when Sadist looks down at my pussy and laughs, I can't find the strength to keep fighting. If he had a knife… if I was being held down to be murdered, butchered on this table like a pig, I'd still be full of rage and spitting fire.

But instead, it's a finger he pushes against my flesh. A precursor to his cock – weapons I can survive if I just relax and don't fight back. And that betrayal from my own body, that instinctive need to survive even when I want to go out fighting, when I want to resist so I can scream I didn't want this, that I tried everything I could to stop it... That betrayal makes me hate myself.

Makes me feel dirty in my own skin, my soul blackened even beneath the touch of his poison.

So as Sadist traces a finger over the tattoo on my pussy, I don't fight him.

I can't.

I just lie here, the survival instinct forcing me still.

"Well, fucking hel. Look at this, boys," Sadist purrs. "This whore's the property of Varius Shadow."

There's a sudden hush in the cafeteria. The grips on my hands and feet unconsciously loosen. One of the men not holding me down even steps back with a nervous energy, and a flare of hope ignites within me.

"Maybe we shouldn't be so rough –" one starts.

"If Varius finds this place –" another says.

"He won't," Sadist snaps, irritated that no one is sharing in his fun.

And now I laugh, relief pouring through me and making me sound mad. "He will," I promise them. "Because we're fucking bonded, and he can feel exactly where I am." I lift my head up off the table as I look at Sadist, but I don't strain against the men holding my arms. Not yet. "He's coming for me even now, and when he gets here, he's going to take every last one of you back home with us." I shift my gaze to the two men holding my feet as I let my words penetrate the heavy air.

"The ones who helped me will be healed from whatever Antonio did to you. You know his mother can do it." There's another ripple around the table. More hope flares through me even as Sadist's glare gets harder, the fury in his eyes burning bright. I hold his gaze head-on. "But anyone who fucking hurts me will be tortured far worse than whatever you do to me. Whatever Antonio's done to you already."

The silence is crushing.

The fear so palpable, it makes me want to weep.

I'm going to be okay. I'm going to make it through this.

But then the door opens.

And I don't need to turn my head to know Antonio has just walked in.

FIVE
HER

The men immediately tighten their grips on me, the fear of their own Boss keeping them in line. But Antonio's mere presence isn't enough to jolt them into action when Varius' wrath will be coming for them if they do.

As Sadist moves aside, Antonio takes his place between my legs. If he were human or a witch, my eyes would be on his hands, checking for weapons, for the upcoming strike. But he is a werewolf, and he doesn't need his hands to deal damage. His teeth will work just as well.

So my eyes stay on his, meeting his approach with false bravado. I sneer at him, injecting laughter and certainty into my words. "He's going to kill your entire Family."

"They're already dead," he says as he passes something to Sadist. My eyes dart down to their hands to see what it is. I jerk on a scream, now fighting like a hellcat, violent curses and threats spewing from my lips.

Laughing, Sadist raises the phone.

The holds on my arms and legs suddenly lift as the men step back, away from the angle of the camera. A few turn to hide their faces, and I clock them even in my wild fury, in my raw desperation to escape. If they're hiding their faces, that means they fear identification; it means they might have something or *someone* Varius can get to to hurt them.

But my attention is on Antonio right now. On sitting up and swinging my elbows into his face, on doing anything I can to get him to stop. I open my mouth to call on the dark magic that swarms around every witch, that fills our souls and sings siren's songs when we are at our lowest, our most desperate.

I was there when Antonio first ripped my baby from my womb. I pulled back when I realized calling on dark magic might end up killing every Shadow brother. It could choose them as the blood sacrifice as I'm not experienced enough to control it.

But I'm back at my lowest point.

At my most desperate.

Because if Varius sees the video of my rape, it'll break him. Break me.

I'd rather risk trying to find him in the next life, hoping that our bond is strong enough to pull us together across all the worlds and timelines even though it isn't finished. Even though there's no guarantee – hel, not even a good chance that we'll ever find each other again.

Because I can't bear the thought of my husband seeing me this weak and helpless. Can't bear him witnessing my shame. My body's eventual betrayal.

So I open my mouth to sacrifice the entire fucking world if I have to.

But Antonio's hand wraps around my neck and slams me back down onto the table. My attack did nothing but cause more pain to flare up my arms. And yet, I still try, bucking against him and slapping at his hand as he calmly cuts off my air. He stares down at me, cold and efficient, until my head goes fuzzy and my limbs drop, unable to defy biology.

Then he loosens his grip just enough for me to breathe but not speak. He wants me conscious, wants me to suffer for the video, and my heart slams around in my chest.

"Fuck, look how hard her nipples are," Sadist purrs as he reaches forward to pinch the one closest to him. Tears burn my eyes as I struggle to inhale. "All that adrenaline has got her wet."

No, it hasn't, I want to say.

He's lying.

I don't want this.

But I can't say anything due to the damage to my larynx. Can't defy biology purely because I will it.

When Antonio casually raises his free hand, Sadist pulls back. This alpha doesn't need to speak for his orders to be heard. He holds up one finger, and it shifts into the claw of his werewolf form; being over two hundred years old, he's mastered the ability to change only parts of himself at will.

Then he lowers his claw to my stomach.

It's sharp, more like a knife, not quite a scalpel, and as his other hand pins me down, only allowing me the smallest amount of air, the bare minimum to not pass out, he starts to carve into my flesh.

Agony hits me hard as he slices me apart. I want nothing more than to flinch away, but I can't move. Can't fight. I can only lie here and bear the pain.

The cuts burn. The agony builds. My brain begs me to dissociate, to separate my mind from what they're doing to my body, but I can't. I need to be fully aware to try to get a message to my husband. Because despite what I said about him tracking me through our bond, I know he can't feel me. His hybrid curse is eating the blood I gave him, making it impossible for him to feel the bond at all.

So I need to get some messages through the recording

and make one good thing come from this horror.

As Antonio continues to carve into me, I lift my left arm and cover my face like I can't bear to watch. Normally, I'd sign a message with my fingers, but the damaged tendon in my wrist denies me. So I use my whole arm to point at the man beside my head. He turned away earlier, but now he's back, pulled in by his own dirty arousal. Hopefully, he's in view of the camera.

Find him and you'll find me.

Save me, Varius.

Fucking save me before I die in here.

For one moment, I curse him in all the colorful words I know, in all the hatred for him I suddenly feel. If he hadn't tortured me, I'd still be able to control my magic. I would have a chance at escaping.

So fuck you, Varius.

Fuck. You.

I hope you can feel my pain watching this.

I hope it fucking breaks you for what you did to me.

This is all your fault...

I scream inside my mind, hating him, blaming him. All the agony and the pain and the anger I have been keeping down for these last four weeks as we've worked through his betrayal erupts inside of me.

And I hate him.

I hate him so fucking much for what he did to me.

But then I clench my teeth tight and squeeze my eyes as hard as I can because I can't let those thoughts destroy me. Can't break my own mind while Antonio and his wolves break my body; I won't survive it.

And I want to survive.

I want to live long enough to kill Antonio Garcia with my own damn hands.

And Sadist.

And every other man in here.

So I trap my anger at Varius down and refocus it on what Antonio's doing. He's just lifted his claw, finished with whatever he's carved into me. I lower my arm to try to look, but his grip on my throat still pins me in place, and there's so much blood, I can't make anything out.

But Sadist must because he laughs as he holds the phone closer to my stomach. "Look at that, Varius. Your whore has a new master."

He moves the camera gleefully, capturing my belly at every angle. "If you wanted to keep your toy," he chuckles, "you should've kept a better eye on it."

Antonio releases my neck, then slices his claw across the top of my pussy. I scream on raspy chords as pain wraps itself around my heart. I don't need to look down to know he's cut a line through the top half of the tattoo there.

~~Property of~~

Another swipe of his claw leaves me broken.

~~Varius Shadow~~

Those words weren't just tattoos on my skin. They were akin to a wedding band and all its vows – a promise of love, devotion, and protection. It was the strongest tie I had to home, and now it's been violated and destroyed. Exactly like I will be soon.

Tears burning my eyes, I try to call out for the dark magic again, but my voice box won't work enough to shape a spell into existence. I am utterly defenseless and at the mercy of these men.

Antonio steps back and takes the phone off Sadist. He stands coldly to the side, his eyes on mine, his camera pointed at me. Sadist grabs my hips and hauls me to him. With his pants already shoved down to his knees, his hard cock presses against my naked pussy. I will myself to sit up again, to keep fighting, but my body's been too deprived of oxygen and blood, and my limbs and brain are sluggish.

A palm slaps across my face, whipping my head to the

side before cruel fingers grab my chin and yank me back to face him. "Come on, whore," Sadist sneers as he forces my mouth open. "Don't stop fighting me now."

He shoves the fingers of his other hand into my mouth, rubbing them against my tongue. I gag on reflex, and he laughs before releasing my face and backhanding me across it. My head hits the table. Blood seeps from my cut cheek and busted lip. Pain radiates inside my skull, but I find it in me to pull one leg up and kick him in the chest. He staggers back as I sit up, delight curling his lips, and I know he let me shove him back. There was barely any strength in that blow.

But if he wants to draw this out, then I'll use this time to get more messages to Varius.

I scoot back towards the other end of the table, where the men who were holding down my arms are now hiding their faces. If I can get them in the shot, Varius can search the country for them, then he can figure out what city I'm in. If I can get the camera to pan around the room, maybe he can figure out the building.

But I barely make it off the table before I'm grabbed by Sadist. He hauls me back around and punches me in the liver. The explosion of agony makes my knees buckle. I drop like a stone, but I'm caught before I hit the floor, then I'm tossed back onto the table.

My legs are wrenched apart by other men. Sadist steps up between my legs.

"I knew you'd like this," he sneers as he rubs the head of his cock between my naked pussy lips. Disgust fills me, thickening with every stroke he does. My stomach burns from all the cuts, and the men holding my ankles spread me even wider.

"You have a fucking ugly cunt," Sadist says. "It would be better to fuck a pig, but you're just begging me to take you, aren't you, whore?"

I'm not. Varius, I swear I'm not.

"And I'm nothing if not a nice guy." He shoves into me with one hard thrust.

I arch up on a soundless scream.

Sheer agony burns through my pussy, like I am being sandpapered inside, like a hot knife is being thrust into me. He's tearing me apart, ripping me into a thousand pieces, a thousand cuts that are then filled with salt. With acid. With fucking fire.

I scream despite the bruising of my voice box, emitting only a raspy wheeze that can't express the volume inside my skull. I twist on the table, trying to flee. I beat at him with numb hands, trying to make him stop. But he doesn't stop, and I can't flee.

He grunts as he rams into me, pulling out and shoving all the way in; each movement is tearing me apart. His fingers dig hard into my hips. His pelvis bruises my thighs.

"Wrap her legs around me," he orders as he grabs my breasts with both hands. He squeezes them painfully, then slaps them to make them jiggle. This entire time, I'm hitting him, each whack sending agonizing pain through the holes in my wrists. And there's a part of me wondering if I'm still 'seducing' him, if he's only raping me because I'm allowing it. Have I made the wrong choice to fight back? By knowing he's a sadist, should I be lying still so he can't get it up? Is me hitting him a twisted way of giving consent?

Am I leading him on?

My throat grows tight as all these thoughts ram into me. This confusion and disgust and pain and self-loathing. I am not Micha Black right now. Not even Micha Shadow.

All I am is a victim.

A thing for him to use.

Not human.

He fucks me faster, harder. The two men wrap my legs around him, forcing me to cross my ankles, to hug him like I want him, when in reality, I want nothing more than to die.

It hurts so much. The burning in my pussy, the dirtiness of the act, and the knowledge that Varius will watch this. Will he blame me for making the wrong choices? Will he see my pathetic blows as me just 'playing hard to get' with a sadist?

I cry, my whole body shaking, and I don't know what to do anymore. Fight back or lie still? I just want to go home. I just want my husband to burst through those doors and take me home.

"She's so fucking wet, Varius," he says as he fucks me on camera. "I'm sliding into her pussy like it's a Slip 'N Slide."

I'm not! I scream. I'm not wet at all. But it's his word against mine, and I'm terrified Varius will believe him.

Sadist's hand closes around my throat, and I know he's getting close to coming. My relief that he's going to finish quickly wars with the knowledge that he's going to come inside of me. I don't want him to fill me with his poison. I try to move away again, but both my legs are held firmly around his back.

He lifts me up by my neck, forcing me to sit on the edge of the table. I slam an elbow into his nose, snapping it to the side. Blood pours down his face. He punches me in the jaw with his free hand. Once, twice. Then he headbutts me, and as I'm left reeling, he releases my neck to wrestle my arms behind me.

"That's it," he grunts. "Fuck me like the whore you are." He releases my wrists, only for someone else to grab them. They yank my arms back, keeping my palms on the table, and I cry out as pain shoots up my shoulders. I bend back to stop my arms from dislocating. They crawl onto the table, their knees pinning down my hands. My breasts jut up into the air, two little perky mounds, and the newcomer reaches under my arms to cup them both. Their body's a terrifying presence at my head. Pinning me in, blocking off any hope of escape.

"You like the feel of her nipples, Grubs?" Sadist pants as he watches the other man grope me. "They're already so hard. She's really enjoying this."

I'm not! Stop saying that!

"Pinch them for me," he orders as he fucks me harder. My body is such a monument to pain that I can barely feel the clamping of Grubs' fingers, but there's nothing to numb the added disgust and shame.

Varius is going to watch this, and he's going to see me get taken by two men at the same time. I'm going to be raped a dozen different ways, one right after the other, and he's going to bear witness to it all.

With a sudden roar, Sadist grabs my hips and steps back, jerking my ass off the table. I cry out in utter agony as both my arms snap at the shoulders, my hands still pinned down by Grubs' knees. He shoves forward again, hitting my back against the edge of the table before forcing my ass on top of it. Grubs releases my hands and pushes me up into a sitting position as Sadist shoves his thumbs into two of the cuts on my stomach. Then the latter buries his teeth into my right shoulder and bites down hard.

He orgasms as pain floods through me.

I jerk, and I scream, but he just holds me tight, and Grubs soon helps him, scooting up the table to kneel at my back. Reaching around me, he rubs his hands all up and down my body, pinching my nipples and squeezing my breasts. Then he touches me lower, sliding his hand all the way down to where Sadist has forced his way inside of me.

His lips trail across my neck.

"I'm sorry," Grubs whispers, but it doesn't stop him from touching me. "I'm sorry."

Sadist bites me again, this time on my breast. The guy behind me offers my other one up to him, and he bites that one too.

I squeeze my eyes shut as I cry.

I want to go home. I want to go home.

I want someone to save me.

But no one is coming – proven when Sadist pulls out of me, and I'm immediately hauled back onto Grubs' cock. He pushes inside me with one thrust, and the burn in my pussy intensifies.

Like sandpaper.

Like fire.

Like utter disgusting shame.

And the camera captures it all.

SIX

HER

Grubs fucks me slowly, peppering kisses along my neck and shoulders. He drops one gnarly, twisted hand to my clit as he rocks in and out of me. His other hand pinches my nipples. He slides back along the table, pulling me with him on his lap, and my feet are forced onto the edge by two other men at Sadist's command. My knees are now bent and my legs spread wide with my back pressing against Grubs' chest. Sadist takes the phone from Antonio, then moves it in close.

"Spread her pussy open," Sadist says. "I want to capture how wet she is for Varius."

Tears fall down my cheeks as his words burn shame into my soul. *Don't look, Varius. Please don't look.*

Using both hands, Grubs slowly spreads me open.

"Look at that, Varius. She's not your property anymore, now is she? She's got my cum inside her. See it dripping out of her sloppy pussy? And that there ain't your cock either."

He leans in and licks my pussy as he holds the phone above him, angled down.

"Fuck!" Grubs jerks in surprise. His cock slips out of me, but Sadist just grabs it with his free hand and angles it back against my pussy. I twist out of the way, trying my best to not get impaled as Grubs claims he isn't into "that gay shit."

But he isn't pulling away from Sadist…

In fact, he's soon grabbing me to hold me still.

Sadist chuckles as he rubs the other man's cock between my pussy lips. Grubs groans as his breathing quickens. His fingers tighten on my hips.

"Look at all that cum dribbling out of our new whore," Sadist says as he points the phone right at my pussy. He releases Grubs' cock to scoop some of his cum up with his finger, then he pushes it back inside of me.

"Fuck, she's so greedy for this. A real fucking whore, happy to take any cock she's given. Ain't that right, bitch?"

I nearly close my eyes, wanting so badly to disassociate, but I need to stay aware as long as that camera is still on. I could be anywhere in the country, and Varius needs me to narrow down where I am.

Sadist brings the camera up to my face. "Look at how much she loves this."

I turn my head away, tears in my eyes. If I look into the phone and imagine Varius on the other end, I'll break.

So instead I focus on looking around the cafeteria and taking note of anything that will help Varius find me. The tables aren't bolted to the floor, and the seats are benches, not individual stools; it is unlikely this used to be a prison. A hospital cafeteria would have chairs – makes it easier to clean. So I'm probably in a public school – an old one given the lifeless design of the place. Modern ones are brighter, a ploy to show we care about our kids' mental health. Let in more sunlight but ignore everything else to actually curb teen suicide.

Sadist scoops up another bit of cum, but this time, he pushes it into one of the cuts on my belly. I grit my teeth as pain rushes through me, sharp and burning, but I don't react in any other way. Fighting him didn't get him to end this quicker. So now I'll ruin any fun he can get.

His finger presses into me harder. His smirk turns cruel. He hates that I'm not resisting him. Fear flares inside of me, but I force it down. *Antonio won't let him kill me.*

Moving the camera off to the side, he grabs my jaw with his cum-and-blood stained hand. He forces me to look back at him as his fingers dig into my cheeks. My mouth pops open as pain flashes through the joints of my jaw. Leaning forward, he kisses me.

The tears fall freely now. I try to turn away, but he holds me brutally still. I can't close my mouth to bite him. Can't headbutt him in the face. I just have to accept his tongue as it pushes inside my mouth, filling it with blood. His severed tip is blatantly missing as he kisses me, and I vow to take the rest of it as soon as I get the chance.

Stroking his tongue against mine, he violates every part of my mouth. He passes the camera to another man so he can lower that hand to my pussy. He grabs Grubs' cock and strokes it between my lips. With every touch he forces on me, I hate my body more.

Part of me wants to antagonize him so badly he kills me.

The other part wants to survive so I can pay him back a thousandfold. I will brutalize him before I leave this place.

As angry and painful tears roll down my face, I focus on the details of the cafeteria. The four windows are boarded up. The white paint on the walls is flaking off. The ceiling's made up of that horrible gray fiberglass so iconic to schools. There's nothing personal to help locate this place, no school colors or faded mascots anywhere in sight.

Lifting his head, Sadist sneers down at me. "You're so fucking wet from that. Does Varius know how much of a dirty whore you are?" He lifts his hand from my pussy and shows me his fingers.

I flinch at the sight of them glistening in the warm lights of the room. *That's his cum, not mine*, I tell myself.

I don't want this...

His grip on my jaw tightens, and my eyes widen as I realize what he's about to do. I try to turn my head, try to struggle as much as I can, but it's hopeless.

He forces his wet fingers inside my mouth. The taste of his cum makes me gag. Tears flow down my cheeks faster and faster as I think about how Varius is going to suffer knowing another man has touched me. Will he even want me anymore? Will he bother coming for me at all after he sees how much of a whore I am?

Or will he leave me to die in this place, seeing it as a fitting crime?

He gets so jealous...

No... He loves me...

And even if not, Dayne will come for me.

I jerk forward on a sob as I remember the last time I saw him though. Dayne is dead. Antonio killed him when he took me. He punched a hole in his stomach and left him to bleed out.

No one is coming for me.

I'm going to die here.

But not before I'm bred.

Not before I'm raped so much, my vagina tears to my ass and I'm begging for mercy.

Feeling the walls of my prison close in on me, I close my eyes and cry. Sadist forces me to lick off more cum from his fingers, dipping them back to my pussy before bringing them up once more to my mouth. And all the while, Grubs is sliding the head of his fat cock between my pussy lips.

The only solace I have in this moment is that Sadist's fingers aren't just covered in cum. There are traces of blood on them – proof that I'm dry as a fucking dessert. *Please let Varius be able to see that...*

"Look at you..." Sadist says as he finally releases my jaw from between his vice-like fingers. "You're so desperate to be used."

His eyes shift to the man behind me, whose hands are stroking up from my hips to my breasts and back again.

"So use her, Grubs. Fuck her in the ass like she wants."

Grubs' breathing quickens as Sadist's smile widens.

I don't want that!

Stop!

Don't!

"I'm so sorry," Grubs says as he releases me to grab his cock. He groans as he pushes the tip against my ass. I tense, squeezing my hole in an attempt to resist his penetration as much as I can.

But he just grunts and pushes into me harder, his hand now back on my hip. He pulls me down with his gnarled, twisted fingers as Sadist wraps one hand around my throat. He kisses me again, forcing me to fight them both at the same time. I try to chomp down on Sadist's tongue, but he jerks back and punches me hard in the face. His grip on me tightens, cutting off my air as pain flares across my cheek.

Grubs' cock pushes into me. He's going slow, but it isn't making it any easier to handle. I feel like a red-hot poker is being shoved up my ass.

"Relax," he grunts as he kisses my neck. "I don't want to hurt you."

Grabbing my hips, Sadist shoves me down all the way.

I jerk on a raspy scream, my voice box too damaged to really portray the pain I'm feeling. Agony ricochets all up my back, spreading through every part of me. I feel like I have been impaled by Vlad III, like his dick will render me in half, popping out of my mouth as I bleed out from the trauma.

My body can't take any more. *I* can't take any more, and I pull on my assassin training to dissociate despite the sheer agony attacking every part of my body.

It isn't easy. Every thrust of Grubs' dick inside of me wants to call me back to the present. Every movement of the phone, every sick touch of Sadist's hand or mouth, all the vile words he spits at me, calling me a whore or telling Varius that I'm so fucking wet, my cum is what's acting as lube for Grubs – it all shouts for my attention.

But I ignore it and focus on a spot on the wall, a peeled bit of paint that almost looks like a dog – if it'd been hit by a car that then reversed.

My mind is too broken to see pleasant pictures in my pareidolia. I can't see a happy dog wagging his tail. Can't see Krypto sneaking a piece of chicken with his eyes closed so Leno can't catch him in time. All I can see is a dying splatter of matted fur beneath the wheels of a truck that doesn't stop.

It doesn't stop.

The pain.

The agony.

None of it stops.

It just keeps going.

Tears burning pathways down my cheeks, I focus on that spot on the wall.

On that damn dog who's howling for help, dragging its crippled body towards the yard it never should've escaped from.

I focus on the vision of his little girl in pigtails and a blue cotton dress finding him and screaming.

Screaming like I want to scream.

Sadist moves back and demands another man, this one nicknamed Bear, to take his place. Sadist takes the phone as Grubs grabs my dislocated arms and pulls me down onto his chest.

Pain flares through me so intensely, I throw up. Sadist just laughs. Grubs wraps his arms around my stomach and apologizes as he rapes me. His touch aggravates all the cuts on my belly, but what makes it worse is I can't see that dog anymore. Can't focus on another horror that isn't mine.

I'm forced to live through Bear stepping between my legs as he jerks himself off. His cock is only half hard, and I pray he can't fix it enough to penetrate me.

I'm already burning so badly with Grubs' dick in my ass. I can't take one in my pussy at the same time.

The look on his face is a mixture of grim determination laced with panic. I stare at him with a silent plea, begging him not to do this.

He freezes as his eyes widen. His hand stops. His dick hangs limp. Then Sadist shoves him in the shoulder, and he jumps, ducks his head, and immediately starts jacking off again.

Don't.

Stop!

Please!

He steps right up to my pussy. It burns from all the tears and cuts it's already suffered. I can't survive this. I can't.

Desperately, I look at the gray ceiling as Bear leans over me, searching for anything to help me dissociate from the hel he's about to inflict. My eyes latch onto a water stain. My brain races as it tries to come up with a story in time.

Bear slides the head of his cock against my pussy.

My heart runs wild as I try to think.

Breathing hard, he pushes against me.

I close my eyes as agony flares through my pussy and stomach. I hurt so bad, I want to be sick.

Grubs starts to pant hard behind me, and all I can focus on is that horrible noise.

I open my eyes again, desperate to see something in that water stain. But instead, my gaze snaps to the Bear's scruffy jaw and his fear-filled eyes.

He starts to say something, then stops, and I realize he hasn't put his cock inside me. He lies soft between my lips. He jerks his hips, but he's just humping me like a dog with a leg.

For one brief moment, I wonder if I have an ally. If he can't get it up because he's disgusted with this whole thing. The fear in his eyes says he's under duress.

"Help me," I mouth.

His face twisting, he shakes his head slightly, then looks away.

I look up at the ceiling, my throat tight with screams I can't emit. I focus on that water stain again, but just as I think I might have something to visualize, Grubs digs his fingers into my hips and grunts, "Fuck, I'm going to come."

Bear steps back with relief. He catches my gaze, and his relief turns to shame.

Grubs lifts me off his dick, reaches down to grab himself, and then shoves into my pussy.

My back arches. Both my holes burn.

Grubs' fat cock pulses inside me. I can feel every twitch of the damn thing because I'm so dry, so tight against his invasion.

My stomach churns as he groans against my back.

"Thank you," he says.

I flinch, those words hurting me more than the slur of 'whore.'

Thank you.

Thank you.

Thank you...

Like I wanted this.

Like I *offered* him my body.

"Thank you."

My lips wobble as I try to find that damn stain in the ceiling.

Thank you for being our whore.

SEVEN

HER

Grubs rolls me off him, then scoots off the table. Another man instantly takes his place, ramming his cock into me. I'm on my side this time, lying on top of a dislocated arm. It hurts like hel, throbbing even harder as my body is rocked by the thrusts going into my pussy. The men holding my feet have released me. Everyone can see all the fight's gone out of me.

Varius can see...

Does he think I'm accepting this now?

Consenting?

Closing my eyes as Sadist puts the phone in my face, I bite back a sob and wait for my rape to be over.

Three more men come inside me before I'm turned onto my stomach and dragged towards the edge of the table. The cuts on my belly burn like fire, but they're too shallow to cause me to bleed out.

My legs fall to the floor as I'm bent over at the waist.

With all my weight on my stomach, my entire body throbs with pain. He pushes into me from behind, his hips slapping my ass. My pussy burns like it's being rubbed across the carpet, like someone's taken a rod of sandpaper, dipped it in lemon juice, and then shoved it up my cunt. The whole area burns, and my stomach churns as I'm shoved into the edge of the table with every thrust.

Sadist hops onto the table in front of me. His cock is hard again, and he strokes himself right next to my face. I can see him thinking about putting it in my mouth. Pulling on all the strength I have, I bare my teeth.

He laughs, then strokes himself faster. As my sixth rapist comes in me, Sadist leans down to rub his dick across one of the bruises he's left on my cheek. I don't try to bite him. I'll miss, and it'll only make him harder. It might tempt him to rape me properly again rather than just rub himself against my face.

The next four men leave me in the position I'm already in, fucking me from the back. The fifth one, though, is Hourglass. I stabbed him as many times as I could before I was tackled from behind, and his wounds still bleed as he hobbles over to me. But his eyes are as venomous as Sadist's are right now, and I know he'd rather die fucking me than miss this opportunity to hurt me.

My pulse rises rapidly as he steps up to my ass. He spits in his hand, and my heart jumps into my throat. I don't need to turn my head to know where he's going to aim.

I jerk forward as he thrusts deep into my ass. Fire burns all the way up my back as he fucks me hard and fast and viciously. He's punishing me for what I did to him, and despite the agony I'm already in, he amps it up even more.

Grabbing my biceps, he wrenches my arms back. I arch on a scream, my dislocated shoulders blaring in protest as he rapes me.

My belly, which is the only part of me now on the table,

churns with pain. I throw up, hitting Sadist's dick. My eyes roll as sweat breaks out across my back and forehead. My body starts to shake from the intensity.

Sadist's eyes darken with lust as he leans in to suck on my breasts. He bites me hard enough to draw blood. His hand quickens on his cock, rubbing the chunks of scrambled eggs and bacon I had for breakfast.

Grabbing the back of my head with one hand while still holding my right arm with the other, Hourglass jerks my head back and forces me to look at him. Tears burn my eyes as his cock burns my ass. A look of cruel satisfaction twists his ugly face. He spits on me, a great big glob of mucus. I flinch as it hits me right below the eye. His breath stinks so bad it makes me want to wretch again. It smells like he's eaten his own shit.

"Sit down with her on your lap," Sadist says as he lifts his head from my aching breast. "I want to fuck her with you."

Hourglass hesitates, like that isn't something he's into. I pray for one dumb moment that he won't.

Horror paints itself across my face, uncontrollable and raw, as he grabs both my arms again and turns us around.

I cry out in pain as I'm forced onto his lap as he sits on the edge of the table, both our legs hanging over it. His dick presses so deep into me. He wraps both of his arms under mine and then places his palms on the back of my head in a Nelson hold. The pain of it twists my stomach, and I cough, but I'm not sick again.

Not that Sadist seems to care. He hasn't even bothered brushing my vomit off his dick.

My pussy shrivels up as he steps in between my legs. But there's so much cum and blood dripping from my vagina that I know I won't be able to stop him from penetrating me.

I want to plead with him to stop, to please not do this, but I don't. Instead, I focus on the peeling bit of paint I saw before and try to dissociate. It still looks like a dying dog – exactly how I feel.

My body trembles as Sadist touches it. He runs his hands up and down my belly, making sure to brush across every cut he can. "You're our property now, whore." He digs his thumbs into two of my wounds. "So beg me to use you."

I grit my teeth and lift my chin despite knowing it'll only lead to more pain. They can have my body –"can have," as if I still have that choice to give... But they won't break me.

Sadist grins, and I know I made the choice he wanted.

Gripping his vomit-covered dick, he lines it up with my pussy and pushes in. The pain that explodes inside of me is all-consuming. He doesn't fit, not with Hourglass already in my ass. So he tears me apart, making my insides burn and bleed. The thought of the chunky bits of bacon and eggs rubbing all inside me makes it worse. It's like I can already feel it getting infected.

I tremble as he pushes on my shoulders, sending pain flaring through my chest. My arms scream in even more agony as Hourglass lays down on his back, his hands still on my head. My breasts jut up in this position as my body arches against his chest. Sadist grabs my left tit as he looks down at my pussy, pinching the nipple hard before rolling it in between his fingers. He waits for Hourglass' dick to move on the backwards thrust.

Then he shoves in balls deep.

I clench my teeth hard as tears rain down my cheeks. The agony is indescribable, the shame even more so. I'm being taken by two men against my will, and the whole thing is being caught on camera to show my husband.

Sadist tugs on both my nipples as he lifts his gaze to them. "Look how fucking hard these are. You like having two cocks in you, don't you, whore? Yeah, everyone can see it." He releases my left nipple and slaps my chest, leaving a red mark.

Pulling his cock out until it's just the tip he has inside of me, he gives Hourglass the space to ram in. They slip into a rough rhythm together, tearing apart my ass and pussy. Blood and old cum runs down my legs as fire rages through my lower half.

I try to focus on the peeling paint, try to separate my mind from the body they've stolen, but my entire world is consumed by the pain.

And the shame.

And the knowledge that I will never get clean again.

I might be able to rinse the vomit out of my pussy. I might be able to scrub my skin raw. I might get all of my broken, bruised, and bleeding parts healed.

But I will forever bear their marks on my body.

I will forever be *theirs*.

Sobbing silently as they both rape me, I wait for my hel to be over.

Sadist lifts a hand to my neck and squeezes. He leans in close to my ear and whispers, "I'm going to kill you, whore. Then I'm going to fuck your corpse. You won't ever escape me, not even in death."

Hourglass groans behind me.

The two of them pick up their pace, their hips slapping against my ass and pussy. Releasing me from the Nelson hold, the man behind me twists my nipples hard.

"I'm going to come," Hourglass says so Sadist can move out of his way. I'm to be bred; not a drop of cum is to end up anywhere but my pussy.

Grabbing my ass, Sadist lifts me off Hourglass' lap. He fucks me while holding all my weight, pumping into me as he bounces me on his cock. "Such a fucking needy whore," he says as he steps away from the table, carrying me with him. "You're just begging us to both take your pussy, aren't you? You want us to come inside you at the same time."

"I'm not rubbing my dick against yours," Hourglass says.

"Now hand her over."

"I'll do it," Grubs says, breathless and keen. "To uh, help prepare her for Chucky." The werewolf with all the scars on his face. He still stands in his wolf form, watching and waiting for his turn.

My pulse spikes, and I try to struggle again, but I'm too exhausted, too much in pain. I can't do anything other than wriggle on Sadist's cock.

He laughs at Grubs. "Ever the gentleman."

He laughs at me. "That's it, bitch. Ride me like the whore you are. Show Varius how fucking wet you are for us."

He kisses me as he turns and sits his ass on the table. He lies down, pulling me with him and keeping our lips locked together. Our legs dangle over the edge of the table. Then he licks my cheek with his severed tongue.

I tremble in fearful anticipation. Grubs steps up to my ass, his presence a screaming warning in my gut. But then he's shoved aside, Hourglass wanting his due. I tense. My legs are forced onto the table, but my knees are bent, so my ankles still hang over the edge.

Sadist grabs my ass with both hands and opens me up wide, spreading my pussy. His cock jerks in and out of me, causing searing pain with every thrust. Hourglass lines his cock up with Sadist's. He leans forward so his chest presses pain into my dislocated shoulders.

Sadist squeezes my ass hard. Then one hand leaves me to grab Hourglass. The man tenses behind me, but like Grubs, he doesn't pull away. He just presses his cock against my pussy and waits for Sadist to come out. Then together they push in.

I cry out as I am stretched so terribly wide. My pussy burns as they violate it with both their cocks. I feel like a whole fist is shoving deep inside me, wrapping its fingers around my intestines, and yanking them all out.

They continue to fuck me together, thrusting in and out

as one great, big cock, but then their speed picks up, and they move in an alternating rhythm. It's a bit more bearable but just as dirty.

I hate my body.

I hate every single part they touch.

And all the parts they don't touch too.

I turn my head away from the camera. If I had my magic, I could've at least destroyed that.

Instead, I am helpless.

Completely at their mercy in every way.

Hourglass grunts as he comes inside me. It was quick. I feel a bit of relief, but as soon as he pulls out, Grubs steps up and pushes into my pussy. I know it's him because he apologizes, tells me he's only doing this to help me prepare for Chucky's cock – as if anything he does with his short fat dick will help me take one bigger than my forearm.

The werewolf in question stands off to the side. His hard purple cock twitches as he watches me. He knows it's about to be his turn. Grubs is rutting me like an animal, kissing my back and grabbing my ass. He's sliding against my body and rubbing his tongue against my neck. He isn't going to last long.

"Fucking hel, you're so wet, I can barely feel you," Sadist says. "A proper fucking whore's pussy. Just a sloppy, loose mess. Maybe we should sew you up, make you tighter. Make this actually fucking enjoyable for anyone other than you."

I flinch at his words, wanting to protest that I'm enjoying any part of this.

Grubs moans. "Am I taking good care of you, princess?"

I want to be sick. His words feel more disgusting than Sadist's. At least Sadist knows he's hurting me; that's what gets him off. But Grubs acts like there's nothing wrong with what he's doing. He sees himself as a *good guy.*

"Tell him," Sadist teases. "Tell him he's being a good boy."

Fuck you.

"I can see her face, Grubs," he says, looking me dead in the eye. "She's about to come."

My head jerks towards the phone, finally wanting Varius to see me. *Look at me and know I hate this.*

I let my tears fall.

I let him see all my fear.

My pain.

My horror.

I let him see every weakness inside of me. Every ounce of shame and self-disgust. I let him see how close I am to breaking.

I'm not about to come, Varius. I swear I'm not... Look at me and see.

Please don't believe him.

Please don't leave me here as punishment.

Grubs groans as he comes inside me. The smell of his cum and sweat adds to the sickness of the room. The whole place smells of sex and blood and violence. It's scorching memories into my brain, making sure I remember this damn scent forever.

Sadist strokes my face as he comes soon after.

I'm so rubbed raw, I can't feel a damn thing other than pain down there. Can't even feel the cum that's definitely leaking out onto my thighs.

Grubs kisses me and says, "Thank you, princess," before pulling out of me.

My stomach revolts. I'm tempted to turn my head and let him see the disgust on my face, to ruin his damn illusions about himself, but Sadist rolls me off him and tosses me off the table.

Bouncing off the bench, I hit the floor on my back. My arms sear with pain that nearly makes me pass out. My vision blurs as my entire world narrows into nothing but screaming nerves all up and down my body.

A giant furry hand wraps around my face. His palm

suffocates me as he lifts me high into the air. His grip is blinding me, covering my eyes so I can't see anything. My fear increases as I'm stuck in the dark, unable to see where the next attack is coming from. I can't prepare myself for it.

I kick out blindly, frantically.

My feet make contact with his muscled stomach, but I'm too weak to make him drop me. He grabs my right leg and pulls me down.

I know his dick is throbbing and dark-purple with a red tip. The girth is on par with a can of tomatoes, and there's no way it would fit at all if not for the small nub at the end, allowing it to spear its way inside a human body.

I kick frantically with my left leg as my heart races, my brain screaming in its need for oxygen. Panic is overriding my system.

When is it coming?

When is he going to hurt me?

My face flushes hot as I wait for the invasion that will rip my pussy to my ass with one hard thrust. Every hair on my body rises in cruel anticipation.

I'm flinching at every shift of air.

At every little noise.

Is Chucky grabbing his cock?

Can I hear his paw rubbing against it?

Who just moved behind me?

Is it Sadist?

Antonio?

Has he shifted his cock into its werewolf form so he can fuck me too?

Fuck!

I can't breathe.

I can't see.

I can't do anything but kick uselessly and wait.

The grip on my leg tightens.

Chills race down my spine.

Is this it?

Will he fuck me to death before Antonio can stop him?

Antonio is their alpha, but a man with his cock buried in a whore might not easily stand down.

My heart pounds in my ears.

Fuck! How far away am I from his cock?

Am I going to die in a few minutes?

Is this how it's going to end?

Is Varius going to watch me get fucked to death after suffering through hours of my rape?

Fuuuuck!

Fuck!

Stop!

Don't!

Let me go!

My lungs burn as my panic eats up all the oxygen.

I need to know who is behind me.

Who the fuck is behind me!

The blindness is terrifying me.

The uncertainty.

The unknown.

I jerk on a soundless scream as something hot and hard pushes against my pussy. The claws wrapped around my head dig into me, like five sharp knives waiting to skin my face off.

Threatened into submission, I force myself to still. Tears can be healed in a day. Internal bleeding, damaged organs, dislocated shoulders, and bruises – they can all be fixed by a good healer in no time at all.

But anything severed like a face skinned off? That'll take time to regrow (unless it's healed over by magic, in which case it'll be permanent), and as a witch, if I get sick enough or suffer enough trauma without receiving immediate care, my magic will break loose from its tight controls and kill me.

So now I'm too tense, my body rigid against the cock pushing against my pussy. It makes it hurt more. I want to scream, but my lungs are on fire too. I'm going to pass out. I'm going to die in here.

My life starts to flash before my –

The hand on my face lifts free.

I suck in a harsh breath as I fall back, the cuts on my stomach making it impossible for me to hold myself upright. The werewolf is now grabbing both of my legs. My mind and vision spins as oxygen rushes back through my body. I blink hard against the light.

Just as my eyes start to focus though, I close them on a soul-wrenching scream.

The werewolf yanks me down with both his hands at the same time as he thrusts up. The small nub on the end of his dick enters me swiftly, but the rest of his bulbous monster cock is stopped by my pelvic bone. I feel like I have been hit by a wooden baseball bat, with a splinter having snapped off and stabbed me.

Growling, he lifts me off him. He releases my right leg and places a claw at the entrance of my pussy.

I might be struggling to think through the pain and fear coursing through me, but I still understand what he's about to do.

My eyes snap open –

Only to immediately shut again as he cuts an incision between my ass and pussy.

I convulse in pain.

He lines his monster cock up with the cut.

Grabs my leg.

My stomach churns.

He yanks me down.

Thrusts up.

His nub enters me easily. The head of his cock stretches the slice he has made, ripping it like he's tearing a piece of paper in half. Or perhaps a bit of cardboard, something with a little more resistance. Leaving more jagged edges and bits of flesh dangling down the sides.

He grunts as he yanks me down some more, tearing that line even further. Pain sears through me like nothing before. My entire world focuses on the agony of my pussy being torn to my ass. Not just one small horizontal tear, but the entire wall separating the two is being ripped apart to make room for his penis.

He yanks me further down his cock. Each thrust of his hips feels like a pole has been lined up with my vagina and then hit with a mallet. It slams into me, piercing into my cervix, then out through my womb before tearing through my colon.

I can feel him thrusting into my intestines, moving them around to make space. He's finally in balls deep, and when he pulls out, the flared head of his cock takes some of my intestines with him.

I scream, destroying my voice box even more. The pain is intense, and I know I'm bleeding internally. The smell of copper hangs heavily in the air as it runs down my legs, mixing with the cum and sweat that's already so prevalent.

Chucky slams his weapon in deep, his hands still forcing my legs apart. He pulls out, shoves back in. Settling into a rhythm, he starts to fuck me faster.

His balls hammer against my pelvis. His cock stabs me like a knife, then drags my intestines out like a hook. I can feel bits dangling out between the hole in my pussy and ass.

My body starts to shake from shock.

My organs slip down further, following the intestines.

My vision darkens.

Chucky slams inside me again, and pain explodes in my stomach. I cough up blood.

He keeps ramming into me.

I barely hold on to consciousness.

But Varius is going to watch this. I need to know what he sees... The idea of him witnessing more than I'll remember, seeing all my shame when I don't know what to be sorry for... That will break me. I won't be able to face him. I won't be able to go home.

So I dig my claws into this world and refuse to leave it just yet.

But I'm only hanging on by a thread.

Chucky thrusts into me a few more times, rearranging my insides until my body feels alien.

Wrong.

Deformed and disgusting.

Then he slams in balls deep, grabs both of my shoulders, and pins me down on his cock.

His knot swells inside of me.

A second later, he throws back his head and howls. His cock pulses, jerking against my intestines. I cough up more blood. Cum shoots inside me. I cough again, and due to the hole he bludgeoned in my stomach, this time it isn't just blood that comes up.

I pray Varius can't see it.

Pray I'm only imagining the salty taste mixed in with the copper.

As I'm pulled off the werewolf's cock, a wet *slurp* sounds from between my legs. I look down, wanting to know how bad it is.

About six inches of my intestines sway out of the hole he ripped through my vagina and ass.

My eyes roll back in my head as my rapist drops me like discarded tissue.

Used.

Disgusting.

Worthless.

The pain of hitting the ground jolts my eyes back open. I catch sight of Sadist walking up to me, holding his cock in his hand. He stands over my body, one foot on either side of my ribs. As I lie on the floor, bleeding out, he takes aim.

Then pisses all over my face.

EIGHT

HIM

I scream in rage as Aleric phases away, leaving me to plummet towards the earth. I can't open my eyes. The wind is ripping across my body. I won't survive a fall from this height. I am helpless to stop it.

As I tumble out of control, I cup a hand over my chest and protect that little smear. It's all that remains of my little girl. If I'm to die, I will die with her in my arms.

I wish I could hold Micha one last time.

Wish I could save her from whatever hel she's in.

Wish I'd never panicked at the thought of losing Khalid or her to my enemy. I should have trusted her. Despite all the evidence, I should've believed in her like she did me.

Regret fills me as I rage against an entity I can't defeat. The night sky swallows my screams of vengeance without a care. Gravity pulls me down.

Down.

Down.

Blinded by the wind, I can't see when death is coming, so I'm anticipating it every second. But beneath my anger, I'm holding on to a silver lining: maybe I can find Bambi in the Underworld. Maybe I can be the father to her I never got to be.

I hit the ground feet first.

My bones break all the way up from my toes to my hips. Shattered fragments sever veins and arteries. The knives I always keep on me stab and slice into my flesh. Broken ribs pierce my lungs. My spine gets crushed in multiple places. My aorta snaps free, and a reaper of death comes for me.

But then she stops.

Backtracks.

Hesitates on the edge of my vision, her smoky wings spread out, her glowing green scythe in her hand. Various souls cling to it in shapeless blobs. One end of them is tethered to her blade by a fading wisp; the other end's a face screaming in rage – or perhaps agony. She is a keres, and her kind comes for those who've died a brutal death, those with unfinished business. No one she takes ever wishes to go.

Her long green hair, matted with blood, hangs over her face, and she stares at me with cruel black eyes between the strands. More blood stains her clothes, and she smiles at me, each tooth long, thin, and sharp. Two rows of poisonous needles.

"Not yet it seems," she coos, her words both a roar and a whisper. As her power hits me, she vanishes.

Pain explodes through me.

My eyes snap open.

Aleric is shoving a woman I don't know into my face. Her throat has been slit, and her head's been pulled back. Blood gushes from her wound, filling my mouth, and the Craving hits me full force.

I try to resist, only wanting to feed from my wife, but I'm

not just starving now. I'm dying, and the bloodlust inside of me has already had a taste. It will not be denied.

And still I fight it.

The vampire above me rolls his eyes as he pulls the dying girl off me. "Stop being a child," he says as he drops her to the ground.

He grabs my jaw and snaps it hard to the right. It breaks with a loud *crack!*

"Aleric!" a woman shouts.

"He's fine." Grinning, he grabs my chin. "Fight me now, asshole." Forcing my mouth up and down, he puts on a stupid accent. "I am Varius, and I have a small penis. I got it from my father."

"I swear if you don't –"

Ignoring her, he looks down at his crotch in surprise. He gasps, then shouts, "Who the fuck cut off my dick?"

"I'm fucking about to," a man mutters.

"I'll hold him down."

"Just say the word."

"Aleric." Short. Clipped. A fucking warning growl.

Laughing, Aleric shakes his head. "I'm fucking hilarious, and no one gets it," he says before leaning down to grab the girl again.

"Or did you get the joke?" he asks as he shoves her to my lips. "When I said you have a small penis that you got from your father," he explains cheerfully, "it sounded like you inherited it, right?"

I imagine ripping his voice box out even through the onset of the Craving.

"But the joke was you cut it off me. You *got* my dick. Get it now?" He laughs as my body shakes.

I try to resist for a moment longer, but the blood is in my mouth. I can't resist with my broken jaw, and with a cry of defeat, I start swallowing the woman's blood down in great big gulps. I clasp my hand over my chest, protecting Bambi from her filth as it runs down my chin and neck. I growl in both disgust and anger, but I don't stop drinking.

Can't.

My rage claws beneath my skin almost as fiercely as the Craving does at my throat. I scream at my body to move, to shove her away, but I'm trapped in this broken shell.

Though even when it starts to heal, the blood pushing magic through my veins, the bloodlust doesn't let me stop.

After I drain her dry, I still want more.

Need more.

Feeling watched by other predators, I glance around as I bare my teeth. Mother, Khalid, Maddox, Ezriel, and Leno are all spread out around me in a large circle. A pack of hyenas waiting for their turn to eat. I growl, a lion standing over a kill.

"If he dies –" Mother starts.

"I know, I know," Aleric says as he pulls my meal away. I want to grab her and hold her to my lips, but the only hand that's working is the one protecting Bambi. My fingers dig into my chest, shielding her, choosing her above all else.

"You'll chain me to your bed and spank me like a bad, bad boy," Aleric says as he tosses the body aside. Then he winks at me and whispers, "Ya know, not gonna lie, I kinda wanna let you die now."

"Aleric," Mother growls.

He grins as he gestures to one of the women sitting in a line at his feet. They're bloodbanks, nothing but property, and they know better than to run. The first woman stands, her blue eyes glazed with whatever drug she's shot up with, and stumbles over to us. She doesn't react at all when he stabs her throat with his knife and then shoves her in my face. Perhaps, for her, this is a mercy.

I drink with less resistance now, but I don't sink my fangs into her throat.

She isn't Micha.

Any intimacy isn't right.

When she's nothing but an empty husk, he grabs another for me to drink. Then another and another.

My body slowly heals.

The Craving slowly dies.

But the agony doesn't wane.

It fucking amplifies.

With a broken scream, I jump to my feet. The fog in my brain has lifted, and I can finally feel my wife through our blood bond. She's north. Somewhere far away. A part of me knows I should head for the cars, but I can't bear to detour long enough to find the keys and get an engine running. She needs me now.

I can feel her dying.

She's dying, and it's all my fault.

"Var–" Ezriel yelps, snapping my attention back to my surroundings.

Shit.

I'm a split second away from barreling into him.

I don't have time to stop. I don't even have time to pivot around him. All I can do is duck my shoulder and slam into his. A loud crack resonates from his body as he goes flying. A hit like that normally wouldn't hurt him, but I'm running at hybrid speed, desperate to reach my wife.

I can feel her terror of pain, her fear that she'll never be saved, that she will die in Antonio's compound. I can't lose her.

I won't.

"Varius!" Khalid says, his voice just loud enough for me to hear him.

Danger flares across my neck, and I twist my head to the right. Mother is tending to Ezriel, bathing his chest in a white light as he struggles to breathe. Beside them Khalid raises the reaper mask to his face – a black skull with four golden horns at the top and a death rune on its forehead.

His mien is one of emotionless indifference. In his right hand, his only hand, is a double-edged scythe, a cursed tool. One cut from it, no matter how small, will cause me to bleed out.

If I want to escape, I'm going to have to kill him.

Pain squeezes in my chest, but the irony of this isn't lost on me: how I'm forced to hurt him now in order to save my wife. I love him, and he's the only person I trust, the only one I confide in. But if it's between him or Micha...

Pivoting towards him, I grab a knife.

Only –

Some fucker removed them all while I was out.

Shit.

I'm just going to have to rely on my speed. My increased strength. If I can take the scythe from him, I might actually stand a chance.

I take a step towards him, and a thousand blades of grass shoot up from the ground. They grow rapidly, crawling up my waist, wrapping around me, and slicing me apart with their sharp edges. A thousand cuts. A thousand more. I tear the strands off me, but they're instantly replaced by fresh shoots. Still, I keep fighting, knowing Leno can't keep this up for long. The ground is already half-dead from whatever Antonio did to it, so he's pulling on nature from a hundred yards away. That's a massive drain on his body, and I'm recently fed. But the danger isn't coming from the grass.

The fucking reaper is stalking towards me, and he'll get here long before I can break free.

Leno whistles three sharp notes of different pitches, and Krypto comes tearing across the yard towards me. I look at him dryly. It's such a fucking ridiculous thing to do – to get his dog to attack me too, that I can't help myself. Useless overkills is just so Leno.

But he does something that makes me still completely.

Krypto stops in front of me, his hackles raised, his teeth

bared, and growling low. Only, he's isn't facing me.

He's facing Khalid.

My brother will kill without mercy; when he dons that mask, there is no pleading with him. No begging. Nothing will save you. But there are two things that will cause him to hesitate.

His kira.

And an animal standing in the way.

In over a decade of being a reaper, Khalid has only killed one creature. It was an accident, but it still haunts him.

My head jerks to Leno, but he doesn't see me, his eyes on Khalid. My chest burns with shock and disbelief. He put his own dog on the line – his best friend.

Why would he do that...?

More movement snags my attention, and I turn to see Maddox joining the mutt in front of me. "Come on, Khalid. Don't do this."

"Move, Maddox," he says softly. "He's lost to the Craving. We can't save him."

Ezriel joins the two in front of me. He breathes out low, like he would rather be anywhere else, like he thinks it's the worst idea ever to stand against the reaper.

But he's there.

And my throat closes a little bit more.

"He's our brother, you dick cheese," Maddox snaps.

"Personally, I would've said he isn't lost to the Craving. He's just acting like a little bitch, like your dad did when Sau went missing," Aleric pipes in cheerfully.

Everyone stills at his words.

Then slowly, they turn to face him.

"But what do I know?" he continues. "As your MILF so often points out, I should shut up more."

"I'm going to cut out your tongue," Mother vows.

He turns to her and purrs, "If you want my tongue, love, all you have to do is sit on my face."

She takes a step towards him, a promise of hel in her eyes, but then she pivots towards me.

"Don't release him, Leno," she says.

I lunge forward, snapping free of the grass, but more just sprouts up out of the fucking ground.

"Let me go," I snarl. "I need to get to Micha."

"You need to rest. You go after her now, and you'll get you and your brothers killed."

"I'll go alone."

"You can't stop them," she says at the same time as they say:

"The hel you will."

"Are you fucking stupid?"

"I didn't just risk my life for you to kill yourself."

Khalid simply removes his mask and deposits his scythe back into his shadows. If he isn't killing me, then he's going to help me. He always does.

I clench my teeth. It's on the edge of my tongue to tell her they are acceptable losses, but I bite it back. They're words I don't mean, born from the overwhelming anger and fear inside of me.

My chest burning, I rasp, "I can feel her. He's killing her."

My body trembles.

I can't breathe.

I need to go to her.

I start to tear off more strands of grass, but then Mother places a hand over my chest, over Bambi, and I stop.

Shudder.

"We'll save her, Varius," she says as she looks me in the eye. "But right now, you need to think rationally. Antonio doesn't know you've bonded to her, so you have one chance to take him by surprise. If you go in half-cocked, he will kill you. He's planned this for years."

"Fuck off," I snap. "If she dies, you won't even care."

Her eyes don't waver. "You know why I picked her?" she

asks. "Because she saves kids. Because there is nothing she would not risk or suffer through for those she loves. You get yourself killed, and you'll make her feel like she's survived for nothing. You'd be telling her that you think she is too weak to hold on long enough for you to make a plan. That her weakness is what got you killed."

She lifts her hand from my chest, but her eyes don't leave mine, and I can't escape the truth within them. "I chose her, Varius, because she isn't some damsel in distress. She's a fighter. Your equal. Now fucking treat her as one."

My lips tremble as I clench my fists. I want to swing at her.

To curse her out.

To release this utter need for violence.

But none of that will change the fact that she's right.

I'm only going to have one chance to save Micha.

One.

If I fuck it up, I will lose her forever.

Antonio will find out we're bonded, and he'll kill her as a loose end. Can't have me knowing exactly where he is.

Unless... I make it look like I found her through good old police work.

Pushing as much hope and love as I can down my bond to Micha, I give a small nod. I won't let my emotions get my wife killed. Mother looks at Krypto, and the grass falls off me.

Maddox tries to hug-tackle me, but I shove him back. I glance away from him as my breath catches in a hard lump at my throat. My heart pounds so hard, it's all I can hear. I tremble as I build up the courage to look down at the little girl he would've squished in his hug.

"He killed her," I say, swallowing hard to push out the words. I want them to know that when I go for Antonio, it won't just be to save my wife. It'll be to kill the fucker with the same amount of mercy as he showed our daughter.

"Who?" Ez asks, but Maddox elbows him in the stomach, and his face instantly pales as it registers. "Shit... Varius..."

I ignore him as I take off my shirt. Slowly. Carefully.

Trying my best not to desecrate her body even further.

My eyes burn as I stare at the dark-red splodge lying on the cotton. She's surrounded by the blood of all those I have fed on, but none of it touches her.

In that way at least, I protected her.

A poor fucking solace.

Rage pulses through my veins, helping me to focus past the pain.

"This is all he left me of her," I say as I lift my gaze to my four brothers and Mother. Aleric stands stiffly beside them. He knows he's my father, knows this is his granddaughter he never got to meet.

She was our little girl.

Our firstborn.

Murdered at eighteen weeks.

We never even settled on a name for her. Micha wanted to call her Bambi. I offered up Rafiki as a joke.

A joke...

I made a fucking joke because I thought we would have time to come up with something that fit her perfectly.

My eyes land on Maddox – cold and dangerous.

He stiffens, knowing what I'm going to say.

But I don't give a shit about his silent protest.

He hasn't claimed her.

He hasn't blood bonded with her.

Her life is mine.

"Get me Zita Garcia."

NINE

HIM

I stand in the kitchen with Maddox and Khalid, in a new shirt, agitation crawling across my skin. The pull north is damn near excruciating. Micha's emotions are sluggish and muted, and I don't know if that means she's about to die, pass out, or has just dissociated; the inability to fucking do something about it is making me feral.

"Hurry the fuck up, Maddox," I snap as he stands in the middle of the empty space, our dining table having been shoved to the side. Mother would've preferred us to do this in the basement, where we have a dedicated spell room for shit like this, but that would have taken longer to walk to, and every second spent being here rather than out there running towards my wife is killing me.

Khalid clasps me on the shoulder and squeezes, a silent command for me to get my shit together. Maddox is moving quickly; his shadows are already swirling on the floor. It just always takes him a while to pull the cage free because the monsters living in there fight to keep it.

"She's your wife, Varius," Khalid says when I stay tense beneath his palm. "But she's our sister now, and you know how protective Maddox is of family."

My jaw tics, but the fucker is right. Maddox is obsessed with Zita to the point none of us would be surprised if he claimed her. Yet, still, he's willing to let me use her. She'll be risking her life to save my girl, coerced to obey me or die. And that's far from being the worst thing I'm going to do to her... or ask of him.

Closing my eyes briefly, I hold on to the blood bond I share with Micha.

Then I block it off.

Lock my emotions down.

I need to become the heartless monster I normally am. The ruthless Boss who never lets his feelings get in the way of business. If Zita catches one whiff of weakness, there won't be a threat large enough to convince her to join our side. Antonio is the boogieman to her, the nightmare that can never be killed. She needs to believe we stand a chance of freeing her from his chains.

The cage finally pulls free in its entirety. Its bars are bent and covered in blood and saliva. Antonio's granddaughter sits in the middle of her prison, her bony knees pulled to her chest, her thin arms banded around them to make herself as small as possible. Still, numerous wounds cover her naked body from where the monsters were able to reach her.

She keeps her head down, protecting her eyes from the harsh light of the garage. The Plane of Monsters is pitch black, and she's been in there for days. Her skin hangs on a skeleton of starvation. Her once long white hair is showing her natural auburn at the roots. It's a bird nest of broken strands.

Maddox opens the cage, which was locked by magic, and steps inside. Grabbing her by the arm, he hauls her to her feet, then guides her out. She follows without protest, her violet eyes blinking rapidly as she struggles to make out her surroundings.

She is lowered into a chair. She looks first at Maddox, then at me. Despite having been tortured for over a month, her eyes are still bright and sharp. Are Micha's? Maddox has only been playing with his toy; Antonio wants to break his.

Burying those thoughts, I step up to Zita. Maddox moves back. A chair is placed behind me, and without taking my eyes off her, I sit down to face our captive.

She looks at me warily. But the longer I allow the silence to stretch, the more that wariness turns to confusion, then calculation, then triumph at figuring out the puzzle.

My entire makeup has changed with the breaking of my curse, including my scent. Hybrids don't smell any different to other sups, but she knows what I smelled like before. And with her little nose twitching, she knows what I smell like now.

"So you've finally hit your ascension," she says as I study her. She doesn't like the silence. Or perhaps she's just trying to build a rapport, a connection between us so I see her as human rather than a thing to break.

"I was a late bloomer too," she continues. Rapport it is. Good.

If she was nervous under pressure, she would be of no use to me. Antonio would kill her as soon as she got home, paranoid we'd managed to turn her. But her intelligence will give her a chance to talk her way out of an execution. It will give Maddox a chance to sneak in. He's been learning how to summon stronger demons from Lou, Micha's sister, so if he gets inside, he can create the perfect opportunity for us to strike.

"You're going home," I say.

Her eyes widen. She glances at my youngest brother, no

doubt expecting him to protest.

"You'll tell them you escaped when our ward was down. Maddox pulled you out for an interrogation. Rudy's magic spiraled out of control, so you took the opportunity to run."

"Antonio isn't going to buy that. He's as paranoid as you are and even quicker to kill. I'm not being your mole."

"You don't have a choice."

She yelps as her arm twists out of her socket and keeps going, the bone bulging against her skin, so close to tearing free.

"Go ahead and kill me." Sweat beads across her face as she pants from the pain. "I'm not a traitor."

"Your Family would have to care about you for you to be a traitor."

She glances away, that remark hitting hard. In the weeks since her capture, not once has someone tried to rescue her. She's nothing but the omega to them, the werewolf with the lowest rank. They bully and beat her as a way to build pack morale.

"But we're not going to kill you if you refuse," I say as I glance briefly to the side, at the curved zebrano wood that divides the cooking area from the table.

She holds my gaze, trying her hardest not to look.

Then she does.

Her face pales as she watches the grain and knots shift, a creature lurking beneath the surface.

She doesn't know it's there willingly, so I let her believe it's a person imprisoned. A captive who didn't do as they were told.

"Except, in your case," I say, "we will tie your soul to a toilet."

Forever trapping her in a world of piss and shit.

"Olivia can taste the food we put on the counter," I say, letting her own mind turn against her. "She'll never leave that place, even if the counter is burned to ash."

Her head jerks back to me. Her eyes fly to Khalid, no doubt believing it's his magic that's responsible. In fact, it's Mother's, and I don't know if she can do the same to Zita, but Zita doesn't know that either. She's seen the impossible happen with Antonio's hybrids; she'll believe this.

"Fuck," she mutters, knowing her fate is sealed.

My brother pushes his magic through the soul doll in his hands. Carved out of alexandrite, the dark-green stone has been molded to look exactly like her. A piece of her hair lies inside it, given to him by Maddox earlier, and it ties her soul to the doll. He fixes her arm, and she sags back in her chair. But there isn't any relief on her face.

"When you get there, you're to help Micha as much as you can. If she dies, so do you. Khalid will be watching you at all times, and if he gives you an order, fucking follow it."

She looks at him warily, no doubt knowing exactly how he's going to communicate with her. A pen can't write on stone, but he can carve words into her flesh with his magic.

She glances dryly at Maddox. "And here I thought you were the worst brother." She looks back at me, not giving him the chance to respond; the bitch knows how to push his buttons, alright. He hates not getting in the last word.

"I'll do everything you ask of me on one condition," she says. "When Antonio finds out about our deal" –she lifts her chin, utter certainty in her eyes– "give me your word that you'll kill me."

Seeing the terror behind her bravado, I wonder what the fuck he's doing to Micha. Zita's his granddaughter. Micha's the wife of an enemy.

My control slipping, I stand with a quick nod. It's a lie; we can't spare the alexandrite. We only have three pieces of it left, and once it's used to kill someone, it's gone forever. But I will break every vow to save my wife.

As Khalid escorts her out of the house, I open myself up to the blood bond again. Relief hits me when I can still feel my wife. A part of me feared she died the minute I shut her out.

My chest tight, I resist the urge to turn in her direction. Instead, I look at Maddox. "Are you sure about this?" What he's willing to do for me is going to be the most dangerous thing he's ever done.

He blows out a breath as he rotates a shoulder and cracks his neck. "Yeah..." he lies. "It'll be fiiiine."

"If he kills her –" I start.

"I'll be fine," he cuts in as he pats me on the shoulder and smiles. But I can smell his fear despite his easy grin. "Now go find Aleric before he gets distracted and wanders off," he says before heading past me to head down the hall. I need the vampire's ability to phase. Otherwise, I'll be driving for days as I try to pinpoint Micha.

After a quick search, I find the vampire outside. He's staring at the dead earth in front of the house.

"Let's go," I say.

He doesn't look at me, his eyes scanning the yard. The stillness of his body is making me uneasy. The ward isn't back up yet. If Antonio attacks us now, we're fucked. I gaze out, trying to spot anything that's out of place. I push out with my senses, checking that way too. Nothing.

"What are you looking for?" I demand.

"The source of a disgusting smell," he says, but for once there isn't any humor in his voice. He's fucking serious, and a chill runs down my back.

"Werewolves?"

"No." Grabbing my arm, he phases us north. We land in a walk-in closet full of brand name clothes, shoes, and purses on every wall. The room is dark, the only light coming from the crack under the door. A shower runs not far away.

The pull towards my girl is weaker now, and panic hits me. Does that mean she's weaker, on the verge of death? Or just that we jumped too far? "That way," I snap, flinging an arm out in her direction.

"First, tell me how Caden died."

"We don't have fucking time for this."

"Then walk. The door's there."

My jaw tics as I glare at him. The fucker'll actually leave me here; no one matters to him but himself.

"He killed himself cursing her," I snap.

He grabs me, and we phase again. The bond is weaker. My panic is stronger.

"What's the curse?"

"Every time she uses magic, it drains her life."

On the next jump, the pull to her is even weaker again. Fuck! She has to be dying.

"She doesn't look weaker."

"She's a healer," I snap. She can hide such things with her magic, topping up her physical looks while the inside of her is a hemorrhaging mess. A part of me wonders how close she is to dying. The other part of me doesn't give a shit. She set Micha up so I would be paranoid enough to torture her. And although Talon was really the one who set that fire, Mother had set up the kindling. Now Micha is without her magic because of her.

No. She's damaged because of me.

Fuck! I'm so sorry, little monster. I'm so sorry.

I spin in place, feeling her pull. My frustration mounting, I try to figure out how far to jump. "Go half the distance that way," I say.

He doesn't move.

"Aleric! I will fucking sell her to you. Just go."

"I don't need to buy her when she'll crawl to me on her knees."

I lunge for him. He grins. We phase, and the pull to her is now stronger. I turn my head, trying to figure out where we are. Where we've been. Try to put it all together to –

Aleric knees me in the balls, and I go down.

I twist towards him, knocking out his legs. He falls onto his back. We're in the woods, and as I jump on top of him, he grabs a handful of dirt and throws it in my eyes. I flinch away automatically, but I still manage to punch him in the face. He hits me in the spleen. Pain explodes throughout my body, and I fall to the side, blinking rapidly to clear the dirt from my vision. I get a brief warning of moving air before a rock bashes into my skull.

I crumble. He phases away, and I hit the ground as he stands over me, tutting. "You take after your mom when you're angry."

Blood pours down my face. My head thrums hard as my vision blurs. Stumbling to my feet, I pull out a knife.

He laughs. "Now, your love of patricide – that you got from me." He cocks his head, not at all concerned. "Then again, that could've come from Caden too. Nurture versus nature and all that."

Cursing, I put my weapon away. Fighting with him will only drag this out more. "Ask your fucking question," I snap.

"You're normally not this much of an embarrassment, so what gives?"

I blink.

He smiles, enjoying how much he's caught me off guard. "Come on, Vay Vay, talk about your feelings with your old man."

Of course he knows Maddox's fucking nickname for me.

"When we're finished with Antonio, I'm going to kill you," I vow.

He winks. "You'll have to fight your mom for that honor."

I breathe out through gritted teeth. Glancing around me, I wonder if I'd be better off on my own, but we're in the middle of fucking nowhere. Trees stretch in every direction, and the clean air and colder temperature tells me we're on top of some mountain. It'll take me hours to get down, even longer to drive. She'll be dead in that time, so I force myself to speak. "I can feel her dying."

He snorts. "Doubtful. Antonio won't kill her this quickly, and if she was doing it herself, she'd be finished by now. So sit." He gestures at a tree beside me. In the blink of an eye, he's where he just pointed, perching on the branch near the trunk. The fucker is even kicking his feet. The urge to set this whole forest on fire is doused only by the knowledge that he'd just phase away.

"Come on up," he coos. "There's room for two."

"I'm not climbing the fucking tree," I snap. "I answered your question. Now phase –"

"It feel any different?"

"What?"

"The bond."

I still, realizing it feels the same as when we first arrived here. It's weaker than in St. Augustine, but it isn't weak. It's stable.

"The stronger a bond feels," Aleric explains, "the farther away you are. Connected souls don't like being far apart, so they practically scream at you until you get back together. Annoying, right?"

"How do you know all this?" Blood bonds are exclusive to witch partnerships.

A chill races through me as I recall Mother mentioning Caden left because of something she did. Did she fucking blood bond with his ass–

"I read it in a book," he says. "Your father –" He pauses. "Your fake father was pathetically 'in love'" –he air quotes– "with Sau. He wouldn't have cursed her. So tell me how he really died."

"He found something out about her, left for nearly two decades, then came back and killed himself cursing her. If you want the next answer, fucking phase."

He stares at me for a moment, eying me up like prey. Then he's gone. I curse as I reach for my phone. Before my fingertips enter my pocket, he appears in front of me.

"Done," Aleric says. "But I phased twice to come back, so now you owe me two –"

I pull out my phone to call Khalid.

He laughs as he transports us to another part of the woods. "No cell service here," he says cheerfully.

"Aleric," I warn. Vlad, his second-in-command, might not want to lead the Blood Fangs, but he's about to not have a fucking choice.

"Tell me what really happened," he says, "and I'll hold all my other questions until after we find Micha."

My jaw tightens, but I shove my phone back into my pocket. "Caden killed himself cursing her, probably because he figured out I was fucking yours. And if you don't think my father was capable of doing that, that's because you didn't fucking know him. Now phase me that way." I point to my right.

"Oh, I knew him pretty well. He's quite a talker after a hard fuck." He grins as he studies my face. "Now you have questions too. Good. I won't have to hunt you down to have our chat." Grabbing my arm, he phases us out of the woods.

He stays true to his word. The only questions he asks are how strong the bond feels so he knows how far to go. We jump another half-dozen times, narrowing down where she is, but vampires can't phase anywhere they haven't been and memorized.

The closest we can get is still too fucking far away. I'm left with a search area that's hundreds of square miles wide, somewhere in the mountains of West Virginia, well inside Death Hunt territory. We can't linger for more than a few seconds at a time either, lest a werewolf catches our scent.

When we land back home, I'm fucking furious. At Aleric. At Antonio. At Mother.

At anyone and everyone in this world other than her.

But most of all, I'm furious with myself. I didn't leave

enough guards on her because of my paranoia. After Talon betrayed us, I haven't been able to trust even my brothers. And I wasn't smart enough to realize what Antonio had planned. I promised her I would protect her.

I promised her.

But all I've done is failed her and our little girl.

Back in my room, I stare at the red splodge on my folded cotton shirt. She has been placed on my bedside table. On Micha's side of the bed.

I couldn't bring myself to let Khalid take her into his shadows. I'm not ready to let her go, so she's frozen with magic, waiting for her mother to come home.

Waiting for her to say goodbye.

Turning from her, I open my laptop to start detailing the area we need to search for my wife.

I'm going to get you out, little monster.

Then we'll bury our daughter together.

TEN

HER

I come to in a different room, lying on my back in bed. A bright overhead light shines in my face, so I turn my head while blinking fast. My eyes focus on a metal counter full of surgical tools. The white walls of the place mock me with their sterile cleanliness; all I feel is dirty.

Used.

Rotten.

Infected with the touch of Grubs and Sadist and all the other men who raped me.

Hating the feel of being on my back, I go to stand. As soon as I sit up, I find my hands and legs are strapped down with thick padded cuffs. A chill runs through me as I glance down at my body. I'm naked and tied to a hospital bed by my wrists and ankles. The surgical tools finally register, and my heart jumps into my throat. I need to get out of here.

Sadist and the others were experimented on.

I tug against my binds.

My skin burns from the pain.

I grit my teeth and pull harder.

My skin rubs raw.

I twist and yank and fucking curse.

But the cuffs still bite into me, deep and unyielding.

Fuck!

Breathing hard, I give up trying to free myself. Fighting against the impossible will just make me break faster. I am not naive enough to think I'll never break. That I'll survive this place with my mind intact. It's the number one rule to torture: *everyone* breaks eventually. Whether during their time of captivity or afterwards.

So I need to keep my goals realistic, need to give myself something I "can" control. I can't get out of these binds, but I can keep my dignity. I can take whatever they do to me today. I can survive until tomorrow.

I can learn valuable information – like what was done to the fourteen men who raped me, if they're still undergoing experimentation, and who does it. I can use that to build a rapport with them, a shared hatred, a shared pain. Then I can work on manipulating them. Get them to see me as more than a pussy. Maybe even get a few of them to help me escape...

The idea of that, of playing nice to the men who raped me curdles my very soul. But I'll do what I need to in order to survive.

The door opens, and a man with short black hair comes in. He doesn't smile at me or glare at me with cold malice. He doesn't look at me at all as he moves over to the counter with all the medical tools.

"I'm going to fucking kill you," I snarl.

I don't need to ask him who he is; his face is one I will never forget. This bastard is the one who helped Antonio portal me here. He was the one who stepped on my hand as I reached to hold my little girl for the first and last time as she lay in a puddle of blood – a mixture of both mine and hers. He stole that moment from me, and so I will steal his life.

It won't be easy though. He knows transportation magic, so that means he's a strong witch, intelligent, and fucking crazy. Given he's also the guy who experimented on all the wolves, though, is a good thing. Maybe I can convince them to help me kill this fucker in between raping me. *I'm not trying to leave you, Grubs. I just want to beat the shit out of Eduardo and then shove his face into his excrement until he chokes on it.*

He picks up a bone saw and comes over to me. It takes everything I have not to tug against my bonds. Show no fear.

"Are you right or left handed?" he asks.

Goosebumps spread across my body. "Go to hel."

He leans in and strokes his free hand down the side of my face. "This is hel," he whispers, "and I'm your god here."

Lunging forward, I clamp my teeth down on his nose. He screams as he jerks back – all defense; he isn't a fighter. He is a coward who hurts people tied down or drugged. I'm going to enjoy killing him, making him feel all the pain he inflicts.

I shake my head hard, like a dog with a hare. He screams as he tries to shove me away. I lock my jaw. Swallow the blood. He finally starts to hit me with his fist. Pain explodes in my skull. I don't let go. He picks up the saw, but with a last wrench of my head, I tear his nose free.

Eduardo howls as he stumbles back. Dropping the tool, he clasps both hands to his face as white light streams from his fingers. He can stop the blood gushing down his face, but he cannot clean the stains off his shirt, cannot erase the evidence of my insult to his masculinity.

That's only a temporary reminder though, gone when he changes clothes.

I want him to remember what I've done to him every day of his fucking life, what little of it remains.

I want him to fear what I'll do next.

Fighting back my nausea, I start to chew. He looks up at me with murder in his eyes. He can't immediately regrow the nose I've taken, but he can reattach it.

"Give it back!" he screams. He doesn't advance. He's too afraid. Too cowardly.

I look him in the eye as I swallow.

My gut churns, but I beat back the urge to retch it up.

Snarling, he bends down and grabs the saw. He takes one angry step towards me, his foot slapping hard on the tiles, and I wonder if I miscalculated. Antonio doesn't want me dead, but he isn't here, and this guy has a god complex with anger issues. All it'll take is one snap moment for him to kill me by "accident."

"You want to make a fool of me, bitch?"

"It's not like you need help." I lean over the side of the bed towards him and bare my bloody teeth. He can't reach my arm without getting in range of my mouth.

So he goes for my feet.

Grabbing my right one, he starts to hack at me just above my ankle. "I'll show you a fool!" he shouts as he drags the saw over my skin.

The first slice is bearable. I have been cut enough times. Pain and I are old friends. "I can already see you, dipshit," I grit out as he makes the second slice.

He's rough, inefficient, and powered by rage. The cuts aren't together, one neatly on top of the other. They are a crisscrossing mess of blood and flappy flesh. The pain turns into agony, and it's harder for me to keep my head together. I fall back on the bed, fighting the urge to scream.

Right as he reaches my bone though, the door behind him opens. I catch sight of a blurred streak, then Eduardo is being yanked off me. The bone saw is pulled from his grasp and flung across the room hard enough to embed into the wall like a spear.

"Heal her," Antonio snaps as he shoves Eduardo back towards me. He keeps one hand on the back of the witch's neck, ready to crush it if he so much as hesitates.

"She bit my nose off!" he whines, but he raises his hands instantly. White light streams from his fingers. A warmth spreads through my limb as he repairs what he destroyed.

As soon as he's done, Antonio shoves him away. He does not need to tell him to hide in the corner and stay quiet. Eduardo's enough of a coward to do it on his own.

"My hero," I say sarcastically as I sit up to face the alpha of the werewolves. Sweat trickles down my face, and despite my newly healed leg, my body still trembles from the earlier pain.

Antonio stands at the foot of my bed, his arms crossed. His biceps bulge against the sleeves of his simple black tee. His golden eyes are sharp with intelligence and a desire to break me. "Who was the father of your child?" he demands, and a wave of sheer rage pushes out my lingering pain.

"Fuck you."

"You fucked someone else to complete the blood bond. Who was it?"

"None of your fucking business."

"Tell me, or I'll let Eduardo take your leg."

My jaw locks. I glare at the fucker in front of me. That wasn't a bluff. I don't need my foot to get pregnant. But I can't tell him Varius is the father.

If the Shadow Domain finds out he's a hybrid, Antonio won't even need to destroy our Family himself. They'll turn on him like a starving pack of wolves. If Khalid doesn't kill him, all of our allies and associates will. Or perhaps they'll just jump ship, moving to do business with our enemies. We will be attacked by every fucking sewer rat wanting a piece or street cred, and our Family, a multi-billion dollar empire, would crumble overnight.

"Aleric," I spit out, my voice one of disgust. There's no way Antonio will be able to hold him here. Although, he's taken other born vampires who had the ability to phase, he forced them to breed with werewolves. They were poisoned day after day, their body melting from the inside out. They had no chance of escape.

But a witch's bodily fluids aren't poisonous to vampires. If he brings Aleric here to fuck me, he might as well release me himself.

Antonio studies me like he doesn't believe me, but I don't waver from his gaze. Nor do I offer up any more details to "sell" the lie. The only time I'd tell him shit willingly was if I was lying, and he knows it.

"Is the bond completed?" he asks.

"Yes." If he knew the truth, he'd kill me. I'm of no use to him if I can't make it to term, and the bond, as much as I cherish it, is a ticking time bomb.

Although Varius and I shared a lot of blood yesterday, I have also lost a lot. I can barely feel him now. It's like he's a word on the tip of my tongue or a shadow just on the edge of my peripherals. I can't feel his emotions raging inside me anymore. Can't feel where he is. I reckon I only have four, maybe five months left before the bond demands blood in one way or another.

I expected Antonio to be concerned about the bond being completed though. If Varius can find him wherever he is, he will have to move me constantly. The added stress of being on the run nonstop, combined with the increased risk of me escaping during transit should garner some sort of reaction, but he doesn't look concerned at all.

"I'm bait," I say with a mental curse.

He smiles for the first time.

"Tell me about the Shadow family, and I'll put you with the other women," he says. "You'll have a room to yourself, and you'll only be bred during certain hours. Refuse, and you'll room with the men you've already met, available to them twenty-four seven. Then I'll force the answers out of you anyway."

I lean forward as far as I can. "Fuck. You."

He stares at me for a moment, then turns to leave. "Draw her blood," he says to Eduardo. "Then put her in with the men."

ELEVEN

HER

Eduardo looks too fucking happy to be alone with me.

The binds on my wrists and ankles seem to grow tighter as he advances with a scalpel in his hand, but I keep my chin up, my fear down. "I'm going to take your ear next," I say with a lick of my lips.

"The only thing you're going to take from me," he sneers, "is my cock."

I jerk against my cuffs, unable to help myself. I'd rather he cut into me a thousand times with that scalpel than know what his cock feels like slamming into my pussy. "If I even see it, I'm going to tear it off and then use it to fuck that new hole in your face."

He stops, his eyes narrowing. Fury and fear clash in his gaze. He'd have to turn me over to rape me without getting his jugular ripped out, but as soon as he freed my hand, I'd find a way to kill him – scalpel to my throat or not.

Turning to the counter, he puts the blade back down, and

a burst of relief hits me, followed by optimism. I controlled that. I'm not entirely helpless in here. I will survive until I escape or Varius saves me.

Eduardo grabs a hypodermic needle and a blood bag. He walks over to my feet, places the bag on the bed, then grabs my toes. He leans my foot back so the veins are clearer, then lines up the needle. "Imagine this is my cock sliding into your cunt," he says as he pushes it inside me.

"It's that small, huh?" I snort to hide the fact that inside I'm panicking. I can fight against a scalpel. I can't fight against his words, against the memories slamming around my skull. My pussy can feel it, and I want to be sick. He looks between my naked, open legs. I want to close them, but I can't.

Can't move against my cuffs.

Can't show any weakness.

"It's so small, I could put it in your urethra," he says, and nausea hits me hard.

He pulls the needle out of my foot, then stabs me with it again. I grit my teeth as I try not to imagine him fucking my pee hole. The pain would be intense.

Stop.

He wiggles the needle as if he can't find the vein, but I'm sure he's just being a dick. "I'm not allowed to come inside you," he says, "so maybe I'll just take your earlier suggestion and make my own holes."

A cold tremor rushes through me.

"I could fuck every single one of your limbs. Your organs. Make my own bingo card."

He jabs me with the needle, over and over again, looking for the vein. I grit my teeth as pain crawls up my leg. I keep my face flat, but I'm screaming inside my skull, yelling at myself for giving him the idea, blaming myself for being in this situation. My heartbeat runs wild at the idea of being violated by this sick freak.

"Not such a talker now, are you?" he sneers. He stabs the needle into my vein. "The next time one of the mutts knocks you out" –he grabs the bag to connect it to the needle– "I'm going to fuck you in your left lung, close enough so I can feel your heart thudding against it. I'll heal you so you're awake for the whole thing."

My throat closes as I stare at him in horror.

"Not so tough now, are you?" Squatting down, he sucks my toes into his mouth.

I jerk my leg so hard the cuff cuts into my ankle.

His teeth scrape the skin off my toes.

The needle hits a nerve, and intense pain flares up my leg.

Grabbing my foot, Eduardo runs his tongue in between my digits. He drags his teeth across my flesh.

I fall back onto the bed with a silent scream I refuse to emit. My hands fist. I close my eyes and imagine thrashing against my binds until I can escape and beat him to death. Outside my head though, I stay locked still, not giving him any other response. No weakness.

Eduardo groans as he starts to jerk himself off. Angry tears burn my eyes. I hate how helpless I am. How pathetic. I am an assassin, the mafia queen to the Shadow Domain, wife to Varius fucking Shadow himself. I should be able to do something.

But I can't.

And I don't know who I hate more in this moment.

Him.

Or me.

My foot throbs as the needle's placed back into my vein, but it's the wet slurp of his mouth, the slide of his tongue, and the hard bites of his teeth that are making me wince. He's leaving his mark on me. I try to comfort myself over the fact that it's not as permanent as the mark I've left on him. I'm winning.

I don't feel like a fucking winner.

He releases my toes and stands quickly. I keep my eyes on the ceiling as the hot spurt of his cum hits my foot. It seemingly burns through my skin, right through my fucking bone.

Perhaps his mark is more permanent than mine after all.

Fuck.

No.

Keep it together, Micha.

You stopped him from raping you. Focus on the win.

"Surprise, surprise," I say, working hard to keep my voice sounding bored. "You're a minute man." I lift my head to look at him. "When I fuck your face with your own dick, I'm filling it with needles first."

He snatches the bag of blood up and quickly steps back. Once he's a few paces away, feeling safe, he starts to gloat. "I hear you can feel when your mate dies. It's agonizing to experience." He holds the bag up to his face and looks at it in awe. "It's poetic, really, that your blood is what's going to kill Varius. Terra will use this to create a disease that infects only him. Then we'll release it all across St. Augustine, and if he so much as breathes in that city, it'll kill him."

I jerk against my binds, my heart hammering. I play it up, let my fear out so he can see it across my face. See my panic. My terror. He just gave me a name, vital information I can pass on to Varius when I get the chance, and I want him to keep talking.

His eyes light up as he looks at me, thinking he's won, thinking he's found a way to hurt me without getting close enough to risk his life. "You're going to be with me when he dies so I can study the effects of the blood bond. Then I'm going to fuck your urethra as he takes his last breath, and you're going to tell me how it feels to feel him dying."

"You're lying. No one is good enough to make a disease that specific, and if you spread it all over St. Augustine, you will infect enough people to call in the SCU." The Special Crimes Unit really doesn't like magical pandemics. They'll come in hard and fast after only a handful of cases. Then Antonio will be screwed. They've left our Families alone so far because the power vacuum that'd occur in our absence would damn well trigger World War III, but cross one of their lines, and they're as merciless as we are.

He smirks gleefully. "Terra Harrison is that good."

"She's been dead for decades. Not even a necromancer could bring her back."

"No, she never died, just nearly did, and now she's here, working for Antonio." He takes a step forward, grinning like the Cheshire cat. "Who do you think broke the ward at your house and killed all of Leno's plants?"

My blood chills. Shit. When she and Cara Jervis went to war over a hundred years ago, they almost took the entire world with them. Both disease witches, their magic went haywire, and over a third of the population died. The SCU went after them hard. Soldiers were rounded up left and right. Capos were killed on sight. Even their associates were not safe, and many of them ended up in prison off world.

The only reason Cara is still here is because she changed her face, forced her Underboss to take hers, made a disease that made them utterly convinced they were her, and then practically served them up to the SCU. Now that person is serving life in Damaculus, the worst prison on the Seven Planes – a place only reserved for the most dangerous of criminals. Varius, Antonio, Aleric – none of them would warrant a spot in there.

So if Terra really is alive...

"Your man is as good as dead. Then we'll kill the rest of the Shadow family one by one."

My pulse crashes against my skull, beating hard in my ears as I struggle to keep focused. Their plan is just that. A plan. It can be foiled. They don't even know we have Cara

Jervis; they think she's in Damaculus like the rest of the populace. So focus on that and keep him talking. "Why is Antonio doing this?"

He shrugs with a demeaning scoff. "For love. He wants to bring Siome back from the Underworld."

My mouth drops. Venturing into the realm of the gods is insane. "He's never going to succeed." I try to put the pieces together, my mind racing. It doesn't matter what I say. He's arrogant enough to correct me if I get it wrong or gloat if I get it right. As long as I keep talking, so will he. "That's why you're making hybrids. You're juicing him up to survive the Underworld. You're a fucking idiot. That's never going to work."

His dark-brown eyes flash with anger. "I'm the only one smart enough to pull this off. No one thought you could turn someone into a hybrid, but I've done it. I just need to tweak a few things, and –"

"Tweak? The men look like twisted piles of shit."

"Those are the failures," he grinds out. "What I've done is pure genius."

"What's so genius about men with deformities? I could make someone just as ugly with a hammer."

His jaw tics. "My masterpieces are not deformities. They are faster, stronger, bigger, better in every way. Their shifted forms are a combination of other creatures –"

"So you've made chimeras, not hybrids."

"They're hybrids."

"Uh huh. How many have you made then?"

"Fi–" He stops, having finally caught on that I have been interrogating him. His eyes narrow. Antonio is going to be pissed he's shared this much with me.

I grin savagely at him. *I hope he fucking kills you for it.* No.

I hope Antonio just beats him senseless for it. Then I can still kill him myself.

"It doesn't matter that you know all this," he says with a sniff, trying to blow it off. "You're going to die in here."

I don't say anything, and he puts the needle and blood bag down on the counter. Then he rolls me out of the room, the wheels of the bed squeaking across the floor. He pulls from the footboard, still too nervous to come anywhere near my head.

I smile at that.

He takes me down a hall. We're definitely in a school, though this part of the building has been renovated. The walls are a cool teal. The door frames are painted black, and the doors themselves are a crisp white. Bronze knockers rest on them in the shape of a howling wolf sitting on a crescent moon that's been turned sideways. Classrooms have clearly been combined to create bigger homes, with no doors sitting across from each other.

All the old school lockers have also been removed, and now long wooden troughs full of flowers and herbs sit along the walls. Paintings of mountains and rivers dot the place. They've been painted in layers to give a 3D feel to the scree slopes and pebbled banks. I like the décor, but it isn't going to stop me from burning this place down if I get the chance.

A door opens in front of us, and a little boy no older than two darts out. He's squealing with laughter. He doesn't have any bottoms on. A well-built man, dripping wet and without any clothes on at all, runs after him. He grabs his son in a few strides and lifts him under his arm like a football. The boy squeals and giggles. "How the funny bunny did you get out of your pen?" he mutters as he disappears back inside. Their door is shut well before we reach them.

I swallow hard and pin my gaze to the ceiling. My empty womb sends a flare of pain all the way up to my heart. I lost my little girl, lost all those moments, and I didn't even get a chance to say goodbye.

But Varius will.

He'll get to hold her.
Bury her.
Be the parent I'll never get to be.
A tear streaks from the side of my eye.
As much as I love him, I can't help but hate him for that.
You better come save me, you fucking neanderthal.
Because if I have to do it myself...
I'm never going to forgive you.

TWELVE

HIM

My bedroom door slams open just as I've finished talking to Katie Wilks. She runs our extortion operations, targeting politicians, billionaires, lobbyists, anyone and everyone in power from all over the world. She'll know whose arm to twist to get every government agency in America to crack down on the Death Hunt without digging further into our own crimes. While the wolves are distracted by the police, we'll go after Micha.

I jerk my head up as I stand, expecting it to be Khalid in my bedroom. He made a soul doll of my wife a few minutes ago and has been watching and hearing everything that's been happening to her. I tried to order him to let me listen in, but he refused, so I have been imagining the worst ever since.

"Is she –" I start before I clock it's Dayne.

His eyes cold with fury, he lunges for me, but with a burst of speed, I tackle him into the hall. If he's going to beat the shit out of me, I don't want him damaging the room. All of Micha's things are in here, our memories. And Bambi sits on my bedside table. Although she's protected by magic, if he even gets close to harming her, I don't give a shit if he's Micha's best friend or not. I'll kill him.

As we hit the ground, he elbows me in the face. My head cracks to the side, and he uses the momentum to roll me under him. Kneeling between my legs, he tries to punch me in the jaw, but I raise my left arm to block him at the same time I throw my right fist into his liver.

He falls forward from the pain, but he takes that as an opportunity to headbutt me in the face. Stars explode in my vision, followed by a sharp pain as his teeth scrape across my cheek. He would've torn a chunk out rather than just damaged my flesh if I hadn't managed to shove him back. Godsdamn, the fucker fights dirty. The fact he isn't using his magic, though, tells me he doesn't want me dead... Yet.

But as much as he deserves to kick the shit out of me, and as much as I want to let him punish me for my sins, I don't have time for this. I have a dozen people I need to call and a hundred arms to break until I get my fucking wife back.

So I shove my elbow into his throat, pushing him back to free up space to move my legs. Swinging out from under him, I stand, grab the back of his head, and then knee him hard in the face.

He falls back, and I jump into the air, having expected him to try to kick at my legs. I twist horizontally and land beside him. He arches back to jump to his feet, and my eyes narrow at how fast he's recovered. He isn't a healer; that knock should have kept him down.

"Wait," I order. Despite his grievances, I am still his Boss. There is a moment, when Dayne lands on his feet and looks at me, that I don't think he's going to listen, but then he stills. The rage in his eyes doesn't die, but it is controlled.

Family brawls aren't punishable; disobeying a direct order is.

"I know it's my fault she's gone," I say.

"We could have had a chance if she didn't have to keep going for that stupid wand," he growls.

I have seen how fast Antonio can move, but Micha's fire could've actually saved her. It eats magic, and it can burn through a werewolf's natural resistance to spells. She could have had time to get to the safe room in the basement if she hadn't had to run upstairs first for her wand. Or she could have stood outside it, standing behind a line of fire Antonio couldn't cross.

"I know," I say, feeling that guilt harder than anything he could ever pack into a fist. "But right now we need to focus on saving her."

"Which I could've done already if you hadn't removed my fucking tracker."

"We know where she is." Roughly, but when we go in, I can lead us directly to her.

"How?"

I think about lying and just telling him Khalid made a soul doll of her, but my paranoia is what got her into this mess. I didn't trust my brothers enough to tell them we had bonded, so Talon thought she'd be an easy patsy. I didn't trust her when I tortured her for Khalid's whereabouts. And I didn't trust any of my men to watch her while we went after Antonio. It's about time I trusted someone other than the reaper. If Micha trusts him, then so will I.

Breathing out slowly, I say, "We've bonded."

"You sonofabitch. You're not happy enough just ruining one of her lives? You have to ruin them all? So what the fuck are we still doing here?"

I start to tell him the plan when I sense Khalid hurrying down the hall. I turn just as he reaches us. The look on his face makes my stomach drop. "What is it?"

"Terra Harrison is alive, and they're using Micha's blood to target yours."

I start to push past him to go find Aleric, but the vampire phases in front of me, his eyes on Khalid.

"Do they know Cara is here?" he demands.

"They didn't mention her."

He disappears, hopefully to bring her here. If Terra really is alive, Cara's the only one who has a chance of countering her diseases.

"It will take her a few weeks to create something," I say, forcing myself to concentrate on the news rather than my imagination as I think about every vile way they could be taking her blood. Cutting off her limbs. Hanging her upside down with her throat slit, healing her just enough she stays alive. "So that gives us a deadline." I turn to Dayne. "I need you to take Maddox's face until we rescue Micha. Antonio thinks you're dead, so your absence won't cause suspicion, but his will."

"Where will he be?"

"With Zita. He's plan one. If she isn't killed on sight, she will smuggle him in. He'll then take Micha into his shadows and get out."

He shakes his head. "They have a witch. They will screen for –"

"They won't find him."

His eyes narrow as he tries to figure out how Maddox is going to pull that off, but I don't have time to explain it to him, then argue about the statistics of it actually working. I am already worried I've just given my youngest brother a death sentence; I don't need to see his concern too.

"Who's changing me?" Dayne asks, and I like that he isn't just agreeing to anything to get Micha out. It means he still has his head on his shoulders, able to calculate risk and return. He's no good to me if he's a slave to his emotions.

"Mother."

Relief flutters across his face, followed by a grimace. This isn't an easy thing I've asked of him. Changing one's body with magic comes with a lot of risk. He could be killed or permanently disfigured or have his brain turned into mush. Talon used to handle these things, so Mother is a bit rusty in this area, but she knows the body well.

"Alright, but if I die, you tell Micha I survived Antonio. I don't want her blaming herself for my death."

She'll just blame me.

So I might lose her anyway.

My throat tightens.

But at least she'll be alive.

I nod at him, and he walks away. Taking a deep breath, I turn to Khalid. "What are they doing to her?"

His eyes bore into mine. "She bit off a guy's nose, then ate it," he says instead. "She'll survive until we get to her."

I glance away, both proud of her and horrified. If she antagonizes them too much –

He clasps a hand on my shoulder. "Trust her to handle herself, Varius."

She shouldn't have to.

Swallowing hard, I nod. Tears burn my eyes, and I look away. He drops his hand. "Anything else?" I ask, my voice rough.

"He wants to bring Siome back from the Underworld."

My head jerks to him. "How?"

"Don't know."

But if we can figure that out, we can finally be one step ahead of him. "Get Rudy on this." It's a job that'll keep him away from everyone and give him a chance to recover.

Khalid looks at me, his face a mask. "You haven't been to see him, have you?"

I tense, guilt twisting my stomach. When we attacked Antonio's men at the crocodile park a few hours ago, Rudy fought one of the hybrids on his own. He was cut to pieces, mauled, bitten, damn near torn in half; if he were anyone else, he'd be dead. But he's terrified of being stuck alive in a body that's long since died, so he turned his own nightmare into reality. He won that fight, but it cost him too much.

When he helped me reach the site of Micha's abduction, with one arm around my waist, practically walking for me, I could feel his magic boiling beneath his skin. Normally, he would hide in the Plane of Monsters for weeks, maybe even months while he regained control of it, but with my wife missing, he's stayed here to help.

"No... How is he?"

I push out with my senses, searching for his heartbeat. It is easier for me to detect now with my curse broken, but I don't relax when I find it beating calmly. It should be erratic like it always is when he's on the verge of losing control.

"Stormie wrapped him in a shield," Khalid says, his jaw tight. He doesn't need to say anything more for me to know what happened.

Stormie Green, the daughter of an old family friend (now dead), became engaged to Enoch for a political alliance. She grew up with the twins and was a firecracker, always rough housing with them before she hit her ascension and was taught how to be a lady. One day, after she learned how to control her shielding magic, Rudy roped her into helping him do something stupid. He damn near gave me a heart attack then, and I feel like I'm suffering one now.

Spinning on my heels, I head for his bedroom and enter without knocking. My heart is lodged so far up my throat, I am choking on it.

"Are you –" I start to shout, but then I find him sleeping.

He looks peaceful for once.

I just know what that peace has cost him.

Breathing out hard, my body shuddering, I walk over to him. I sit down on the edge of his bed, knowing he's out cold. There have only been two times in his life that I've seen him at peace. When Stormie shielded him as a kid and now.

"Fucking hel, Roo," I mutter as I stroke his red curly hair like I used to do when he was a kid. For once, his head isn't damp with night terrors.

The first time I saw him sleeping like this, I was so happy for him. I finally got a night's sleep myself, having been up in his room every night previous, protecting him from the horrors of his mind as his magic pulsed out of control. But then I found out *how* he'd been able to find such peace, and I nearly killed Stormie for it.

She's a shielder, able to wrap her magic around people so nothing can escape the bubble – not their body, their own magic, or even any monsters they call forth. But she can only stop that power from escaping; she can't stop it from manifesting.

When I cornered her for answers that first time, having found her shaking and vomiting and looking close to death, she told me that inside her bubble, Rudy had released every nightmare, every fear, every agonizing terror his mind could come up with. He had lived a hundred deaths, watched us all die in a thousand different ways. He'd been raped and beaten and eaten alive – then all three at once. He was set on fire, beheaded, strangled with his own intestines. The entire bubble filled with rats and snakes, and when they ran out of space, they started to eat their way into his body. And those were all the 'easy' things.

When it got too much, Stormie turned the shield opaque to protect her own mind. She refused to speak of the last thing she saw. His torment went on for hours after that.

He did it then so I could have a single night's rest.

He did it now so I could rely on him in the coming war, so he wouldn't have to hide in the Plane of Shadows while we fought this battle without him.

"I'm supposed to be the one protecting you," I mutter.

Yet another thing I've failed at recently.

Feeling so damn tired, I'm tempted to lie down beside him. I used to share his bed when he was a kid, jerking awake every time he flinched or whimpered. It was one of the most stressful times of my life, and yet, listening to him sleep was sometimes the only way I could fall asleep myself.

I give his shoulder a squeeze, then climb to my feet. As much as sleep calls to me, I can't rest until I save my wife.

THIRTEEN

HIM

I make my way to the garage. Enoch and Ezriel have been cleaning up the yard and have moved those "lucky" enough to have survived Mother's monsters into the cells hidden beneath the building. When the trapdoor is shut, you can't hear their screams of pain or cries for help, but at the moment, it's been left open, and wails and howls and little pathetic whimpers echo up the stairs.

They know something worse than death is coming for them.

I head down into the harshly lit room, the bulbs so bright as to hurt the eyes. But though it's bad for me, it's worse for the wolves. Despite being born on Earth, their kind evolved on a world that never sees true sunlight due to a constant coverage of clouds.

Around two to four pups lie in each of the three cells. Normally, it's one person each, but these are not hardened soldiers, an elite task force that was trained to fight Mother.

These are nothing but rogue pups that were promised a position in Antonio's pack if they fought well. They weren't even told we were the target; else, they wouldn't have come. All they are is cannon fodder. I doubt they will know any of Antonio's secrets, but if there's a chance one of them has overheard something they shouldn't have, I need to check.

"Heal me... please," a young mutt begs as he lies on his side on the floor, scooping up his spilled intestines with shaky hands. He pushes them into the hole in his stomach, but they keep falling back out. He needs to lie on his back to have a chance of keeping them in, but even then, his odds of survival without a healer are slim. He's lost too much blood, his skin pale and sweating. "Please..."

Cries for mercy flood the place.

"Let me go."

"Please don't kill me."

"I don't want to die."

"Antonio forced me..."

I glance at a blond-haired boy who is missing both his legs from the thigh down. The fact that he's still conscious means he has just entered his ascension. The healing magic inside of him has a fresh well to pull from, and it's working overtime, but eventually, it will fail. He can't be more than nineteen.

When he finds me staring, hope fills his eyes. He's too naive, not knowing it's worse to have the attention of your enemy. He wouldn't have spent any time in the Death Hunt.

I start to turn away to pick someone else to interrogate when he says, "He has my sister... Please help her... and I'll tell you... everything."

"What do you know?"

"Help –"

"Only if you have usable information."

He struggles to sit up. His desire to talk to me like a man rather than lying on his back has me recalculating what he might've been through. Kids don't handle pain that well if they come from happy families.

"Antonio is breeding… hybrids," he says. "My sister was forced… into the program four… years ago. I tried to rescue her… but they chased me out." He takes a heavy breath, then another. Sweat glistens on his brow. The puddle around him grows, and the stench of iron is making my teeth ache. I clench my jaw, fighting back my urge to feed. I am more than my base desires.

"I have been rogue ever since, but I know… where they are keeping her and the other women. He… bought a whole town and turned the school… into a… a facility…"

My blood runs cold. Micha is in a school. If he's fucking breeding her –

His eyes start to close.

"Where?" I snap, praying he isn't going to say the area I just fucking marked out.

"Morning Springs, West…"

"Virginia?"

He nods, looking as pale as a ghost.

A dark energy claws at me, begging for release. My body shakes as I struggle to control it. She's been there for hours. How many times have they –

Stop.

Concentrate.

You can't help her if you lose it.

Gritting my teeth, I breathe in hard. My fists clench, but I stop the rest of my body shaking. "How many wolves?" I demand.

"A few hundred… There's not… much security… in the school itself… But it's in… the middle… of town… Please… help… Katie…"

His eyes start to close, and I storm up the stairs to get cell service to call Louise Warner. She's our second best healer (Mother is currently out with Aleric and seven of his vampires, searching the area I outlined for her hours ago), and I want this boy alive. I can use him to turn his sister into a mole, recruiting her through Zita.

Despite it being three in the morning, Louise answers on the second ring. "Yes, Boss?"

"Come to the house."

I hang up, knowing she'll be here in a few minutes; she doesn't live that far away. I text Mother the town she should be searching for, and she replies back, saying she's already found it and is waiting for the vampires to study the area enough to phase us in. Which means she'll be back well in time for the raids.

In three hours, every government agency in America is going to crack down on the Death Hunt. They'll attack their compounds, businesses, and every place they like to hang out in an organized sweep, creating the perfect distraction we need to go after Micha.

Once that starts, all we'll need to wait for is for Zita to smuggle Maddox inside the school.

My heart rate increases as I call Khalid. He's with the rest of my brothers and Stormie, working on creating a new ward around the house. He doesn't answer, but I feel the air buzz with power, giving me the reason why. A shimmering blue wall, visible only to sups, shoots up around our yard. Then it goes black, crackling with energy as Stormie feeds it the bubble of magic she took from Rudy. My anger towards her ignites, but I push it down. I can't kill her. I need her for this raid.

She's a shielder, meaning she can contain my powers if I start to pulse. No one knows when I'll hit my ascension or even if it'll happen, but if it does, it *will* spiral out of control, exploding out of me and hitting everything in its path at random intervals. Given we don't know what abilities I'll be blessed with, I could kill everyone nearby, so she needs to stay by my side during the rescue.

We're only going to have one shot to take Antonio by surprise, and I won't be the reason we fail.

My phone rings as Khalid calls me back.

"What's the update on Zita?" I ask as soon as I answer. The last I heard, she'd managed to steal someone's phone and text Antonio, telling him in a coded message that she had important news she needed to tell him in person. He never answered her, but she was driving up to find him.

"Antonio's men picked her up in South Carolina. They're interrogating her."

"They going to kill her?"

"I don't think so. She's using the intel about the raids she 'overheard' as leverage to move up from omega."

She's smart. It makes her seem selfish rather than a rat. And if we lose, she still comes out better for it. I can see why my brother likes her.

"And Maddox?"

"In position."

My grip on my phone tightens. Everything so far is going to plan. I could have my wife back in a few hours. But if they don't buy Zita's act, I've just killed my brother. "Call me as soon as there's change."

"I will."

I start to hang up, knowing he won't answer my other questions about Micha. He wants my head in the game, but just as my finger moves towards the end call button, I blurt, "Are they breeding –"

But the line is already dead.

Burning with a need to move, I start to head back down the fucking stairs. I'll get the kid to tell me what they're –

My phone vibrates, and I glance down.

My feet instantly root in place.

My breath is squeezed out of my fucking lungs as I stare at the notification on the screen.

Antonio: *You've violated something sacred to me, so I've* *returned the favor.*

My hands shaking with rage, I open the text. At the sight of a link beneath his message, an eruption of darkness burns through my veins, clawing at my skin, begging for release.

The fucker's posted her torture on the dark web.

I tap the phone.

Micha's body appears, beaten and broken. Her clothes are torn, her breasts and pussy bare. Antonio is pinning her to a table with one hand on her throat.

My rage burns cold as I hover on the play button so I can see how long the video is.

Four hours. Thirty-eight minutes.

Four hours. Thirty-eight minutes.

Four hours…

Thirty-eight minutes…

"Don't!" Ezriel shouts my name from outside the garage. My phone jerks out of my hand, pulled by his telekinesis, but I dart forward and grab it again before it can go out the door. My muscles strain as I fight against his magic. I hit the play button.

"Fuck, look how hard her nipples are," the man behind the camera says as he reaches forward to touch my wife. "All that adrenaline has got her wet."

I'm going to kill him first. Skin off every piece of flesh that touches her. My blood boils as Antonio raises his free hand and shifts his forefinger into the claw of his werewolf form.

The phone starts to be pulled from my grip, Enoch now helping his brother steal it from me.

Snarling, I wrap my other hand around it, my eyes glued to the screen. Antonio starts to carve into her flesh. Into *my* flesh. My fucking heart.

As she raises a hand to cover her face, my brothers race towards me, eating up the yard in long strides. Stormie is running with them, and the air crackles with magic.

With rage.

I'm going to kill him.

I'm going to kill everyone in that fucking town.

Khalid said there were kids, but I don't care.

Antonio took my baby from me.

My wife.

Anyone who stands with him deserves to die.

Micha is shaking as he cuts into her. I'm shaking right along with her, my body vibrating with an energy I need to release. I can't stand still. Can't fucking wait for my Mother to get back. For Zita to get into position.

I want so badly to gather my wife in my arms, to bring her home before the rest of this video happens.

But I can't.

It's already passed.

Four hours. Thirty-eight minutes.

She suffered all of that because of me.

I fucking *failed* her.

Antonio pulls back his hand as he finishes carving into her belly. I drag my attention from my wife's face, her pain and drop it to what he's taken so much care to write.

Screaming, I drop to my knees as an explosion of energy rips its way out of me. Shadows pour out from under me, crawling across the ground like fingers of death. I've wanted magic all my life, devoted hours of every day for years as a kid, trying to trigger my ascension or bond with a wand. But all I can focus on right now are the words he carved into her.

Property of Antonio Garcia

The phone moves in closer. "Look at that, Varius. Your whore has a new master." It swivels around, letting me look from every angle. "If you wanted to keep your toy," the man chuckles, "you should've kept a better eye on it."

Antonio releases Micha's neck. Then he lines his claw up with the tattoo on her pussy. On my mark. My vow of love and dedication. My ring before we married. Before I could even admit to myself that I wanted her regardless of her ability to carry to term. Micha Shadow isn't a fucking toy. She's my wife.

And now Antonio is trying to take her from me.

He slices a line across my name, ripping out my heart.

Micha's mouth opens as she tries to scream. Her throat is so damaged, she can barely make a sound. Yet, still she tries, her grief too great to keep in, and seeing that level of pain on the woman I love destroys the last of my control.

My magic explodes.

My shadows shoot through the entirety of the garage, then race down the stairs, billowing out like fog from my feet. Screams ricochet up from the cells. My brothers reach the door, only to backpedal quickly as my shadows climb up off the floor. The Craving hits me just as strongly as when I was starving, but it's darker now. It isn't after blood. It's after –

"Krypto!" Leno's scream is one of pure panic.

The dog is much lower to the floor, and the shadows are cramming themselves into his nose, eyes, and ears. He yelps as he shakes his head, then starts pawing at his face.

"Stormie!" Khalid shouts as he drags Leno back. Ezriel and Enoch have to help him. Leno's so desperate to get to his dog. The screams coming up from down below intensify. Then they stop.

Leno screams again, his voice cracked.

Breaking.

Shrill and terrified.

His best friend whines as he falls to the ground.

My shadows crawl over him, so hungry to consume, so out of control.

"Don't!" Enoch shouts as he turns his head to his fiance, torn between who to stop. He starts to let go of Leno, but Stormie throws up a light-pink shield around herself, then steps into my shadows, going where he cannot.

The smell of her fear teases the Craving. It wants me to turn to her, to focus my power on consuming her life, but all my attention is still on my phone, on the torture my wife is going through. Alone.

Four hours. Thirty-eight minutes.

I need to get to her now.

Climbing to my feet, I walk towards the door. Stormie wraps me in her magic before I can take two steps. I slam my shoulder against her wall of pink, furious and desperate to get to Micha. The fucking wall holds. Her magic hums with power as it feeds on mine, coaxing me to release more. The more I do, the stronger it gets, the weaker I become. My shadows fill the bubble as I continue to pulse, and I start to panic as it gets harder and harder to see my phone. To see Micha. To be with her in the only way I can.

I'm bathed in total darkness. Even the screen's light is gone. But I can still hear that man talking, and now I can hear my wife getting slapped around. How many men have abused her in those four hours and thirty-eight minutes?

Exhaustion hits me like a fucking semi running a red light. I struggle to keep my eyes open as my shadows start to disappear, my magic drained by Stormie's shield.

My limbs feel like lead is coursing through my veins, and I sway on my feet. My eyes stay latched onto the screen. The phone has been passed to Antonio, and the man who was behind the camera is now in view. I finally have a face to go with the voice of the man I'm going to kill.

And a body.

And a cock.

My heart bursts. My power pulses beneath my skin, wild and furious but too drained to be released. Just bleeding eternally. I can't help her. I can't stop this.

They're holding her down, forcing her legs apart, and he is lining up his cock with her pussy.

"I knew you'd like this," he lies.

She doesn't like any part of this. That's so fucking clear.

Once I get my hands on him, I'm taking his off. Piece by piece, I'll butcher him slowly over four years, thirty-eight days.

"You have a fucking ugly cunt. It would be better to fuck a pig, but you're just begging me to take you, aren't you, whore?"

I'm going to feed him to the fucking pigs he loves.

"Give me the phone, Varius," Khalid says as he moves in front of me. Stormie's bubble is gone, as are my shadows.

I pull away from him, my eyes unwavering. I can't stop watching it. I can't leave her alone.

"And I'm nothing if not a nice guy."

He thrusts into her.

She arches in agony.

Rudy snatches the phone out of my grasp, my fingers too weak to hold it.

I scream at him, but he just tosses the phone aside, then throws his arms around me. He hugs me. Holds me back.

I try to push him away, not wanting to take any comfort when Micha doesn't have any.

But he doesn't let me go.

He clings on.

Squeezes me tighter.

"Tell me he's going to be okay," Leno begs, his broken words piercing through my grief. Guilt slams into me as I stop struggling against Rudy and turn my head to look at Krypto.

He is lying on Louise Warner's lap. I didn't notice her come in, but she's sitting on the floor with him. One hand rests on the mutt's head, the other on his chest. I can hear him breathing, but it's raspy and weak. Tendrils of smoke-like shadows seep out of his nose and mouth.

Her face scrunched up in concentration, Louise lets her

magic flow out of her fingers. Krypto isn't a true familiar. He's a witch's pet, with a special bond and some magical attributes, but he isn't magical himself. He's just a dog, and Louise only specializes in humans.

"Please tell me he's going to be okay."

Khalid places a hand on his shoulder.

My stomach twists with guilt. "Leno, I'm sorry. I couldn't control it."

He shakes his head, unable to speak.

Louise doesn't answer him either.

Shit.

If he dies...

He can't die.

He's one of us.

He's family, and I can't lose any more fucking family.

"Louise, *please*..."

I turn from them. Needing to do something I can control, I push Rudy away. He lets me go this time. I'm not mindless with rage anymore. I'm wielding it like a fucking weapon.

"Phone," I demand as I hold out my hand.

Enoch studies me for a moment before retrieving it with his telekinesis.

Stepping away so I don't break Louise's concentration, I look down at my phone. The video has been paused with the fucker's cock halfway in my wife. Dark energy claws at my skin, demanding vengeance and violence. My rage burns cold, and I tear my eyes from the video, looking below it instead.

Posted one hour ago.

Sixty thousand views.

Nine comments.

Closing the page, I call Stefaan Black. He answers on the first ring.

"I'm hiring every single one of your assassins. All their other jobs end now."

"I can't –"

"Antonio has your daughter, and he posted a video of her torture. I want Goodbye World" –the best hacker group in the world and part of his gang– "to scrub it from the web and any device it's been downloaded to. I want messages made out of every single fucker who has viewed it. I don't care what the price is to make that happen."

His voice goes deadly quiet. "Where is she?"

"Get your men on the video, Stefaan. I want it fucking down, and everyone who's seen it tortured."

He snaps out an order to whoever is beside him, calling all of his assassins back temporarily (so as not to void their contracts), regardless of what they're doing. Then he returns to me. "Where. Is. She?"

"Morning Springs, West Virginia," I say just as Mother arrives with Aleric and the other vampires. "We hit in an hour."

FOURTEEN

HER

The men might've enjoyed what I did to Eduardo's face, but it isn't enough to make them see me as one of them. As soon as I'm wheeled into their living quarters, they drag me out of the hospital bed and force me onto a breeding table.

An actual, bonafide fucking breeding table.

It's in three parts. One table with leather straps for my arms and two separate pillars with ties for my ankles. The pillars are on locking wheels so my legs can be moved to wherever they want them.

I fight like a hellcat as they throw me down onto my back. They drag me across the table until my ass is near the edge. Hourglass pins me down by my throat while Sadist, Grubs, and Chucky get me strapped in. I kick Chucky in the balls, so he punches me in the face until I pass out.

I come to a few seconds later, as the last strap gets pulled tight on my elbow. By not tying my wrists down, I can still give them handjobs. My head is killing me, and one of my eyes is swollen shut. As I struggle to see past the blood and the stars dancing behind my eyes, Grubs steps between my legs and spits on my pussy. He rubs his saliva over me as he takes out his short, fat cock. "You're such a good girl, letting me make love to your pretty little cunt," he says. He lines his cock up with my hole.

Just as he's about to thrust in though, Softie, the guy who couldn't get it up earlier, says, "Fuck her in the morning, Michael. I want to go to bed."

His real name might be Michael, but I am still going to call him Grubs. He doesn't deserve that level of respect.

"But –"

"That table's loud as fuck."

Grubs looks at Sadist, but he just yawns and walks away. Even monsters need their sleep.

Sighing, Grubs puts his dick away and backs off. Softie shoots me an empathetic look that says, *That's all I can do.*

In this moment, it is enough. I breathe out slowly to hide my tremors as he steps through a door that I assume leads into his bedroom. We're in the gym, the court-painted floor and high rafted ceiling dead giveaways, but there are over a dozen square pods set up around the edges for the men to have their privacy. I lie in the middle of the communal area, beside sofas and a TV, my pussy spread open for all to see.

Left alone, I try to relax enough to close my eyes. Sleep increases the healing process, and if I don't get some rest, I will lose my edge and my ability to think clearly. I won't survive this place then.

I already know that tomorrow I'm going to break. That's when the breeding will start for real. When I'll be forced to take V after V as they rape me in their werewolf forms.

My heart rate increases as I force myself to think about it, to imagine every detail of what's coming in an attempt to prepare myself. I can't stop what's going to happen come the morning, but by confronting it in my thoughts, I can work my way through the trauma before it begins.

Hopefully.

Theoretically.

Probably not, but it's giving me a sense of control, which is something I desperately need right now because Vs don't just change a woman's anatomy so she can take monster cocks without dying. They increase her arousal, heightening the sensitivity of her g-spot and clit. I won't be able to stop myself from orgasming as they rape me, and when they ejaculate inside of me, it'll trigger the V to make me squirt all over them.

I know, logically, that it won't be me doing those things. It will be the drug they give me. It'll be anatomy. Nipples simply stand up in the cold. It doesn't mean the A/C unit turns us on.

But it's still my body betraying me.

It's still my mind associating something pleasurable and intimate with something so fucking disgusting.

It's still going to break me from the shame.

From the knowledge that this won't just be a one time thing. It'll be hour after hour, day after day, week after week if Varius doesn't fucking save me. Because I'm not escaping this bed by myself, and it will take a long time for me to manipulate any of these men into helping me.

By that point, I'll be addicted to Vs. To their touch. The increase of arousal hormones will fuck with my reality. I'll lose my desire to escape. I'll beg them to fuck me day and night just so I can get another fix.

Then eventually, I'll get pregnant.

That reality terrifies me.

Makes me sick.

Makes it nearly impossible for me to go to sleep despite my training. Though even when I do, I keep one eye open. Waking up at every perceived movement or sound.

Varius better fucking come for me soon, I think as I'm

trying my best to sleep.

A pinprick stabs the bottom of my foot, and I wince. I can't get comfortable on this damn –

I jerk wide awake, though I keep my body still so I don't make a sound. Softie wasn't kidding when he said this table was loud. Every movement echoes through the gym.

Another pinprick radiates up my leg. It isn't painful, but the significance of it makes it so damn electrifying, I could cry.

Khalid's made a soul doll of me.

Half a year ago, that would've fucking terrified me. He's the reason I kept my head shaved, not wanting to leave any DNA evidence for him to find. With it, he can create soul dolls, allowing him to torture you from afar, then straight up kill you.

But fuck, right now I am so damn relieved. The range and limitations of his magic is a well kept secret, though there are rumors that he can see and hear everything his victims do. Granted, those are rumors mostly spread by rats. I swear I didn't tell anyone, Boss. Khalid must have made a soul doll of you and found out that way. But I hope to gods it's true.

I open my mouth to start to tell him everything I have found out, but he cuts me off with a series of pinpricks in Morse code.

Dayne alive

Relief burns my eyes and throat. I can't stop the tears from leaking down my face. I only just manage to stifle the sobs. I thought he died. I thought –

Rescue one hour

I close my eyes as a tremble rushes through me. Then I open them again as I whisper, "There are kids here."

I don't want them caught in the crossfire. Whatever the sins of their parents, they are innocent.

We know

That doesn't sound like he cares though. "Don't –"

Zita. Ally. Bye

I don't feel any different when he's gone. There's no way for me to tell when he's here with me. I also still don't know if he can really see or hear what I do or if he can only hear what I say. My throat tightens at the idea of him having witnessed any of my abuse. Then I think about the video Antonio sent Varius. I don't know which one is worse.

Khalid watching in real time "through me."

Or the love of my life seeing it at all.

How can I ever face either of them?

Taking a deep breath, I push those thoughts aside. I can't lose my head right now. I need to keep it together so when Zita comes, I can do whatever she needs me to. Focusing on the tattoo I gave Dayne all those years ago – something I've been terrified to do, thinking I'd feel it gone, I concentrate on his heartbeat.

It's faster than normal. A bit more panicked.

But it's there.

He's alive.

I breathe out on a shudder.

Breathe in on a fractured smile.

Out and in until my thoughts quiet...

As it's done so many times, the rhythm of his pulse soon lures me into sleep.

Just for a little while though.

When I open my eyes, I look to the high windows of the gym. The sun isn't up yet, but the sky's darker than before, telling me the moon's gone. It's perhaps two or three hours before dawn.

A tear falls down my cheek as I focus on Dayne's pulse. It's calmer now, less stressed. He believes in the plan.

They're going to save me before the men wake, before I'm forced to take a V.

Of course, that's when one of the pod doors opens, and

footsteps creep towards me.

FIFTEEN

HER

My heartbeat picks up at the sight of Grubs, but I tell myself I only need to stall him for one hour.

Sixty minutes.

Two sets of half-hour blocks.

Four fifteen-minute sections.

That seems more manageable.

I can do this.

Grubs sees himself as a nice guy. That means he'll be easy to manipulate. I just need to stroke his ego, then get him to do some foreplay without the V. The idea of faking moans with his head between my legs twists my stomach, but I only have to endure this for one hour.

Four fifteen-minute blocks.

For a split second, I think about screaming. If the others like their beauty sleep, they might beat the shit out of Grubs for interrupting it. But there's too big of a risk that Sadist just decides to join in. There won't be any talking with him, no foreplay. And if he beats me unconscious or just breaks a few bones, then I might struggle to walk out of here on my own. If someone has to carry me, it'll fuck us both over.

So I keep my mouth shut until Grubs gets close enough to hear me whisper, a pink vial in his hand. Then I plaster on the smile I use for seducing targets.

"I was hoping you would come visit me before the others woke up," I say as I look him up and down. "The way you fucked me yesterday has me so *desperate* to feel your cock again."

He stumbles a step, his eyes widening. Then his surprise quickly gives way to a puffed out chest and cocky grin.

"I like your cock so much better than the others. You actually know how to use your big, bad boy." I glance down at the small tent in his underwear. I'm laying it on too thick for most people, but "nice guys" are egotistical narcissists. He eats it all up with hungry eyes.

"Can I feel your tongue and fingers today?"

His eyes light up as he hurries the rest of the way over to me. "Of course, princess. You can play with Daddy's cock today with your mouth too, and I can play with your pussy."

His words almost slap me out of my fake persona, but I hold onto it like a fucking professional.

Taking his directional cues, I say, "Thank you, Daddy." I arch my back a little and lift my hips. "I've been dreaming about you all night."

"So have I," he says as he reaches out to cup my breasts.

"Tell me what you've been dreaming about doing to me," I say as I bite my lip.

He stands between my legs, his eyes roaming across my body. "I was thinking about sucking on your tits for hours."

"Oh, please do it, Daddy." I arch my back, hoping like hel that's all he does until Varius gets here. I'll never be able to get clean of his touch, but at least I will be able to live with myself.

Leaning down, he takes my breast into his mouth. He sucks on me like he's a fucking vacuum. I don't think he's ever made a girl come in his life. Still, I start to moan. "Oh gods, Daddy. Thank you. You're so good to me."

He likes me thanking him. Likes me calling him Daddy. If I can get him to come in his pants, he'll need a while to recover. Perhaps an entire fifteen-minute block...

He places the vial of V down on the table, not far from my elbow, then starts to grope me with both hands. I turn my head towards the pink potion, wondering if I can knock it off "by accident." Will that draw attention to it, or will I get away with it?

Deciding to hide it under me so he'll have to spend some time looking for it, I reach for it with my left hand. Fuck. He has placed it somewhere I can't quite get. Gritting my teeth, I strain against my binds while he's distracted by my chest. The leather cuts into my skin. My hand bends so far around it hurts. My fingers flick back and forth as I almost manage to –

Feeling his head start to lift, I slap my other hand over the back of it and hold him to me as I curl my fingers into his hair. "Keep sucking on my tits," I moan as I arch my back, pushing myself into him.

Maybe if I can rock the table a little, I can reach it...

No.

I don't want to make enough noise to wake the others.

"Oh gods, your tongue feels so good on my tits, Daddy. You're going to make me come."

I wriggle beneath him as I increase my moans. He starts to suck on my nipples faster. His technique somehow gets even worse. His teeth scrape across me a couple of times, but I finally manage to grab the damn vial.

Moving quickly, I lift my head up, place the V between my shoulder blades, and then lie back down. I suffer three minutes of his gnawing before I fake an orgasm. I go all out, making him feel like a man, stroking his ego.

I grip his hair hard. Hard enough to pull a few strands loose so I can give them to Khalid in case I don't get to kill him before I escape.

"Thank you, Daddy," I say as I glance at the windows of the gym. Does the sky look lighter now? Either way, that has to have been fifteen minutes. Just three more blocks to go…

"I love making you feel good, princess. I'm going to eat your pussy now," Grubs says as he peppers my chest with kisses. "Daddy's going to make you come so hard." He licks me down to my navel.

"Wait," I blurt, trying to think of a way of stopping him when I'm supposed to be into all this. He's going too fast if that was his idea of 'hours' of nipple play.

"Can you get the V?" I say. "I think I knocked it off the table."

"I don't need that to make you feel good."

"But then you can shift, and you have such a big tongue as a werewolf. You don't want to hurt me though, do you Daddy? I thought I was being such a good girl."

He stills, and I wonder if he's quick enough to realize he doesn't need the V if he's just licking me. Or if he's just so caught up in the moment, he's not thinking things through and just associates werewolf + human = needs V to not hurt them.

"I want to feel your long, wet tongue in my pussy," I say, trying to keep him from thinking straight. "You will be able to lick me in places no one's ever touched me before. Don't you want to be my first?"

The idea of virginity is like catnip to "nice guys." They act like they are such gentlemen, when in fact, they're the most judgmental, women-hating assholes out there – which comes to light as soon as you do something they don't like.

So if I can piss him off by getting him to look for the vial

I've hidden, he might forget to 'care for me' at all and just straight up rape me. At least then, I won't be high on V.

"Okay. Because you're being such a good girl. Just wait here. Daddy'll be right back."

I smile at him as he hurries away, bending over at the waist as he scours the floor for the sex potion. He looks for less than ten fucking seconds before he's back between my legs, shoving his underwear down, and pulling out his cock.

"What are you –"

He shoves into me, and I grit my teeth from the pain. The "foreplay" with my nipples did nothing to prepare me.

"I'm sorry, princess," he grunts as he grabs my hips and rams into me like an animal. "Daddy couldn't wait. I kept thinking about how good you feel, and I just had to get back to you. You understand, don't you? You forgive me?"

I ball my hands into fists as he tears apart my vagina.

"Of course, Daddy," I grit out as I arch my back, a new plan forming in my fucking mind. "I want you to fuck me. I want you to kiss me too. Will you kiss me? Show me I've been a good –"

His lips crush mine. My stomach lurches up my throat as I force myself to part my lips. He is so far gone, he clearly isn't thinking about what I did to Eduardo's nose. He shoves his tongue into my mouth without any hesitation, and I kiss him back, straining against my binds as I moan beneath him.

"I need to touch you, Daddy," I rasp against his mouth. "Untie my hands."

"I can't," he pants as he kisses my neck.

"Just one," I plead. "Please? I want to cup your balls as you fuck me."

He groans as he shudders and falls on top of me. I pray the asshole hasn't just come. Let one fucking thing go my way right now.

"Okay," he says as he kisses my lips. He starts thrusting

into me again. "But I'll have to tie you back up afterwards."

"Of course," I say breathlessly.

He leans back enough to undo the strap on my right arm. As much as I want to clock him in the face, I thread my fingers into his hair and pull him back to me. My heartbeat is utterly calm as I slip into the mindset of an assassin.

I trail my lips down his throat while my free hand slips between our bodies.

He moans.

I kiss his neck, right below his jaw.

Then just as my fingers graze his hips, I bite down hard and rip out his carotid.

He falls against me, gasping and in shock but not dead. I have sixty seconds to torture him before he passes out. Two more minutes after that until he dies.

As blood squirts all over the place, drenching me and the table, I spit out the chunk of his throat. His dick slides out of me, then the rest of him starts to fall off the table. I squeeze him with my thighs before he can thump against the floor.

Weaving my hand under him, I undo the buckle holding down my other arm. Then I slowly lower him to the ground and untie my feet.

Sliding off the table, I don't turn for the door. There's no point running. I don't know the building, and they can just hunt me down by smell. Given I'm covered in Grubs' blood, I'll be easy to find, and that might make it harder for Varius to rescue me.

Besides, I want to make him suffer in his final moments. I really want to take hours with him and make him scream, make him *hurt.*

But only an idiot drags out a death when they're low on time. It's right up there with monologuing as a villain or not killing the hostage after you get busted.

I have forty-ish seconds left.

Crouching over his body, I grab hold of his testicles and

twist them over and over again to remove the elasticity from the area. Planting a foot on his pubes, I jerk to my feet with a hard yank. His ballsack rips free with a satisfying noise that I will remember every night in my dreams.

He stares up at me, pain and terror in his eyes. They're glassy; he doesn't have long.

But I will be the last thing he sees.

Shoving my fingers into his eye sockets, I scoop both of them out. There's a split second of resistance as the bundle of nerves at the back of them pull tight.

Then they're snapping free, and I'm crouching back over his groin, tying his eyes together, and looping them around his pathetic cock.

His testicles, I pop into his eye sockets so he can know just what an utter fucking *ballsack* he is.

I do not wait with him as he dies. He doesn't deserve my company.

Instead, having realized it'd be suspicious if I didn't run, that it might warn them Varius is about to attack, I head for the door.

Slipping out into the hall, I come face to face with Zita as she was about to enter.

"I told you they have a soul doll of her," she says, talking over her shoulder to Antonio, "and they're coordinating her escape."

You backstabbing bitch.

SIXTEEN

HER

I'm shoved back into the room. As soon as Antonio steps inside, noise radiates from every pod. They can smell their alpha and are hurrying to see what he wants.

Eleven doors open around me.

Chucky shouts, "The bitch killed Michael."

The hairs on my neck rise. My adrenaline spikes, and I'm twitching at every noise, every movement. The violence in the air is damn near suffocating.

I take a step back as Zita and Antonio advance, but all the other men push in from every angle.

"I'm going to take you with me when I escape," I say as I glare at the woman in front of me. "Then I'm going to cut you up better than Maddox did."

"Maddox never laid a hand on me, so that's a pathetic threat. But here's one: I'm going to pretend you're Maddox when I torture you. That fucking asshole has so much shit coming, and I'm going to practice everything I want to do to him on you." She pulls out a knife. "Starting now."

"Khalid is going to kill you." Maddox has definitely kept her DNA, but our supply of alexandrite is limited and super precious. I don't know if my threat is fact, but I face her like it is.

"No, he won't." She smiles with utter certainty. "Because I've already been killed and brought back with necromancy. He doesn't have my complete DNA anymore, which means no soul doll."

When a person is resurrected, they're given a bit of the soul of the necromancer, changing their genetic makeup just enough for Khalid's magic not to work.

"And the thing about soul dolls is that once their victim dies, the alexandrite becomes useless. Talon stole their main stash, which means they don't have much alexandrite left, and they're going to use every last stone on you." She cocks her head to the side. "You hearing this, Khalid? We know how to bypass your creepy magic."

Her eyes focus back on me. "Now, since you're bonded with Varius, necromancy is out. It makes it too complicated to bring you back, and Antonio here doesn't want to risk you dying for good." She starts to undo her belt. "So we're going to strangle you, then bring you back with CPR. Over and over and over again until we use up all their precious backup."

My heart rate jumps as someone grabs me from behind. A wet tongue slides across the side of my face, and I know it's Sadist before he even speaks. "I'm going to fuck you while you're dead," he whispers in my ear.

I throw an elbow into his side, but he takes a page out of my fucking playbook and latches his teeth around my ear. I scream as he rips it off my head, the tearing of flesh felt all the way down my jawline.

Instantly, the building rocks with an explosion. The boys are here, and Khalid is watching through my eyes, but I feel no sense of relief.

If they kill me before my bond with Varius is complete, will that destroy it? The idea of losing it when I've already lost so much is damn near crippling.

I fall to my knees as the ground shakes beneath me, and the loss of my ear fucks with my balance.

"That's Varius," Zita says as she stands over me with a cruel smile. "We're going to go kill him real quick, then be right back for you." She turns to Antonio. "You'll need all these men. He's finally hit his ascension."

I gasp at the idea of his curse having broken. There is a part of me that's so happy he's come to kick their asses, but there's another part of me, a colder part that hates him out of envy. He took my magic. How dare he get his own. And what the fuck? He told me he'd have to be okay with giving me up for the curse to break. If he's thinking of saving me only to try to leave me so I'm "safe," I'm going to kick his ass.

"Strap her back to the table," Antonio says.

Sadist hauls me to my feet, then backhands me across my missing ear when I try to fight him off. My vision blurs, the edges going black as my head rings with pain. I'm forced onto the table.

"Cut off her circulation," Antonio says.

I scream as I get my second wind, fighting tooth and nail, but there's too many of them, and they are well rested and healed, whereas I am not. As the straps tighten painfully on my elbows and ankles, I scream for all I am worth. The building doesn't rock this time though. Khalid is no longer watching me, no doubt preoccupied with whoever it is they're fighting.

"Let's go," he says, satisfied that I'm not going anywhere. Zita starts to leave with the men, but he stops her. "Stay here."

"They tortured me," she seethes. "I want to help kill –"

She cuts herself off and bows her head. He's her alpha, and he's just given her an order. Her jaw tics as he leaves. As soon as the door shuts, she turns to me.

"Knife or belt," she says as she gestures with one, then the other. "I'm hurting someone today, and oh, look, you're the only one here."

"Touch me, and –"

My words die as her eyes widen in horror, right before she stabs herself in the stomach. She twists the blade around as she falls to her knees. The belt slips from her fingers. As panic carves itself into her face, I wonder if she's being touched by Rudy's madness. Pulling out the knife, she drops it onto the floor, then shoves her hand inside the hole.

"You fucker…" Zita bites out as she falls onto her ass, her face pale, her body shaking. The pain she's going through must be intense. If I didn't hate the bitch, I might have been impressed. But she isn't looking good, her body already too frail from Maddox's torture.

"Get *out* of me," she seethes as she yanks her arm free, and in her hand…

Is a fucking tapeworm.

Her horror infects me. My stomach twists with the idea of having one of those things inside of me. It wriggles in her grip, but I don't think it's trying to get free. Magic electrifies the air, and my horror intensifies as I realize that fucker is Maddox.

Using her other hand, Zita drags more and more of the worm out of her digestive tract.

The fucker is long.

Three or four feet at least.

Swaying on her knees, she tries to grab the knife she dropped as Maddox wriggles on the floor, his shapeshifting magic starting to amp up. His eyes and ears pop out along the top of his length. His shadows swirl beneath him as he draws on the extra meat he keeps in his locker to increase his size.

Zita manages to touch her knife, but she's too weak to actually grab it. Her eyes roll back in her head as she falls to the ground, blood pouring out of her stomach.

Maddox finishes shifting into his full naked form. Then he turns towards me with a crooked smile. "You so owe me," he says as he walks towards me.

"I've never been more happy to see you."

"It's because I'm naked, isn't it?" His smile falls as his eyes rove over my naked form. He takes in the breeding table I'm strapped to, the bruises and cuts on my face, my missing ear. A darkness cloaks him, wrapping him in its arms like an old friend, and I shiver despite myself.

I've never seen him so serious before.

"I need to do something before I get you out of there," he says softly, "but you're going home tonight Micha."

I take a deep breath, my chest quivering as I bite back my pleas to please get me out of this damn thing first. They have a plan. If Maddox says he needs to do something, it's to help get me out of here and all the boys back home alive.

"How's Dayne?" I ask as I watch him move over to Zita. He kneels down beside her, dips his fingers in her blood, and quickly starts sketching out a summoning circle.

"Alive." His tone tells me he's busy concentrating, so I bite back the rest of my questions even though I really want to know about Varius and Rafiki. Varius is here. Dayne will be too. Neither of them would have stayed behind. I can ask them myself soon enough.

I study the circle Maddox is drawing as best as I can from my position. I recognize a few of the runes as ones my sister created. She's a progeny in summoning demons, and I damn near had a heart attack whenever she asked me to check for monsters under her bed or in her closet when she was little. Nine times out of ten, they were real.

How she managed to survive all this time is the world's

greatest mystery, especially since she's the clumsiest person in said world.

Maddox steps back once his circle is done. Funneling his magic, he chants for a solid minute, and the hairs on my neck rise as I wonder who the fuck he's summoning. Most demons only need one or two sentences to call them forth. Given the amount of limitations and power he is pulling on to bring this fucker forth, they must be powerful. An arch demon perhaps?

The urge to yell at Maddox to free me already increases with every second that passes, with every building of power in the circle of runes. I keep telling myself I'll get out of my binds soon, but it's getting harder and harder to stay calm. I feel so vulnerable on this table. So helpless and weak. If he can't control the demon, I'll be at its mercy just as much as I was at the wolves.

The summoning circle hums with an influx of power. The runes turn black, and a swirl of dark-blue smoke fills the area. Glitters of gold twinkle in and out of the haze, like a galaxy of stars. He's clearly calling forth a pride demon. They always like to make an entrance. In a blinding flash of gold light, the smoke clears, and in its place is an eknor pride demon.

Their kind can take many shapes and forms, but this one is a towering bipedal male with sleek dark-blue fur all over his body. Like the smoke from before, he is dusted with bits of gold – an entire galaxy of stars from a world far away from here. He has the mane of a lion, and two strands, one on either side of his head, have been braided before ending with a golden feather. A tail with multiple heads flicks lazily behind him, like a cat o'nine tails whip. His thick arms are crossed, showcasing his muscles, and behind his back are folded feathered wings.

A loincloth is the only clothes he has on, but there is a golden cuff around his right bicep and a necklace of teeth hanging between his collar bones. It's the cuff that draws my focus. Engraved within its metal –something far more valuable than gold– is a depiction of the sun beside a pretty detailed bird, like an archaeopteryx of sorts, its wing-arms spread, its beak to the sky, its talons wicked and sharp.

He isn't wearing it though.

No.

The cuff's been melted into his skin.

Which means this pretty boy is one of the seven princes of Sin. He is the Prince of Pride. They have no king.

His power makes my heart flip.

Now I no longer feel helpless.

I feel insignificant.

Like an ant in front of an elephant.

Normally, this is when the summoner brags to the demon about how powerful they are and why they must listen to them before giving the demon very detailed and extremely exact instructions on what they are to do. However, Maddox just draws another picture on the floor.

Not a rune this time.

The callsign of my sister. She has a bit of a reputation in the eknor kingdom…

The demon's entire demeanor changes. He's no longer puffing out his chest in a warrior's pride. Not a peacock strutting his power. Now he stills like the true predator he is. His strength is quieter, more lethal, like a lion stalking through the grass.

Maddox points to me, and the demon's head follows his finger. His eyes, gold and burning like the sun as it dips below the horizon, land on me.

I shiver even as I lift my chin.

"She wants you to kill any werewolf you find inside this building for the next thirty minutes," Maddox says.

"But no kids," I add. I'm pretty certain the 'she' Maddox mentioned is Lou, not me. He won't use her name though, doesn't want to give the demon that power over her. But the eknor is still staring at me, so hopefully that means he will listen.

The demon prince inclines his head, his mane shifting like moonlight through an ancient forest. "Sister," he says, his accent heavy and thick, his dialect nowhere from earth.

As I stare at him in utter bafflement, he steps across the line of runes, his arms dropping to his sides. "You are not as good as her," he says to Maddox, letting him know the circle did shit all to contain him.

My nerves spike as my eyes dart between them. If he wants to kill Maddox, there is nothing I'll be able to do.

"Yeah... She said I might get myself killed..." he says, not a single waver to his voice. In fact, he looks fucking pleased with himself. Proud.

The demon grunts, then heads for the door. Sleek like a panther, his muscles rippling beneath his fur.

"All the witches are her friends!" Maddox calls out.

Except for Eduardo. But I don't tell him that. I want to be the one to kill him.

The demon makes no sign of having heard him. As the gym door shuts behind him, Maddox hurries over to me and starts to undo my binds.

"Why did he call me sister?" I ask warily. That is not a name of address for them.

"So that's a funny story," he says as he frees my arms. I try to sit up to help him remove the straps on my feet, but my limbs are too numb and tingly to listen to me.

"I could use some humor right now," I say.

"Mmm. Well, short story, that's going to be your brother-in-law. I think. I think he's planning on kidnapping her now that she's pregnant with his child, but –"

"What?" I shout. "She's sixteen! What did you do?"

"Hey, why is it automatically my fault?"

"She was so *good* until she started hanging out with you."

He grins, proud of himself.

"Maddox..." I growl.

Finished untying my ankles, he helps me off the table. My legs refuse to hold my weight, so he sets me on the floor, well away from Zita.

"What. Did. You. Do?" I grit out.

"Well... I might have, theoretically, allegedly told her to have hot, dirty sex with a more powerful guy than Rudy so she wouldn't have to marry him?"

"*Maddox*," I growl. My savior or not, I'm going to kill him.

"In my defense," Varius' soon-to-be dead brother says as he starts to pull on his shadows, "I thought she was asking for a friend. She said, and I quote, 'What would you advise for a *friend* of mine who's getting married for their virginity to someone she doesn't want to –"

"She doesn't have any friends getting married!" I yell. "She's sixteen!"

"Yeah, I hear you, but she clearly wasn't talking about herself because we don't care if she's a virgin."

My eyes narrow at him as he pulls out the cage he kept Zita in. "No one who says I'm asking for a friend," I bite out, "is ever asking for a fucking friend."

I'm so pissed at him that it takes me a few seconds to clock what his plan is. Then my eyes widen. "Oh hel no. I'm not getting in that."

"You won't survive in the Shadow Domain until the bond is completed, and you're not fit to walk, let alone fight. So in you go."

I grit my teeth. I hate this plan so much.

"Don't you want to survive long enough to yell at her and kill me?" he asks sweetly.

My eyes are fucking slits at this point. "Fine. But when you bring me out, I don't want anyone there. I want to get dressed and showered first." If I'm yelling at my sister, I'm sure as hel not doing it naked. She'll twist the conversation around with all her concern for me, and I'm not having it.

"Varius –" Maddox starts.

"*Varius*," I spit, my anger at him coming back now that my rescue is imminent, "got me into this fucking mess. He can damn well wait for me to get showered and dressed before he goes all neanderthal." I swallow hard. My voice lowers. "Don't let him see me like this. Please." If he's going to try to send me away for my "safety," then I'm going to look like a fucking lady.

His lips in a tight line, Maddox nods. Then he helps me into the cage. He shuts the door, but before he can seal it with magic to keep the monsters out, the gym's door bangs open.

"Shadow form!" I scream as three chimeras race towards his back. They've changed into their monsters, and they are moving fast. There's no way Maddox is going to be able to turn in time.

The only way he can survive this is if he shifts into his shadows. They can't touch him then.

But the little shit tries to pivot anyways, not wanting to disappear long enough for their attention to turn to me.

SEVENTEEN

HIM

My back slams into a wall of the school as I struggle to keep a werewolf from ripping out my throat. Her teeth snap in front of my face, her breath rancid, her spittle flying everywhere. My arms strain from the force of keeping her head away from mine, but by doing so, I've left my sides completely open to her claws.

She starts to rake them across my chest, trying to open me up like a fucking pinata. I kick her in the groin with my steel shank boot, catching her off guard with my unnatural speed. Her pelvis snaps, shatters, completely obliterates. She yelps as she crumbles to the ground, then makes no sound at all once my knee connects with her chin.

The *crack* of her jaw is instantly followed by the *squelch* of the shards as they pummel into her brain. An angry howl comes from down the hall as a wolf charges at me from my right. Shoving my broken opponent aside, I turn to face them, but Leno is already on her.

Krypto wasn't in a good way when we left the house. I did something to him that Louise couldn't fix. My magic wasn't physically hurting him; there was nothing for her to actually heal. It was just... *replacing* his brain, weaving in amongst the neurons and gray matter like a fungus. The only thing she could do was keep him in stasis until Mother arrived, and even she, the best healer in the world, struggled to remove my magic.

Still, the dog was infected for too long. A magical residue lingers inside him, poisoning his blood, causing his organs to fail over and over again every time they're healed. With Louise there, he has a good chance of survival, which is the only reason Leno left with us.

Otherwise, he would've stayed by his best friend's side until he passed.

Wanting to get this mission over with quickly so he can get back to his dog, Leno charges at the wolf. He attacks her like an animal. A beast without restraint. Flowered vines are wrapped around his forearms. Sharpened sticks point out of them at every angle, no doubt dripping with poison. Any time he blocks an arm or a snapping jaw, he's dealing more damage than them. The wolf yelps as he beats her with his club-like fists. He pounds into her, breaking her bones and severing her arteries with every blow.

Leno rarely ever gets his hands dirty, preferring to kill in ways that don't shed blood, but at the moment, he's reveling in the violence. The infliction of pain. The transferring of his agony as he worries about his dog.

Turning from him, I attack the next werewolf standing between me and my wife. The hallway is full of mothers and fathers that have barreled out of their homes to protect the pups hiding inside; we normally leave no survivors, no kids that can grow into soldiers, so they're fighting as viciously as we are.

But eventually, they will all die because I'm not failing

my fucking wife again.

That damn video haunts me as I pull out a new set of knives and dance through the chaos of fur. Over the snarls and shouts of battle, I can hear her desperate screams, the ones her broken vocal cords couldn't handle.

Over the crimson slashes of blood and the white sprays of spittle, over Mother's shadow on the floor racing towards my wife, I can see Micha's broken and bruised body. The unwarranted shame on her face. The pain. The agony. The hopelessness.

It fuels me as I cut down one wolf after the other. My brothers are beside me, as is Dayne in Maddox's form, but we're not moving fast enough. Although I planned for Zita to betray us, only really needing her to get Maddox inside, I didn't expect Antonio to have someone bring her back. That changes everything, accelerates my need to get to her before it's too late.

I studied necromancy a lot when I was younger. It's a skill even humans can learn if they make the right deals with the keres and other reapers of death. If they learn how to walk all the different planes of Purgatory so they can escape at will. But there's only one way to talk to a keres and learn the paths of Purgatory. Only one way to train as a necromancer.

You have to die.

Over and over again because if you stay too long in one visit, your body will get consumed by the souls desperate to return to the world of the living. And without a body, you're nothing more than a trapped soul. Not dead, so you can never move on into the afterlife. Just lost without an anchor for all eternity.

I wasn't allowed to practice. But I studied the art deeply.

I uncovered all of the legends and myths, all the secrets within them.

Including the dark side of it, the illegal practice of killing soldiers right before a mission and then reviving them.

Necromancy requires a vast amount of power. You have to open a portal to Purgatory, heal the body, and reattach the soul. That influx of energy lingers in the patient long after they've returned, making them practically immortal. For the next few hours, they will auto-revive, healing from every injury unless both their heart and head is removed.

So in a normal fight between Zita and Maddox, I would put my money on my brother.

But right now?

When it's only been half an hour since Khalid saw her die through his soul doll, the stone turning black as Antonio squeezed the last air from her lungs?

Whatever Maddox does to her, it won't be enough. Zita will get back up. Perhaps when his back is turned. Then he'll die and so will my wife.

A set of claws scrape across my back, reprimanding me for being distracted. A fucker has come up behind me while I've been engaged with another wolf. I lunge forward just in time to save my spine from being severed. But that's pushed me into the range of my first opponent.

"Leave me!" I shout, seeing Rudy is about to come to my aid. "Get to Micha!"

I can't shift into my shadows like he can. I can't bypass all the wolves in our path, sliding across the floor in a form they can't touch. Mother is already racing towards the gym. I told her about the necromancy as soon as Khalid told us Zita was still alive, but Antonio already nearly killed her once. She can't call out her monsters when Micha isn't our blood. They'll turn on her as quickly as they turn on any wolf. Besides, Mother doesn't even know if they'll come this time. They have recently fed due to the attack at the house, and they are not pets, not dogs willing to defend. They are simply monsters who are happy to eat.

But worse, she is cursed. I don't know how capable of

fighting she actually is. The amount of magic she's used recently has been vast. She could die at any moment, hiding the fact that beneath her flawless skin, she's rotting away, the curse eating her alive.

So I want Rudy with her, as much as I'm terrified I might lose him and Micha at the same time. The two people I love the most. I don't know if I could survive their deaths (Rudy can die if his magic is first drained, meaning he can't bank on his nightmares to keep him alive), but I sure as hel know I won't survive failing to rescue my wife.

What they've done to her…

What they'll *do* to her if we don't get her out today.

Antonio knows now that we're bonded, so he'll move her constantly.

He knows we have a soul doll of her and that we can see and hear through her senses, so he'll kill her over and over again to ruin all the pieces of alexandrite we have left.

"Go!" I shout even as a wolf's claws slice open my chest. If I have to die so she lives, then it is a trade I'm willing to make. "*Please!*"

I will find her in the next life. I don't care that we're not fully bonded, that I won't have anything to pull me towards her. I *will* find the djinni who gave us the possibility to bond with our chosen mates, and I will kick the shit out of them until they return me to my wife.

Pain fills Rudy's eyes. As much as he's a son to me, I am a father to him. But he makes that split second decision I need him to. He shifts into his shadows and races off down the hall, after Mother, towards my wife.

I tumble to the side, my feet twisting out from under me as pain explodes across my back and chest. I hit the ground and fall into a roll. Pulling on my hybrid speed, I regain my feet, but fighting multiple opponents isn't like in the movies. They don't come at me one at a time. They don't wait for me to get back into a defensible position.

I'm tackled while I'm still in the middle of straightening. Teeth latch around my shoulder. I punch the wolf in the jaw. He yelps as his teeth go flying, but though he releases me, the second one is already biting down on my left leg and dragging me across the floor. I scream as she shakes her head, snapping my bone in half. Fighting through the pain, I lean up and slash my knife across her face multiple times. I hit her eye, her nose, her cheek – not precisely aimed cuts, just mad slices anywhere I can reach.

She releases me, but the wolf with the missing teeth is at my back. I can hear him thundering across the floor, and I know I'm not going to be able to turn in time.

Still, I try. I might be willing to die for Micha, but I'm going to fight until my last breath to see her one more time.

I roll over and stand on one leg. I raise my knife, but the wolf never reaches me. Stormie has him wrapped in a pink bubble of magic, and now she's compressing it, tightening it, squeezing it so small the wolf is pretzeled inside. Then his organs and bones pop out of his flesh, all nicely contained within a ball of pretty, glittery pink.

I grab two healing potions from my jacket and quickly guzzle them as I spin around to face the wolf I cut up with a knife. The bone in my leg snaps back together, and the slice on my chest heals, but the one on my back isn't as deep, isn't as serious, so it still bleeds. I'll need another potion to heal it, but I don't have the time right now.

Slasher has regained her feet. With one eye missing and most of her face covered in blood, she lunges for me. I duck, going low and getting in close and personal.

Werewolves stand at seven to eight feet on average, with some fuckers as tall as nine, so forcing them to bend down messes with their balance. Getting into their space removes their reach advantage. They focus on using their mouth and claws; they don't put as much thought into their footwork.

So as I dance around Slasher, I kick out and slice at her

legs. She topples to the ground, her tendons now severed. I quickly step up to kill her, embedding my knife into the back of her neck. With her paralyzed, I lift her head to slice open her throat, but a brother's scream stops me cold.

My focus snaps to the right, and between the fighting crowd, I clock Leno's being pulled apart by two wolves. One has his arm between its teeth, the other has his leg in an iron grip. Leno's vines are wrapped around his body now, trying to keep him in one piece as they tug him hard in opposite directions, but there is blood pouring through the vines at his joints.

Leaving the female, I run towards him, as does Khalid, having just killed the wolf he was fighting with his magic. Enoch, Ezriel, Stefaan, and Dayne are all still engaged with their own opponents. One of the vampires is dead, two of them are dying, having been bitten and infected. Aleric ran down a random hallway soon after Mother left, and I don't know if he's gone to find his own men that are being held here, forced to breed, or if he's caught Antonio's scent.

Stormie runs beside us without hesitation even though she isn't a fighter. She's never been trained in combat. She wrestled with the twins when she was a kid and won more times than not, but as soon as she hit puberty, she had to learn to become a lady. All the fire she was born with was tightly wrapped up behind fancy clothes and thick layers of make-up. But clearly, it was never doused, never snuffed out completely.

As we close the distance to our brother, Khalid builds up a ball of dark-red magic in his right hand, muttering under his breath to shape it. I pull out a gun from a holster on my side. In close, crowded quarters, where allies take up as much space as the enemy, it is a terrible weapon to use. But I can't throw a knife from this distance, so if I get a clear shot, I'm taking it.

Leno screams again.

More blood pours beneath him.

His vines are starting to tear.

Khalid launches his ball of magic at the wolf on his leg. It arcs through the air, a missile of burning energy.

Someone else screams from behind me. But it's a voice I don't recognize, a woman's. One of Aleric's vampires, so I don't turn, don't get torn between who to help. I'm getting Leno home to his dog.

Though fuck, Louise better not let Krypto die. If she does, it won't matter what these wolves are doing to him now. Losing his dog will kill him.

As Khalid's magic nears its target, the werewolf releases Leno. It darts out of the way, and I raise my gun, my finger on the trigger. I aim straight for his heart. But right before I fire, I yank the gun down. One of the man's arms is hanging loose, flopping around like it's missing a bone. I didn't catch the face of the wolf in the video Antonio sent me, but he had a dead arm just like that.

This is one of the fuckers who raped my wife.

I don't want to kill him with one shot to the heart.

The bullet slams into his thigh, so close to his fucking groin. He stumbles to his knees and growls. I can almost smell my wife on his skin. The urge to empty my gun into his face is damn hard to resist, but a bubble goes up around him, and I decide that's infinitely better.

"I want him alive," I say to Stormie. After we get Micha back home, I'm going to gift her this piece of shit. Then we're going to cut him open together. Turn him inside out. It'll be a lovely date night, the first of our hunt as we kill every single fucker who hurt her.

The other wolf, with snow white fur, drops Leno as it charges at me on all fours. Along its back is a row of bone-colored spikes, rising up like hackles. But it's his eyes that are drawing my attention. Violent and cruel and so fucking familiar.

This is the wolf who took the lead, the one who tortured my wife as well as raped her. His death is going to be slow, so fucking slow as everything he did to Micha is repaid a thousand times over.

I charge forward, tackling him before he gets to Khalid, my control breaking, my bloodlust making me mad. I bare my teeth, wanting to rip out his throat like a fucking beast, but I bite it back. Because when I feed from my wife, it'll be with virgin fangs. She'll be my first and last. The parts I sink inside her will never be tainted with the flesh of another.

As we collide in the air, my shoulder slams into his solar plexus. I press my gun against his belly and fire twice. He grunts as we hit the ground. I land on top of him, then scramble up to beat his face in with the butt of the gun. I don't want this fight to be long. I want to get to my wife and come back for him.

Then I will kill him slowly. Over four years and thirty-eight days.

But as I lift my arm, the wolf rakes a hand across the left side of my face, cutting my eye clean in half. Blood pours down my cheek. Khalid can't blast him with magic with me this close, and I'm sure he's cursing me for having lost my fucking mind, but I'm a slave to the madness, to the rage and fury, to the desire for revenge, and the bloodlust of the Craving.

So despite being blind in one eye, I follow through with my attack of hammering my gun into his face. I bust his lip and crack the corner of his eye. He still manages to flip me under him though. He's much bigger than me, and his pain receptors don't seem to be fucking working.

I fire my gun once more, this time in his chest. As much as I want to take him in alive so Micha can torture him, I'm not going to let him kill me.

I'm not letting him take anything more from my wife.

His grip crushes my hand as he wrestles me for the gun.

At the same time, his mouth aims for my throat, his hot breath blowing across my face.

I throw my free arm up to intercept him. Scream when he chomps down on it sideways.

He shakes his head, trying to rip it free, but a blast of magic from Khalid explodes across his back, singeing his fur. He yelps as he lets me go and rolls away from us. He tries to stand, but my first two shots paralyzed him from the waist down.

Dropping my gun to free up my right hand –my left arm shredded and almost dislocated– I pull out a knife. Lunging for him across the floor, I stab the eight-inch blade through one of his legs, pinning him to the ground. He tries to slice me up with his claws, but Khalid hacks off his entire arm with a scythe. His precision with a blade is fucking magical. Anyone else would've cut me at the same time.

I pull another knife out to restrain his other leg, but a blurry form slams into me, knocking the air out of my lungs and my knife free from my grip. I go flying.

I crash into a wall, plaster raining down on me as I go straight through it. A pup screams for her father as I land in their home on my back. Lifting my head, I have just enough time to glimpse the charging werewolf before he's on me.

He isn't as fast as Antonio, and his fur is pitch-black, not red, but his scent tells me he's recently been near my wife. I don't care if he didn't rape her. He hasn't helped her, and that is enough to sign his death warrant.

Grabbing the leg of the bedside table I've landed beside, I swing the whole thing at his face. I clock him in the jaw mid-air, and his head whips sideways, the lower half of his muzzle hanging broken and free. The table splinters apart. He lands on me, causing agony to explode down my mauled arm and across the wound on my back. I push through the pain, grab one of the table's long splinters, and stab him in his back, right through his right lung.

Leaving the weapon inside him so he can't heal, I throw him off me. He wheezes as he struggles to reach me, but his eyes close, and his arm drops to the floor.

I stagger to my feet to rejoin the original fight. Right before I got hit, I clocked another four heartbeats. Khalid is a better fighter than I, but even with his magic, he can't take on four chimeras alone, even if they are 'failures.'

"Khalid!" I scream as I stumble towards him.

He's pulled his double-edged scythe out of his shadows. A cursed weapon, it can kill with one cut, no matter how shallow, no matter where it is on the body. He's no longer trying to take these four wolves alive.

He spins it around himself, forcing them to keep their distance, buying himself time to work a spell. Normally, a witch needs a free hand to do so, but Khalid's learned how to speak magic for his job as reaper. He hasn't mastered it, and the energy he's building is chaotic and wild. It sizzles in the air, forming around him in little sparks of heated magic, a bomb just waiting to go off.

Snarling and snapping their teeth, the four werewolves instantly charge at my brother as one. It doesn't matter if he cuts one or two with his scythe. He won't be able to stop the others from ripping him apart.

But just as they breach the range of his weapon, Leno's vines shoot out of fucking nowhere.

They grab two of them by the back legs, then slam the werewolves into each other. Khalid pivots, smoothly shifting gears to fight off the other two. His scythe slices one across their chest as he dances out of the way of their mouth. He spins it around himself as he finishes his spell, and one of the wolves drops to the ground, their heart having exploded in their chest. The other one gets a blade straight across their face. Knowing he'll be fine, I turn my attention to the two trapped in Leno's vines.

They're dazed from having been knocked into each other,

but the vines aren't wrapped around them anymore. They're lying on the floor, loose and limp. My heart plummets into my stomach as I follow their green trails to my brother.

He's sitting up against the wall, his left arm completely gone, his right leg only attached by the smallest bit of flesh. He didn't heal himself in the nick of time so he could join the fight.

He used the last of his energy to save our brother.

I run towards him despite the pull of my girl, trusting Mother and my brothers to bring her home, trusting her to be strong enough to survive until I get there. Leno has been with me nearly all my life. Only a year separates us. Most of my memories have him in them.

We built pillow forts in our rooms and waged battles on each other in the middle of the night, doing our best to sneak through 'no man's land' (ie: the hall where Mother could catch us).

We taught Khalid how to scribble on the walls and shit in the corner of the house to distract her so we could sneak into the cookie jar.

We snuck out of the house as preteens, learned how to hot wire the family car together. Learned how to drive.

And when he lost his eyes, I found him a dog. A stray who needed him as much as he needed it.

He never backed a single coup to take my throne. He has never seen me as a threat, as an enemy, as anything other than his older brother. Not even when he found out I was a hybrid.

He stood against the fucking reaper to save my life.

I can't lose him.

I won't.

"Stay with me," I say as I drop to my knees beside him, having already pulled out a potion on the way over.

But I only have three vials left, and even in my wrecked state, I know they won't be enough to save him. His injuries are too severe, and he's our secondary healer. Mother's with my wife.

At least, I hope she's with my wife, but what if she never made it? These halls are full of werewolves, the town having shrunk to just this school over four years, since the kid in our garage basement had been chased out.

For a second, I'm torn between the need to stay with my brother and the need to run towards my girl.

But Micha doesn't need *me* to save her. Doesn't need me to carry her out of here like a white knight with a massive fucking ego.

She is my equal, and she is a fighter.

She will survive long enough for me to get a vampire to take Leno home, back to Louise so she can heal him.

So my heart hammering, I raise the potion to Leno's lips. I can hear the beat of his heart splashing out on the ground around us. Can hear it struggling inside his chest.

"Aleric!" I shout. "Vlad!"

Footsteps race towards me from all directions.

"Leno!" Ezriel and Enoch shout.

Khalid reaches me first, pulling out more potions from inside his jacket. Enoch and Ezriel grab his arm and leg and hold them in place while we feed him one potion at a time.

But they're not doing a damn thing. He's too far gone.

"Stop..." he finally says, admitting what we cannot. "Tell Krypto..."

"You can tell him yourself when we get you home." I turn to Vlad, who's standing silently beside us. Only one other vampire has survived, a woman with dark-blue hair. "Take him back to Louise."

He stares at me, then shakes his head. "He won't survive the journey in this state."

"It's his best chance."

"Varius..." My head turns back to him, tears burning my eyes.

"You're going to be fine."

"Tell Kry...pto... he's... a... good..." His words trail off. I lift a new vial to his lips.

"Come on, Leno. Stay with me."

The potion dribbles out of his mouth.

"Fuck," Enoch whispers.

No! I grab another vial, but Khalid places a hand on my shoulder and squeezes.

"Take it," he says.

"Leno needs it more."

"Take it," he repeats, and that is an order. A reaper's duty to keep the Family together.

To keep me together as I stare at the empty husk of our brother.

Fighting back a scream, I close my eyes, then bring the vial to my own lips. I hate myself for giving up on him, for taking the vials he needs.

But Micha needs me too.

I can't let Leno's death be for nothing.

As I swallow the soft-blue liquid, heat courses through my face as the slashes there stitch themselves back together. The vision in my eye slowly starts to come back, but it stays blurry, the potion unable to heal it fully. Eyes are too complicated, and off-the-shelf spells can only do so much. I need to find a proper healer within a few hours. Otherwise, the potion's 'fix' will be permanent.

My hands shaking, my gaze on my dead brother, I down two more vials, healing the wounds on my arm and back. Then I reach forward to close Leno's eyes. My grief turns into rage, into dry ice in my fucking veins.

My hands shaking, I take another potion, healing the rest of my wounds.

"Antonio has a necromancer," I say as I stand, my voice hard and cruel. "Fucking find him."

"Varius –"

"Find him," I snap. "And take those fucking wolves with us."

I look towards the bubble Stormie has up around the wolf I shot in the leg. He killed my brother. He raped my wife. I am going to kill him slowly.

The same with –

My eyes narrow. My jaw tightens. The leader, the sadist who tortured Micha is no longer where we left him. A trail of blood disappears down a hall.

I start to tell Khalid to hunt the fucker down and to bring him back alive, whatever it takes, when my heart plummets into hel. Fear and terror and utter despair slam into me, shooting down our bond.

My head jerks in the direction of my wife.

I take off in a sprint.

"Varius!" Stormie shouts as she tries to keep up with me, but I leave her behind.

I leave them all behind.

Because there is a sickness in my stomach.

A twisted mess of black poison.

Spreading through my veins.

So lethal in its certainty.

A truth that every atom of my soul is screaming:

I'm going to be too late.

EIGHTEEN

HER

"Maddox!" I scream as the three chimeras shove him against the cage, pinning the door shut so I can't get out. Blood sprays in the air and across the bars as they slash him to pieces with their claws.

"Fucking shift!" I snap, my body buzzing with a need for violence I can't release. The bars are big enough for me to push my arms through, but the only person I can reach is Maddox. The three men are on the other side of him, slicing his back open, taking turns, having fucking *fun*.

He didn't even manage to turn around, so he's facing me, his eyes glossy with pain, blood trickling out of his mouth. His right hand twitches with magic, and hope flares through me that he is about to defend himself. He only has a few seconds before he passes out from blood loss or they just rip his head off, but maybe that'll be enough.

Maybe he can force them off him and –

"Don't!" I scream, my heart plummeting as he presses his

hand to the cage.

And that defensive spell I was praying he was forming never sees the light.

Instead, he's taken those few precious seconds to seal the door of the cage with magic. Trapping me in. Protecting me from their reach.

"Brother!" I scream in desperation, hoping that fucking demon can hear me. But Maddox's circle didn't contain him, which means none of the words were binding. The Prince of Pride could've fucked off, using his time of being untethered on Earth to find my sister.

So he can drag her down to Halzaja's Underground, to his kingdom of Sin.

So she can have his baby.

Oh my gods, I'm going to kill her.

"*Shift*, you little piece of shit," I cry as I squeeze his other hand. "I need to kick your ass for giving stupid advice to my sister."

He half-chuckles, half-gives a dying breath. "Don't cry..." he says.

But his words can't stop the tears from falling down my face.

I squeeze his hand harder. "Don't you dare fucking die on me."

He tries to squeeze me back, but his grip is so weak.

"Shift, Maddox, please."

His fingers start to loosen.

His eyes glaze.

And then he's gone, sagging against the cage as his legs give out.

A foot slams into his lower back, keeping him up before he can drop far. The kick rattled the bars enough to make me jump. My gaze jerks from Maddox's face and over his shoulder, landing on eyes that I know too fucking well.

Hourglass.

The bitch I stabbed with my bone knives. The one I didn't get a chance to kill because some fucker tackled me from the back.

I won't be stopped the next time I come for him.

Smiling cruelly, he holds my furious gaze, my promise of revenge as he reaches a hand inside Maddox's back.

The sound of blood squelching around as he digs inside his body makes my stomach twist.

Squeezing Maddox's limp hand, I shake with rage.

With helplessness.

There's nothing I can do to stop them from desecrating his body.

The other two wolves start to howl, throwing their heads to the sky as Hourglass starts to pull. Maddox's body arches back, and I know the fucker has hold of his spine.

My grip on him tightens.

My fury rages.

He pulls hard, and Maddox's spine rips free with a loud squelch. Blood sprays all over Hourglass, painting him for death. Intestines and organs pour from the hole in Maddox's back, splattering across his feet.

Werewolves can't speak in their animal forms, but the rage in Hourglass' eyes is there. He's doing all this because I fucking stabbed him. What a tantrum-throwing pussy.

Dropping his foot to the ground, squelching through the mess, Hourglass raises the spine in the air. Bloody nerves and tendons dangle off it.

Maddox slides down the cage.

His hand slips from mine.

"I'm going to kill –" I start, only to immediately jump back as his entire body slams into the cage. I didn't even see the pride demon enter the gym, but he's here now, his wings spread out, his dark-blue fur covered in blood and bits of brain matter. He pins Hourglass to the cage with one meaty paw on the back of his head. The two werewolves that were howling in celebration now stop short and try to rush him.

Pride's wings flick almost lazily, and his feathers, the beautiful midnight-blue, golden-tipped feathers, slice across their necks like knives, decapitating them so quickly, they still take a few steps before they fall to the ground. He keeps his eyes on me, and I stare at him in shock, wondering what the *fuck* Lou was thinking when she called this demon forth for a booty call.

I'm so going to kill her.

Hourglass snarls as he tries to turn around, his frothing fury snapping my attention back to him.

"Let me out of here," I growl at the prince. "I get to kill him."

"I do not take orders." He yanks Maddox's spine out of the wolf's hand, then he wraps it around Hourglass' throat and pulls back hard, his thick biceps flexing, his eyes never leaving mine.

My jaw drops free as Hourglass thrashes around, gasping like a fish, his eyes bugging out of his skull. He reaches around him to try to scratch his way free, to cut out Pride's eyes, but the demon doesn't release him.

I've seen a lot of shit as an assassin.

A lot of imaginative deaths, but this...

My eyes tear up.

This is so fitting for Maddox.

He would've loved this so much.

"Okay, well *that* was worth the pain to see."

I scream as Maddox's voice comes from behind me.

I spin around, my heart thumping wildly. I swing for his face, wanting to both check he's real and to just hit him for being a fucking little shit if he is.

"Ow!" he yelps as he throws up his hands.

"I held your hand as you died!"

"I said don't cry! I had a plan!"

I throw my arms around him as my emotions run wild.

The amount of stress in my system right now is making me shake hard. He shoves me away.

"If you give me a boner, Vay Vay is going to kill me."

I slug him in the arm, the circulation in my limbs having come back.

"Nice touch with calling the demon back," Maddox says as we watch the werewolf get strangled. He gestures to him. "Cullen Rogers is a fucking cunt," he says, giving the pride demon his name. A token of thanks, a payment owed. "Did you know he used to bully me as a kid because this *one time* I pretended to be his crush, took him on a date, convinced him to let me tie him up, blindfolded him, and covered him in chocolate sauce, then released a bunch of fire ants onto the bed?"

Okay... Maybe he didn't desecrate Maddox's body to get back at me...

Varius' youngest brother takes a step forward, his dark eyes blazing bright as he stares into the werewolf's bulging, bloodshot, desperate eyes. "Die while reliving that memory, you steaming pile of shit." He turns to me, his face serious. "He used my fabric scissors on paper."

I open my mouth, then do a half-shrug and light shake of my head. "Yeah, okay. I mean that's fair."

"Right? He deserves this every day of his life."

I roll my lips in, wanting to laugh despite the pain of it all. But if I laugh, it's going to turn hysterical. Then I'm going to break down and cry.

His eyes softening, Maddox squeezes me on the shoulder. "You're going to be okay."

Hourglass finally stops struggling. He hangs limp, his neck bleeding from Maddox's spine having cut into him.

"You survived," he continues. "Now you're going home."

I survived...

My throat closes as I stare at him. Did he see the video too?

Desperate to change the subject, I gesture to his dead body. "How are you... Is that even you?"

"Uh huh. Hurt like a bitch too."

"What?" I shake my head, so fucking lost. Shapeshifters can't make duplicates of themselves. "How?"

"You know how there's a snake that pretends to have a spider on its tail? Well, I did that but in reverse."

That does not clear anything up at all. "What –"

My head jerks at the sudden blur of motion streaking towards the demon prince. It barrels into Pride, tackling him off Hourglass and slamming him into the floor.

I fully expected it to be Antonio, but this thing's fur is as white as paper, with dark-red veins running through it. His muscles are even bigger than the prince's. He looks like a gorilla on steroids and has a crown of horns atop his head. He throws a fist into Pride's face, and the ground shakes.

"You fucked my mate!" he roars.

"You didn't claim her," Pride snaps as they roll across the body-littered floor, trading blows.

"She's had my mark on her since she was three!"

"Then you should've made it bigger."

"What the fuck is going on?" I shout at Maddox, unable to make out what they're saying.

"Fuck if I know," he says. "I don't speak Eknor. That's a rage demon though, so could be an assassination attempt. Or they could be the best of friends."

I notice the cuff melded into the newcomer's arm. They are moving too fast for me to make out the image, but I do not need to see it to know who he is. There's one prince for every type of eknor demon, and they all rule Sin together. "He's the Prince of Rage," I say.

"Assassination attempt then?"

"Hopefully," I reply just as they roll into the circle of runes and disappear back to Halzaja. If the rage prince kills him, then that would solve one half of my Lou problem.

There's still the baby to figure out, but –

My thoughts die under a crashing wave of guilt and envy.

My little sister is going to have a baby when I lost mine…

I press one hand to my stomach, the other to my mouth as a little sob escapes me.

Maddox opens his mouth to say something, but I shake my head, so he turns towards the cage door. He's about to unlock it and step out when a dozen more werewolves run in.

"Oh, for fuck's sake," he groans. "Leno's never going to let me live this down if he has to rescue me out of a fucking cage."

NINETEEN

HER

"No..." I whisper, none of the humor in Maddox's tone making it into mine. I don't give a shit about the wolves. They're not the ones who raped me, and the cage was made to withstand the monsters in the Shadow Domain. As long as we stand in the middle of it, they can't touch us. Varius and Dayne are coming for me, and they'll slaughter every last one of these fuckers if they need to.

But it isn't just werewolves that have arrived.

It's Eduardo.

The witch who teleported me here.

"Keep looking at her," my brother-in-law says as he steps in front of me, blocking me with his body, misinterpreting why I'm afraid, "and I'll turn your head into a bowling ball."

Eduardo's eyes narrow, but he doesn't stop. We're stuck in a cage. I don't have any magic, and Maddox is the baby of the family, with a lot left to learn. If he tries to hit him with a spell, the fucker will just block it. The summoning circle has been destroyed, meaning the demons can't come back, and over a dozen more guards have just entered the gym and taken up guard by the door. If anyone comes in, they're fucked.

"You have to get out of here," I urge as I grab Maddox's arm. "He's a teleporter."

Antonio wants me alive for breeding, but they'll just kill Varius' brother on arrival – if he's lucky. Thoughts of him being tortured in medical experiments, of being cut open and stitched back together in an attempt to turn him into a chimera makes my fingers tighten on his arm. "Now."

"No."

"*Maddox.*"

"I'm not leaving you, sis."

I want to both hug him and hit him. If I could shove him out of the cage, I would, but the werewolves would just tear him into pieces if he's not in his shadow form.

"Find Varius and lead him here," I say. But we both know he won't make it in time. Varius can feel me now that his curse is broken. He knows exactly where I am, and it's been about ten minutes since the explosion. If he could be here right now, he would be. Maddox making him panic will only distract him, but it's my only chance of convincing his baby brother to leave.

"He won't make –" Maddox starts, only to be cut off as the room breaks out into utter chaos. The werewolves howl and snarl in pain as they start sinking into the floor, like a row of dominos being knocked over, starting at the door and spreading out. Sau's shadow races across the floor, and she has opened herself up to the monsters within.

"Yes!" Maddox shouts, but I'm not feeling his same flare of hope.

Eduardo throws up a ward around all three of us. He's a strong witch, and although Sau might be stronger, it'll take her time to break through his defenses. Time where he can complete the teleportation spell and take us all away from here.

Shifting into her human form so she can use the rest of her magic, but keeping the shadows spreading out at her feet to force the werewolves to still give her space, Sau starts to bring out her monsters. They don't pour free like they did at the house though. Only three of them step out: a giant spider-like thing with two heads and crab claws, a dog with three heads full of shark-like teeth, and a large flying beast that has the upper body of a bat, the bottom half of a serpent, and 'hair' made up of wriggling snakes.

As terrifying as they look, they don't seem capable of taking on seven wolves each.

"What's wrong?" I ask, my panic increasing. If Sau is already struggling, what's going to happen when Antonio finally rocks up?

"Nothing," he says as he launches a series of missiles at Eduardo. The red streaks of magic pass through the bars of the cage, aiming straight for the fucker's head. They explode against a shimmering blue shield. Eduardo didn't even look up as he cast it, his attention on the teleportation spell he's drawing on the floor. With two fingers, he pours his magic into two thick black lines as he circles the cage.

Fuck.

It's only going to take him one or two minutes to get us out of here. I look at Sau as she starts hammering her magic at the ward, but there's a paleness to her skin, too much sweat on her brow. She's used a lot of magic recently, and even if she wasn't cursed, the amount she's used would be dangerous for anyone. With every spell, there's a backlash of magic, and if we use too much too soon, the buildup will kill us.

Blood trickles out of her nose, then starts to gush, and I know that even if she makes it through the ward on time, she isn't going to be able to kill him. Maddox's missiles aren't doing shit. There's too much of a power difference between them.

A werewolf comes at her from the side, having slipped past her monsters, but she blasts it in half without ever breaking the rhythm of her attacks on the ward. Her magic is already getting hard for her to control. More blood gushes down her face, coming out of her ears now, her eyes. She starts to sway, but she doesn't stop throwing energy at the ward, her magic such a dark-red that it looks black.

"Maddox, get out of here," I repeat, forcing myself to think of the worst. "You can help me more by rescuing me after."

"I'm not leaving you."

"Don't be an idiot."

"Can't help it." He throws another flurry of missiles, but this time he aims for the ward where his mother is attacking it. He doesn't have the power to match her blows, but if he can help her get through by even a second, then it might be enough to save us.

I clench my fists, hating Varius so fucking much right now. If he didn't torture me, if he just trusted me despite all the evidence against me, then I would be able to help him. I would be able to help them save me.

But the fucker took that from me.

Part of me almost wishes Eduardo succeeds in his spell out of spite, wanting Varius to fucking suffer over what he caused.

But then I remember how much I love the damn fool. How much he has tried to make up for what he did over this last month. He has already suffered, *is* still suffering, knows he will suffer for the rest of his life even if I'm saved today. Not a day has gone by that he hasn't apologized since we got married.

He's seen to my every desire, giving me foot rubs and back rubs, leaving meetings early to go get me random ass foods when my pregnancy cravings hit. Stopped me from eating dirt when they took an even weirder turn. He spent an hour every day with me, helping me bond with my wand faster. He's told me secrets he's never revealed before, tried to open up, to trust me even though I can feel his fear, his panic at doing so. He has been betrayed his entire life by those he trusted and loved. Being ruthless and paranoid has kept him alive, but he is trying to change his very makeup for me. Trying to ignore all his screaming instincts.

And I've found him researching late at night when he thought I was asleep or in the day when he thought I wasn't paying attention. He's still trying to find a way to give me my magic back. He's looking into calling an audience with a fucking god even though those *never* go well for the caller. He is looking into ways of stealing magic from another. Dark magic. Forbidden magic, outlawed by the archangels themselves.

He will risk his life for my happiness.

A tear slips free as Eduardo nears the start of his circle. He's so close to connecting it, to ripping me away from a future with the man I love and sending us into hel.

Zita's words, her promise of what will happen to me if I'm not saved today slam into my skull, my very soul. I start to shake, and the panic I have been struggling so hard to contain breaks free.

"Get out, Maddox," I try one last time, my voice cracking and high-pitched. I don't wait for him to move before I start calling on my magic. The air crackles with uncontrollable energy.

Dangerous.

Chaotic.

Desperate.

It burns my hands, making the area smell like a BBQ.

"What are you –" Maddox starts.

"I'm not letting him take me."

"Fuck! Don't!" He turns to me, tries to throw up a shield around my hands, but my fire eats magic, and I am a lot more powerful than he is.

"Micha!" he screams in a panic as he throws up another useless shield, but this one is consumed just as fast.

"I won't be able to control it," I say as the fire burns up my arms, wanting out. Eduardo finally looks up from his fucking transportation spell, and his eyes widen. He can't see the purple flames building on my fingertips –they are visible only to me– but he can feel their heat. Once I release the spell, this entire bubble is going up in flames.

I don't know if the fire will die once I do, or if it'll carry on burning until an archangel stops the inferno, but I don't care anymore.

I'm not going back to that hel.

I'm not going back to Sadist.

To Eduardo.

To Antonio.

"Get out, Maddox!"

"She's through!" he shouts as the ward crashes down, and Sau launches a black ball of power at Eduardo. He's forced to stop his transportation spell in order to defend himself, and with a cry of relief, I stop trying to pull on my own magic.

The fire disappears, but my arms are burned raw all the way up to my elbows. I fall to my knees, and Maddox is immediately beside me, trying his best to heal my wounds.

"Never give up hope like that, Micha," he says as white light flows from his fingertips. "We will *always* come for you."

"I can't go through that again," I rasp.

He looks up at me as his magic helps dull the pain. He can't heal me completely, hasn't learned enough, so my skin is still puckered and raw. "Listen to me. If the worst happens today, you keep yourself alive however you have to."

I shake my head.

He grabs my hands and squeezes. "You have your sister to yell at and protect from a demon prince, and you still need to kick my ass, then Varius'. So you *survive*, Micha. We will never stop coming for you."

I stare at him, the panic in my throat making me mute. He knows I might not be making it out of here today. Sau is struggling to stand up, healing herself almost as much as she is attacking Eduardo. He's still on the defensive, unable to get a blow in, but if he can just hold out, eventually, she'll weaken too greatly to heal. One of her monsters has been killed, the other two are struggling to keep the werewolves off Sau, and more wolves keep pouring into the gym.

"I'm stepping out to pull your cage into my shadows now, okay?" He releases my hands. I have a sudden urge to hold on to him, to not be alone, but I wipe my sweaty palms on my thighs and nod. "It might be a while until I can bring you out, but if something happens to me, my brothers will find you. Never give up hope."

My pulse spikes at the idea of being trapped in this cage on the Plane of Monsters, not being able to move from the middle of it without being torn to shreds by beasts I cannot see. I'll be lost in a pitch-black world, slowly and painfully starving to death.

But it'd still be better than my fate with Antonio.

I nod, stronger this time. "Do it."

He squeezes my hands, then slips from the cage, but just as his shadows start to swirl on the floor beneath his feet, one of the werewolves rushes him. A growling black ball of fury tearing up the ground behind him.

"Maddox!"

Sau turns and blasts the werewolf in the face, but it's left her open to an attack from Eduardo. His crimson magic arcs towards her, and she only just manages to throw up a shield. White light flows from the fingers of her other hand as she presses it over her heart. She can't heal any damage the use of magic is doing to her, but she can remove the pain.

If it's in her heart though, how long can she possibly survive?

Smirking like the sleazeball he is, Eduardo attacks her again.

Relentless.

Powerful.

Not letting up to give her a chance to go on the offensive.

Her blue shield wavers under his red blasts of magic, and for a second I wonder why she doesn't just take him into her shadows. Then I see the shield he has erected all around his feet – a circular wall about six inches tall, three feet in diameter. Her shadows can't scale vertical surfaces. There's always a counter to magic if you can find it.

Another werewolf charges Maddox.

Two more.

Three.

He keeps trying to fight them off with one hand as his other pulls on his shadows for me, but every time they fully form, he's forced to use both his hands to protect himself. Then they disappear, and I'm still here.

Refusing to just stand here waiting to be saved though, I drop my eyes to the double-walled circle around the cage. If I can disrupt it, it'll force Eduardo to start his spell all over again. If Sau's here, the boys can't be far behind. Buying another one or two minutes could save my life.

Dropping to the floor, I reach an arm through the bars and bring forth my fire so it crackles in my fingertips. I'm not trying to let it out this time. I know I can't control it, but if I can just get it to burn through me, perhaps that'll be enough to smudge the black lines.

Enough to break the spell.

To save myself.

But I never get the chance to try it.

Sau goes down, her shield shattering, her face covered in blood.

Eduardo blasts my arm sideways, breaking it backwards against the bars of the cage and snapping my bone out of my skin. As the werewolves keep Maddox off him, he starts to complete his spell.

I scream in pain as I try to move.

To stop him.

To save myself before it's too late.

Another shadow streaks across the floor, bypassing all the wolves, and Rudy materializes in front of me. An army of giant spiders arrive a second later and start attacking the wolves.

He swirls his shadows around the cage.

Hope wars with panic inside of me as I try to do the math, seeing who will finish first.

Eduardo is only a few inches, a few seconds away from completing the circle.

Rudy, like Maddox, is now being forced to fend off a pile of wolves. He's having a better time of it, able to keep one hand on calling out his shadows, but Maddox has just gone down, sliced into pieces – hopefully not dead, just shifting like he did before, and the wolves that were fighting him now turn to his brother. The spiders can only stop so many.

Rudy's tackled from the side, his concentration broken. He kills the wolf quickly, but as another of Sau's monsters go down, torn apart by teeth and claws and suicidal guards, Antonio enters with three full chimeras.

They tear their way across the gym. Rudy's trying his best to stop them, manifesting giant snakes, wasps, rats, any and every horror he can pull on, but he's also trying to fight Eduardo, stopping him from completing the spell or erecting a ward. He throws ball after ball of magic.

But he can't concentrate on four different foes at once, especially one with Antonio's speed.

A soundless scream erupts from his lips as Antonio bites him on the shoulder and shakes him hard. Another chimera grabs him on the leg, and they rip him apart at the waist.

Eduardo's breathing hard as I'm screaming.

I stick my other arm out of the cage, try to use my magic to burn through his line, but a wolf just steps on my fingers, crushing them. Making them useless.

Eduardo finishes the transportation spell.

Antonio and his remaining men step inside it.

But as he starts the incantation needed to send us out of here, Rudy's shadows swell across the floor. His magic is keeping him alive even though he's in pieces.

I don't know if he can heal from that. Don't know if he'll live an eternity as severed parts.

But right now, he is saving me, and I will dedicate the rest of my life to figuring out how to heal him.

Antonio grabs hold of the cage, trying to keep it from sinking into the Plane of Monsters.

Rudy's magic is stronger though.

It pulls me down.

Down.

Down.

Into safety.

Into hope.

But just as my head is about to go under, the Boss of the Death Hunt lets me go. Then he grabs both halves of Rudy and brings him into the transportation circle.

I scream in utter terror, knowing that when I come out, it will be at another of Antonio's compounds. Rudy will hold out as long as he can, but eventually, they will torture him until he breaks.

Everyone breaks.

And then he'll pull me out of his shadows and deposit me right back into Antonio's lap.

"Micha!" Maddox's voice calls out to me, coming from

near the door. It sounds the same as always, but somehow I know it isn't him this time. It's my best friend wearing his face.

The man who will do anything to save me.

A flair of hope rushes through me as I scream, "Dayne!"

But the shadows consume me.

Then I am gone.

TWENTY

HIM

My heart damn near explodes when I hear her screaming another man's name.

It means she's there. She's just *right there.*

Another few feet, and I will be able to see her, just like Dayne can.

I'll be able to save her.

Hold her close to me and never let her go.

My heart slamming around my throat, I pass Stefaan in the hall and streak into the gym a second after Dayne does.

Antonio scowls at me from the middle of the room. Black smoke-like magic swirls around him and his gang, but I don't give a shit about where they're going. All I care about is that my wife isn't with them. I only get a second to check, but I'd know her from any glimpse in my peripheral. From any brief sight of her beautiful, strong face. I know the way she stands, the way she moves.

She isn't with him.

He isn't taking her.

Which means she's here.

Thank gods, she's here.

I'm not too late.

The group vanishes in a split second, but I have already turned away from them. I will hunt Antonio and his men down later. Right now, I just want to find my wife.

"Micha!" I scream as I run around the room, searching through the sea of bodies, blood, and severed parts, between the wolves and monsters still fighting. I try to feel my wife through our bond, pinpoint her before she bleeds out, but my heart is racing too fast. My own emotions are drowning hers out.

So I force my feet to root, for me to take a deep breath so I can –

"Varius..." Mother says as she drags her way over to me. She's bleeding from her eyes and ears, her mouth and nose. Her hands are shaky, her body on the verge of collapse, but I ignore her.

When I stopped for Leno, Micha ended up screaming another man's name. I don't give a shit if Dayne's the one who saves her; I just want her saved. I just don't want her to think that I don't care as much as he does, that I haven't been doing everything I can to get to her.

I –

My breath stops.

My stomach fills with a poisonous weight that almost brings me to my knees as my brain finally catches up with what I've already seen.

Dayne is running to where Antonio was just standing.

He's streaking across the gym, scrambling over bodies, not stopping for anything.

His name rings in my ears, shrieked by my wife because she didn't see me. Because I was a second too late.

Because I stopped to comfort a dying brother.

But Dayne saw her.

He knows where she was...

And he's running to the spot where the transportation spell just activated.

No!

I take off after him, my eyes on the circle of nothing on the floor ahead.

No!

No!

No!

She has to be here.

No!

I can't be too late.

Noooo!

I can't have lost her because I stopped to try to save my brother!

My heart feels like it's ripping its way out of my chest, dragging its bleeding, broken form up through my throat and down to my stomach at the same time. Like it's lost, like it doesn't know which way to go, doesn't even know if it'll make it, if it'll survive the agony shredding it apart.

"Micha!" I scream even though I know she can't hear me.

That she isn't here.

That the spot on the floor is merely a memento to her absence.

To my failure.

It doesn't shine with the brightness of my wife, of her fire.

Still, I tear across the room to it, as if being where she was a moment ago will bring her back. Will make me feel connected to her. Like it'll absolve me of the guilt crushing my shoulders because I stopped to try to save Leno.

I should've gone straight to her.

I shouldn't have run to him when I saw him getting torn apart in the first place.

If I hadn't, I would have my wife.

I would've lost Khalid too, more of my brothers perhaps. But I would've had my wife.

Dropping to my knees, I scream an unholy noise that is matched only by Dayne's echoing agony.

He slams into me a second later, his hands crackling with electricity, his fingers wrapped around my head. I'm on my back, and he kneels on top of me, his eyes like a summer's storm.

"She's gone because of you!" he yells, his voice cracking. Broken.

A shell of who he is.

A mirror of me.

"She could have saved herself if she had her magic," he cries.

Pain lances through me. "I know."

"Oh, fuck off. No, she couldn't have," Maddox cuts in as he walks over to us, completely naked and covered in blood but without a scratch on him. He must have shapeshifted recently to heal himself. "Antonio would've just cut off her hands."

Dayne looks like he wants to argue, to attack the man he believes tortured her, but I can see the knowledge in his eyes. As much as he wants to blame the two of us, as much as I am still blaming myself and always will, we know my brother speaks the truth.

Antonio isn't stupid. Everyone knows a witch without their hands and tongue is helpless.

He would've just maimed her as soon as he took her.

"She only has her hands still because she doesn't have magic," Maddox continues. "That's given her a better chance to survive, so stop with this blame and pity party shit and help me find Rudy. He took her into his shadows before they could take her." His brow furrows. "But I had to shift right then so I didn't die, and I didn't catch where he was..."

Dayne and I are already on our feet, streaking around the room, trying to find Rudy. I throw wolves aside left and right in case he's under one of them, not giving a damn that I'm supposed to be hiding the fact that I'm a hybrid from Dayne and Stefaan

"He's gone!" Mother calls out, her voice strong enough to cut through my desperation. I stop, facing away from her, my chest heaving, my brow sweating. The werewolf I just tossed into the air crashes down on another pile of bodies, and like it's the starting gun, I spin on my feet and race back to my mother.

"Who?" I rasp, my heart beating fast, yet feeling like it's not moving at all. I know who she's talking about, in my heart of hearts I know.

But I'm not ready to accept it.

I'm looking for any reason, any smallest sign that she doesn't mean *him.*

The boy I raised like my own son.

"Antonio... took... Rudy," Mother says, knocking the final strength from my knees.

I drop down in front of her with a broken cry.

Her voice is weak once more. It seems she used all her energy to yell, so I reach for a potion, for one of the ones I couldn't use to save Leno. As soon as I uncork it, that *pop* sounding between us, though, she shakes her head. "It... won't... heal me," she says. "The damage... is from... my... own... magic."

"Father's curse," I growl just as Dayne and Stefaan reach me, all of us desperate to hear what she has to say about the woman we love.

"I'm... sorr..." She trails off, and Dayne's hands are on her immediately, glowing white. He isn't an innate healer like she is, isn't as strong, but he's the best one we have left now that Mother's out, and Leno's...

"Where's Leno?" Maddox asks as the rest of my brothers

enter the gym, followed by Stormie, who makes a beeline for me.

"In my shadows," the reaper says quietly. He looks at me. Maddox stops dead still.

"So bring him out," he says. "He doesn't like that place. Bring him out now."

"Maddox –"

"Bring him out!" He shoves Khalid with both hands, his eyes wild, his chest heaving. "Bring him out! You're killing all of our brothers! Just bring him out!"

"Maddox!" Ezriel shouts, but Khalid just grabs our baby brother by the wrist and spins him around so his back is to his chest. Khalid's arms wrap around him. Magic crackles in Maddox's fingers, but then it just snuffs out, dies as he sags forward and cries.

Khalid holds him up, his face stoic, unreadable. "He's in a bubble of Stormie's," he murmurs. "We're bringing him back so Krypto... So he can understand he's gone."

"He can't be gone...." Maddox cries. "I talked to him just last night. He was telling me all the plans he had for the yard... He can't be gone. He *can't...*"

I turn away from them, the grief hitting me hard.

The guilt over wishing that I didn't even stay with Leno as he died now.

That I left him to run to my wife.

Even though by the looks of this place, I know I would have just died. There are over twenty dead werewolves here, two monsters, and way too many spiders to count. I would have been torn apart in seconds.

But I would've been here.

She would've seen me at least trying to get her back...

"Come on," Khalid says as Maddox shudders in his arms. "Let's finish here so we can go home."

Home...

Home is where Micha is.

And she is not at the Shadow house.

TWENTY-ONE

HIM

We arrive back at the house in solemn silence.

The place feels empty. Hollow. Everyone's exhausted, but no one wants to sleep.

"Krypto!" Louise shouts from somewhere further inside, and a split second later, a missile of red fur, big ears, and a wagging tail comes streaking towards us.

Maddox drops to his knees, fresh tears on his cheeks, his arms open. The dog barrels into him, and my brother holds him tight, but he can't get him to stay still. The dog's too ecstatic over our return. He bashes into our legs, moving us aside so he can find Leno. He jumps between us, barking and shaking his entire backside in excitement.

Leno often plays – *played* hide and seek with him...

It was a bit unfair, but Krypto loved it.

"He's made a full recovery, Leno," Louise says brightly as she walks down the hallway, followed by Micha's sister and Khalid's girl.

The reaper runs to his *kira*, his master, the love of his life who owns all his reasons for breathing. Then he's gathering her in his arms and kissing her, taking comfort from her, basking in the knowledge that she is safe.

I look away, the punch of envy in my stomach making me sick. That is the reunion I should be having with my wife.

"Shit," Louise says softly. She knows Leno would've been the first through the door to get to his dog.

"Where's Micha?" Lou asks as she stops in front of me, her neck craning around me, trying to see who's holding her sister. Her heart beats a million miles an hour as hope wrestles in the pores of her skin.

Maddox reaches for Krypto again with a little sob, but the dog bounces away, sniffing the air, searching for our brother. He barks, tired with the game of hide and seek. He just wants to see him come home.

"I'm sorry, Lou," I tell her, my throat tight, my words thick. "Antonio transported her away before we could get to her."

"I fucked up the summoning," Maddox says as he stands, his own guilt hitting him as hard as mine. Tears run down his cheeks without shame.

She shakes her head as she turns to him. "But you told him it was for me, right?" Denial and panic seeps into her eyes.

"Yes. And he helped us, but then another demon – the Prince of Rage came through too, and he dragged him back to Halzaja."

"What? No. No, you're lying."

"I'm sorry –"

"No!"

"Lou," Dayne says, stepping forward and opening his arms. She throws herself at him, crying and shaking, and a tear slips down my cheek.

"Pull Leno out," I tell Khalid, needing to say it now before I lose the ability to speak, the lump in my throat growing too thick. I look at Louise. "Heal Aleric first."

I need him and Mother to go into the Plane of Monsters with me. They know the place the best, and as soon as Leno is buried, we're going.

"Let's do it outside," Maddox says as Lou starts to wail. Her father joins her and Dayne in a hug, although he looks stiff and uncertain. They are my wife's family – a family I'm not a part of.

"He'd want to be with his flowers one last time," Maddox adds, his voice cracking. No one mentions most of them are gone, killed by Antonio's witch. Or perhaps it was Terra's magic now that we know she's alive. Aleric saw her briefly when he went off on his own, but a pack of wolves attacked him before he could grab her. Then Eduardo transported her and the pregnant breeding women away while Aleric fought off the guards.

Khalid pulls his girl with him as he nods for us to head outside. As my brothers start to follow him, Aleric steps up to Louise with a slow smile. "When you put your hands all over me, do you want my clothes on or off?"

She clears her throat, struggling to stay professional.

But if I can sense her increased heartbeat, so can he.

"Sau? You want to answer me, love?" the vampire purrs even though he keeps his eyes on Louise.

I grab Mother before she can fry his ass. "No magic for two months," I growl. "I'm not burying you too."

After Dayne healed her as best as he could, he told me how bad she was beneath her healthy visage. She's missing an entire kidney and a few ribs – all eaten by the magical backlash that's been building up inside her over the last month, and she's at a high risk of developing loka, a magical disease that's always lethal to witches.

It's the same ailment that nearly killed Krypto, but with

dogs, you can keep treating them until the magic is fully out of their system. With other sups, as long as they don't use their special abilities – like, phasing for vampires, shifting for wolves, then they can live a long and healthy life. But for witches, where our magic is ingrained with every part of our body?

You'll have three to four months to live.

I pull her away, down the hall we barely stepped inside, and out the door and into our yard.

Our brothers stand by the only patch of flowers Leno managed to regrow in the few hours we had between the attack and us leaving to save Micha. By the front porch, lies a row of various flowers, spelled to bloom as we look at them. His idea of therapy.

My eye lands on a daffodil.

It opens up like he's watching me.

Smiling at me.

Telling me it's going to be okay.

Krypto whines as he runs around the yard. He starts to streak off down our driveway, searching for the only one he wants.

"Krypto!" Maddox yells as he takes off after him.

"Khalid," I say softly, but I don't look at him. Can't look at him, not with his girl's arm around his waist.

Without a word, he starts to pull on his shadows. They swirl by the row of flowers. Stormie's bubble comes out. Enoch holds her hand, squeezing it as he trembles. I don't think she returns his love, but she holds him now. Comforts him. A friend rather than a fiance.

I look away from them too, my heart feeling like it's about to burst. I shift in place, my eyes on the shadows, on the portal that leads to my wife. She's in there somewhere, stuck in a cage and terrified.

We have three, maybe four days to find her before Rudy pulls her out. He might not break in that time, but he won't risk her dying of dehydration.

Stormie's bubble rises out of the shadows. As the black falls away, so does the pink, leaving our brother lying on the ground, his arm and leg 'attached' by the twins' telekinesis. Mother takes a step forward to heal him properly before he goes, but I grab her arm.

She looks at me, her eyes dry but so damn sad. She told me once that she could never love any of us fully, not after she watched so many of her kids die. She always keeps a part of herself back so she can survive the pain of a grieving mother, so she can continue living well enough for her other children. How many kids has she lost now?

My eyes sweep around my brothers. Rudy's absence kills me. *How many more will she lose?*

Krypto streaks across the yard, barking in excitement as he catches Leno's scent. Maddox isn't that far behind him. He's breathing hard, having run himself ragged, having that burning need to just *move*. To try to run away from his grief.

But it chases him just as fast.

A horror he can't outrun.

Krypto launches himself at Leno's body, jumping on top of him and excitedly licking his face. The twins keep their hands low, but their fingers dance with magic as they keep our brother together under his dog's weight.

Krypto barks, a stress noise. He knows now something isn't right.

His back end stills.

His tail drops.

He lies down with a whine.

Licks Leno's face again.

Tries nudging him to get him to move.

Another whine rips from his throat.

Maddox arrives, breathless and shaky. "Krypto, boy, he's gone," he says as he takes a step towards him. He kneels down, but the dog immediately snarls at him.

He's protecting Leno when Leno cannot.

When we failed to.

I crouch down to tell him my brother's last words.

"Good..." But my throat closes on that whispered word. I can't bring myself to finish the sentence my brother never got a chance to.

"Good boy," Enoch says into the thick silence as he stays standing. "You're such a good boy watching out for him, but you have to let him go now. Leno would want you to let him go, boy."

"You have to let him go," Maddox says as he sits back on his ass, his knees up, one arm wrapped around them, the other picking at the dead ground, the decaying plants and bare dirt that Antonio left in his wake.

I look at that damn daffodil from before. It closed at some point during all this, but it opens now, under my gaze. Giving me that little bit of comfort. That feeling that Leno is still here with us.

I need more than it can give...

"Come on, boy," Enoch says. "You have to get off him. We need to take him into our shadows."

To return his magic from where it came.

To keep his presence with us forever.

"Krypto..." Maddox says. "Come here, boy."

The dog just whines and licks Leno's face repeatedly.

"Should we lift him off?" Ezriel asks softly.

I shake my head as I rise. "No. Let him come to terms with it."

"And if he doesn't?"

My throat tightens as I stare at the dog I picked up for my brother. He was just a pup. A rescue with a mangy coat, underfed and unloved. My brother gave him everything, and Krypto returned that tenfold.

The dog starts to wail, his sounds of distress breaking my

fucking heart.

My throat tight, I say, "Then we will bury them together once he dies of grief."

TWENTY-TWO

HIM

As much as I want to mourn my brother properly, I can't. An army of fire ants are crawling beneath my skin, urging me to move. To run. To get the fuck out of here.

My wife is in the Plane of Monsters.

In complete darkness. Alone. Trapped in a nine-by-nine-foot cage with monsters all around her.

What if one of them manages to break through?

What if the whole cage is thrown off a cliff?

What if Rudy brings her out early because his torture is too much?

I need to get to her *now*.

"Come," I say, that single word vibrating with all my rage and pain and fear. I nod towards the garage and walk away from Leno, my legs heavy, my heart even more so. I've just had an idea, and it's fucking crazy, but I have to try.

I'll risk everything to get her back.

I turn to face my family. Maddox rubs at his eyes, his

face red and raw. Enoch is looking to the sky, struggling to breathe. Ezriel is standing with his head down. Mother is looking behind her at Leno. Khalid's the only one facing me. For a moment, I wonder if they can't meet my eyes because they're blaming me. I gave the order to go in.

He would be alive if I didn't care about Micha enough to go get her. If I had taken the weeks it would have taken to properly plan a rescue, would it have made a difference?

My jaw tics as that weight crashes down on me, adding to all the other guilt on my shoulders. But I force myself to ignore it, to keep going despite the pain. If I break beneath it, I'll never save my wife.

"Micha's in the Plane of Monsters," I say. "We can get her out before Rudy does, then turn the cage into a Trojan Horse."

Maddox drops his hands. The others' heads turn towards me, but there isn't any hope on their faces. We have no idea how big that world is. Each brother opens up a different area when they access their etheric storage. The chances of Rudy's spot being close enough to anyone else's for me to cover the distance in three days is extremely low.

There aren't any roads for me to take a car. A dirt bike would work, but the jungles might be too overgrown even for one of them, and any lakes or rivers in the way would fuck me. A helicopter will be attacked out of the skies by one of the flying beasts. An amphibious combat vehicle will be seen as a threat, and the monsters Mother brings out are the small ones, the ones she can control. She claims there are dragons there, and Olivia, the monster-sister who lives in our counter, is a runt. Her kind can cut through diamonds with their front claws, and they have the ability to phase short distances.

"Our magic doesn't work there," Mother says, her face grim. "We won't be able to open the cage."

"I can shift beforehand and grab her," Maddox says, his

voice cracked. "Other creatures can only put twelve percent of their body through the bars, but I left a loophole for me."

So he could fuck Zita without ever letting her out of her prison. No wonder she betrayed us the first chance she got.

"And what will happen to Rudy if the cage is empty?" Mother asks softly.

My teeth press together hard. "They could just kill him after they get Micha too." It changes nothing. His chances of survival if Antonio doesn't want to play with him are low.

Extremely low.

My heart feels like it's going to fucking explode, ripping my ribs wide open, letting all my organs pour out. Khalid catches my eye, holds it.

"They'll attempt to breed him first," he says, his tone flat but certain. "That'll buy us some time."

I nod.

Hold on to that hope.

Mother's lips press into a thin line, then she's opening up her shadows, swirling them beneath my feet. "You felt her when she was in West Virginia, so use that as a comparison to judge the distance. It needs to be half that strong for us to have a chance of getting to her in three days. Aleric has a... map of sorts. I'll get him to bring it."

I nod, hope building in my chest.

I'm pulled into the Plane of Monsters.

The bond instantly snaps into place.

A soft cry escapes me.

I close my eyes, wanting to drop to my knees as I feel her emotions coursing through me. She's afraid. The monsters must be slamming against her cage, trying to reach inside. But she's alive.

My girl's alive, and I'm going to find her.

But the bond is too strong. Easily double what it was when she was up in West Virginia, meaning she's further away. Too far for us to reach.

Still, I take a step in her direction, desperate to feel closer to her. I push as much love and hope down our bond as I can. *I'm coming for you, little monster. I'm going to bring you home.*

But as soon as my next foot follows, I'm being pulled back to Earth. I shake my head as I face everyone, once more in our backyard. Maddox swirls his shadows around me next. If he gets me the closest to her though, he won't be able to come with me to bring her out. He'll need to stay here to work the portal.

As I sink down, I am both relieved and fucking gutted at how strong the bond feels. Hope and depression war inside me as I'm pulled back out. That's two out of five down, but I still have three more to go.

Three more possibilities.

Three more chances.

Three more prayers.

My heart beats like crazy every time a brother sucks me into their shadows, hoping that this is the one that gives me the chance to save my wife. And it beats even harder on the way up, that hope brutally dying.

Shit.

Three down…

Come on…

Four…

Fuck.

Enoch is my last chance.

Micha's last chance.

What if Leno's shadows would've been the closest?

My throat tight, I nod at Enoch. He breathes out as he sucks me down into the dark.

My heartbeat picks up.

Faster.

Faster.

Please gods, let her be –

I fucking scream.

TWENTY-THREE

HER

A light appears about a football field away from me. The entire time I have been in here, it has been pitch-black in all directions. I've been huddling in the middle of the cage, my legs up, my arms wrapped around my knees so none of the monsters can get me.

Now I lurch to my feet, my heart racing.

"Varius!" I shout, stumbling forward even though I can't see anything but that blare of light, getting dimmer by the second.

"Varius! Varius, I'm here!" I wave an arm, then scream as a tentacle wraps around my wrist, its poisonous suckers stinging fire through my flesh. It drags me towards the edge of the cage, a low growl sounding from somewhere in the dark.

Throwing myself backwards, I scramble to dig my heels into the metal floor. I reach for my magic, knowing it's the only chance I have of stopping it from eating me once I get to the edge of the cage. If I can just burn –

I cry out as I slam into a solid wall before I even make it to the bars. Pain flares through my broken arm, and I slide down the barrier with a gasp. The monster releases me with a yelp of pain, shocked by magic, and then I tumble forward as the wall disappears.

Maddox, you little shit...

I wondered how he stopped the monsters from eating us through the bars, but I didn't want to get close enough to find out in case there wasn't a fail safe and he just relied on Zita not wanting to test it either.

As I drag myself back to the middle of the cage, I can't help but understand why she betrayed us. She was trapped in here for months. I have only been in here for a couple of hours, and I already want to kill him.

I can't move more than a foot without being attacked.

I can't see anything at all, the darkness making me mad.

I can only hear the scrape of claws and the gnashing of teeth across the bars, setting my ears on edge. I'm flinching at every noise, always wondering if this time they'll be able to get through the spell. If I'm a second away from being dragged out of here and eaten alive.

Struggling to my feet, I look towards the direction where I saw the light. Nothing but darkness greets me now.

My pulse hammers inside my skull, I turn my head left and right, looking.

Searching.

Waiting...

Why didn't the idiot bring a fucking flashlight?

"Varius!" I scream as I catch a flicker of light.

My pulse beats so fucking *hard* as I wait for a response. Any response as I stare into the darkness.

There's no light anymore.

The minutes tick by.

Come on.

Please.

I didn't imagine it.

Fuck. Did I imagine it?

Fuck!

I imagined it.

I scream, letting out all my helpless pain. A high-pitched wail I'm too exhausted to be ashamed of.

A monster roars not far from the cage, and I jump out of my fucking skin. I am on edge, my heart racing like mad. I want so godsdamn badly to be hopeful. But at the same time I'm terrified of it.

I was so fucking hopeful when Khalid talked to me and again when Maddox arrived.

I can't take another disappointment.

Can't take –

There!

I take a step towards the light before I force myself to stop. I shuffle back. "Varius!" I wait a beat. "Varius, I swear to the fucking gods if you don't get your ass over here, I'm going to drown you in your own piss after I beat it out of you!"

My arm is throbbing in pain. The bone is still sticking out of my skin from when Eduardo broke it, and the fall just made it worse. I'm tired. I'm hungry. I'm in so much agony, I would've been sick a dozen times over if I had anything in my stomach. Antonio didn't give me any food or water.

"Don't give up hope, Micha," I hear in my head as I close my eyes. Maddox's voice keeps me standing when all I want to do is sag to the ground and cry. *"We'll always come for you."*

I swallow hard, shoving the rising sobs back down my throat.

Wetting my cracked lips with a dried tongue, I scream again, "Varius! I'm here!"

A light darts sideways through the terrain, and I realize

he went back for a flashlight.

He knows I'm here.

He can feel me through our bond.

Closing my eyes, I drop to my knees, my chest shaking so hard, I'm struggling to breathe.

"Oh gods…"

In the back of my mind, when seemingly everyone else came to rescue me but Varius, I thought…

I thought he might've died.

I have been refusing to think of it, refusing to let even a single thought fully form in my brain, but it's been *there.*

A subconscious fear niggling at the back of my mind.

A terror too great to face.

But he's okay.

He can feel me.

He hasn't lost too much blood like I did.

Tears stream down my cheeks as I fall forward, pressing my palms on the ground. My shoulders shake. My breaths come out hard and raspy.

"Micha!"

At the sound of his voice, my head snaps up. I struggle to my feet.

"Varius!"

"Micha!" His voice cracks, and I might not be able to feel him through our bond, but I can *hear* his desperation, his pain, his happiness at finding me through that single call of my name.

He lights up my cage with his flashlight, and I raise my hand to shield my eyes. I blink rapidly, trying to see as fast as I can.

He's close.

So godsdamn close.

I lower my arm.

My chest swells with hope and happiness as I watch him near the cage. The monsters have gone, scared off by this mad neanderthal, but there's a massive anaconda wrapped around his upper body. I stumble forward, blindly trusting that he wouldn't have brought a giant snake to eat me, and I reach my ~~good~~ better arm through the bars, waiting for the last few seconds it'll take him to cover the rocky, barren terrain to get to me.

My eyes widen as he screams in agony.

"Varius!" I shout, so godsdamn terrified that a monster's managed to grab him despite the protection of his blood.

But then I notice that the light filling my cage has just got brighter.

Because there's another lightsource.

One coming from above.

"Noooo!" I scream, my body shaking with utter terror, with the death of hope.

Varius peels the snake off him. He's still thirty feet away.

He launches the anaconda at me, and I watch as it sails through the air.

But it's too late.

Rudy pulls me out of his shadows.

TWENTY-FOUR

HER

The light of a new world explodes all around me.

I squeeze my eyes shut, trapping in my urge to scream.

My chest heaves.

My body shakes.

Varius was so fucking close to reaching me...

I don't know what the snake was for, but I know he had a plan to get me out. I was so close to going home.

Gods-fucking-dammit!

A sob of frustration rises in my throat, but I swallow it down, then kick it to death with my will to survive. I can't focus on close calls, on the hope dying inside of me, on the vortex of despair that just wants to drag me down. I have to block out Varius' scream. His twisted voice of pain. How he ran so frantically, so desperately across the black landscape, trying to reach me. Trying to take me home.

My lips tremble.

I can't focus on green grass when I've just been pushed

back into hel. So I take a deep breath and open my eyes into a squint, the light hurting my brain.

It takes me a second to register what is in front of me...

Then I'm jerking back, my heart hammering, a horrified scream ripping out of my throat. I lunge forward in the next second, rage shoving down my disgust and pain, and I slam into the bars of the cage. "You fucking bastards!"

Everything inside of me is boiling hot, burning away even the pain of my injuries.

I can't feel anything but a need to kill, to punish these sick fucks. "I'm going to kill you!"

Rudy is lying on the concrete floor, still ripped in half, with his intestines hanging out of his waist and with his legs not far from him. His eyes are wide and panicked, so heavy with guilt and sadness as he looks at me.

But I understand why he pulled me out of his shadows so quickly.

Why he's already so fucking compliant.

Because behind the ward we are trapped in, behind the shimmery blue sheen that's only just visible in the air, like a ripple of heat, is a dog.

A white pit bull.

Muzzled but unchained.

It's missing its tail and two back legs, and there is blood all over the workshop's floor. Blood I can read, having killed enough people over the years to know how it looks when they run.

The dog was brought in, happy and unsuspecting. There's no wild splatters at the start of the trail, nothing to show that it tried to fight off Eduardo before he cut off its tail with the machete he's still holding, blood dripping from its blade.

The dog then jolted forward, blood flying everywhere as it ran in circles, making wild hops of pure panic.

Then it pivoted towards Antonio. Seeking help.

It *trusted* him.

It cowered behind his legs as Eduardo approached, blade in hand.

It whined.

Pushed itself against Antonio's legs, begging him to do something.

Eduardo kept walking towards it, but it kept hold of its damn hope, waiting for the last second until it bolted.

It didn't get far, its severed limb only a foot away.

Now the blood splatter changes.

Becomes chaotic as the dog stumbled around, trying to figure out how to walk with one leg missing. It kept falling over, leaving pools of blood rather than streaks.

Then Eduardo cut off its other leg, and still desperate to find help, it started dragging itself towards Rudy.

Now it lies just outside of the ward, trembling, going into shock from blood loss. Death would be a kindness.

Rudy knows that.

It's not the reason he pulled me out.

The reason is in Antonio's hand.

A little girl still in diapers stands silently beside him, her left arm stretched up as he holds her wrist. She sucks on the thumb of her free hand. No tears line her face. She is well used to violence, though the lack of blood on her clothes tells me she was brought in after the dog was brutalized.

After Rudy still refused to bring me out.

"I'm sorry," he signs, shaking with grief as I finally look at him. "I tried to kill myself…"

But his magic wouldn't let him.

My heart twists in my stomach as he turns his attention back to Antonio.

"Let her go," he signs.

So optimistic even with all the nightmares he sees.

Perhaps he has to be in order to survive.

"Put your hands on the floor," Antonio says, his tone flat, like he's giving instructions over a fucking intercom.

"Heal the dog." Shadows swirl beneath my feet. Rudy brought me out to save these two innocents, trusting I will be strong enough to survive whatever happens to me. But he won't sacrifice me for nothing. Already, his guilt pulls at him. He loves Varius so much, and he knows Varius wants me back. Any other brother would've left these two to die, and that guilt that he wasn't strong enough, that there is a reason he is brought in after all the business is done and the crime scenes just need cleaning, is eating at him.

Tearing him apart.

Making him waver in doing what Antonio wants.

Seeing that just like I can, Antonio nods to Eduardo, and the witch drops the machete to the floor. It clatters on the concrete, sending up splatters of blood. He takes his time collecting the severed tail and legs before he walks over to the dog. The canine's had all his hope ripped from him that he doesn't even try to move. He just gives a half-hearted growl inside his muzzle, knowing there is nothing he can do.

As Eduardo heals him, Rudy spreads his arms out on the floor. Compliant because he knows there's no way we can fight our way free. Even if he shifts into his shadows, he can't get out of the ward. If he tries to break it, as I suspect he's already tried, Antonio will kill the girl, hacking her into pieces until he stops.

"Rudy," I rasp, my heart racing, knowing the pain he's about to suffer.

There is only one way to contain a witch.

Most use metal gloves or a witch's chain to bind them.

But these fucking *assholes* are going to cut off his hands.

They're not going to just take his magic; they're going to take his ability to talk.

His chance of reasoning with them. Of soothing their bursts of anger as they torture us.

Then they're going to kill me over and over again to

destroy any soul dolls Khalid tries to make of me, and I don't want him blaming himself.

I'm an assassin.

A Black.

A Shadow.

I am strong enough to take it.

I will not be the reason Rudy breaks in this place.

"Rudy," I say again, clearing my throat and squatting down inside the cage.

He looks at me, his face pale.

Reaching out, I touch his arm. "It's okay," I say as I look into his tear-stained eyes, letting him see I mean it. "You did the right thing."

He shakes his head, so much guilt in his eyes. Varius would've held out. He would've listened to that dog's howls, would've let that girl die because he'd sacrifice everyone to save me.

But Rudy...

Sweet, beautiful Rudy can't bear to see anything suffer.

Finished healing the dog, Eduardo picks up his machete and walks over to us. The ward's about to come down. Then they'll separate us, torture us. I squeeze Rudy's arm as tears clog my throat.

"It wasn't your fault. Okay? They are the only ones to blame."

He swallows hard as he gives the briefest nods, but he doesn't look like he believes me. *I tried to kill myself...* My throat tightening at the idea of him losing himself in here, I squeeze his arm again.

The shimmer in the air disappears. The electrical buzz on our skin, so faint it's only felt in its absence, vanishes as the ward comes down.

"Don't give up in here, Rudy. You stay alive. We're both getting –" I swallow down a string of profanity as Eduardo hacks off Rudy's fingers, leaving only the thumb on his left hand. I try to tell myself this is a good thing, that they're doing this because they want him alive and able to take care of himself, but the twisting knot in my stomach just grows.

Tightens.

Becomes a fucking tumor as Eduardo raises the machete again.

He lets it linger in the air this time.

Drawing out the anticipation.

The torturous wait.

Rudy doesn't try to fight back at all; they've found his weakness, and by the gods, they've found mine.

The blade comes down and *thwack!* It slams all the way through his fingers and into the concrete floor.

Rudy looks at me, craning his neck. A tear runs down the side of his face, but he somehow still finds the strength to smile at me. To comfort *me*.

I'm okay, he seems to say. *It's not your fault.*

But it *is* my fault. He wouldn't be here if it wasn't for me.

And *I* wouldn't be here if it wasn't for Varius, I think with a burst of rage.

Except...

I look at Rudy's severed fingers. Having my magic would have made things worse for me.

I couldn't have killed Grubs.

I couldn't have even attempted to defend myself in the cafeteria. Antonio would've hacked off my fingers as soon as I'd arrived at the school.

Then there would've been fourteen men raping me rather than the twelve I culled them down to.

And without my fingers, without any way to actually fight back... I might've broken already.

My anger at Varius dwindles at those thoughts, but it doesn't disappear completely; it sits like embers beneath my skin. Just because there is a silver lining to his torture does not make his betrayal much easier to bear.

"Open the cage, heal her, then stitch him back together," Antonio orders Eduardo. The witch hurries to do as he says, and although I want nothing more than to try to kill him while he's in range, I catch the warning in the alpha's eyes. *Harm him, and I'll kill Rudy.*

I also don't know if Varius' brother can survive on his own like this, if his magic will grow him a new body, or if he'll simply die when his magic runs out. It's already taxing him greatly, most likely using up all the power he has left. So I can't risk killing the only person who can save him.

As soon as all of the wounds on my body are healed, Antonio beckons me out of the cage.

"Let her go," I say, trying to give Rudy a bit of peace. To let him know that he at least saved this little girl.

Antonio walks her to the door and shows her out. Then he stands on the other side, holding the door open, and pins his gold eyes on me. *Come.*

It's time for me to die.

Over and over and over again.

I glance at Rudy. "You did the right thing," I murmur to him. "I'm going to be fine."

"I'm sorry," he mouths.

"It's okay," I say. "We're both getting out of here."

Feeling Antonio's growing irritation, knowing he won't let me linger any longer, I look at Eduardo and growl, "Hurt him anymore, and I'll find a horse's dick to fuck that face of yours."

He glowers at me, but he keeps his cowardly mouth shut.

Moving stiffly across the room, I walk towards Antonio.

Towards my death.

Chin up.

Head high.

Vengeance in my eyes.

I will kill you.

Just not today.

TWENTY-FIVE

HIM

I'm pulled out of the shadows in a fucking rage. I was so *close* to getting her out. I should've had the thought to go in sooner. I should've had Enoch take me in first. I should've run faster.

"Fuck!" I can feel her in this world again. My head whips in her direction. Northwest. Further than she has ever been. I'm hit by the urge to call Aleric, who left with his men as soon as they dropped us off, and demand he take me to her. But I know it won't matter. Antonio will just transport her again. We need a plan to deal with that fucking witch now that Maddox failed in his task.

As my youngest brother is pulled out beside me, still in his snake form, my rage ignites into ice cold, merciless fury. I start to lunge for him, wanting to tear him apart for what he's caused, but Enoch's magic has already wrapped around my clothes. My feet stay rooted, and I know Khalid ordered him to restrain me as soon as I entered this world. He saw what happened in the Plane of Monsters through Micha's soul doll, saw her get taken from me again, and he knows I have been struggling to not blame our little brother for what happened at the school.

But I can't hold it in anymore.

"You were supposed to save her first!" I yell as Maddox appears beside me in his human form, tears in his eyes, guilt on his face.

"I'm sorry!" he rasps. He doesn't try to explain, doesn't try to defend his decision under the weight of my pain and the weight of his own shame.

Power rages beneath my skin, an overwhelming need to let it all out. To kill him to release some of the agony inside of me. My muscles straining, I struggle to reach my brother, but Enoch's magic holds me back.

"Varius," he murmurs, his voice cracking. He doesn't say anything else though. Perhaps he can't.

But he doesn't have to.

We all know why Maddox did it.

He did it to save us, knowing that we'd gone in without the numbers, without enough planning because I couldn't wait after getting that video of my wife. He heard Zita sell us out as he hid in her intestines, and he knew that Antonio was ready for us.

If he hadn't summoned the demon, Leno wouldn't be the only one dead. The number of slaughtered werewolves and chimeras in the hall outside the gym would have joined the ones we were already fighting and overwhelmed us. I can't get Leno's screams out of my ears, the sight of him being pulled in half out of my mind.

Krypto cries on top of his chest only a few feet away, and my sorrow turns thick in my lungs. I glare at Maddox, my chest vibrating with pain, and he stares at me with tears falling down his cheeks.

"I'm sorry," he whispers again, and there is so much pain

in those words, so much guilt and sorrow and regret.

I know he means it. He likes my wife.

I recall him standing between me and her when I wanted to torture her for hurting me. I had to knock him out and cuff him to a radiator to get him out of the way, and when he woke, he just chewed off his own fucking arm to get free. To get between her and me.

"I'm sorry," he says, his voice raw, his emotions thick. His tears run faster, as fast as they did for Leno.

My legs give out from under me, and it's only Enoch's magic that keeps me standing. The urge to scream bubbles up in my throat. I just lost my wife. I just lost my fucking wife!

But I don't let it out, knowing if I do, it'll break me.

Cripple me.

Destroy me.

I stare at Maddox, wanting to hate him for fucking up the order I gave him.

Micha was supposed to be his only priority.

We failed to save her because of him.

My throat closes, thickens, hurts so fucking much as it traps down the scream that is clawing at my chest, ripping its way through my lungs and heart and ribs.

Because the truth is *we* didn't fail at the school because of Maddox.

I failed because I banked on plans A (asking him to go in as a tapeworm, something he had never tried before) and B (having Mother race to Micha immediately) without having a plan C.

Because I didn't know Mother was that fucking broken, and I *trusted* my brother to listen.

To put her first above everything else, including us.

I never should've trusted them.

Tears burn the back of my eyes as rage, grief, and guilt tear every atom of my soul apart. I want to give into it, to let it rip me into pieces without purpose, to abandon me in a pile of shattered glass, so fragile, so broken, so utterly and completely useless to anyone.

But I can't.

Because Antonio still has my wife – and Rudy.

I can't break until I get them back.

So I blink away my pain and grab hold of the control I'm well known for. I look away from Maddox. I force myself to forgive him for making the wrong choice.

But I'll never trust him again.

Not when it comes to her.

I take a moment to collect myself, to bottle up my grief and rage and guilt, and I focus it into something usable.

Something useful.

"Let me go, Enoch," I say, my voice calm and flat. The emotion gone, the ruthless Boss back in its place.

He looks at Khalid, but the reaper is holding Micha's soul doll in his only hand, his dark eyes distant. He's focused on whatever is happening to Micha and Rudy rather than on us. So Enoch starts to look at Mother instead.

"*Enoch*," I say, and this time I am not asking as a brother.

His magic releases me, and for a second, the grief pounds down on my shoulders, wanting to shove me to the ground. Steeling myself, I walk over to Khalid.

"Show me," I demand.

His eyes focus on me, searching to see if I'm ready to see and hear what's happening to my wife. Pain flashes in his eyes and then he turns towards the house.

I walk past Mother as I follow him. "Bury Leno where he lies," I say. Krypto isn't ready to give him to the shadows.

And neither am I.

She nods, her sorrow dry and silent.

But there is a question in her eyes, one she can't quite hide: *how many more children will I lose?*

Turning from her, I head into the house.

I meet Khalid outside the room of runes on the ground floor. It was first built by our ancestors hundreds of years ago, and every time we moved, it was packed up and carried with us by magic. The door is made out of solid black stone, but on this side of the hall, it's been spelled to look like part of the wall. No seams mark its location; no handle is there to turn.

"Does he want Rudy alive?" I ask, my throat tight as Khalid steps up to the wall. Normally, my brothers place a hand on the area and push their magic into the square room hidden on the other side, but with Micha's doll in his only hand, Khalid instead leans his head against it.

"Yes," the reaper says before he murmurs an incantation in Drazic, a demonic language that most of our spells are rooted in.

I glance up as the tension in my shoulders loosen a little, then I swallow hard as I prepare myself for what I'm about to see. Ever since Micha was pulled out of the shadows, I've been wondering if Rudy only did that because he was dying. If he feared she would be lost in there forever, left to die in that fucking cage. Did he pull her out because he knew Antonio wants her alive and that her chance of her survival would be higher with him than alone in the dark?

But if Antonio wants him alive too, that means I'm not about to enter the room of runes and see my brother dead through Micha's eyes.

A small victory.

It isn't enough.

Smoke pours out of Khalid's mouth, then washes over the wall. The hidden door moves back, a soundless slide of stone as it gives us access.

We step into a completely square room. The walls, floor, and ceiling are all the same. Shiny black stone with runes etched into its surfaces. Some glow a soft red for aggression, others blue for protection, and the rest green for our family power. It's the same color green as the pins Khalid pulls out of thin air when he wants to torture his soul dolls. The same color green as the soul whips that Delun, Sau's father, used to kill Antonio's parents – those infamous weapons that could tear through even a werewolf's natural defense to magic.

Perhaps one day, Khalid will learn to wield them too, but right now, my brother is focused on pulling on the power of our ancestors to allow me to see and hear everything Micha does. The runes themselves aren't magical – just like the tattoos on his skin aren't either. They're simply trappings for power, this room having been charged by our family for over eighteen hundred years. A battery bank for us to pull on.

Khalid places Micha's soul doll in the center of the room, on a runic symbol that looks like a twisted heart. As soon as it glows green, a chill rushes through the room, sweeping around us like a ghost seeking vengeance. And perhaps it is, this room having trapped the souls of various men over the years – our enemies whose souls were pulled from their bodies and interrogated by the witches in our bloodline who could control soul magic.

Cid Garcia, Antonio's youngest son, is in here, killed by Khalid not too long ago. Perhaps he is responsible for the chill across our skin.

The temperature in the room quickly rises back to what it was, Khalid's magic controlling the restless souls. They're not quite spirits, not conscious beings just stuck on another plane. They're more like the characterless husks that we become before the gods reincarnate us as new people. There are no whispers of memory, no real personality. A 'fetus' of the soul, a new beginning that is not marred by the sins of their past. But they will never be reborn, not until this room is destroyed. No one can even release them for once they are stored in the runes, they are removed from this world and placed on the outer planes of Purgatory. The amount of power needed to free them would be too volatile for any one witch to control.

My soul itches beneath my skin. My pulse races, and for the first time, I can feel the pull of the runes. The temptation of power. The dark whisperings of magic demanding I set it free.

Crossing my arms, I dig my nails into my bicep and side, fighting the urge to listen to its lure. Magic is dangerous, and until I learn to control it, tapping into the power of the runes would be a death sentence.

My blood screams in my ears, a demanding screech. I scratch my nails across my flesh, forcing myself to focus on the pain. My heart beats harder though, running wild, and my gaze pinpoints in on a single rune. It starts to glow red, and the air whooshes out of my lungs as if pulled by –

"Varius," Khalid snaps, his voice sharp, and I startle, my eyes tearing from the rune and shifting to him.

I lock my jaw as I glare at him, warning him not to say the words I know he wants to. If he tells me to leave, I won't be able to hear or see my wife. Khalid isn't strong enough to share her senses with me outside of this room. But if I stay and lose control, if my magic tries to fight his inside this room, he'll most likely have to kill me to get it to stop.

I'm under no illusion that I will win in a magical fight against him.

"Show me," I demand.

His lips tighten, but he nods, and the runes flare bright red and green, their light reflecting in Khalid's eyes as he twists his hand in the air, tracing tightly controlled shapes with his fingers, binding the spell to be exactly what he wants it to be.

"...fuck that face of yours."

I step forward at the sound of Micha's voice, my heart urging me on before my brain can catch up and tell me that she isn't here. Her voice is merely echoing from the runes. There's no woman for me to run to, no one to pick up in my arms and hold to me as I cry in relief.

Clenching my fists at my sides, feeling the weight of her absence, I force my feet to still.

Khalid looks at me, but I don't return his gaze. Instead, my eyes fly around the room, searching for a visual of what she's seeing. "Where –"

"I'm not skilled enough," Khalid says. It doesn't matter how much power this room can give him if he doesn't know how to shape it to get what he wants. It's a lot harder to pull an image into the air than mere words.

Then again, it could just be an excuse. I know he doesn't trust me not to lose it if I see what's being done to her.

And honestly, I can't tell him that I won't.

"Antonio's separating her and Rudy," Khalid says flatly, his emotions well hidden, and I force myself to do the same. They need us thinking logically. Coldly. We can't save them otherwise.

So I lock it down, cross my arms, and say, "Tell him I'm willing to trade. Micha and Rudy for –"

Micha grunts in pain as she's slammed into something solid.

"I could just take your eyes and pierce your eardrums instead of killing you," Antonio says. "Then it won't matter how many soul dolls they make of you."

My eyes snap to Khalid. "– control of his territory again," I finish sharply, my tone verging on the edge of desperate. After today, with all of Antonio's capos arrested or on the run, Aleric and I can easily pick apart what remains of his gang. But if he just gives me back my wife and brother, I'll turn on Aleric. The Blood Fangs are too weak to fight us off.

"But I want you to hear them come for you," Antonio says. "I want you to see what they do to you, how your belly will swell with their children."

"Khalid!" I snap. An order. A plea. No one can control the soul doll but him. I can't just grab the green figurine and carve a message across my wife's skin. Khalid has to push his magic into it while he does it. "*Tell him*!"

He looks at me, but he doesn't move. He wants to see where this conversation goes. Playing our hand too soon could force us to give up everything, and Khalid isn't just my brother in this moment. He's the reaper; it is his duty to protect the Family, even if I would sacrifice it all – all our businesses, our streets, the fucking portal.

Anything to get my wife and brother back.

"Still..." Antonio says, his voice coming in from every angle. "Varius got the police to raid most of my businesses, and that can't go unpunished. So which one shall I take?"

My heart hammers at the idea of her losing either. I've already taken her magic. If he takes one of her senses, will she give up? Will she kill herself before I can get to her?

"Why don't you take," Micha says slowly and clearly and without any of the fear eating me up inside, "that giant stick out of your ass and fuck Eduardo's new hole with it. Then deep throat it until you fucking choke."

I swallow down a raspy cry. She's still holding on, still fighting.

I have to do the same for her.

She doesn't need my emotions right now. She needs –

"I wasn't talking to you," Antonio says.

I still, that little flare of relief at her words dying a brutal death, then decaying inside of me, turning into rot.

"Pick, Varius," he orders. "I know you're watching."

"No!" The word is torn from me as I stagger towards the soul doll. "Take mine! Trade me –"

"He can't hear you," Khalid says softly, his tone flat.

"Tell him!" I snap as I turn to him.

His eyes bore into mine. "I'm not trading you."

"Leno is dead!" I yell. "You're secondborn now, so if I'm

gone, *you* will lead. The Family won't fracture –" Not like it would if Leno was still alive. He couldn't make the ruthless decisions Khalid and I can. That Caden could when he used to rule, sacrificing his own kids to save the Family, to save Mother.

"I'm not trading you," he simply repeats.

Micha grunts in pain as a *crack!* reverberates through the room. He's broken something of hers.

"It's just a finger," Khalid says, as if that should fucking matter. "He's going to kill her anyway." If she were anyone else, I would ignore her pain and not let it affect me from making decisions. The reaper is right; Antonio is going to kill her regardless. He has to stop her heart to stop us from using her soul doll – the alexandrite burning up as soon as she dies.

But that is my wife.

Her screams of pain still haunt me from when I tortured her myself. I haven't slept a single night without reliving her cries, without seeing all the blood pour from the blows of the hammer. Some nights I watch her miscarry. Other nights I can't stop myself from raising that hammer to her thighs...

I can't stand by while she suffers again, even if it's 'just' a fucking finger.

"Choose, Varius," Antonio says as if he's talking about the fucking weather.

"Khalid!" I snap, this time taking a step towards him. The runes flare red beneath my feet. The power hums inside my blood.

He stills like a predator in the grass. "Choose her eyes," he says. "She's smart. She'll interrogate –"

"I'm not hurting my fucking wife!"

"Antonio –"

"It'll be my choice!" It doesn't matter if I'm not the one picking up the scalpel. *I* would have hurt her if I decide.

And I can't do that to her again.

I can't be the reason she loses her eyes.

"Dammit, Khalid. *Please.*"

His lips tight, he kneels down beside the soul doll. I don't know if he's going to carve what I've told him to or if he's going to make the decision for me, but there's nothing I can do other than beg. I am completely helpless in this situation.

Powerless.

Only Khalid can affect the alexandrite.

Only Maddox could infiltrate the school.

Only Aleric can phase me to my wife.

I've never felt so fucking *weak.*

My body trembling, I watch as Khalid picks up Micha's doll.

I can't breathe.

My chest feels too tight.

Like I'm being crushed from every side.

I open my mouth to suck in more air.

My lips wobble as I struggle to stay calm.

But every second is dragging out.

I can't –

"Take the tattoo!"

Micha's voice punches me in the gut, slamming up into my chest, and I fall to my knees on a wretched cry.

I know it's just a mark on her skin, something I can redo, but her desire to remove it feels worse than a demand for a divorce. Like a rejection of *us.* A sub removing a collar. A dom demanding it back to put on someone else.

But fuck, if it saves her eyes... if this is the choice... hurt me or hurt her...

I will pay it a thousand times.

She is my *wife.*

It is my job to protect her.

So I will gladly have my heart ripped out to save a single strand of hair on her head.

She is my wife...

"You want to hurt him, right?" Micha says. "Punish him for what he did to your gang? Then take the tattoo. He does not give a shit about me as long as I'm still his property."

My throat closes as I fall forward. My hands barely catch me before my face hits the ground. I know she's only saying this to manipulate him, but the words cut deep.

The fear that she believes them.

That even if she doesn't, maybe one day, while trapped in Antonio's prison, she will come to think that they're true.

"So cut it off," she says, a ringing hatred for me so clear in her voice. "Show him that he's failed and I'm no longer his."

I squeeze my eyes shut on a silent scream. My hands fist on the floor as her words beat down on me.

Because I *have* fucking failed her.

She should be home. With me. With Bambi. Smiling and laughing and planning a nursery. Antonio should be dead, cut down by our ambush at the crocodile farm. Instead, we killed his double while he ran into our house and murdered our baby girl, then kidnapped my wife.

Now Bambi lies as nothing more than a red smear on my bedside table, waiting for her mother to come home to bury her.

My fists tighten as I struggle to keep my emotions in check. I want nothing more than to give into my grief for just a moment.

But I can't.

Not when Micha's still fighting.

She's going through hel and isn't giving up.

I won't insult her by acting like she's already lost to me.

"I chose her, Varius, because she isn't some damsel in distress. She's a fighter. Your equal. Now fucking treat her as one."

Mother's words slam into me, shaming me, and I push

my palms against the floor as I let out a ragged breath. My fingers press hard into the stone.

Micha hisses in pain as Antonio skins my mark from her skin.

I tremble as I kneel on the floor, listening to her being in agony but unable to help. Clenching my jaw, I force down my grief. She doesn't need me to be her husband right now. She needs me to be the Boss of the Shadow Domain.

A cold, ruthless businessman who'll tear apart Antonio's entire Family so there's nowhere left for him to hide.

I have failed my wife too many times.

I will not fail her in this.

Climbing to my feet, I look at my brother. His eyes fasten hard on mine, and I push out the words I know I must say. "Release her soul doll."

As much as I want her to know she isn't alone when Antonio kills her that first time, we can't afford to lose the alexandrite. We only have two pieces left, and if we're to go after that fucking teleporter, we might need it to kill him.

A flash of approval in his eyes, Khalid pulls the drop of blood from Micha's doll, and the room falls silent. My heart twists over the loss of her voice, but I tell myself I'll hear it again soon.

My wife's a fighter.

My equal.

It's about time I fucking treat her as one.

TWENTY-SIX

HIM

I walk outside to find my family. Lou's trapped Krypto in a nine-foot-wide containment circle, and she and Maddox are sitting outside of it, trying to calm him down as he rages around the small patch of ground. His hackles up, his ears down, he snarls and barks nonstop. His eyes never leave the hole in the ground right in front of the flowers.

The twins are solemn as they finish packing the dirt in on top of Leno. Dayne, still in Maddox's form, Khalid's girl, and Stormie are grouped together off to the side, outsiders looking in. Mother stands stiffly beside Enoch, her back to the door, but as soon as I open it, she turns to face me.

Her cheeks are still dry, unlike everyone else's, including my own. But there is an emptiness in her eyes, a dying part of her soul.

Despite my need to talk to her as a Boss, my eyes go to Krypto, and my throat tightens, making it hard to speak. He looks so lost, so utterly broken. Maddox is crying in front of him as he begs him to not give up, but I know in my heart that the dog will die from grief.

"Stefaan left. He got a call from Goodbye World," Mother says softly, pulling my attention away from Krypto.

"Did they take it down?" I demand as I turn to her. It'd take fucking ages for a normal person to do, but the three women who make up the hacker group: Mickyla Hatch, Kati Vosika, and Ashley Quiett, all are specialized in electronic magic like Talon was. They are able to make Trojan horses to trace them back to the source or some shit like that. I'm not entirely sure as none of that is my forte. All I know is that they are the only people who can scrub stuff off the internet completely and make sure any downloaded copies all become corrupted too.

She nods. "He's gone to organize the start of the kill list, but I told him to only make an example out of those who downloaded the video."

I start to open my mouth in anger, wanting the Blacks to kill them all in the worst ways they can imagine, but she stops me.

"That many deaths, all with the same calling card, will call in the SCU and put more attention on the video. People will be looking it up out of curiosity."

I clench my jaw as I'm forced to remind myself I can't be Micha's husband right now. I have to be a Boss. Otherwise, I'll never see her again because I'll make stupid mistakes like that.

I nod slightly, letting her know I understand. Then I turn towards Krypto as Lou releases her containment spell. The dog immediately runs to Leno's mound, then starts digging at it with a whine.

"Stop!" Maddox begs as he staggers over to him. He tries to drag him away, but Krypto twists around and bites him on the arm. My brother jumps back, tears rolling down his cheeks, but I know he isn't crying out of pain. He knows what I know. What we all know as we watch the dog start digging again.

He snarls as Maddox takes another step towards him, but he doesn't stop pawing at the ground. Maddox waits just beside him, his shoulders shaking as he sobs, "Please, boy. Come on. Stop."

My heart twisting, I order, "Enoch."

Breathing hard, my brother raises his arms, and a second later, Krypto is lifted away with his telekinesis. The dog howls in the air, a heartbreaking wail of desperation. After he's deposited on the ground a few feet away, I order Lou to draw a containment circle on top of Leno.

Krypto doesn't need to be trapped; I don't see him trying to go anywhere, but the circle will stop him from being able to dig his way down. Then our brother can rest in peace, and perhaps his dog will eventually tire himself out and just lie down on top of him.

Once Krypto is placed inside the circle, Lou closes it with a small sob. Then she falls to her knees and watches as he immediately starts trying to dig his way to the person he loves the most. Maddox collapses beside her and pulls her into his arms. She clings to him, and he squeezes her like she's a teddy bear being crushed for comfort.

My throat closing, I turn from them. I catch Khalid's eye as he hugs his girl to his chest, both his arms around her. His lips press into her hair. I gesture at the garage, and he nods at me over the top of her. She squeezes him tighter before she lets him go, but instead of following me, he lifts her chin to kiss her. I let him take the moment he needs; as reaper, he suffers too much.

Striding towards the garage, I say, "Stormie, Dayne," in a clipped voice.

The two follow me instantly. Krypto's cries hound at our backs, making each step feel heavier than the last. But when I tortured my wife, I had to listen to her screams, and they claw at me now, drowning out his.

"You're not to kill the captives," I tell Dayne as we enter the garage. "That's no one's right but Micha's."

"Agreed," he snarls as we head for the stairs. "But why aren't we going after her while Maddox gets them to talk? Every second she's with him –"

"I know," I cut in, hating how fucking useless I am to her. "I can *feel* her."

She's trying so hard to stay strong, but deep down she's terrified. Antonio hasn't started killing her yet either, and that's making me paranoid. Is he still trying to talk to me? What if he didn't accept my lack of an answer? What if my silence causes him to take both her eyes and ears? What if I made the wrong fucking choice?

Gritting my teeth, I force my panic down. He has my number. He doesn't need a soul doll to communicate with me. If he wants to torture her so I'll do what he wants, then me having Khalid 'hang up on him' and act as if I don't care about her anymore is the best way for me to protect her.

I just have to keep bluffing even when he tries to call it.

"And you're able to *ignore her*?" Dayne spins on me, the air around him becoming electrified. His eyes darken – literally. Not just with emotion like how it's meant in books, but with color, his sclera graying, his brown irises turning black. I am reminded of when I hit him with my hybrid strength. I should've knocked him unconscious then, but he stood up like it was nothing.

My eyes narrow in curiosity, but I file the questions away for later. Right now, all that matters is my wife.

"We need a better plan," I say, ignoring his accusation. If it was just us two, I would tell him the truth, that feeling her suffering is breaking me bit by bit, but I don't trust Stormie. She's right behind us, and though her parents died fighting on our side during one of the coups, she might blame me for their deaths. So instead, I just focus on the facts as I head into the basement.

"Antonio wants to bring his wife back from the dead. Micha's only a small part of that plan, so if we can figure out –" I stop mid-sentence. Mid-step, halfway down the stairs.

There is a moment of silence, and then Dayne breaks it. "What the fuck?"

Not knowing how to answer him, I continue down the stairs. The dying werewolves that were thrown into the cells earlier were all in pieces and bleeding from multiple holes. Now they're standing in a single line behind the bars. They haven't been healed though. Their wounds are still gaping, but seeping black smoke fills them. The boy I talked to, the one without legs, stands on two solid replacements – matte rather than gloss.

Eerie silence deafens our ears as we draw closer. They were all screaming, crying, or pleading the last time I was here. Now, nothing.

"Fuck. I do not do zombies," Stormie mutters. I can smell her fear, but she doesn't run back up the stairs. She watches our backs as Dayne and I stop in front of the first cell.

They don't react to our presence at all.

"Their eyes..." Dayne murmurs.

They're filled with the same smoke-like substance that's inside their wounds. Tendrils of it are still leaking out of the edges, curling out before they vanish. Is this what I would have done to Krypto if Louise hadn't healed him?

My arm hair rises as my fingers twitch down at my sides. A foreign feeling tugs at me, like a newborn whale's instinct to swim to the surface. A dog's prey drive being activated as soon as something small takes off.

I can play with these things in front of me.

Control them like they're dolls...

All their heads snap in my direction.

"What the fuck?" Dayne jumps back, his hands raised.

Electricity crackles between his fingers.

Stormie throws up bubble after bubble as she shrieks in fear. As terrified as she is, at least she's being smart about it.

Closing my hands into fists, I kill the urge inside of me.

All my life, I have wanted magic, but with my wife gone, this moment just tastes like ash. Colorless and numb.

"Release them, Stormie," I say, somehow knowing they won't do anything unless I tell them to. Yesterday, I would have stayed down here all night, too excited to sleep, testing the limitations of the gift I have been given, but today, all I want is my wife.

Turning on my heels, I head for the exit. Khalid's just entered, and his face is expressionless as he scans the room. "We'll do this upstairs," I say, and without a word, he heads back up before me, then sucks the cars into his shadows.

The three of them spread out in the now empty space, and each one starts drawing two circles of runes, one inside the other. Red energy pours out of their forefingers, glowing neon as they create a rune by pushing their power into it. Then the light fades, the magic becoming dormant until it's activated. It's going to take a few minutes for them to draw them all, so I stand with my arms crossed, trying my best not to focus on the pull of my girl. If I do, I'll run to her, and she doesn't need a headless fucking chicken.

My shoulders tight, I look over at Dayne. I don't know anything about his past, and though I will continue to trust him just because Micha does, I need to figure out what he's hiding. Is he a hybrid like me? Does Micha know? Is that why she didn't bat much of an eye when I told her what I was? All she was concerned about was how she managed to get pregnant when all hybrids are infertile.

I study him as he moves in a crouch, making a circle barely big enough for a person to stand in. He looks normal, isn't moving any faster than expected. Perhaps I should get into a proper brawl with him when there are no witnesses, see what he can actually do.

Khalid finishes his containment circle first, and he pulls his shadows into it immediately. A small pink bubble rises out of them, holding one of the chimeras. The beast shifted into his human form in an attempt to give himself more room, but Stormie's magic just shrank around him so that he's forced to lie on his back along the curvature of the wall, scrunched up, with his legs in the air. There's no room to stretch out at all. He has been like that for hours, and he's struggling to breathe what little air remains in his cage.

The bubble pops, and his limbs splay out uncontrollably. As soon as he touches the runes, a web of bright-red energy shoots up in a cylinder around him. The smell of burning flesh permeates the air, and he screams as he jerks his arms and legs in. He scoots into the middle, then tries to stand, but his legs are too weak. He collapses immediately, hitting the edge of his cage and burning himself all over again.

The second wolf Khalid pulls out, inside Stormie's circle, is lying in his own piss and sobbing, but despite how easy he'll be to break, it's the third one I want the most. The one with the limp arm. The fucker who helped kill Leno. The one who raped my wife in his werewolf form.

The two of us stand in front of him, radiating with a need to rip his bald head off his shoulders. He stares up at us, his green eyes full of a bravado I'm going to enjoy destroying.

"How's your brother?" he taunts as he climbs to his feet. Careful not to touch the runes, he leans towards us with a sneer. "I enjoyed tearing him apart almost as much as I did your wife."

Dayne yells as he charges from behind us. Khalid throws up a barrier in front of Micha's friend though, and he slams into it, then falls to the floor. The reaper knows what the wolf's trying to do. Containment circles are near impossible to break from within, but a single brush of the outer ring will shatter them easily.

"When I ripped her cunt open all the way to her ass –"

Khalid isn't fast enough to stop me.

Swiping my foot across the runes, I destroy the spell so I can throw a fist at his face. The wolf would have been ready for it had I been a mere witch, but I'm a fucking hybrid.

More, I'm *pissed.*

So my knuckles slam into him hard enough to dislocate his jaw. He staggers to the side, and I kick down at his knee. It cracks apart, bone pushing out of his skin. As he drops to the ground, I grab his arm and pivot behind him, yanking it up at the shoulder.

He screams, finally able to fucking register that his piss-poor attempt at escape is never going to happen. Slamming my foot between his shoulder blades, I shove him forward hard as I rip his humerus completely out of its socket. His skin tears at the joint, but his muscles and tendons still keep it attached.

I pivot to the side, tossing him over onto his back. I slam my heel into his balls, then drop on top of him, straddling his waist. Able to imagine all too well what he did to Micha, I hammer my fists into his jaw. I'm careful not to hit his nose though. I don't want to send any shards into his brain, don't want to kill him and let him off that easily or take that right from my wife.

His jaw fractures, then shatters, cutting through his skin like pieces of glass. Blood covers my face, arms, and chest. He wheezes harder, unable to breathe through the mess that is now his face.

My body shakes as I imagine all the pain this fucker caused my wife.

I want to kill him.

I want to shove a dildo up his ass so deeply that the only way his shit can come out is through his mouth. I want him to choke on it. I want him to suffer. I want him gone from this fucking world because he doesn't deserve to breathe on the same world as my wife.

But she might want to kill him herself.

She might need to in order to heal after all they've done to her.

Emitting a broken, hoarse cry from the void in my chest, I punch him one last time. Then I shove to my feet and face the other captives. Blood drips from me – his and mine, my knuckles having split apart in my rage, my fingers broken.

Breathing heavily, I demand, "Tell me about his plan to resurrect Siome."

He's hurt my girl.

Now I will hurt his.

TWENTY-SEVEN

HIM

They're pathetic.

Squealing like fucking pigs, the two try to talk over each other, desperate to gain my favor. As if they think there is anything they can say that will save them from pain. I know what they did to my wife. They will never know a moment's peace until the day they die.

"She's in the Underworld."

"He has to undergo the Elusive Mysteries first. It's a big thing. One of the last steps."

"Eleusinian," the first werewolf corrects. "He has to go to Greece for it."

"When?" I demand as I walk over.

He shakes his head as snot and tears pour down his face. "I don't know." His shoulders hunch forward. "We're only the rejects. He doesn't tell us anything."

"Then how do you know this?"

His head snaps up as his eyes widen in fear, thinking I'm

going to punish him for lying. "Eduardo told me."

"Me too," the second one adds, shuddering as he still sits in his own piss. He lifts his right arm, twisted by medical experiments, the bones rotated to give it an awkward angle. His hand is permanently slanted twenty-odd degrees to the outside. "Antonio let him cut into us as a reward for finding out what the Mysteries entail. He was on a high for weeks."

"He likes to talk while he's *working*," the first wolf says, his voice breaking, but I don't give a shit about what they've suffered through. I don't care if they were ripped from their families and forced to join Antonio's gang as nothing more than bodies to be dissected. *They raped my wife.*

"What do they entail?"

The wolf sitting in his piss starts to sob uncontrollably. The other one shakes his head in terror. "I don't know. He didn't say. But please... let me go. Antonio would've killed us if we didn't fight. But I can leave. I can leave and never come back. Please... just, please... My name's Jona," he says, trying to humanize himself to me but only managing to piss me off. "I'm a good guy."

"You're a rapist."

He flinches.

Dayne steps up to us, radiating with the fury he hasn't yet been able to release. He glances at me, a silent request for permission to break the containment spell and kick this fucker's ass. I nod at him as I turn to the piss-sitter. I only need one of them to talk.

"The white wolf with the purple eyes," I say. "What's his name?"

He whimpers.

Jona screams. He tried to attack Dayne as soon as he opened the circle, but now he's down on his knees, his back arched in agony, his body convulsing, and all Dayne's done is grab his arm. He can control electricity, but he doesn't shoot it like Talon did. He wields it elegantly – precisely and controlled. Small lethal attacks rather than the crushing bursts of power my brother preferred.

Stepping behind Jona, Dayne places his free hand on the side of the guy's head. The werewolf stops convulsing, but he doesn't move, doesn't fight. Frozen by Dayne's electricity through his brain, his every moment now being controlled, he just stares at the ceiling in horror. Dayne places his other hand on his head.

Then Jona reaches down to his soft cock and grabs hold of it with his right hand. Tears fall down his cheeks. The captive I'm talking to cries just as hard, perhaps knowing he will soon suffer the same fate.

"Tim...othy," he sobs in answer to my question about the sadist. "He tortured me too. I didn't want to... do that to her. But he forced –"

He screams, loud and shrill. Pure terror that causes him to jerk back, right into the runes still surrounding him. He shrieks again as he's burned, but it's nothing on the noise Jona is making.

He squeezed his dick so tight it became purple. Then he yanked his arm, fast and hard, away from his body. He did not manage to tear his penis off, not enough power, but he's degloved it. The skin's been severed from the base, and now it dangles in his grip. A bloody sock.

His eyes dark clouds of vengeance, Dayne forces Jona's hands towards his mouth.

The wolf's screams grow higher; he knows what's about to happen.

But he can't stop it.

He's locked in, a prisoner in his own body.

Still screaming, he sticks his tongue out and slides the skin of his cock onto it. Then he grabs what remains of his penis with his other hand and starts jerking himself off, chaffing his exposed nerves, veins, and tissue, sending bits of blood spraying with every movement.

"I swear I didn't want to," the other captive sobs. A lie to save his own skin. I have seen the video. I can never forget that fucking video.

He fucked her as she lay unmoving, trying her best to dissociate and survive. He did it enthusiastically. He did it willingly. And even if he hadn't, he hadn't saved her. That is enough for me to punish him.

Feeling my own guilt for not stopping it, I step forward and rub my foot across the outer circle of runes. He doesn't try to fight like the other two did. He just sobs harder.

"Please... don't... I can be of use. I can tell you what they are working on."

I stop just to give him hope before I take it away. "Talk."

He shudders in relief. "Eduardo has made chimeras. Not like us but finished ones. And he's trying to get that other witch to create a disease that'll enhance us. Like rabies or myso – myso..." He breathes out heavily as he struggles to remember the words. "Myostatin hypertrophy!" he blurts. "She hasn't managed it, but she's close."

I recall the souped up wolf we fought in Morn Tower. It was going to die even if we hadn't killed it; whatever it had in its blood was terminal. I don't doubt Terra Harrison, the infamous witch who helped wipe out nearly a third of the world's population barely more than a century ago, could perfect her work with time. But we've just taken down the majority of the Death Hunt. Now they don't have enough soldiers to infect.

I stare down at the pathetic man before me.

His hope dies in his eyes, and I relish in the fear that soon replaces it. He starts to hyperventilate as he tries to think of something else to say.

"Is that all?" I ask mockingly.

He gasps, falling to his hands in front of me, kneeling down as he begs for mercy. "Please! My name's Alejandro. I'm a victim! Eduardo would cut off our hands and use them to jack himself off if we didn't obey! I –"

Dayne charges in front of me, tearing through the circle. He grabs Alejandro by the top of his head. He hauls him to his feet, then moves his grip to be around his neck. "What did you just say?"

I glance at Micha's best friend, studying him warily. He was enraged before, but now he's lethal. Calm. Buzzing with a volatile energy that sits right beneath the surface. The air around him becomes charged.

Sobbing, Alejandro tries to collapse back to the floor.

Dayne simply lifts him into the air, his feet now kicking as he struggles to breathe. His body convulses as jolts of electricity fry him from the inside. When he is dropped, he hits the ground with a thud, then curls into a ball. Dayne squats down in front of him, but before he can touch him again, Alejandro blurts out what he wants to hear.

Eduardo cutting off their hands clearly means something to him. His eyes blazing, Dayne stands and looks at me.

"Take me to her," he demands.

"I can't phase."

"Then we drive."

My eyes narrow. "He'll move her before we get there." As much as I want to be her fucking white knight, I can't waste time on pointless endeavors.

Pivoting on his feet, Dayne roars as he throws a bolt of lightning at the wolf I knocked unconscious.

"Stormie!" I snap, not wanting the fucker to die. I barely left him alive.

A bubble pops into existence, blocking Dayne's attack a second before impact. Crackling white bolts spread across the pink surface with a deafening boom. Jona tries to take the moment to run, but Stormie throws up a bubble around him too, catching him mid-stride. He slams into the inside of his prison, then screams as it shrinks around him, forcing him into a stress position. Khalid just stands there watching everything, ready to step in only if he's needed. I know he wants to use his energy for other things; it's been clear in his pheromones ever since we got back.

"What do the hands mean?" I ask, ignoring the smell of my brother's desire.

Dayne turns to look at me, his lips flat, his anger back under control – barely. "There was a serial killer targeting sups a few years ago. He'd have three or four victims at a time, and he would keep them in dog cages until he wanted entertainment." His jaw tightens. Tension rolls off him in fucking waves. "Then he'd force them to fuck, maim, or kill each other, using the... *improvements* he'd given them."

My stomach churns, able to guess where this is going.

"He would cut off their hands – sometimes after they died, but mostly while they were alive and able to watch him use them." He clenches his fists as he struggles to stay still. "The SCU eventually went after him when he took one of their families." He glances away, his eyes darkening like they did before. A trick of the light perhaps, considering when he looks back at me, they are his usual dark-brown with white scleras. He shakes his head, furious with himself. "I thought the fucker died, and I never knew his name. He's changed his face too."

He shifts on his feet, and I am acutely aware he hasn't shared this story with many people. The body remembers, and his trauma is carved deep into his skin, a festering pool of infection. "When Micha and her dad found me," he says, "I was still locked in my cage, only a day from death." He smiles cruelly, a mixture of fond memories and dark humor. "I was so hungry, I tried to eat her."

"He did experiments on you?" Stormie breathes in shock.

He stiffens even more – damn near rigid. Stone-like. Full of shame and self-loathing. "No. He kept me alive as a *pet*. I was to be killed after my ascension."

"He took you as a child! Did you ever find your pare–"

"He is my father."

Stormie gasps.

"My mother was his 'favorite,'" he says bitterly.

My heart races. If Micha knows this, she'll try to kill him herself. He was strong enough to fend off Mother, and my wife doesn't have any magic anymore because of me. That won't stop her from trying though. She is a fighter. A Black, a fucking talented assassin.

Dayne starts to shake as he looks at me, and my heart beats even faster, terror pumping through my veins. "I was feral when Micha found me," he says. "I only knew violence. Eduardo –" He stops, as if he's trying the word for the first time, finally putting a name to the face in his memories and nightmares. "He rewarded me for that. He thought it was funny whenever I tried to fight back because I was too weak to do anything. But Stefaan didn't like that. He wanted to put me down, and Micha is the only reason he didn't."

He crosses his arms, then drops them, his hands fisted. "She taught me how to speak and read. I rarely left her side for the first six months, and the reason... The reason I felt comfortable enough with her to calm down wasn't because she saved me from that cage." He's fucking vibrating now, unable to stand still. His need to move is so great, that his own body is betraying him. "I liked her..." He takes in a deep breath through his nostrils. His teeth clench tight as he struggles to push out the words. "Because she reminded me of my mother."

I reach for my phone, wanting to call Aleric and tell him to take me northeast until I find her, but then I freeze.

She doesn't need a husband right now.

As hard as it is, I force myself to breathe. "Antonio wants her to breed hybrids," I say, my tongue thick, my throat dry. I don't know if I'm trying to convince Dayne right now or myself, but either way, I push the words out. "He won't give her to Eduardo and risk causing a stress miscarriage. And once she is pregnant" –the words dig their claws into my throat, not wanting to be born– "Eduardo won't be able to transport her." The risk would be extremely high. "That is when we go for her."

"That could take months," Dayne seethes.

"He'll be using Vs." It's what I'd do. "There's one that can almost guarantee pregnancy." They're expensive as hel, the potions requiring the sacrifice of a fertile womb and a set of testicles. When mass is 'created,' it must first be taken from somewhere else. The Ricks and other Vs can get by with any meat being used, but when the spell requires more than just physical creation, specific items are needed.

Dayne's jaw tics, but it's not his wife who might decide to keep another man's baby, too traumatized by having lost one already. It gets harder to breathe as I push my senses out towards the house. Through their heartbeats, I can tell Maddox and Lou are still sitting with Krypto, Mother is in the kitchen with Khalid's girl, and the twins are asleep in their rooms. When at war, it's important to rest whenever you can. But there is one heartbeat I can't feel, who I never got the chance to learn.

Sitting on my bedside table is all that remains of a future that could've been.

The urge to scream claws at my throat again, but I shove it down.

"What's the rest of the plan?" Dayne demands, as ready as I am to put it into play.

I start to tell him when a wave of fear slams into me. My lips freeze as my head snaps to the northeast.

I ball my hands into fists. He's fucking killing her. It isn't quick. He's making it hurt, and she's trying so hard to fight back. I can feel her resistance, her refusal to go down easily. There isn't any hope inside of her, but there is fire. There is *fury.*

Now there is numbness.

And then nothing.

"What is it?" Dayne demands, but I barely hear him over the rage screaming around my skull. I want to be her white knight, her fucking husband. I want to slay her dragons and uphold my vows to protect my wife.

Except I never made those vows, did I?

Micha's stinging words come back to me, how I didn't have to offer her anything due to barbaric Shadow *tradition*. I brushed it off then because that was simply how the vows had always been said and I was so focused on trying to fix my bigger fuck-ups. I thought it was minuscule in the face of the torture and rape, but right now, the absence of them feels crushing.

"Varius."

I look at Khalid. He's always been my voice of reason, and his mere presence grounds me now. I exhale slowly. It helps that I can feel Micha's revival. She's groggy, but her willingness to keep fighting is still strong.

Fuck. This is going to kill me to do.

"How do I block the blood bond?" I ask him, knowing it needs to be done. If my control slips and I try to push as much love and strength down it as I want to, I could use up what little blood of hers remains inside of me. Then I won't be able to feel when she's pregnant. I might not even be able to track her down, and the thought of running out right as I'm about to reach her is terrifying. What if I fail to save her again and Antonio takes her away from me forever? She'll die if we don't complete it.

No.

I'll kill myself before it kills her.

A chill runs through me.

And subject her to a lifetime of torture?

Hating the choice I might have to make, I concentrate on what my brother is saying.

"... want it."

Fuck, I missed most of it.

"What?" I ask.

"Want it."

I stare at him, waiting for him to expand on that.

He does not.

Realizing I'm not going to get anything more from him, I decide to ask Mother. "He's killed and revived Micha," I say as I move towards the house. "Once she's pregnant, we will make a new soul doll of her."

My phone buzzes inside my pants pocket, and I pull it out as I walk. The sight of Antonio requesting a video call makes me stop abruptly.

Dayne passes me a step before he turns around. Khalid is already beside me, looking at my phone.

"You don't have to take it," he murmurs.

I don't acknowledge him as I stare at the screen. At the red or green choice in front of me.

We all know what it's going to be. Another video of my wife. Live this time.

Still... I can't ignore it. What if he wants to trade now that we've crippled his organization?

I finally look at Khalid. "Get him out of here." I don't trust Dayne not to give into his urges to rip the phone out of my hand and scream at Antonio. Hel, he might even be able to shock him through the device, but I know whatever he tries, the wolf will be faster. And he'll take out his anger on my wife.

Dayne curses as he's herded up to the house. Stormie stays with me, ready to contain my powers should I lose control. Trying not to feel the presence of the husks below the garage, I turn so my back is facing a wall, then hit the play button.

"If you're calling to beg for your territory back, the only trade I'll consider is for the alexandrite," I say in a tone that is strictly business. I know he isn't going to give me Micha without first trying to use her to manipulate me. I'd trade my whole kingdom for her in a heartbeat, but if I tell him that, he'll just torture her more severely. He knows I can't give him back everything Aleric and I have stolen from him, especially with most of his soldiers now in jail. All he has left is to hurt me like my mother hurt him, to make us feel that same loss he did. So I'm going to have to pretend I do not give a damn about either her or Rudy.

I'm just the cold, heartless Boss. The nightmarish bastard who's so infamous in his cruelty.

"You're going to choose," Antonio says as he turns in place, his phone held out until a grubby mattress appears on the floor behind him. Single-size. Stained. They're definitely in a fucking human trafficking house.

My wife is dragged into the shot by that fucking white-haired sadist, then shoved down onto the bed, and it takes everything inside of me to keep my face flat as he strangles her.

"She's no longer my property," I say, keeping my voice as emotionless as my eyes. "Do with her what you will."

My heart hammering, I go to end the call.

"No!" Antonio snaps just as my finger hovers over the button. "You are going to *feel* what I did when your mother killed my mate. I'm going to take her eyes or her eardrums. And if you don't choose, I will take them both. Then I will take her legs, her hands. I will cut her apart piece by piece until you do. So... which one do you want me to take from your lovely bride?"

The bastard! I want to jump through the screen and beat him to death. I want to blurt out an answer to stop him from going through the rest of his threat, but I *know* he will not stop. He will just keep me picking between the choices over and over again. Eyes or ears? Fingers or tongue? Breasts or clit?

Struggling to keep my arm from shaking, my rage and

fear burning bright, I narrow my eyes. Pretending I'm only annoyed at him for wasting my time is the hardest lie I've ever had to sell.

But I do it for her. Because I know that if I break now, he *will* torture her for the rest of eternity to get to me. Micha is staying strong while suffering through this; I can't fail her by being weak just for hearing what she might go through. I hurt her once, and that nearly destroyed us. I cannot hurt her again.

So I don't focus on my wife's legs as they kick frantically against the mattress. I don't focus on the air being squeezed out of her lungs and the panicked fear that's raging down our bond. I simply focus on the alpha with the golden eyes I am one day going to kill. "She's your problem now. If you have trouble deciding, flip a coin. Now –" I break off when I feel her die, but I manage to cover it up by glancing off the screen, as if I'm focusing on someone else. Just as I work up my ability to start talking again though, I catch Timothy in the corner of my eye.

He's fucking her hard, jerking the mattress across the floor. Eduardo hasn't revived her yet.

My grip tightens on my phone so hard my screen cracks at one edge. The werewolf husks down in the cells call to me, a shrieking darkness that demands to be used.

"Call me when you want to trade that alexandrite," I bite out. Then I hang up before he can see me break.

Screaming, I crush my phone in my hand, then launch it across the fucking yard. It shatters through a window of the house. Pivoting on my feet, I slam fist after fist into the garage wall, making the whole building shake.

Rage pours through me as I imagine what's happening to Micha right at this moment. How she's lying on that damn mattress, completely fucking vulnerable, and he's shoving his cock inside her limp body.

Magic flares beneath my skin, burning hot and wild,

chaotic energy urging me to set the world on fire. To let my husk soldiers rise from the ashes and slaughter anyone who remains.

Screaming, I slam both fists into the wall, punching right through the material, and let my power rip free. Shadows pour forth from my feet. The husks' bloodlust runs through my veins, so pale in comparison to mine.

He's hurting my wife.

He's hurting my wife!

Closing my eyes, I roar as I rip my hands free of the wall. Before I can take off towards the northeast though, a pink bubble forms around me.

"Noooo!"

I rail against it, slamming my shoulder into the curved wall over and over again, but it doesn't give. So I start to use my magic, flinging out whatever I can – an uncontrollable, volatile energy.

Pain ruptures across my body as I'm hit by the ricochets, but cracks are starting to form in the pink. Roaring, I dig deeper inside of myself, willing to offer up everything I am to my magic. It can take a kidney, my muscles, my entire left arm if it means I can get out of here and to my wife.

But I'm struggling to extend my arms now. The bubble is shrinking rapidly. Forcing me to bend in half. For my knees to come up to my chest. For my neck to curve painfully.

And still my prison shrinks.

Smaller and smaller until every part of me is touching.

Until all that's left to breathe is the black smoke that sits thick in my lungs.

My vision narrows.

My anger grows.

I gasp as I strain to keep trying to escape.

But my limbs won't listen.

My lungs won't breathe.

Unable to fight it, I pass out just as I feel Micha coming

back to life.

TWENTY-EIGHT

HER

Pain.

Agony.

A few broken ribs. A crushed esophagus. Four-by-three inches skinned off me.

That's how I know I'm fucking alive.

Then comes the awareness of movement.

The understanding that someone is cradling my head in both their hands as a healing warmth flows through me.

And another person is on top of me.

Inside of me, their thrusts rubbing raw against the walls of my pussy, jerking me up and down the mattress as I lie motionless, my body screaming in pain.

But my fracturing mind shrieks louder.

He's raping me.

He killed me. Then he raped me.

So fight!

Get him off!

Snapping my eyes open, I jerk up to bite off his lip, his nose, a chunk of his throat – I don't fucking care. It's pure panic running wild through my veins. If I can't fight him off now, I won't be able to at all. He'll just kill me again and get unrestricted access to my body.

He jerks back, grinning with his tongue out. Then his fist flies towards the side of my face. I try to throw up an arm to block it, but all my energy went into my attack. I've been starved, tortured, and killed. I'm not fighting in my prime.

His knuckles slam into me. My teeth cut into my cheek as my head whips sideways. My eyes roll, stars dancing, and then he starts to choke me with both hands.

I grab his arms, but I don't have the strength to fight him off.

I want to call on my magic.

I want to burn him as it runs uncontrollably through my veins.

But I know I'll fail.

He'll kill me faster than I can draw on it in my weakened state.

Then I will wake up to both my arms having been sawn off at the shoulders. The sight of Eduardo severing Rudy's fingers slams into me.

Weakens me.

There is nothing I can do.

It doesn't matter how well I've trained.

How many people I've killed.

I can't stop him from raping me.

As tears leak down the sides of my face, I pass out.

Five minutes later, I die.

The next time I come to, I fight on instinct.

He doesn't stop raping me.

And I still die.

I'm brought back to life in a vicious cycle of a crushed esophagus to kill me and broken ribs to revive me – CPR never as gentle as it is in movies. I don't know how many times I have died. How many times I have woken up to find Sadist's cock buried in my pussy as he kneels between my legs, with Eduardo's hands on my head, pouring his magic into me.

But it's been long enough that I'm no longer fighting.

As Sadist rapes me, I keep my eyes closed and dissociate, just waiting for it to be over.

He slaps me in the face? I ignore him.

He pulls out of my pussy to rape me in the ass? I ignore him.

He tells me how much I'm enjoying this? I ignore him.

But then he says:

"You want to fuck her, don't you, Eduardo? You want to slide your tiny, little cock into her wet, sloppy pussy?"

Now panic slams into me, hitting me in the solar plexus and finally jerking my attention to him. I can't breathe. I need to fight. My limbs are too heavy though. I don't have it in me, no energy. My mind's screaming, trapped in a body that's too exhausted and weak to move.

"Are you imagining how tight she is?" he grunts. "You've been staring at her pussy all this time."

Our bodies slap together. Harsh breathing sounds from behind my head.

"Do you see how wet she is sliding on my cock? She's such a fucking whore."

Eduardo's fingers stroke my ears, running around the outer rims. The one on my left is starting to push inside, but it's too big to go in any further than the tip. That doesn't stop him from trying different angles though, and my skin crawls every time he does.

"How tight is she?" Eduardo rasps as he rocks his groin against the top of my skull. My hair has grown out a little bit from the clean shave it was when I first met Varius, but it isn't nearly enough to feel like any sort of barrier.

I want to be sick.

I want to fight.

But I have nothing in my stomach to expel.

And I have no control over my limbs anymore. I've died too many times; the drain on my body has been too great.

"Fucking loose." Sadist presses a finger on my clit. "But you can fuck her ass, can't you?"

Eduardo's finger jabs me harder in the ear. "Can I fuck her urethra?"

Sadist laughs as he pulls out of me. "Be my guest."

Fucking fight back!

I beg my body to listen to me. I need to kick him and run. To do anything other than fucking lie here like I want it, my legs open in invitation. My pussy wet from the constant use.

But they've turned my body against me.

It isn't mine anymore.

It's theirs.

As Eduardo crawls onto the bed and kneels between my legs, he grabs my hip with one hand and his cock with the other. He wasn't lying when he said it was small, an inch or two max, but it's still too big to go *in there*.

I brace myself for the pain as tears of frustration burn my eyes. I try to dissociate once more, but my mind is too tuned in to what's happening, a horrified pull I can't break free from.

I beg for Varius to save me.

For Dayne to come bursting through the door.

Antonio is no longer in the room with us. I don't know when he left, but he isn't here. There's no guard in his place.

They have a chance to save me.

Eduardo's cock pushes against a hole too small to take him.

Helpless tears run down the side of my face. No one runs through that door though. No one comes to save me.

I try to pull on my magic, but it's like a lighter that's out of fuel. I flick the wheel harder and harder, faster and faster in my desperation to get it lit. The darkness crowds in on me though; all the monsters rush me at once, and they grab me with their teeth and claws, ripping me apart.

Eduardo shoves his cock inside me.

I scream inside my locked-in state. The pain is intense – burning and all-demanding. The betrayal of my body hurts even more. Why won't it fight? *Why won't it fucking fight!*

"I told you I'd fuck you," Eduardo hisses as he grabs hold of my breast with a talon's claws, digging his nails into my skin. "Not so tough now, are you, bitch?"

He slaps me across the face, then grabs both my hips as he pulls out of me. He starts to push back in, but as he does, he falls on top of me with a grunt.

No, not falls.

He was pushed by Sadist.

Now I realize what I didn't before. My thighs aren't wet with his cum. I stopped fighting back, but he needs that fear to orgasm.

"Get off me!" Eduardo shouts as Sadist pushes down on him. The witch thrashes above me, wriggling like a fish in an attempt to turn over and protect his ass, but Sadist has both Eduardo's hands pinned to the mattress, and without his magic, the fucker is as weak as I am. He's much smaller than Sadist, and he isn't a fighter.

He tries to buck the wolf off him, but Sadist just laughs, then groans, "That's it. Rub yourself against my cock."

"Get off!"

His panic is damn near palatable. A delicious feast after

all the shit I've been through. His cock slipped out of me when he first started to fight too, so now I'm able to 'enjoy' the feel of him being forced flat against me. I start to laugh as he screams, high-pitched and full of fear. My laughter is more of a broken wheeze, a soft release of air. But I can feel it in my chest.

Manic.

Delighted.

Fuck this fucking piece of shit.

In one swift movement, Sadist shoves his cock into the witch's ass. Eduardo arches up on another scream. His dick is rubbing against me somewhere, but it's so fucking small, I can't even feel it.

My laughter grows louder. Stronger. With each shriek of pain and terror Eduardo emits, I regain a little bit more of my energy.

"That's it, Ed. Squeeze me with your fucking ass. Milk my cock like the whore you are."

He thrashes on top of me. Screaming. Crying.

I pull on all of my strength as Sadist rapes him on top of me, every last molecule I can scavenge. Then I snap up – probably really moving at a snail's pace, but a snail he is distracted from by the hot poker up his ass, and I sink my teeth into his Adam's apple.

He tries to jerk back, but Sadist is pinning him to me. There is nowhere for him to go but sideways, and in his panic, he does. Blood spurts into my mouth as his flesh tears between my teeth. I don't have the energy to move, to rip my head side to side like a rabid dog, but he's doing all the work for me, his instinctive need to get away from the pain causing him to try to shake free.

More blood coats me.

More strength runs from him.

Sadist laughs as he fucks him harder, clearly able to see what's happening. He doesn't care that they're on the same side. All he wants is to cause pain for his own pleasure.

Eduardo soon drops limp on top of me, blood pouring out of his throat. I don't think I managed to kill him; the carotid arteries are on the side of the neck. But he's passed out from either shock or pain.

Sadist groans as he shoves deep inside Eduardo's ass. He's filling him with his cum, and I finally release my prey's neck. I don't have the energy to bite him again. I used it all up in that one attack.

As I collapse back onto the mattress, Sadist crawls off the witch, then pushes him off me so he can look down at my unguarded body. Keeping his violet eyes on mine, he shoves two fingers into my pussy. I don't even try to close my legs anymore; I know I can't. I know it's useless. Grinning, he grabs hold of my chin with his other hand and forces me to taste myself. Disgust rolls through me as his fingers sweep around my mouth, touching every part of it.

Releasing me, he then turns to Eduardo. He takes his wet fingers, and he works them into the man's ass. The witch whimpers, but Sadist pulls his fingers out before he wakes up. Then they're back at my mouth.

I gag at the smell of them. A chunk of brown –

My eyes widen as I jerk my head to the side.

Grinning, he grabs my jaw. It doesn't take much for him to force my lips apart. Then his fingers are inside me, the taste of shit is on my tongue, and I'm retching on reflex.

He laughs as he pumps the full length of his fingers in and out of my mouth, keeping it open with his other hand. I try to move my tongue away, but he just follows it, making damn sure I taste every chunk of Eduardo's shit.

My stomach churns.

My brain screams.

But my nightmare doesn't stop.

Satisfied that I don't have *any* strength left to fight him, he crawls up my body until his cock is at my lips. The smell makes me vomit up air, nothing left in my stomach. The sight, though, makes me start to hyperventilate. It's covered in cum, blood, and shit, with chunks and streaks of brown. Chuckling, he squeezes my jaw tighter, making sure I can't close it, then he pushes his cock into my mouth.

I retch at the mere waft of taste, nothing quite touching my tongue yet. Then comes the contact, the soft mush on top of a half-hard dick. Along its length. He pulls the end of his cock back and rubs his bare head on my tongue, forcing me to taste it all. I try to turn away, but he holds me still.

It's extremely bitter with a mix of bile and exactly how it smells. I know I'll be tasting it long after it goes down my esophagus. I'm torn between trying to spit it out or swallow it quickly so it's gone.

The latter choice wins. With tears of disgust falling down my face, I gulp down the saliva and shit mix. I can feel it sliding down my throat, coating me in its slime.

With a retch, I throw it up again, the force spewing half of it down my chin. Sadist laughs. His cock starts to harden, but then he's torn off me, his penis ripping across my teeth. The taste of copper mixes with the bitterness and salt, and I turn my head with a cough, desperate to get it all out.

"I didn't kill him!" Sadist shouts as Antonio pins him to the wall with one arm, his other changing into that of his wolf. "I tried to warn him not to get close to her mouth, but the arrogant fool didn't listen."

Antonio turns his head to look at Eduardo. Seeing the witch still breathing, he releases the chimera and steps back. The tension in the air reduces. Sadist keeps his back pressed to the wall and his shoulders hunched. His eyes stay glued to the ground. Non-challenging and submissive.

"How many times have you killed her?" Antonio asks.

"Twenty-nine."

Fuck.

No wonder I can't move. Eduardo might've taken on the

bulk of the work needed to heal me, but it's still my body that had to produce the blood cells and stem cells. He's used up all of my stored energy and some of my muscle mass by reviving me that much.

"Get him a potion," Antonio orders. "I need him to heal her eyes."

My eyes?

There's nothing wrong with –

I jerk towards the door as blatant horror pounds into me. I roll onto my side, then drag myself towards the edge of the mattress, desperate to get away. My limbs are too fucking heavy though. My body has a different master, and I barely make it a full body-length before Antonio grabs me by the back of the neck and hauls me to my feet.

As he shoves me towards a wall face-first, I try to lift my arms before impact, but I'm too slow, and my face smashes into the plaster. He leans in close behind me as pain radiates across my jaw. My heart rate spikes. He presses into me. All six-and-a-half feet of solid, dangerous muscle.

Now every instinct is screaming at me to stay still, to freeze rather than to fight or run as that will only give the predator something to chase.

"If I even *sense* your magic," he says, his chest vibrating against me as he talks, he's that fucking close, "I will rip off your arms before you can use it."

His hands cup my shoulders, sending chills all down my spine. As I tremble against the wall, I'm forced to admit that even if I'd fought him in my prime, with all my magic and a group of bodyguards beside me, he would've still won. The power difference between us is too vast.

"Bite another one of my men again," he says, his fingers digging into me, "and I will pull out all your teeth. Disobey me, and you'll be punished. Your little tantrums stop now."

Stepping back, he spins me around to face him. My legs wobble, and I nearly fall over, but he wraps a hand around the lower half of my face. His fingers and thumb squeezing into my cheeks, he keeps me standing. With his other hand, he pulls a switchblade out of his pants pocket and flips it open. He drags the blade up my neck, following my carotid artery, and it takes everything I have not to flinch away. But I can't stop the goosebumps from exploding across my skin as he raises the knife to my ear.

Then across to my eye.

"Varius has made his choice," he says.

Pure agony erupts from my mouth as my knees buckle. The scream comes from the very depths of my soul. I could have survived losing my eyes, but my husband's betrayal is cutting deeper than any knife. It's destroying every part of me, hurting me more than anything Sadist has done to me.

My body shakes uncontrollably as the grief drowns me in my own tears. I tried so hard to stop this from happening, knowing it would break me. That's why I offered up Varius' tattoo even though I knew how much it'd hurt him. Because I *knew* I wouldn't survive his betrayal.

The breaking of his promise to never hurt me again.

You fucking promised! I scream at him down our bond. *You promised!*

Tears rolling down my cheeks, I start to hyperventilate. Antonio stabs the knife into the wall beside my head, but I don't even flinch, the agony in my chest desperate to be outdone.

He digs a finger into my eye, and I merely welcome the pain. It feels so much better than the black hole growing in my chest, consuming every inch of me. I'm breaking apart, collapsing inwards. No piece of me will survive.

I never should have given Varius a second chance.

You promised... I sob inside my skull.

You fucking promised!

Antonio pulls my eye out, and finally that pain overrides my broken heart. Then he crushes it in his grip, sending fire through my nerves, and I scream for all I'm worth.

I hate him.

I hate Varius.

I hate how I gave him a second chance, listening to all his fucking *lies* about how he was sorry and how he'd never hurt me again.

As Antonio reaches for my other eye though, I start to laugh.

Maniacally.

Brokenly.

Happily.

Because now I can feel it coming. I'm about to pass out from the pain, and I'll gladly take that over suffering from a broken heart.

TWENTY-NINE

HER

I don't feel any better when I wake up, lying on a bed in some new place – one that doesn't smell of sex and blood and shit. The pain in my eyes... my eye *sockets* is gone, as is all the physical damage Sadist dealt to me and the patch of skin cut from my pussy.

But the agony in my chest still burns with a crippling heat, and the fractures in my soul are still spreading out like a web across broken glass.

He took my eyes.

Varius told him to take my fucking eyes.

Furious rage pours through me as I think about all the lies he told me this last month. About how he was so called "devastated" over what he did to me, how he hated himself for listening to his brother and mother and the pain in his chest when he thought I had betrayed him. He swore to me he'd never hurt me again. He vowed to spend the rest of his life regaining my trust, and he'd fucking started to do it too.

Tears burn my throat as I think about what an utter fool I was. An utter fucking *fool*.

My brain refused to forgive him, giving me nightmares every night about that hammer and screw and those cold, cold eyes that blanked me out as I screamed. But my dumb fucking heart swallowed up all the stories he told me about how he practically raised Rudy while their mother was busy with newborn Maddox and the other boys. It swooned over the fact that he conditioned himself to have a phobia of line-dancing goats just so Rudy could have something funny to concentrate on in crowded rooms, when his magic would grab on to all the terrible things people feared and demand he bring them to life.

And then...

Then it practically threw itself at him when I ordered a goat plushie, and he full-on freaked out when he saw it. It still sits with a knife through its face down in the basement, six rows of containment circles around it. He didn't want to throw it away, considering it was a gift I'd gotten him, but he didn't want to take the risk it could come to life either.

So I fell hard because he knew just what stories to tell. Stories that mirrored me taking care of Lou when our father was dealing with depression. And he did little acts that felt like genuine change. He showed me the ledger – the real one that not even his brothers (except for Khalid and Rudy) know about. He put his entire kingdom in my hands, and he was tearing down his walls for me, giving me weaknesses to exploit, trusting me even though I was angry at him.

Even though his paranoia was beaten into him by his friends, his first crush, his uncle, his cousin, his brother, his mother. He's been fighting his instincts and twenty-odd years of experience *for me*.

And so I believed that he could change.

That he could eventually love me like I loved him.

But it was all just a fucking lie.

Varius is still capable of hurting me.

My chest aches so hard, I struggle to breathe.

How could he do that to me?

How could he *choose* to take my eyes away?

Or did he wish to punish me because I offered up his tattoo? Because I revealed his weakness at the first sign of torture?

That thought almost breaks me, and I press my face into the pillow. Biting down on it, I touch the patch missing from my skin.

He poured his soul into that tattoo. His *trust* when he never trusts anyone.

It was a symbol of his vulnerability, a declaration of his weakness.

A rebellion against all the rules he had to put on himself in order to survive being betrayed by those he loves.

It was hope.

It was fear.

It was *him* in all his jagged pieces.

With that simple scribble of ink, he claimed me, but he also gave himself to me. A collar to a sub. A ring to a wife. His heart in his eyes, he begged me never to remove it.

I knew offering it up to Varius' enemy would break him. There's no sugarcoating what I did.

I just thought that there was a chance he could forgive me for it. That he would understand I was only hurting him to save myself just like he'd hurt me to save Khalid.

Whereas, I knew I would not be able to forgive him for choosing which sense I lost.

Yet, he went and did it anyway. He *chose* to hurt me. He thought about it and decided that it was acceptable.

We're never going to come back from this.

Tears claw at my throat as that truth resonates inside of me.

The last month I've spent trying to forgive him was for

nothing.

The anger comes back now, pushing aside the grief.

I hate him.

I hate him so fucking much that all I want to do is break out of here so I can yell at him. So I can torture him like he tortured me.

An eye for an eye only works with enemies. It leaves only bitterness, no second chances. No returning from one's mistakes. But we are already too broken to fix, and my rage is all I have left to carry me through this nightmare.

So I use it. Wield it. Letting it burn furiously through me, I rub my face against my pillow. I need to figure out where I am. With me blind, they might lower their guard around me now. So if I keep being smart about it, I can escape. Maybe not today, but eventually.

Then I can kick Varius' ass.

With a strengthening inhale, I push myself up and search for the edge of the bed. My fury falters a bit under the panic that slams into me from being unable to see. I'm only doing something simple, yet I feel like I'm climbing a sheer rock face with a hundred-foot drop. A river raging below without mercy.

I shudder as I breathe, trying to find my focus.

It's just a bed.

But what if I'm on a top bunk? Or there's glass or trip wires on the floor to keep me imprisoned without the use of chains?

He wants me alive to breed, but I don't need to be able to walk.

Moving slowly, I scoot forward on my ass until my feet find the edge of the bed. I hold my breath as they swing off it, the anticipation of pain sending needles across my skin. I reach down, stretching my legs.

Fuck.

Where's the floor?

My pulse starts to pick up.

I point my toes.

There! Hard wood presses against my soles, and I exhale with relief. Pushing to my feet, I spread my arms out around me and inch forward.

Something grabs my wrist and hauls me towards it.

My body recoils.

My heart rate spikes.

The fear in my belly tells me it's Sadist, and I swing for him with my other hand. He laughs as he dodges, then kicks me in the stomach. My legs buckle, but before I can hit the ground, he knees me in the face. My head jerks back. Pain explodes all down my jaw and neck. My teeth bite into my tongue, and blood fills my mouth as I start to fall. He shoves me, angling me towards the bed, and I hit it on my back.

Panic rushes through me. I need to sit up. I need to –

His hand wraps around my throat; he drags me beneath him, up the mattress, as he crawls on top of me. I try to kick him, but it doesn't throw him off. He lies down on me and licks the side of my face.

His hard cock rubs against my thighs.

At the feel of it, I immediately stop fighting. He wasn't able to finish when I was dead and unresisting. Perhaps he will tire of me quicker if I just don't react to anything at all.

Pressing his lips to my ear, he murmurs, "You're going to come for me today like a good fucking whore."

Bile claws its way up my throat. I tremble beneath him, unable to hide my fear. I know my orgasm won't be because I want it. He's going to give me V, and there'll be nothing I can do to stop it. It shouldn't be that big of a deal; my body already isn't mine. They took it, tainted it. What should it matter if it does something else I don't want it to do? It has already betrayed me.

But the thought of orgasming with the sick fucker on top of me...

No!

Jerking my head towards him, I aim to bite his cheek, but a hand slaps down on my face, pinning me before I can.

"Don't," Bear pleads as I struggle against him, and Sadist laughs. "Antonio *will* take your teeth."

But I don't care.

I can't go through this.

Reaching between our bodies, I grab hold of Sadist's balls and squeeze.

Hard.

He yelps as he pushes off me, but I clamp my fingers, not letting him go. Kneeling between my legs, his balls being crushed in the palm of my hand, he screams like a fucking manwhore. Bear's shoved back; his hand dragging across my face. Then two fists swing into me, splitting my lip and busting my nose. I bask in the pain, knowing that he is feeling as helpless as I am, that he's desperate to stop me. But he can't.

I jerk my arm up with everything I have.

His testicles rip free, blood spraying across my chest and face.

I laugh maniacally as he screams. Will Antonio kill him now that he's unable to breed me? It'll be a loss, not getting to do it myself, but at least the fucker will be dead.

He won't ever be able to hurt me again.

Won't ever be able to make me come on his cock.

It takes only a hundred and ten pounds of force to tear off a ball sack – well within the average pull strength of a woman. He should've known better than to crawl onto the bed. He should've checked what he was wearing if he didn't want this to happen. My laughter turns into pain as dark humor bleeds into my thoughts. I just want to go home. I want to be held by Varius even as I stab him for taking my eyes. I can kill him, then taxidermy him. Then he can hold me without hurting me with his presence.

My laughter gets more fractured.

My breathing turns hollow and sharp, the air dragged into my lungs, kicking and screaming and doing everything it can to escape. I want to open my eyes.

I want to do something so fucking simple, but I *can't*.

Varius took them from me like I took Sadist's sack.

Phantom pain erupting behind my eyelids, I squeeze the balls in my hand harder, making them *pop*.

Crack!

I scream as my arm is broken at the elbow. I couldn't see the attack, couldn't prepare for it, or even know it was coming, and that adds to the fear, the helplessness. My dark humor vanishes, and all that's left is pure terror because I know that wasn't Sadist.

Antonio is in the room with us.

"You better hope Eduardo can fix these," the alpha says as he grabs my hand. With it broken at the elbow, I don't have enough strength to keep my fingers closed.

He pulls them apart and takes what he wants.

Then someone's hands are on my jaw and nose, forcing my mouth open. The pop of a vial sounds beside me, and I know they have a V. I jerk my head side to side, trying to resist.

The potion pours down my cheek, missing my lips. One of the men curses as I take the small win. But a blow to my temple soon knocks me into compliance. I struggle to think through the rattle of my brain, and the rest of the V's forced down me. It tastes of pomegranates and chocolate.

Desperately, I spit it out.

"Enough," Antonio says, and I hate how fast my body obeys him, freezing in undeniable fear. He isn't like Sadist or Eduardo, who have to curb their darkest desires because their boss won't like it. He is the Boss, and I am nothing but a toy for him to break.

He grabs my chin and pours an entire vial of V into me.

His hand slides down my throat, a silent threat.

I tremble, my pulse jumping erratically against his palm, but I do not swallow.

"I can cut off your hand for what you did to Timothy," he says calmly, "or you can convince me that you now know how to listen. The choice is yours, Micha."

He rips out my soul with those words. If I continue down this path, he will cut me into pieces. Eyes here, hand there, tongue next, then arms, then legs. Bit by bit, he'll destroy every part of me. There will be nothing left for Dayne to rescue. A hollow husk with a broken mind.

I need to be smarter about this if I'm going to survive.

And I *need* to survive.

Lou is going to be a mother; she'll need my help.

Dayne will spend the rest of his life looking for me, so I can't give up first.

And Varius... Varius needs to get his ass kicked, so I have to keep my arms and legs to do it.

Fighting back the tears, I deafen myself to the screams inside my skull telling me that I'll be *consenting* if I do this.

That I'll only have myself to blame when I come.

That I should stay strong.

But I *am* staying strong.

I'm just choosing to protect my mind over my body.

To survive instead of die in this place.

A cock is a weapon, I tell myself. As lethal as any knife. It is okay for me to stop fighting...

There isn't any shame in this.

Liar.

There isn't any shame.

My lips shaking, I swallow down the V.

THIRTY

HER

The triggering of arousal is instant. My pussy pulses, wanting to be touched by whoever's willing, and my nipples harden, wanting to be sucked into the first warm mouth. My mind recoils, imprisoned inside my own body. I withdraw into myself, trying to get through this. If I'm not mentally here, I can't truly consent.

My body isn't mine.

It doesn't matter what they do to it.

It doesn't matter what it does because of them.

It is only my brain that is me anymore.

And I do not consent.

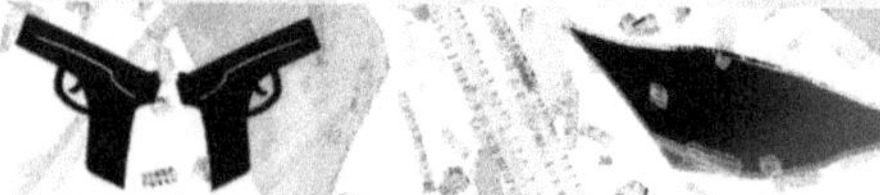

She's lying on a bed. There are men around her, ready to have intercourse with her. Two of them start to shift into their wolf forms. She can hear the cracking of their bones and their grunts of pain.

My name is Micha Shadow.

She shivers in anticipation. Her vagina throbs in desire. Her legs tingle, already close to the edge of an orgasm. Her nipples are hard and sensitive. Her eyes are closed, her lips parted as she pants.

My best friend is Dayne Killeen-McCarthy.

Two large strong hands grab her hips, and she tries to spread her legs in invitation, but the werewolf ignores them as he flips her over. He's so strong. She's just a toy to him, and he easily positions her how he wants her. At the edge of the bed, on her knees, her ass in the air, her face pressed into the fresh sheets.

I have a sister called Lou.

His penis lines up with her labia. She pushes against him on a moan, begging for him to enter her.

I will survive this.

He pushes in slowly, his clawed hands squeezing her hips. She arches downwards as he fills her up, moaning and panting. Her vagina pulses around his penis. Her nipples ache. It's not going to take much for her to come, the V in her blood running hot.

My name is Micha Shadow.

He rocks inside her, and she's never felt more full. Due to the V, her insides have moved and changed to accommodate him. The original g-spot has grown three times as large and become more sensitive. Another one's been created where the head of his penis hammers into her.

My best friend is Dayne Killeen-McCarthy.

He moves inside her slowly, leisurely, and she twists and moans beneath him. She wants this. Is hungry for this.

I have a sister called Lou.

She pushes back onto him, wanting, needing more. She's on the verge of her orgasm. Her vagina kegels around him. He grunts above her, a primal wolf. An animal. His speed picks up.

I will survive this.

A clawed hand presses down on her back. Her face is forced into the sheets, making her gluteal more prominent. She curls her phalanges into the fabric as he picks up speed.

My name is Micha Shadow.

He rams into her. She starts to scream. The pleasure that is rushing through her is so fucking intense. She's a dirty little slut. A willing participant. A cheater.

She has a husband who loves her, who is trying to save her. The scream he emitted in the Plane of Monsters erupts in her ears, that heartbroken cry, that desperate yell of pain and misery. She tenses.

But only for a second.

My best friend is Dayne Killeen-McCarthy.

She wants that dick. She's a bitch in heat. She ruts him hard, sliding up and down his cock without shame even as tears run down her cheeks.

I have a sister called Lou.

His knot grows inside her, pressing on her pleasure spots and signaling that he's about to come. But she beats him to it. Her body shaking, she squirts all over him. It runs down her legs, soaking his hairy balls.

I will survive this.

She hates herself.

My name is Micha Shadow.

He comes in her, filling her up and making her stomach swell due to the magic of the V. Her growing belly presses against the sheets.

She cries out in pleasure, pushing back onto his cock. She can feel each spurt of his cum and rocks her hips, milking him for more.

My best friend is Dayne Killeen-McCarthy.

His hands tighten on her hips as he waits for his knot to go down. She spasms against the bed, her orgasm still going.

It runs through her body with an intensity that leaves her a writhing hot mess. She's never come so hard.

She's never hated herself more.

I have a sister called Lou.

He pulls out of her, his knot gone. She wiggles her ass, wanting, needing another cock inside her.

Over and over, numerous werewolves rape her.

I will survive this.

But how can she claim it's rape when she's coming all over their cocks?

When the V wears off, I wish it didn't.

My body is "mine" again, and I fucking hate it. I want to tear my flesh off my bones. I want to set fire to all the parts they touched. I want to hurt Varius like they've hurt me. He caused this. He took my magic and made me helpless.

He's the only reason you still have your hands.

He took my eyes.

Did he?

I bite back a scream. I don't want to listen to the damn voice in my head. I want to yell at it. I want to throw things at it. I want to rip it from my skull and skewer it on a knife. It's supposed to be on my side. It's the *only* thing left on my side!

Tears build in my throat, but I force them down. I don't want to cry, and gods fucking dammit, I'm going to do *one* fucking thing that *I* want to do even if it fucking kills me.

And right now, I want to tear these damn sheets off the bed.

I roll onto my side, hating the feel of the wetness sliding around on my legs. I grab a handful of dry sheet and angrily wipe myself down. My broken arm has been healed, but it gives me little pleasure to know Eduardo fucking touched me at some point while I was spaced out.

"That's pointless," a man says – the same guy who cursed after he missed pouring the V down my throat.

My teeth grind together. "Guess you never wipe your ass then, huh? Just going to shit again."

My stomach growls, the hunger sharp and cruel. My nose twitches at the smell of something spicy and meaty nearby. Doing my best to not look interested in whatever he has, I climb off the bed, then turn around and start tugging at the sheets.

"Touche," he says, his voice moving around to the other side of the bed. There's a light clatter. A plate being put onto a side table, perhaps?

I still for a fraction of a second, my stomach controlling my movements. Then I'm jerking on the sheet again, more annoyed than before. I want to yell at him to get out of here, but if I do and he doesn't, then he'll remind me that I'm at everyone else's mercy, and just for one pathetic moment, I want to pretend that I'm not.

"Eat," he says. "It's jambalaya."

"I don't want it," I snap just to be difficult.

"Too fucking bad. Antonio told me to make sure you eat, so either you get your ass over here and eat, or I'll pin you down and shove it in your mouth."

"You'll lose your fingers," I growl.

"And you'll lose your tongue."

I clench my teeth tight.

Stiff and unyielding.

The growling of my stomach undermines my defiance.

"Just fucking come eat. Then I can take you for a shower before you're raped again."

I turn towards him. Most rapists don't like to admit it's rape. Except for the fuckers like Sadist. The fact that he's so blatant about it oddly makes me more at ease. And I hate that. I hate that I can feel a *kinship* with one of my rapists.

Was it rape if he made you come?

"What's your name?" I demand, mostly to quiet the voice in my head and to distract myself from the shame in my belly.

"Why?"

"So I can tell my friend to kill you slowly when he gets here."

He laughs. "It would be a shame if you lost your tongue. There's no one here for me to talk to."

"I don't want to talk to you."

"You talk a lot for someone who doesn't."

I purse my lips together again.

He chuckles. "I'll show you how to get to the shower on your own if you come eat."

"Why?"

"Because being malnourished is shit for pregnancy."

My pulse spikes at the idea of carrying the child of one of these fucker's inside of me. The only solace I have is I will die before I ever make it to term due to the blood bond not being fed. Or Varius or Dayne will rescue me, and I'll get an abortion.

"So is being stressed," I say, "and he doesn't give a shit about that."

"If your lover boy didn't attack the school, you would've got moved into your own quarters after you got pregnant. That's what he does for all of them. But now, well, space is limited on a boat. So –"

"I'm on a boat?" The air drains from my lungs, those words taking every last bit of it. If Eduardo or Terra is able to cloak large objects, we'll never be found.

"A super yacht. So there's ample space, but not many berths."

Something this big, they might not be able to cloak –

"Eduardo can cloak it on his own," he says.

But he's used a lot of magic recently, having kept my

brain alive while Sadist killed me, then reviving me twenty-nine times. He has to be short on –

"We're drifting afloat somewhere in the Pacific Ocean, so give up your hope," the man says. "You will survive better without it."

Tears choking me, I go back to tugging off the sheet. It comes free of the bed, but now I don't know what to do with it. Angry and terrified, I squeeze it in my fists.

"Come on," he says. "I know you're hungry."

My damn stomach hasn't stopped growling.

I drop the sheet, wishing I had a knife so I could open myself up and pull out the fucking traitor. Desperate to hold on to some semblance of power, I snap, "Can I at least eat at a fucking table?"

"Oh, right. You can't see I'm standing beside one. Walk three steps to your left."

I hesitate for a moment, but I need to learn the paces of the room. I need to build it up in my head. So I breathe out and shuffle three paces to the left.

"Two more steps," he says. "You didn't walk far enough." Then, "Turn right. Now walk towards my voice. There is nothing in your way."

I move faster this time. I've sparred blindfolded before with Dayne and other members of the Blacks, and although I was never great at it, I wasn't terrible either. But that was in a gym, where I knew the only things to get hurt by were the things that moved. I could feel the air shifting, hear the fabric of their clothes as they tried to strike fast. There was knowledge to pull from, but in this room, with him standing still, there is no input for me to use.

"Stop," he says, and I do instantly.

There's the sound of a chair being moved backwards. It isn't far in front of me. I reach forward.

"Put your – A bit further. Down..."

I touch the back of a cushioned chair. It isn't straight. It's curved, posh. Too big for me to pick up and hit him with.

He chuckles. Then the clutter of silverware sounds. "Now you get to eat with your hands," he says.

It irritates me that he's able to read me, especially when I don't have any fucking eyes to decipher.

"I was in your place not too long ago," he says softly, and a flare of hope ignites in my chest.

"We could work together."

He snorts. "You can't even walk across the room on your own. What good are you to me? The only way I get out of this is if I get you pregnant with a hybrid."

"Antonio will want you more then," I say, wary about how little that makes sense.

"It's not Antonio I'm trying to escape. I have no life on the outside, no family or pack. But Eduardo's 'hybrids' are infertile, so I'll be pulled from the experiments if I'm more useful elsewhere. Now eat. At least one of us is to rape you every hour until you're pregant."

Panic hits me in the stomach, and my knuckles whiten on the back of the chair. I want to lash out at him – kill him and escape, but I need to be smarter about this if I'm going to survive. I'm only going to have one chance to pull this off, and doing it before I know the layout of the room, let alone the boat is suicide. And where would I even go? I can swim, but I doubt we're anywhere near land. Vampires can phase to where they can see.

Begrudgingly, I feel my way around the chair, then sit down. He taps the table in front of me, showing me where the plate is.

"Can I at least have a spoon?" I ask, not wanting to dig my hands into the rice. My right one touched Sadist's balls and is still covered in his blood, and my left is covered in Grubs'.

He taps the silverware on the table twice before laying it down, the clinking of movement deciphered by my guess of what he's doing. I reach for it slower than I actually need to. I don't want him to know how confident I can move without my eyes. As long as I have sound or movement, I can map it easily thanks to my assassin training. I know he's being nice by deliberately making noise and that if it came down to a fight, I would lose, but I want him to drop his guard around me.

Antonio isn't going to be on this boat all the time. He has things to do, evil plans to put in place, the Shadow family to fuck with. So I'll be left with the men who rape me, the men who aren't as paranoid or as terrifying as he is. I'm *going* to survive this place.

I just need to pick my moment.

"So how did you end up here?" I ask as I grab the spoon and awkwardly aim for my plate. The Cajun spices tickle my nose, and my stomach growls in approval. The flavors explode on my tongue, utterly delicious, and I struggle to eat like a lady rather than scoffing down the rice. It doesn't matter that I *know* Sau isn't here; the constant 'corrections' I got from her makes me wary to break her rules even in hel.

Can't get a fucking break anywhere.

Oddly, that brings a small smile to the hollow part inside of me. Outside, my lips don't move except to eat and talk.

"I was a lone wolf sniffing around without permission."

Males are often run out of their packs a few years after their ascension. The majority of packs are female, with an alpha at the top (normally male, though twenty percent of them are matriarchies) and a few beta males ranked under the women. Breeding is allowed throughout, unlike in actual wolf populations, but this set-up gives them the best chance of having a large pack without an excess of testosterone causing fights and allows the troublesome males a chance to actually make it to adulthood without being killed by the alpha or one of the women they annoy.

But it also means lone wolves don't have the safety of a pack. There's no retaliation if you kill one – or kidnap it and use it as a test subject for your experiments.

"How long have you been here?"

"Two, three years? So believe me when I tell you there's no way out of here. The sooner you give up your hope, the better your life will be."

That might've worked for him, but it's not going to work for me.

I'm going to get out of this place.

I'm going to see my niece or nephew grow up.

I'm going to be at Dayne and Quinton's wedding – or the latter's funeral, whichever way that goes down.

And I'm going to kick Varius' ass.

Picking up another spoonful of jambalaya, I keep asking him questions about his life. If I can figure out my enemies, then I can manipulate them. If I turn him into a friend, then I can turn him into an ally.

And if I can do either of those things, then my chances of surviving are a lot higher.

Antonio might've taken my eyes and stolen my body, but he hasn't broken me.

Not yet, that little voice whispers.

But everyone breaks eventually.

THIRTY-ONE

HER

Under the spray of the shower, I rub at the cum dried on my legs. It comes off with a bit of water and soap, leaving my flesh bare. But it doesn't clean *me*.

It doesn't remove their touch, which sticks like fucking tar.

Like a tattoo.

A branding.

Forever marking me as a whore.

I *came* with them.

I rocked my hips against theirs.

And I *enjoyed* it.

I didn't, I tell myself as I scrub at me harder. *I* hated *it.*

Desperation lances through me. My eyes are open, but I can't check if I got it all. Maybe I feel disgusting because I missed a bit of it somewhere. Maybe there's cum and blood still on me, and if I can just remove it, I'll feel like myself again.

Tears mix with the spray as I duck my head and rapidly drag the rag across me.

My thighs start to sting beneath the pelt of the water as I rub off my top layer of skin, and all the anger that has been keeping me going since I came off the V now retreats under an overwhelming urge to break down and cry.

I am a Black, I tell myself as I fight down the scream building in my throat.

Dayne is waiting for me.

As is Lou.

And I need to kick Varius' ass for taking my eyes after he *promised* me he'd never hurt me again.

How could he do this to me?

I've never felt so helpless.

So crippled.

Straightening, I force myself to move away from my thighs – and those thoughts. I can't give into despair. I need to stay strong. Keep my head on my shoulders until I can figure a way out of here.

As I continue to wash myself, starting with my face and moving down, I go over the ways for a captive to increase their chances of survival.

Don't draw attention to yourself. Stay calm and clear-headed at all times so you can study your abductors and their routines. Learn what they like, what their morals are, what things they respect about a person. Then mimic their beliefs. Become human to them, an ally that doesn't need guarding.

And set goals to keep your hope alive.

I'm going to see my family again.

But can I even face them like this? With all the disease rotting away inside of me? What if I infect them? Lou's about to be a mother. She doesn't need my trauma around her and the baby.

I press my hand to my stomach as a sob threatens to

break free.

I want to feel my own baby inside of me.

I want Rafiki to still be growing there.

I want her to be born healthy.

I want a future with her and her father.

One where we're all running around the house laughing or cuddling on the sofa with her in my arms and Varius' arms around me. I wanted the chaos and the frustration and the love and the joy.

I just want *her*. And I want him.

Fuck, I still want him.

Even though he took my eyes, I still want him to hold me. To break onto this boat and save me. As mad as I am at him and as much as I know there's no fixing us anymore, my heart yearns for a different outcome. It mourns over the reality it's in.

He chose to hurt me, and as much as I want to make excuses for him –he wouldn't have done it if he hadn't been forced; he picked the same sense I would've because I need to be able to talk in this place, to win allies and gain intel; I would have done the same in his shoes, terrified Antonio would've taken his ears instead– I know I will never trust him not to hurt me again.

And a relationship cannot last without that.

Wiping away the tears, I force myself to think about my situation here rather than the one I am never going back to. If I can't keep my head on my shoulders, I'll break.

So I start to compartmentalize and set myself goals.

1. The biggest threat to me right now is V. I don't know how long it'll take for me to get addicted if I'm being forced to take it every hour, but the outcome's inevitable. So I need to convince them to fuck me in their human forms. Sadist, at least, will be easy. He can't get hard if I'm willing, so I'll make it "fun" for him. I'll only fight him if there's no V. The idea of engaging in "foreplay" with him makes me sick –

not so much the pain and depravity he'll inflict on me but the knowledge that I'll be participating. *Consenting* in order to survive.

I scrub myself harder.

Force my thoughts to shift to the next goal.

2. I need to make allies. Sadist is out of the question, but there's Sunny, as I've decided to call the guy who fed me due to his oh-so-sunny optimism, and Bear, the guy who couldn't get hard at the school. The two of them might not help me escape, but I might be able to convince them to show me around the boat so I can learn its layout. I can also tease information out of them.

3. Eduardo is the only way on and off this super yacht. Teleportation magic uses a lot of energy, and he must be running on fumes given how much he has done recently – reviving me, cloaking the boat, healing himself and Sadist. Which means he and Antonio are going to be here for a while while he recovers... unless he's taught Terra how to teleport. With his entire gang on the run, she's probably here with us. Antonio will want to keep her close and safe.

So the other breeding women and Rudy might be here too...

I stiffen. *Did he hear me scream? Did he hear me beg for their cocks?*

My lips wobble. *Does he hate me for being the reason he lost his hands, while I'm over here* enjoying *it?*

He never should've tried to save me. I *am* the reason he is here, and by the gods, I will get him home.

Clenching the rag tight in my hand, I force it to glide across my face. I focus on the feel of it. On the rough cotton dragging across my lips. I ground myself in the now. I need to concentrate only on the present. On my goals. On staying alive long enough to go home.

Dayne will not stop coming for me. And Varius won't give up on the brother he practically raised.

He won't give up on you either, my heart whispers.

But even if I could forgive him for taking my eyes, why would he choose to stay with a tainted cripple like me? I'm disgusting. I'm broken. I'm dirty. I came on all their cocks... As soon as he realizes what I am, he'll cut his losses. He'll turn his back on me even if he still loves me, just like he did when he believed I betrayed him.

I cannot rely on him to come for me, so I won't. Putting my faith in him again, just for him to break it will destroy me.

But I know Dayne will not stop regardless of how tainted I am.

So I put my faith in him.

And I put it in me.

After all, I am a fucking Black.

Wiping my body down one last time, I give up trying to clean my soul. Then I turn off the shower and exhale slowly.

I have this.

I will survive –

I twist on my heels as the shower door is wrenched open behind me. Knowing it's either Eduardo or Sadist, I kick out in front of me. My foot slams into their chest. They grunt as they stumble back, and registering it's Sadist, I charge at them. Eduardo wouldn't have sounded so happy to be hit.

I make sure not to fight as well as I actually can. I want him to underestimate me until I'm ready to finally break out of here. His fist slams into my jaw. I stumble to the side, and he shoves me against the wall. His body presses against me. His cock is hard against my belly, and his fingers dig into my jaw.

"You're going to pay for what you did," he sneers as he leans his face close to mine, his breath fanning across my cheek.

"For fucking your mom last night or for making you squeal like a little bi–"

He headbutts me in the face, slamming the rest of the words back down my throat. A migraine explodes in my skull, and I fall to the side, my knees buckling.

His grip tightens on my face, holding me up and forcing my mouth open. A cork pops nearby, and the urge to really fight back courses through me. The aroma of chocolate and fucking pomegranates assaults me, and it takes every bit of training I have to stay still.

To become the doll rather than the fighter I know he wants.

His cock starts to soften, and I start to believe in this plan. But then he says:

"You're going to beg me to fuck you."

I snap my arm up to elbow him in the face as my other hand shoots out towards the area I heard the *pop.*

I connect with his jaw at the same time I smack the vial out of his hold. It spills across the floor. He stumbles back, his hand dropping away from me, and I jump off the wall with my knee leading. It slams into his chest. He falls to the ground, and I try to stomp on his head, but he rolls into my legs, knocking me to the floor.

He scrambles on top of me and starts to choke me. I grope for his face, but his arms are longer than mine, and all I can reach are his shoulders. Changing tactic, I slam my fists and feet against the floor. I'm just trying to make noise now, to get Antonio's attention.

He doesn't want me dead, but in this moment, Sadist does, and he might take it too far. It takes five minutes to kill someone by suffocation, but just three minutes without oxygen can fry my brain permanently. Eduardo isn't here to keep it from damage. He might not even be on the boat at all, and if he isn't, then Antonio probably isn't either. But maybe Sunny or Bear will hear me and come running; as long as they're more afraid of Antonio than Sadist…

My chest burns. My limbs drop. Just as unconsciousness

starts to take me though, the pressure on my throat lifts, and I suck in air between coughs of pain. I roll over onto my side, then to my knees.

The sounds of a fight fade into my sluggish brain. Then my instinct is screaming at me to run in crystal clarity. Stumbling to my feet, I head in the direction I hope is the door, my hands out in front of me. I hit a wall and slide my fingers along it, searching for the exit. Grunts and blows of pain echo behind me.

"Eduardo isn't here to heal her!" That's Bear. I want to turn around and help him, but being blind in close quarters, I'm unable to distinguish who's who. I could accidentally hurt him as easily I could Sadist. I need to get help.

Finding the open door of the ensuite, I run out into the room. I picture the layout in my mind, trying to figure out where the door to the hall will be. With the bed on my right and the table I ate at further along, I take a guess and hurry forward.

A sickening blow sounds behind me. Something's been smashed into the floor. Now someone is scrambling onto their feet and running for me.

I pivot just as they reach me and kick out at them. They grab my leg, move in closer, then lift me for a throw. I elbow them on the top of their skull. They drop to the ground, dragging me down with them. Panic flares; grappling is not my fucking strong suit, and Sadist is bigger and stronger than I am. He can also fucking see.

It doesn't take him much time at all to pin me down and start strangling me again.

"I'm going to enjoy turning you into my personal whore," he says.

A part of me takes comfort in the fact that he isn't going to kill me.

The other part screams that this is worse. He's going to break my body in every way he can. He's going to make me crave his touch. With the V in me, I won't be able to deny him. I'll be desperate for an orgasm, and if he denies me for too long, I won't even be able to dissociate. Every part of me will be focused on getting that high just out of reach, and eventually, I will break.

I try to bang against the floor again, but this time no one comes. As I black out, my limbs fall still, and then I come to on the bed. He ties me up with straps already prepared for me, both my arms and legs. Either he did it before entering the bathroom, or they were always there, a mimic of the breeding table they had me on at the school.

My mouth is pried open and a new bottle of V is poured down my throat.

I try to spit it out, but he cups a hand over my lips and pinches my nose. Desperate to breathe, I suck it down, and he laughs as he releases me. Sharp arousal spreads through me. I fight it as much as I can, but as soon as Sadist starts stroking my body, I can feel my pussy growing wet.

"You want this, don't you, whore?" He rubs my breasts, then tugs on my nipples.

I shudder and clench my fists even as my legs spread on their own accord. He chuckles as he slides a hand down to my pussy. "I bet you're already soaked." He slips a finger inside of me, working it in and out. "Oh, yeah, you are. I can see how much you want this."

I tremble against my binds. Desperate to distract myself from what he's forcing my body to do, I focus on Dayne's heartbeat. I can feel him through the tattoo I gave him years ago – a promise that I will always protect him. He gave me a similar one, but Varius had me burn it off, and in this moment, I'm thankful. I don't want him feeling me as I suffer through this. His heartbeat wouldn't be normal then. Wouldn't be calm, and I need to feel that right now.

Sadist shuffles down the bed. His head goes between my legs, and as his deformed tongue laps against my lips, I hate myself for feeling pleasure.

For rocking my pussy into his face.

For cradling him with my thighs.

I tug on the binds, desperate to break free, but they hold fast.

He licks me, and I can feel it coming.

I squeeze my eyes shut, begging my body not to do this to me.

My orgasm builds. I'm not going to be able to stop it.

But just as I start to near the edge of no return, Sadist pulls back.

I cry out in frustration even though I don't want him to continue.

My thighs tremble as my hips lift, seeking his face.

He laughs at me.

I scream at me.

Moving off the bed, he says, "Beg me to shove my dick into your wet cunt."

I clamp my mouth shut. Try to concentrate on Dayne's heart rate to override my own.

The words burn at the back of my throat, but I refuse to let them free.

Ba thump

Ba thump.

I love you, Dayne.

Once again, he is saving me. There've been many restless nights where I wasn't able to sleep without focusing on his heartbeat. And I know he's done the same.

Ba thump.

Ba thump.

Blocking myself off to whatever Sadist is saying, I focus on what I can control.

Ba thump.

Ba thump.

I bring my heartbeat down to match his, and I wait for

Sadist to tire of me.

THIRTY-TWO

HER

He doesn't tire.

He stays with me for hours, keeping me on the edge of my orgasm but never letting me fall. The V is boiling in my veins, creating a fever in my soul. I twist against my binds. Sweat pours down me and soaks the sheets. My brain is sluggish. Dayne's heartbeat has long faded from my mind. Every part of me is focused on the pulsing in my pussy, that desperate need for the high the V will give me.

I hate myself.

But that doesn't stop me from wanting this.

In my delirium, I start to think about Varius. How he used to touch me, how easy he was able to make me come. I don't want to taint those memories with the disease in my veins, but I need the release Sadist isn't giving me.

I imagine him here with me, lying on top of me, his cock between my legs.

For a moment, I hate him even in the daydream. *You*

promised me...

"*I had to, Micha.*"

I blink back the tears. I don't give a shit if he had to. I accepted his apologies before; I won't do it again.

"*I'm sorry.*"

I flinch at those words, said in his voice, then repeated in Grubs'. I *hate* that phrase.

"*Fuck me like you hate me.*" Varius' voice rams into me, and I arch back as a cock slides into my aching pussy. I jerk my hips up.

I clench my teeth together, refusing to beg Sadist for my release.

My thoughts are all jumbled. He mixes with Varius and Grubs and then Antonio takes the forefront. He said he'd get off watching me get raped, but he wasn't even hard at the school. I don't understand him. I need to understand him in order to play him and survive.

Antonio pinches my nipples, and I cry out. Any coherent thought disappears. Any understanding about what's really going on fades under the delirium.

All I want is to get off, and my thoughts twist and turn like dreams, like nightmares, as my brain tries to give me what I want.

Varius is fucking me.

Then Antonio.

Sadist is hurting me.

Then Grubs.

Varius is back between my legs, coaxing me like he used to, and I arch off the bed, feeling myself get close.

"*That's it, little monster. Let me see you come.*"

The cock pulls out of me, but it's too late.

I laugh madly, then scream as I orgasm.

Varius beats me with his fists.

Hurting me over and over and over again.

I pass out from the high though, unable to feel the pain.

My body feels too damn good.
My heart cries.

I come to as another vial of V is being poured down my throat. Jerking my head to the side, I spit it out. My heart thunders in my ears. My jaw is grabbed and yanked back towards the ceiling. A towel is put over my face, and a fountain of V is spilled onto it, making me choke. I can't help but drink some of it though, and the arousal hits me hard.

I've barely come off my last high.

He doesn't bother to tease me this time.

He shifts into his werewolf form and slams his cock into me. I don't know if it's Sadist or Sunny. I wouldn't think the former could get it up with me being this willing, and the latter wouldn't waste the opportunity. I'm his ticket out of here, and unlike Bear, he didn't try to save me.

He ruts into me like an animal. I jerk my hips in rhythm to his. His technique doesn't matter at all, the V doing all the work. My body flushes hot. My orgasm builds, and I'm soon squirting all over his cock.

Another V is forced down my throat as I'm shaking from the high.

I've never felt so good.

I swallow it like a whore.

The wolf keeps fucking me – perhaps he's taken a rick for his own stamina. He comes in me; a fountain of it pours into my womb, making my belly swell. I tense at the idea of it being this big with a baby, but then my orgasm is ripping through me, triggered by the cum, and all my thoughts leave me.

Another V goes down.
Another orgasm is forced on me.

Over and over and over again.

Until it finally stops, and a man's hand roughly grabs my chin.

"Beg me to fill your wet, aching cunt," Sadist growls.

I press my lips together, fighting down the words. My body is beyond sensitive. Just the air is making it hurt for more V. I don't know how many hours have passed, but my stomach is tight with hunger.

"She's not going to beg yet," Sunny says from somewhere in the room. "Get off her. She needs to eat."

"I'm not done."

"So start again afterwards. Antonio told us to keep her fed, or do you want me to tell him you're the reason why she's malnourished and unable to get easily pregnant?"

Sadist grunts as his fingers dig tighter into my cheeks. Then he releases me and moves off my body. I tremble in gratitude for Sunny's interference. For Antonio's order that I am to have at least a little care.

My wrists are untied a few minutes later. I'm handed a bowl of chicken and dumplings, but my hands are numb from all the pressure on my wrists, and I nearly drop it.

"It's okay. Take it easy." It's Bear in front of me, and a part of me is glad to hear he's alive. An ally. He lowers his voice. "Take your time eating. It's the only break you'll get. Eduardo could only reattach one of Tim's balls."

A broken smile curls my lips. "I'm going to take his cock one day."

"I don't doubt it."

I take a few bites in silence, trying to get my mind to focus on a game plan rather than the itch for more V. I am already craving it like my next breath. He's flooded my system with it, and the addiction is gnawing at every nerve inside my body. I'm trying to fight it, but I don't know how much longer I can resist.

"Did Antonio force you into the program too?" I ask the

man beside me.

"If you call agree or die a choice," he says.

"How did you end up here?"

"I got run out of my pack in the seventies for being born *wrong*," he says with such bitterness that I don't ask him to elaborate. The fact that he hasn't been able to get hard with me makes me realize all too easily what he means. He's only here because he's gay.

My stomach twists as I think about how hard this must be for him. And then I think of Rudy.

Is he being bred like me? Forced to take ricks so he can fuck the female wolves who are capable of birthing hybrids?

"Is there a Shadow brother here?" I ask.

"We're not supposed to tell you –"

"Please," I say, knowing there's good in him. "He's only here because he tried to save me. Is he okay?"

There's a heavy pause, then he sighs. "He's doing better than you."

"He's on the boat? Can I see him?" I flinch at the word 'see.'

"Maybe one day... If you're good. Antonio rewards those who obey him. He's strict, and he can be cruel, but he's also fair."

"He just wants to hurt me to get to Varius."

"You're more valuable as a breeder. Play your hand right, and you might just convince him to keep you alive and in one piece."

I snort as I wave a hand at my eyes. "It's too late."

Ever so softly, he says, "There's so much more he can take from you."

A chill runs through me, and the air thickens, suffocating any other attempt at conversation. I finish my meal. The bowl is taken away. Bear retreats, and Sadist comes back into the room with another vial of V.

I fight him, trying to get him hard so he doesn't force the

potion down my throat.

But though his cock presses into me, so does the vial, and I am lost to the addiction again.

For five days, he keeps me high every moment I'm not eating or sleeping. My body is well past being mine, and I am starting to crave the enhanced orgasms as much as I am escape.

But I still fight the administration of V.

And I still refuse to beg Sadist for his cock.

On the evening of day six, everything changes. When Sunny crawls onto the bed to rape me, he stops right before he penetrates me. He presses his face against my neck and inhales. I can feel his smile, and I just *know.* Even through the haze of the V demanding me to spread my legs and think of nothing else, I *know.*

My stomach drops.

A scream builds from the deepest part of my soul.

Hopping off me, he says, "She's pregnant."

I jerk against my binds as the scream erupts, breaking every piece of me on its way out. My body convulses from the sheer force of it, the pain tearing me apart. An ear-splitting noise of raw, primal agony.

The sound of a mother who's just lost her child all over again.

Who's come back and found it replaced with a monster of the fae.

I scream myself hoarse as I thrash on the bed, wanting to rip the creature from my womb, to remove it from a place it should've never touched with its sickness. That's Rafiki's spot. That's where she should still be, growing every day until she's ready to come out and be held by her mother. My baby was taken from me, and now someone else is in her home, and that knowledge is breaking me apart.

Destroying me like Sadist never could.

I hate this child inside of me.

I want it out.

It's a rape baby.

A monster's baby.

It isn't *mine*.

It isn't *her*.

It shouldn't be there.

"Get it out!" I scream. "Get it out! Get it out! *Get it out!*"

I jerk my arms down hard, tearing the skin off my wrists as I struggle to free myself. If I can just get a hand free, I can dig the imposter out of my stomach.

I'll find a knife.

I'll use a broken bottle.

I'll antagonize Sadist so badly, he'll beat me to death.

I just need it out.

"I'll get Eduardo!" Sunny shouts.

I tear my left arm free of my binding, ripping the skin off my wrist and hand. I grope around for something to stab myself with, but finding nothing, I simply start tearing my nails across my flesh. They haven't been trimmed in weeks, and the thick keratin scratches through the first layer of skin. Someone grabs hold of me as they curse, their fingers tight around my skinless wrist. Pain flares down my arm, but it's nothing compared to the shards stabbing their way into my heart.

I don't want this monster.

It isn't right.

Rafiki should be the one in there.

I shouldn't be holding another child in her place.

I can't do this.

I can't keep this creature.

I have to get it out.

I jerk against the person holding me. A fist slams into my

face. I try to free my other arm.

"Hold her still!" Eduardo snaps as he enters the room, but there is a tinge of fear to his voice, the whine of a coward who doesn't want to approach anything less than a sedated lion.

Heavy muscles pin my arms down. Someone sits on top of my chest. My screams turn into gasps as the air is pressed out of me. A hand rests on my belly, and warm magic flows from its fingers. I sob as I realize he's going to keep the monster alive. I do not want the disease in my belly. I want it out. I want it fucking out of me.

"Is it a hybrid?" Antonio demands, his words flat without a care. The calmness of his tone cuts through my fear, and I swallow the rest of my cries as I tremble, waiting for his answer.

A few moments pass, then, "No."

"Then abort it and breed her again."

I sag in relief, hiccuping tears of gratitude. Losing the last part of Rafiki I have will break me. Feeling another baby moving around inside of me, passing all the milestones I should've had with her...

I won't survive that.

So despite how much I hate Antonio, I'm grateful to him too. He's letting me keep that last memory of my baby alive. I want to press a hand to my stomach. I want to curl up and cry. Sobbing as I think of Rafiki, I thank the alpha between my tears. It's the only solace I've had in this place. The last connection I have to *her*, and I cannot express my gratitude enough for him having killed the other *thing* in her place.

Thank you.

Thank you...

Nine days later though, I get pregnant with a hybrid.

THIRTY-THREE

HIM

"I'm not interested in anything you have to tell me," I say as I slide a knife across Alejandro's flesh. It's a shallow cut across the tip of his penis. Number nine hundred and one out of a thousand. He screams for mercy, howling in the chair he's tied to, the silver chains around his arms and legs draining away his strength, making him weak.

Helpless.

Just like my wife and Rudy.

"Take comfort in the pain of today," I tell him as I cut a short line down the length of his cock. He offers up more secrets about the Death Hunt, trying to get me to stop.

I don't.

He has already told me Antonio tells them nothing, so anything he spits out under torture will just be lies said to get the pain to end.

It won't.

"For tomorrow will be worse," I say calmly. "As will the

day after that." Another cut, this one around the base of his cock, right above his balls. "And the day after that." I slice open his sack, following the crease in the middle. "For the rest of your life." Cupping him, I squeeze a testicle out of the hole I've just made. He screams, high-pitched and hopeless, and I meditate to that noise, to these actions.

I normally go nine rounds with a bag when I can't sleep, but that just isn't fucking cutting it these days.

Not when I can feel her pain even through the wall I've erected. It's a dull ache in the back of my mind, a constant weight on my shoulders. I want to lower it and feel her fully, to experience it with her so she's not alone, but I can't risk using up any more of the blood bond. We already have a deadline of only a few months before it kills her. If I decrease that any further, it could prove fatal. Besides, Antonio needs to think I've given up on her, that I have abandoned her like an empty bottle. Otherwise, he'll take more than just her eyes.

My fingers tighten on the blade, my control slipping as my emotions rear their volatile head.

A week and a half ago, I went to meet one of my capos. After destroying the Death Hunt nearly overnight – with only a few loose threads still needing to be trimmed, Aleric and I have been busy running our expanded territories and businesses. As much as I have wanted to focus all of my energy on finding my loved ones, I am still the Boss, and playing that role has helped me sell the lie that I don't give a shit about either of them.

But when I came out of that meeting, with Maddox, Enoch, and Stormie beside me, there was a small box sitting on my windshield. Dark teal with a blood-red bow. The colors of the Death Hunt. Inside was a pair of eyes I would recognize anywhere despite how badly they were crushed. I'd never had a favorite color before I'd looked at my wife.

But I knew he would be watching.

Unable to let my grief show, it took everything I had to drop the box onto the pavement and climb into the car. I did not let the others see what it was. Maddox would've lost it. He's already on the verge of breaking over Krypto. The dog hasn't moved off Leno's grave except to use the bathroom. He isn't eating. He isn't drinking. Maddox is syringing him food and water every night, but the mutt is a pile of bones just waiting to decay.

It will not be much longer until we bury him with our brother.

The door to the garage opens. Dayne walks in, unable to sleep either. Ever since we learned that Antonio had taken his breeding women with him, we've been in here every night.

When I saw the mess he had left behind at the school – female werewolves with their stomachs ripped open and their babies torn from them, I assumed he had only taken those who were childfree. But according to Jona when we tortured him for info about it thirteen days ago, showing him photos of the dead, he told me Antonio had taken the only women who had successfully given birth to hybrids, all of whom were pregnant at the time we attacked. The others were only carrying full wolf pups; that's why they were left behind.

Which means my earlier idea of waiting until Micha was pregnant before we rescued her isn't going to give us the advantage I hoped it would.

"What's the time?" I ask Dayne as he moves over to Greyson, the wolf with the missing bone in his arm.

"Four-ish." Pulling out a knife, he starts carving Micha's name into the man's flesh. Over and over again. We cut out Greyson's tongue days ago, and now he's just a pathetic, whimpering mess.

I continue my count of a thousand cuts across Alejandro. My hand stays steady despite the increase of my pulse. We only have one more hour before we need to go.

Ryker Ezwail'ik, the Boss on the other side of the portal connecting Earth to one of the Seven Planes called Blódyrió, has found me two highly skilled teleporters. It's taken him fifteen fucking days and cost me a hefty fee five times the normal rate, but I would've paid it a thousand times over.

Without them, we have little hope of rescuing my wife and Rudy. Vampires can't phase to somewhere they haven't been to if it's out of sight. I could track her down through the blood bond, but it'll take weeks for us to catch up to the super yacht (if we manage at all), and they'll spot us from miles away. I highly doubt their boat will be unarmed either. They could easily sink our ship or teleport her out of there before we ever board.

So we need someone to hijack Eduardo's teleportation network, but if we hire a witch from Earth, there's a good chance Antonio will be alerted. Then he'll know what we're planning and that I care very much about what happens to his captives. For now, I have managed to convince him that Micha is broken goods, yesterday's trash, and Rudy is a defective Shadow, unable to kill like the rest of us. A softie, a liability, and Antonio taking him has been nothing but a favor.

If we don't save them in our next attempt though, they will be cut into pieces.

I jerk my knife as intense pain crashes down the blood bond. Alejandro screams as the shallow cut I was aiming for slices off the head of his penis. I push to my feet, no longer squatting between his legs. My heart pounds hard as I turn northeast. Dayne is in front of me a second later.

"What's happening to her?" he demands, his haggard eyes full of rage and pain.

Khalid enters the garage, Micha's soul doll is in his hand. The two of us turn to him, but I don't need to hear him say the words I already know.

"She's pregnant with a hybrid."

"Abort it," Dayne demands, and I want to tell Khalid the same. She should be carrying *our* child. Not one of theirs.

But if Antonio finds out we still have some alexandrite, he'll take more than just her eyes. He might even kill her and Rudy, deciding to cut his losses and bank on the three breeding women he already has to juice him up enough to rescue Siome. Micha's only alive because she isn't too much of an inconvenience. I can't risk changing that. Can't risk revealing our hand just to give her momentary relief.

"No," I say, turning to Dayne, forcing down my own desires. "They won't want to risk causing a miscarriage. She will be tortured less while pregnant."

His jaw tightens, but he nods, and I turn back to Khalid. "Call Vlad. I want an updated list of locations."

Aleric owns half the police force in this city, and his men have been interrogating the members of the Death Hunt they rounded up. The capos and the higher fish have been transferred to more secure facilities, but he has connections in most of those places too.

When phasing, a vamp jumps to a known coordinate – with a bit of magic to push them out of any solid objects – assuming it goes well. With teleporting, a witch has to make the portals first, etching them into the ground or other flat surface, then connecting them together. Once the gateways are established, they can step onto the portal area and draw a black circle within it. This is the 'key' that lets them open the door, and it allows them to only take or send the items they want to go through.

However, the creator isn't the only one who can hop between them. Any witch who can read their workings can do so, which is why they need to be secured through other magic. An average witch would put the spell around the portal. For someone like Eduardo though – smart and paranoid, they'll weave it into the portal itself. Meaning a brute force attack will most likely trigger an explosion that destroys it or an alarm that alerts him to tampering.

I'm hoping the witches Ryker is sending me today are good enough to bypass Eduardo's security. If not, we'll kill them and get some more. There isn't a causality number too high when it comes to rescuing my wife.

Rudy will hate me for killing innocents to save him, but he can hate me when he's back home.

I head to the front of the house to check on Krypto before we go. My chest tightens with every step, expecting that this will be the time when I find him dead. Dayne does not say anything as he follows me. Khalid goes inside the house through the side door to make the call, then to rouse Stormie and Enoch.

She'll need to come with us as I'm still unable to control my powers. It's common among those who pulse to struggle for months or even years. It's the equivalent of being tossed a bomb and having to stop it from exploding. The eruption of power is too intense, too blinding and deafening to even hope to know what to do. It took Rudy two and a half years to stop pulsing. Every time it happened, Mother sucked him into the Plane of Monsters. To save the rest of her kids, she had to terrify him. The pain she's endured holding this family together...

I understand now why she doesn't believe in true love. If I have to choose between Micha or Rudy...

Krypto, thankfully, is still alive. Barely though. His ribs are countable. His fur grubby. But his chest is still rising and falling. I focus on that rather than the choice I might have to make. Perhaps, though, I should ask Mother how she decides.

And how she lives with herself afterwards so if it comes to that, I don't hesitate in the moment and end up losing them both.

"If this fails," Dayne says, finally breaking the heavy

silence, "what's plan B?"

"We kill your sperm donor. And every other teleporter on Earth." We'll still have the issue of finding the ship, but if we can kill or run off Eduardo after he's teleported Antonio to land, then we'll have a much better chance of rescuing my family.

Of course, tracking him down will be the difficult part. A coward like him won't venture off alone.

"*Eduardo*," Dayne says, an almost hiss full of trauma and fury. "I get to kill him."

"Micha –"

"Will want this for me."

I glance at him, the words of refusal on my tongue.

I bite them back though. Micha might be my wife, but no one knows her better than Dayne. I might not trust my family when it comes to her, but I trust him.

Because she does.

"He's yours," I say. Then I go back to waiting for the next rise of Krypto's chest.

A part of me wonders if I can fill him with my magic. The... *things* in the garage basement are still alive. I don't know if their minds are trapped in the husks they've become or if everything that makes up them is gone. But if I learn to control it... If I can take him over just enough to give him back the will to live...

My chest tight, I squat down and run my hand through his red fur. His bones are so prominent. He doesn't react to me at all.

Perhaps it'll be best to kill him now. We're only dragging out his pain for our benefit.

"Dayne," I say softly after making sure none of my brothers are around. I signal for him to join me on the ground, then nod at Krypto. "Will it be peaceful? If you stop his heart with your magic?"

He looks at me in horror.

Then pain.

Then understanding.

Given his upbringing, he'll know better than anyone if the dog's level of suffering is worth surviving.

"I can stop him from feeling any pain," he murmurs.

I take a few seconds to pour all my love into a few pats, wishing I could do more for him than this. He still doesn't acknowledge me in any way though. Doesn't focus on or want anything other than his best friend to come home.

My throat closing, I fist my hand in his fur and bite back the tears. My nose burns as I shudder. I glance up at the flowers, needing to see them bloom. Needing to convince myself that I have Leno's approval. He wouldn't want his dog to suffer when there's no hope of recovery.

The flowers open up in front of me. I can almost see Leno's face in the reds and yellows and blues and pinks. I can certainly feel him in my heart.

Fuck. I want my brother back.

I want Krypto to live.

I want to hold my wife in my arms as Rudy stands beside us.

But wishes don't just come true.

As a single tear falls down my cheek, I find the strength to nod. "Do it."

Reaching forward, Dayne places his hand on Krypto's chest.

I can feel the air electrifying with his power.

I look away, my gaze landing on a closed daffodil as I yearn so fucking hard for Leno to come back to life.

It should've been me.

I should've watched our six instead of running towards my wife. I should've told Leno to stay home, to stay with Krypto while we recovered.

I just want him back.

"Stop!" I shout, shoving Dayne away as the daffodil

finally blooms.

It's the flower of rebirth.

The start of a crazy thought.

Insanity made acceptable under the flag of grief.

Perhaps.

Or perhaps this would be going too far.

But I have to try. Krypto is family.

"Did you –" I start, my voice cracking in desperation. I could just look over at the dog and see if he's still breathing myself, but I don't. I keep my eyes, my hope on Dayne.

"No."

Jumping to my feet, I rush inside to drag Maddox out of the house. He's still asleep when I barge into his room, but he jumps up with a jolt. "Krypto –" he asks, so much terror in his eyes, fearing this is the night he doesn't make it to morn.

"Would you be willing to hold Leno's –" I stop, choking on the words. On the fucked-up request I am asking of my brother. "Form –" My throat closes at the thought of seeing Maddox with Leno's face and mannerisms.

Will he smell like him? Will his heart beat like his? Or will I know something isn't quite right through my senses? Will this fuck my brothers up, having "Leno" around all the time until Krypto dies? Make it impossible for them to face their grief and accept that he's gone?

Maddox cries as he understands what I am asking him. He throws himself in my arms, and I cling to him like he does to me.

"I'm sorry," I rasp as I'm reminded of just how young he is. He's just a kid. His brain isn't even fully developed. He can't do this. It'll destroy him to live as Leno until the dog is gone. "I never should've asked."

He cries harder, and I'm made aware of movement at his bedroom door. Behind me. The hairs on my neck rise. The paranoia.

But it calms at the sound of Dayne's heartbeat – the closest connection I have to Micha.

"It's time," he says.

Maddox squeezes me tight, then lets me go. He rubs at his eyes.

"Bruh," Marrabelle says, her usual chirpy voice replaced by one of sorrow.

He looks over to his bed, still shaking from his tears. She holds up a tissue that's almost as big as she is, the end of it still trailing on the mattress.

Collapsing onto the bed, Maddox picks up the tiny, tiny woman who he turned into his pet years ago and lifts her to his face. As weird as the sight is, there's no denying the bond between them. A pet and a master simply becoming two friends.

Leaving him to grieve, I turn towards Dayne. I rub at my face, duct tape the broken pieces inside of me, and force down the pain. "Let's go," I say.

I can't save Krypto.

But I'll be damned if I fail my wife and brother.

THIRTY-FOUR

HIM

After picking up the teleporters, we bring them to the house, then march them into the garage. They have black hoods over their heads and steel gloves over their hands, which are tied behind their backs with witches snares, thin golden chains spelled to be unbreakable. Dayne touches the two of them on their arms, dropping them to their knees with his magic. He pulls the hoods off them, and they blink rapidly at the influx of light into their retinas.

The older of the two is a woman. Light skin with high cheekbones and runic tattoos weaving across her chest and face, wrapping around her neck and over her arms. Her bubblegum-pink hair is shaved on one side and long on the other, a complementary color to her lime-green eyes.

The other one is a young male, probably around Rudy's age. Even lighter skin with platinum-white hair ruffled about his face. His pale-yellow eyes makes him look washed out.

Their gazes land first on me, standing in front of them, then on the three chimeras strapped to the chairs behind me. Pools of blood and severed bits lie at their feet. Their heads hang down – looking dead to the newcomers rather than just passed out.

Jerking back in horror, the two of them scream.

I squat down in front of them as they try to scramble backwards with their hands tied behind their ass, and their feet kicking across the floor.

"*Zohfiik ije,*" I say in Drazic. *<My rules simple.>* meaning *// The rules are simple.*

The language is guttural, harsh, and angry, almost like a mix between German and Spanish. It's a primitive tongue despite being the second oldest language in all of the Seven Planes; the demons are always looking for a reason to fight, so why bother fixing communication? Magic is also wild despite our attempts to tame it, and the chaotic creativity of Drazic allows it to breathe like it needs to.

So all witches share this language.

"*Vicara, ke aloze.*" *<Win/victory/success, [moving action] your home.> // You do what I want, I'll smuggle you back home.*

Their screams stumble into choking whimpers as they stare at each other in horror, no doubt thinking I want them to fight to the death, and only the victor will get to go home. My jaw tics at the complexity of the language, but I can only hope they'll understand as I keep going. Given neither of them speaks Eknor (which Lou does) or English, this is the only one we have in common.

"*Hojez, alovanajez,*" I continue. *<Disappointment/failure, your shameful/horrible death.> //You don't, and I will kill you slowly.*

As threatening as that was, they perk up a little, hope flaring in their eyes. If they were fighting to the death, then I wouldn't have to kill them for failing. So now they realize

I want them for a job.

"Heevan, alokimal vanajez." <[fuck-up/expletive], your family dies shameful/horrible death." //You make a mistake, and I'll torture your entire family.

I lift a hand and snap my fingers. Seven chairs drop from the ceiling and land behind me, each holding a dear family member of the two in front of me. They're tied and gagged and free of any wounds – for now.

And those two words are crystal clear, screamed by the captives we've already carved into pieces and shouted by the cruelty in my eyes.

The teleporters fall forward, begging me in their native tongues, no doubt, to let them go. To not harm their kids and other loved ones.

But there is not a person I will not sacrifice to save my wife. There is not a death toll too high. An innocent too fucking pure.

Rudy might've traded her to save a dog and a two-year old girl from being butchered.

I will fucking not.

"Kiv," I snap. *<Stop/end.> //Enough.*

When they do so immediately, I know I got my point across. Enoch and Ezriel dropping the chairs might have been a bit theatrical, but I need them to focus. To skip the whole phase of trying to fight back and escape.

"Si alovicara si?" the man rasps as he looks between me and his sons. *<[question] your victory/want/desired effect [question]?> //What do you want from us?*

I tell them about Eduardo's network, and I make it clear that if he finds out we've hijacked our way into it, then their family will live a very long life in this garage.

I snap my fingers, and my shadow husks walk up the stairs, controlled by the twins' magic, not mine. They move to stand behind the seven chairs, and my hostages, having finally woken up from Khalid's spell, all scream and cry behind their gags. The smell of fear permeates the air. A few of the children piss themselves. The teleporters yell at me, and Stormie's fingers twitch down at her sides as she waits to see if either of them are foolish enough to try to attack.

The odds aren't in their favor. The risks are too great. We can kill their loved ones far faster than they can speak a spell – if they even know how to do that.

But push a desperate man…

And he will turn into an animal.

Take those I love…

And I will become something far worse.

When neither of them make a move, I nod at Dayne, and he removes the gloves from their hands, then the chains from around their wrists.

The two teleporters rub their hands and flex their fingers, but whereas the woman looks at her children, the man looks at us, clocking where we all are. Biting back a cruel smile, I turn away from him, goading him to take the shot.

There is a reason I asked for two.

One of them is only here as an example for the other.

As the air crackles behind me, I dart over to the first boy of his. He doesn't even get a chance to scream before my knife slices across his throat. A quick death. Merciful.

The man roars behind me. A bolt of red fury slams into a pink shield as I turn to face him. A half a dozen other bolts slam into various shields of blue as my brothers all protect themselves. His attack was impressive, trying to take us out all at once, but Dayne already has him down on the ground, one hand on his shoulder. Forced to be still and quiet, only his eyes can scream.

My gaze moves to the woman. Shaking, she tries to calm her own screaming children, shouting words that are meant to be soothing, but her partner, a woman with blue hair to her pink, is rocking her chair back and forth as she shrieks behind her gag. As their terror rolls through the air, the

Craving hits hard in my stomach, and my teeth ache. It has been weeks since I've eaten, and the urge to feast grows stronger every day.

Fighting it down, I walk calmly over to the man's second and last son. "Elivici," I say, addressing the woman. *"Chi."* *<<See/watch.>> //Pay attention.*

Holding her terrified gaze, I slit his throat. She clasps a hand over her mouth. The man's wife jerks her chair up and down, trying to free herself so she can fight back. The man's eyes grow wider, terror eating him up inside. Dayne looks away, unable to stomach watching the kids die. But he does not stop me either, and he does not let the man go.

I kill his wife next.

Then Dayne kills his hostage quickly, stopping his heart with barely any movement of his fingers. He releases him, and he drops to the ground with open eyes. He might have died fast, but he died full of rage and fear.

I turn to look at Elivici.

She trembles and cries in silence.

"Vicara, ke aloze," I repeat, reminding her there is only one way she and her family go home.

Her lips trembling, she nods.

Cleaning my blade on the dead mother's back, I gesture for Elivici to come with me. Then I slip the knife into its sheath and lead her out into the night.

Vlad is already waiting for us, ready to take her to one of Eduardo's circles. He got a dozen locations by interrogating the captured Death Hunt members and has been scouting them out to see which one would be the best to hit without drawing attention. Morn Tower, where Antonio took Khalid and his girl after kidnapping them, is the closest one, but it's owned by civilians. The police might've rounded up anyone associated with the Death Hunt they could, and Aleric and I have been killing or recruiting anyone who's remained, but enough innocents have their fingers in Morn Tower that we can't touch it. It gives Antonio an instant way back to the area, but the fact that he let us know about it by dragging my brother there makes me suspect he has another one nearby. There's no better way of sneaking into a place than by going through the back door that no one knows about because everyone is busy guarding the front.

My eyes soften as I walk up to the vampire. He looks as shit as Dayne and I do. There was a moment when him and Rudy were... something. A *thing* sounds too solid for what they were. Not Romeo and Juliet sneaking out behind our backs. Not in love. Not just sex.

My brother loved everyone but the man in front of me. He went out of his way to antagonize him, and the two of them got into blows more than once. Vlad is the only one Rudy has ever deliberately affected with his magic, and he'd do it all the time – a type of pushing away, of destroying it before it destroys me.

But at some point, they started sleeping together. Rudy came home smelling like Vlad, and he kept that scent for the next few months. I pretended like I knew nothing; their relationship would have caused an all out war if the Death Hunt thought our two gangs were forming a secret alliance. Ironically, we went to war anyways, so I wonder if Vlad regrets keeping Rudy in the closet. If he regrets that lost time now that my brother is gone.

Then again, they haven't smelled of each other for over a year. Even though their relationship would no longer cause any strain, they've stayed apart. Bad blood festers between them, and yet...

Vlad is only here because of him.

We don't exchange pleasantries. We might share a love for Rudy, but we're not anywhere close to being friends. In utter silence, he grabs Dayne and phases him to the school Micha was being held at. It's risky going back there with the SCU crawling all over the woods now, but it's the only place we can be sure that Antonio isn't watching. Dayne can keep them hidden with his magic, but he's willing to risk getting caught in order to save Micha.

After Vlad takes the teleporter, I head back into the garage to help clean up the bodies – a task normally left to Rudy. My brothers can't take them into their shadows as that'll call the monsters to their storage area, increasing the risk of losing the items they hold there. So we'll burn them into ash – the fire reminding me of Micha, then bury them deep underground, beneath the new flowers we plant in Leno's honor.

Memories. Honor...

I want more than that.

And I don't care how much of the world I have to burn to make it happen.

My jaw tight as I help dig a six-foot hole, I vow to bring my wife and brother home.

THIRTY-FIVE

HER

They keep me tied up for the next two weeks. Every time I'm free, I try to tear the monster from my stomach. Try to protect the last part of Rafiki's memory even though I can feel it fracturing into pieces inside of me. They carry me to the toilet, my hands tied together, my fingers interlaced.

If it's Bear or Sunny, I get wiped. If it's Sadist, I don't.

They feed me like I'm a foie gras duck. A funnel is forced down past my tongue so I can't spit anything out, then soup is poured into it until I can't do anything but swallow. I try to let it kill me, first by refusing to breathe, then by trying to inhale it into my lungs, but it's damn near impossible for me to overcome my survival instinct. Yet another way my body betrays me.

I don't stop screaming. My throat is sore, the chords made raw. But I can't contain the agony inside of me. The broken shards of my heart stick out of my skin, cutting their way free.

It gets Sadist hard. He fucks me more than when I was on V. They have taken me off it because it can negatively affect the hybrid pregnancy. But I don't care what he does to me anymore. Nothing can surpass the pain of a mother losing her child. To have a rape *thing* take its place.

I never even got to hold her.

Because Antonio ripped her from me.

Because Eduardo stepped on my hand when I tried to reach for her.

My chest heaving as snot and tears run down my face, I don't fight Sadist as he rapes me.

And I don't fight Eduardo when he kneels between my legs during a "health check" and starts to sew up my pussy so his tiny fucking cock can feel *snug*. I don't have anything left in me anymore, nothing but crippling agony in my soul and a desperate need to escape it.

So I welcome the damage they inflict on my body.

I welcome that nicer pain.

My pussy burns with every thrust of the witch's hips. The stitches tear from his roughness, sharp tugs I chase just to escape the utter despair eating its way up my womb and consuming every part of me.

I can't survive to term.

I *won't* survive to term.

I search for the bond I have with Varius, desperate to use up any drop that's left. To take more than what it has to give so it'll take my life quicker. But all the blood is gone. There's no link for me to pull on. To manipulate into being my executioner. All I can do is beg Varius to kill me from afar. To wish for that so deeply that he'll find a way to get some more alexandrite just so Khalid can make a soul doll of me. Just so he can stop the pain inside of him, pushed on by me.

I pray that he can feel it.

That he'll kill me.

But the days pass, and I'm still here.

Brutally bred and being forced to carry a monster to term.

Varius, please, I beg as I heave dry tears, my body too broken to produce any more. I scream against my ball gag. It stops me from using dark magic. If only it would stop the pain.

Kill me.

Release me from this hel.

Varius, please.

If you've ever loved me…

I'll forgive you for everything.

Just please…

Do this for me.

Kill me, Varius.

KILL ME!

THIRTY-SIX

HIM

I charge into Dayne's room, wearing only a pair of pants, the button and zipper not even done. He's on his feet in an instant, fully dressed and ready to go. He's been sleeping like I have, with one eye open and one foot out the door. This is the second night he's been back from guarding the teleporter, and although he's supposed to be resting before he returns to her, he's on edge every second of every day, hoping this is the moment she's cracked it.

"Has Elivici –" he starts.

"No." I shut the door behind me, turn on the light, then sign for the silence rune. As soon as he wraps the room in privacy, I blurt, "Micha wants me to kill her."

He freezes like a deer in headlights. I feel like the fucking truck. Out of control. Barreling down a hill with no brakes. Her agony is ripping through me, killing me, making it so fucking hard to breathe.

I stride over to the armchair, then collapse within it, my

legs having used all their energy to get here. Dayne stays standing, his face beyond pale.

"No," he says, his voice both raspy and strong. In denial.

I want to agree with him. I want to save her so fucking badly, be her white knight, and bring her home. But Micha is begging me to listen to her. Just like she did when I had her tied to a chair. My breathing quickens as I see her tears all over again, hear her screams that are never far from my mind.

It was agony to block her out the first time and do what I thought needed to be done in order to save my brother. I barely managed it, pulling on my anger and jealousy and utter *fear* that I would fail Khalid. That I would arrive too late just because I let my feelings get in the way. Because I couldn't do what needed to be done to get the information out of an enemy I barely knew, who I believed had helped kidnap him. An outsider I had just started to love versus a brother who had been there with me my whole damn life. I was able to suffer through her screams because I thought I was saving him.

But now there is no one to save but her.

Her death won't change Rudy's chances of survival.

Though even if it did... My heart tightens.

She is my wife.

I love Rudy like a son. I'd sacrifice everyone in this house to save him, myself included.

But...

She. Is. My. Wife.

I tremble as that truth slams into me. That utter terror at loving someone so deeply when you know you're just about to lose them.

My power pulses beneath my skin, and I know if my curse wasn't already broken, torn asunder by seeing Bambi for the first time, it would be shattered in this moment. In this horrible, terrible instance where I would be willing to give her up, to let her leave me for her own happiness.

Her own blissful release in death.

She might be an assassin, but she saves children. Surely, the gods will not punish her too severely...

And then she will be reborn. Given a new life. With no memory of me. No tie given the blood bond isn't complete.

And yet... I would still set her free.

If she really wants this.

"You know her better than anyone," I rasp, keeping my eyes on a random spot on the floor, unable to meet Dayne's, unable to find that strength. I hate how little I actually know her, regret all the times I treated her like a stranger when she first came to the house instead of milking every last opportunity I had to be with her. I hate myself for torturing her, for not believing in her, *in us*. I mourn for the future we will not have. The days I will live without seeing her face or hearing her voice.

Krypto's broken shell fills my mind – a glimpse of a future, a reflection in my own mirror. It has been a month, and he is nearly gone, a wasted shell only still alive due to Maddox desperately syringing him food and water.

No.

No, I won't die like that.

I'll kill myself immediately after. Then I'll at least have the chance of finding her in the afterlife. For once we are reborn, all of our memories are wiped clean. A new slate. A *broken* slate in my mind.

But despite that desperate hope, deep down, I know the ugly truth.

If I do this, if I honor her wish, I will lose her forever. I could search for a thousand lifetimes, refuse to be reborn when the gods say it's my time. I will keep searching until I forget her name, what she looks like, pulled only by the hole in my heart, and still, I will never find her.

Because the gods do not take kindly to those of us who

have rejected their gift of a lifemate and chosen to create our own blood bonded mates.

But for her... I will do it.

I will suffer for the rest of eternity.

"Would she really want this?" I ask, my voice breaking, splintering into a million jagged pieces, my walls no longer up to keep the judgment out. "Can she survive this?"

Or will I be saving her, only to gift her with decades of pain? I can feel the agony she's in. It jerked me out of my pitiful sleep, this soul-wrenching madness, this desperate need for it to stop. He is breaking her, killing her, leaving nothing but a husk behind.

What if I bring her home, and I just end up imprisoning her like Antonio has? Forcing her to endure something she doesn't want to for my own selfish needs? I might be doing it out of love, but for her, will it be any different?

Or will she just suffer like Krypto? Where every living moment is one of heart-breaking agony?

"When Lou was born," Dayne says slowly, his words no less impactful from that creeping hesitation, "Micha became a mother. In that same moment, she lost hers and her father. She suffered that grief alone for years. Stefaan was going to marry her off, wipe his hands of her, and she convinced him to let her stay and train as an assassin. She suffered the cruelty of that training for Lou. For herself too because Lou was all she had. She was just a child."

He hesitates for a moment, letting his words carry. Like stones placed upon my chest, they crush my lungs, hinder my ability to breathe.

"Then she cared for me," he says softly. Another pause. "And the kids that no one wanted, their names plucked from boards they never should've been on." From forums on the dark web, offering up money for their deaths.

Mother's words of why she had chosen Micha in the first place come back to me: because she saves kids rather than kills them as her reputation says.

My chest tightens as I realize she has an entire part of herself, a secret so entwined with who she is, and I know nothing about it.

I never won her trust enough to know.

But fuck, do I want the time with her to win it, to have the chance to prove my loyalty and devotion to her so that she wants to share these things with me, so that she trusts me to fight to protect the things she loves. The people she loves.

But I won't be selfish with my decision.

She is begging me to do this thing for her, to listen to her cries and show her mercy.

A tear slips down my cheek as I feel her scream, feel her tearing apart at the seams. She's fracturing into too many pieces to save.

But I don't know her like Dayne does.

So the choice will be his.

Whether or not my wife lives or dies.

My throat closes as I desperately wait for his next words.

He takes his time, giving weight to his thoughts, and my heart beats faster with every passing second.

"As long as she has someone to fight for," he finally says, "she will survive this."

I shudder, breathing out hard. I feel as if all my blood has poured out of my limbs, leaving me hollow and exhausted. "She has you," I rasp, thankful as all fuck that she has him. "And Lou."

Dayne stares at me, cautious now, wary. Like fingers reaching for a gun. Hairs rising to tell him something is wrong. Off. Not quite *right.* "And you," he says slowly. A question hidden in those two words.

I lift my head now, look him right in the eyes.

Micha told me never to tell him, knowing he'd try to kill me, then die by the reaper's hand, but he needs to know. He needs all the facts to make his decision, needs to understand all the pain Micha is going through. It isn't just Antonio that has broken her; it is me.

And she might not be able to heal from her trauma when she's living with the cause.

The silence rune hums around us. He can kill me before Khalid ever realizes we're fighting, but if he thinks that is the best decision for Micha, then I will let him do it.

I would die for her a thousand times over if it would help her heal.

My voice raw and honest, I say, "Perhaps not. I'm the one who tortured her, not –"

With a roar, he lunges for me.

I have time to bolt out of the chair, roll across the floor, and pull a knife, but I don't. Even knowing the pain that's coming, recalling Jona's screams as he ripped off his own dick, I stay seated until both of Dayne's hands wrap around my bare shoulders and yank me to my feet.

Burning pain explodes down my arms and arcs through the rest of my body. Each tiny bolt is precisely controlled to do the most damage, to fry my nerves without removing their ability to feel pain. I seize up, my muscles locking as thousands of needles stab me in a thousand locations, each one heated like molten metal. The pain is excruciating, but my jaw is locked so tight, I can't scream.

I hit the ground, convulsing hard, the damage to my nerves so intense, I can't remember how to breathe. Dayne squats down beside me as my heart races, and I gasp for air, his fingers resting lightly on my arm.

"The only reason I have spared your life," he says, "is because I know she loves you. So I will not kill you until she asks me to. But know that I know exactly how many times I can do this –"

My body jerks, spasming on the floor as sheer agony rips through me once more. Every nerve. Every thought. Every bit of my existence has been reduced to a burning agony.

"Without killing you."

Pain flares. My nerves all scream. He keeps electrocuting me over and over again, but I know I deserve an entire hour of this. An entire day. A week. A fucking lifetime for what I did to her – an act that will stay with her for life. A betrayal by someone she loves.

Eventually, he stops though, and I suck in air through gritted teeth, my jaw feeling like it's been welded shut, my two rows of teeth seemingly melted into one.

His fingers leave my arm, but his handprint stays burned into my skin. A silent, permanent threat.

"Now," he says as he stares down at me. "You get the *hel* up and find another way to save Micha because if we don't get her back –" His voice cracks over that, the fear that she isn't coming home. "I'll rewire your brain so that everything you feel, every bit of heat or cold, every smell and sound, every brush of fabric on your skin will translate into pain. I will make it so you'll live in hel long after Khalid kills me."

I sit up, sweat beading across my body. Every muscle feels tight and strained, every nerve dipped in acid and broken glass. I work my throat, but the chords feel fried, over-used, as if I have been screaming non-stop for hours. The words drag along my throat, kicking and screaming and doing their damnedest not to touch the air, to stay down so they don't scrape against the raw flesh inside, but I push them out.

"Being away from her is hel..." I take a breath, my lungs burning in protest. "So save your threats for Antonio." His eyes narrow as I lean against the chair, the lingering pain taking the air out of me but not the fire. Never the fire when it comes to her, and now that I know Micha will survive this, that fire roars into an inferno.

She still screams down the bond, begging me to set her free into death's embrace, that pain more crippling than the attack from Dayne. I don't ignore it, can't when I can hear her cries, but I do endure it.

I push to my feet...

Stare him in the eyes.

"Promise me you've not made this decision for yourself."

His jaw tics. "She'll survive even without you."

I flinch, recoiling from the pain.

I couldn't survive without her.

But if that is what she needs to heal from all this, then I'll set her free. Watch over her only from the shadows.

Turning for the door, I lock down the husband side of me and step back into the role of Boss. Elivici has a wife and three children. It's time to motivate her to work faster, and if she can't, I'll kill them all and get another teleporter in. After all, Eduardo's only a genius on Earth.

He isn't shit on the rest of the Seven Planes.

And I don't care how many people I have to kill.

How many families.

I am bringing my wife home.

THIRTY-SEVEN

HER

I've cried myself dry. I've screamed myself hoarse. I've emptied myself of everything I am until nothing remains but a hollow pain.

A constant ache that burrows into my soul.

This is a wound time will never heal.

A mother should never outlive her child.

I stare into nothingness, feeling like I'm looking inside of me. Rage flickers like a flame, but there's no oxygen for it to burn. No energy. I just lie here grieving, hating how easily I draw breath.

Hating Varius for letting me suffer.

I don't want to live anymore.

I don't want to keep fighting to survive when I don't even have anything to go back to.

What about Dayne? a little voice asks. *And Lou? And whatever helspawn she'll give birth to?*

I hate her for being pregnant.

I *hate* her.

And I hate myself for turning on my own sister. For being bitter and jealous over her pregnancy. It's not like *hers* will make a difference to *mine*.

But that doesn't stop me from hating her.

I open my mouth to scream but nothing comes out. I'm empty inside.

Except I'm not.

I have a monster in my womb.

A parasite.

A disease.

It's killing me.

I want it out.

I want it out!

I want it out!

Varius, please, I beg.

Please just kill me.

You promised you would protect me...

The world has lost its colors.
The birds their morning song.
My pulse no longer beats,
How can I live...
How can I live when you are gone?

I don't want to hurt anymore.

I don't want to work through the pain of losing my baby and come out stronger.

What the *fuck* has being strong ever gotten me anyway?

Self loathing.

Humiliation.

My stomach churns as the bitter taste of shit drags itself out of my memories and across my tongue.

Being *strong* got me disfiguring the face of a little girl on my first mission as an assassin. Her screams still haunt my sleep, and her trauma's tattooed on the back of my hand.

Being *strong* got me married to Varius. Got me tortured by him and then broken by his next betrayal.

Being *strong* got me kidnapped because I didn't hide in the basement and let Sau and her monsters handle it all on her own.

Being *strong* got my eyes ripped out.

My throat burns from unshed tears.

Being *strong* killed my little girl.

So perhaps it is time to be weak.

To take the easier path...

The next time Bear comes to feed me, I beg him for some V.

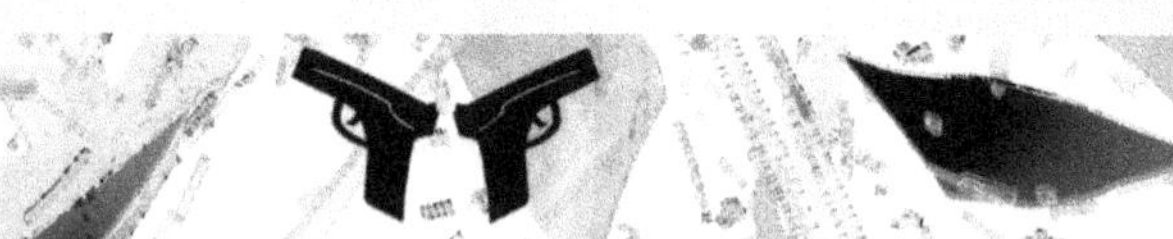

"I can't," Bear says, his voice strained as I cry without shame. I know it's hurting him to see me like this, so I let it all out. Use it to manipulate him. He's a good guy, the only one who hasn't raped me, but he's also afraid of Antonio.

"Please... you have to. The baby..." My throat tightens as I think about that *thing* inside of me, the thought of helping it survive. But the pain is just too much, and I know there is only one way to escape this hel.

Now that I know Dayne is alive, I won't risk using dark magic to kill myself. It might take him as the sacrifice, and that is one loss I cannot bear.

I hate myself for thinking Lou would be an acceptable

payment... Simply because she's pregnant when I am not; I am *infested*. That cruelty burns itself into my soul, changing me into something I'll never come back from.

The pain increases.

My need to escape it becomes unbearable.

"Please," I sob. "It'll help with the stress. Antonio wants the baby... to live, right?" I cry harder, hating the idea of giving birth to this *thing*. "It won't make it without the V."

"The risk –" he starts, but I don't let him continue. Can't let him talk himself out of helping me again.

"Is less than Tim and Eduardo raping me."

"What?" he breathes, so much horror and terror wrapped up in that single word. The empathy...

And the knowledge that he can't do anything to stop it.

"They're not supposed to fuck you." His voice shakes. "I can tell Antonio. I can get them to stop."

I shake my head, crying louder. That's not what I want. I want the V. What Sadist and the healer are doing to me are nothing compared to feeling this *thing* inside of me. I don't want to feel it anymore. I don't want to be aware of it at all. I need the V.

"You know it'll be too late," I say. Antonio hasn't been back on the yacht since I got pregnant. Aleric and Varius have been keeping him busy by hunting down the last of his connections. He's running out of funds and allies – his bank accounts being closed or emptied, his associates changing to the winning team. With him scrambling to solidify what he can in terms of money and resources, no one knows when he'll be back.

Eduardo gives me a 'health check' once a week and fills him in on my status. That's when he takes the time to sew me up and rape me, then heal me so no one will know.

Sadist fucks me at night, when the others are asleep. I've been crying and screaming at all hours, so no one's noticed when he's on me. And considering he pisses and shits on me for kicks and giggles throughout the day, no one can tell that the smell he leaves on me isn't just from that either.

"They'll keep raping me until you give me V," I say. The stress of what they're doing to me is nothing compared to the knowledge that it's not Rafiki growing inside me. Not *my* girl. Not a wanted child.

And while I'm in this much agony, I'm more desirable to Eduardo and Sadist. They won't be able to stop themselves even if they're punished for this, not while Antonio is away. When he isn't here to keep them in line.

"No," Bear says, denial in his tone. "No, stress doesn't cause a miscarriage."

"It *does*."

"It doesn't, or rape babies wouldn't happen, but the V –"

"*Please!*" I shriek, my voice cracking. "*Please! Just help me!*" I thrash against my binds, my arms and legs flailing against the mattress, rubbing my skin off until it burns.

"Micha! Micha! Stop! You're going to hurt yourself!"

I scream, arching back on the bed, all my pain ripping out of me. I can't live like this. *I can't.* I just can't. I can't make it through another day.

But I will.

Because they will force the food and water down my throat.

They will carry me to the bathroom and bathe me.

They will change my sheets so I'm not lying in filth, so the risk of catching a disease is slim.

They will heal me from any wounds.

They will keep the *thing* inside me alive.

Because their alpha wants it to make it to term.

With the three female werewolves failing to get pregnant with hybrids, Rudy's magic too strong to share the womb, I am currently his only option. So I will live.

Because Varius doesn't love me enough to kill me.

Screaming myself hoarse, I thrash on the bed until I'm so

exhausted, I pass out.

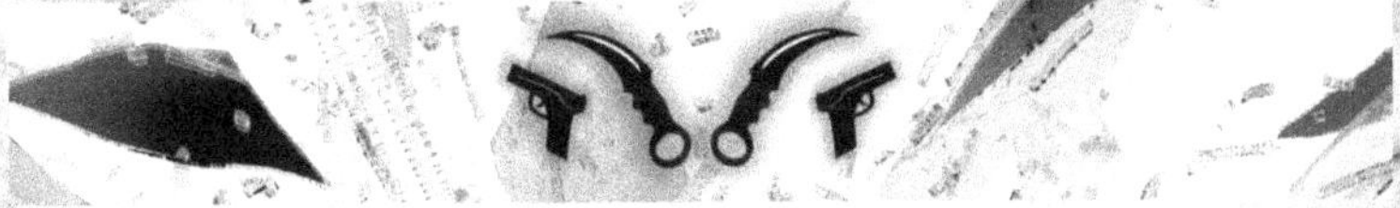

I wake up in a sweat, Micha's pain pushing down the bond despite the wall I've tried to erect. They're torturing her right now, making her hurt more than she ever has. My heart beating rapidly, I throw my covers off and sit up. I can hear her screams as if she was in the room with me. My magic crawls across my skin as I run my hands through my hair and tug.

I want to help her. I want to do what she is asking of me simply because *she* is the one asking me.

Help me, Varius!

You can stop the pain.

Why won't you stop the pain?

Her words echo inside of me, soundless as we're not telepathic, but I can *feel* them. The hatred for me. The *need* to get it all to stop.

I want to help her.

But Dayne knows her best, and he's confident she will survive this.

If that requires her to hate me, to never want to come back to me, then so be it. But she will live.

And she will heal.

And I will love her from afar.

Breathing out harshly, I rebuild the wall in my heart like Khalid told me to do. Each brick I lay is a solid commitment to losing her in order to save her. But even with it up, my skin itches.

For another loved one of mine weeps, their pain so deep, their desire to die so pungent on the air.

It's a giving up.

A plea for someone to end the misery of being forced to stay alive.

My eyes closing, I shudder over the sickness I can smell in the air, my senses having sharpened with the breaking of my curse. Krypto is desperate to reunite with Leno, and it is only because Maddox is forcing food and water down his throat that he's still alive.

But what life is he living? Lying on a grave his heart has already been buried in? Suffering for our own selfish want to not suffer another loss.

He's already gone.

And unlike my wife, he will never heal.

My brothers just refuse to admit it.

Knowing they will stop me in the light of day, I stand up and walk silently across my room to my weapons cabinet. I open the door and look at the gun Leno gave me when we were kids. My first one. A suppressed Ruger MK II.

"Hey, dickhead," he said, tossing me its case. "Have this so you're not so fucking useless."

I hesitate for a moment, not wanting to go through with this.

But urged on by Krypto's pain and the knowledge that my brothers will never let him go, I grab it, load it, then slip out into the hall.

A part of me wants to call Dayne back from babysitting the newest teleporter so he can euthanize him instead, but that wouldn't be right. Krypto isn't his responsibility.

He's mine.

The mutt doesn't look at me as I step out onto the porch.

I shut the door softly behind me, then walk over to him. He's still lying on Leno's grave. We built him a lean-to a couple weeks ago to keep the harsh sun off him, and I duck under the wooden roof.

He doesn't acknowledge me in any way, his grief too harsh a master.

Stroking my fingers through his short red fur, I start to sing "The Dickhead Song" by Miles Betterman, one of my brother's favorites.

My voice cracks over the first mention of "dickhead." It's so different to how he used to sing it – carefree and full of humor. Maddox would belt it out on terrible notes that'd leave our ears ringing, and Leno would laugh as he joined in despite having the singing voice of an angel. Because the song wasn't about perfect notes and beautiful harmony. It was about sharing a love of frustration over an idiot, and we have all been idiots at one point or another.

But fuck, do I think he is a godsdamn dickhead right now for leaving us too soon. For refusing to take the potions I tried to give him.

My pets turn into scratches. Tears burn my eyes.

But my heart rate slows as I solidify in my decision to do this.

To let him go peacefully into the night like he wants to go. Then I'll bury him with my brother.

As I think about Leno and feel Micha's pain, I stumble over the words of the song. I don't want him dead, and I'd give anything to be able to punch him in the face and piss on him if he was on fire.

Falling back on my ass, no longer crouching on my toes, I drag Krypto onto my lap. He growls, not wanting to move off the ground, to have something else between him and my brother, but he doesn't have the energy to snap his teeth at me.

So I slip my arms around him and squeeze him tight.

Rock him back and forth as I continue to sing.

When I get to the chorus again, I switch off the safety of my gun.

Line it up above his eyes.

But just as I'm about to pull the trigger, the door bangs open as Leno runs out of the house, butt naked and yelling at me to stop.

I freeze.

My heart plummets into my stomach and rolls around in the acid.

My jaw drops open as I stare at the impossible.

I'm on my feet, scrambling out from under the lean-to, and Krypto is on his too for the first time in weeks. He wags his tail and barks in joy as Leno runs towards us, his arms open, his eyes on his dog as tears rush down his face.

But then we realize it at the same time.

How something isn't quite right.

How the man in front of us is *wrong.*

Fake.

It's just Maddox wearing Leno's face.

Krypto's tail stops wagging before my brother can even get off the porch. The red dog skids to a stop, then pivots around, desperate to return to his best friend. He collapses back on Leno's grave, howling a note of pure agony.

"Krypto, it's me!" Maddox cries as he rushes down the stairs.

But the dog knows the truth and so do I.

Leno's never coming back.

His dog is never going to recover from this.

The flowers bloom as I hate myself with every fiber of my being.

"Varius, please!" Maddox cries, seeing the decision on my face.

Varius, please! my wife begs, her words an essence down the bond.

Locking down my emotions, I do what needs to be done. What no one else has been strong enough to be able to do.

I line the gun back up with Krypto's skull.

Bang!

He drops in an instant. Gone.

Maddox slams into me, shoving me back into the lean-to. As I'm pinned against one of the pillars, the roof digging into my lower back, he swings for my face. He hits me over and over again, cracking my nose, busting my lip. I don't fight back as the front door slams open and the rest of our brothers streak out.

He scrambles for my gun, wrenching it out of my hand before Khalid can stop him. He presses the muzzle against my forehead as he breathes hard. The metal's hot enough to burn.

His hand shakes.

I stare at him, at peace with whatever he chooses.

Dayne will find Micha. He will not rest until he saves her.

And I'll wait for her in the afterlife, refusing any attempt the gods might make to reincarnate me.

Maddox's tears splash down his face.

He sobs as he curls his finger over the trigger.

"Why?" he rasps.

But he already knows the answer. He heard that howl of pain the same as I did.

Krypto knew he wasn't the man he wanted.

He was never going to heal.

"I could've perfected it," Maddox says, his hand shaking so hard, the muzzle scratches at my skin. "I could've saved him."

I don't say anything. Can't.

Micha's pain still radiates through me. An agonizing cry I can't stop. Can't ease.

All of our attempts to save her have hit brick walls. The three teleporters I've since gone through have all told me the same thing: if they even *touch* Eduardo's spells, they'll trigger his safety measures. Even when I killed their kids one by one in front of them, their answers did not change.

And Eduardo's staying on the fucking yacht, so grabbing him isn't even a possibility.

In my desperation, I have turned to hunting Antonio himself, but all that's done is kept him from going back to the boat. It hasn't eased Micha's pain at all.

It's been seven weeks since she was taken, and we're no closer to getting her back. I haven't given up on her. I will *never* give up on her, but I can't help her in this moment either.

Can't help Krypto.

Can't help Maddox.

Can only look him in the eyes while he wears our dead brother's face.

"I could've saved him," Maddox cries, his voice shaking as badly as his hand.

Jerking the gun to the side, he roars and fires a shot into the air just beside my head. He pulls the trigger over and over again. My ears ring from the deafening noise. Then the clip is clicking on empty, and he's falling against me, his face hitting my shoulder. Shaking as he cries.

I stand stiffly for a moment.

Then my arms come around my baby brother, and I hold him as he sobs.

But just for a moment.

One small moment to let my brothers grieve.

Then we're going to get my fucking wife.

THIRTY-EIGHT

HER

I wake up to one of the men screaming in pain, and hope spikes in my chest at the thought of Varius or Dayne having come for me. I lift my head, trying desperately to open my eyes and see what's happening before my brain catches up to me and tells me I can't. Agony burns through me but so does my old fire – that spark I thought I lost forever.

My lips trembling, I clench my teeth and force myself to breathe.

It's about to be over.

I'm going to go home, where I'll spend a hel of a time fighting to overcome my trauma.

But I'm going home.

All my training kicks into gear, and I move on instinct, a mindless machine as I scoot up the bed. I might be blind and tied up, but I refuse to be helpless in my rescue, so the first step is getting out of my binds.

My hands are tied up with witches' snares, thin magical

chains that only Bear can remove (him being the one who put them on), but if I can break the slats of the headboard I'm tied to – as long as it's not metal, then it doesn't matter if they're still dangling on my wrist.

I exhale sharply in relief at the feel of wood beneath my palm. Then I twist onto my stomach, sit up, and scoot as far down the bed as the chains will let me. Leaning back, I place my right foot on one of the slats I'm tied to, then inch my way up to the middle of it. It'll break easier in the center rather than at an end.

Imagining the scene in my head, envisioning where I need to strike, I bring my knee to my chest. Then I snap it forward, kicking as if I'm trying to reach the wall behind. My heel slams into the wood as screams of pain echo from somewhere on the boat.

I wish I could see Dayne's face as he bursts into here to save me, only to find me already free.

A small grin curls at a corner of my lips as the slat cracks clean through. The splinters dig into my foot, but I don't care.

I just want to get out of here.

I want to go home.

It's almost over.

I search for the other slat I need to break with my left foot, then I bring my knee to my chest. I kick out, breaking free, and I quickly lean forward to tug the other ends of the witches' snares over the splintered pieces.

I crawl off the bed, my bleeding feet protesting when they're forced to take my weight, but I shove the pain down. I need to find a weapon. I need to cut out the monster inside of me.

No.

No, focus, Micha.

Escape first.

Then abort.

The door opens, and I tense, trying to figure out if it's one of the wolves or Antonio himself or if it's Varius come to save me. There's no more screams coming from the hall.

"Oh, for fuck's sake," Sunny mutters, and I lunge for the bedside table, hoping it is small enough to lift; I only know it's there because I've heard the clinking of things being put down on it.

My hands scramble to find the edges, but he tackles me before I can even try to wield it. We fall onto the bed, me on my stomach, him behind me, and I instinctively shout for Varius.

"He's not here!" he hisses as he turns me over, forcing me onto my back.

"Da–"

I sputter as a large vial of V is poured down my throat. As much as I wanted it not too long ago, I try to spit it out now. With my rescue imminent, I don't need to turn to it to stop the pain. I'll cut out the *thing* myself.

But Sunny's palm slaps across my mouth, and the V runs back down my throat. He pinches my nose closed with his other hand. I thrash my head, struggling to free myself so I can breathe. I slam my fists into his sides, try to reach for his face to claw out his eyes, but his reach is longer than mine. He hisses in pain as I crack one of his ribs, but he doesn't move off me, so I slam my fists into the crook of his arms instead, trying to get him to drop towards me so I can reach the soft parts of his face and neck. I wasn't prepared to hold my breath when he poured the V into me though, and I can already feel my lungs burning. My limbs losing their strength along with the oxygen in my blood.

Reaching between our bodies, I search for his balls. I'll rip them off him like I did Sadist.

He jerks off me, and I suck in air on a wild gulp. The V slides down my throat on an instinctive swallow. I cough as I scramble to my feet. "Dayne!" I half-shriek, half-wheeze.

Yelling for help isn't a 'damsel of distress' move. It's a damn good tactical decision.

I try to shout again, but Sunny barrels into me, and the word disappears into a grunt. His arms wrap around me, but expecting him to try to lift me off my feet, I'm unprepared for when one of his hands slips between my thighs.

The potion has me reacting instantly, my knees buckling, my breath catching. I straighten my legs, digging into my assassin training, my need to escape this nightmarish hel, to fight the effects of the V. Twisting in his embrace, I slam my elbow into his ribs. He grunts. I pivot further around, then lift my knee towards his groin.

He dodges it – just.

He shoves me back hard enough to make me lose my footing. I try to correct my balance, but with one leg in the air, it takes me too long, and he drops low, then takes out my remaining leg with a sweeping kick.

I crash to the ground and immediately try to roll onto my feet, but he's on me too fast, pinning me down on my belly.

"Stop it," he snaps as he wrestles my arms behind me so I can't use them to push off the ground or keep fighting.

Jerking my head back, I try to headbutt him in the nose, but his fucking eyes give him too much of a warning. He leans back and bends one of my thumbs the wrong way. My head falls to the ground as pain radiates up my arm. I lie on the hard floor, seething.

But I don't give up. Varius or Dayne will come for me. They'll be here any moment. Then I'll kill this fucker on top of me.

"No one is coming for you," he says.

My heart skips a beat. "You're lying."

"The screaming you heard was Bear attacking Tim."

No.

No.

He's just trying to get me to stop resisting so he can turn

me into a better hostage. Tie me up. Make me weak. Then ask to trade me for his own freedom. "Varius is going to kill you," I grit out.

"Probably, but not today."

The honesty in his tone is starting to freak me out.

"You're lying."

"You've said that."

I shake my head, trying to hold on to my hope even as my heart starts pounding against its cage, screaming to be let out. "Bear wouldn't go against him," I try.

"Not normally, no. But then you went and told him Tim was still raping you. Now, Bear might be a bit of a coward, but he likes to think of himself as a good guy, and well, he couldn't just stand back and let you get raped when the big old Boss told us to take care of you."

I tremble, my hope fracturing in my chest.

"So he waited until Tim was coming to see you tonight, then he attacked him in his werewolf form. He's currently breaking his arms and legs and then he's going to tie him up somewhere because he knows Antonio won't punish him for this. He might even reward him for handling Tim and his crazy in his absence."

Shit. Shit! That all sounds too believable.

No.

No!

He has to be lying.

Dayne is coming for me.

"Which has given me time to come in here and sneak you some V."

I grasp onto that last statement, using it to convince myself he's lying. Bear might go up against Sadist, but he won't dare defying Antonio. "He refused to give me any."

Sunny chuckles. "Oh, I'm not part of his plan. I'm doing my own shit. You see, the bastard in your belly –"

I flinch. My panic is rising too fast to hold back now. I

can feel that *thing* eating its way through me. Can feel the disease of its soul.

"– isn't mine, which means I'm going to have to suffer fucking months of experiments before I get another chance to stop them. So this is what we're going to do. I'm going to give you V, and in exchange, when you miscarry, you tell Antonio it's because of Eduardo."

The truth of his words hits me so hard, I can't breathe. Now that Sunny's learned the two of them have been raping me, he's made his play. There was never a rescue attempt. Neither Varius nor Dayne have come for me.

Tears burning in my soul, I cry out, and all my bandaged fury, all the fire I pulled on for this last desperate attempt to escape, is blown out with a single breath.

There is no end to this.

I'm going to die here just like Antonio said.

"You don't have to suffer anymore, Micha," Sunny says as he kisses my shoulder, and a bolt of arousal is triggered by the potion he forced down my throat.

Only, this time, I don't have the energy to resist it.

Don't have the desire.

Instead, I let the high course through me, let it take away the pain that's dug its claws into every nerve of my body, every piece of my soul.

"Just stop fighting it and accept that this is life." His lips trail across my skin to my shoulder. He still keeps both my wrists in his hands, but I don't struggle anymore.

"It'll go so much easier once you do. Trust me." He licks his way up my ear. "I've been exactly where you are."

My lips tremble as self-loathing and disgust roll down my cheeks. I hesitate for a second, that last flickering flame in me struggling to hold on despite the wind and the rain and the pitch black of nothingness baring down on it.

Utterly defeated, I arch my neck.

I give in to the effects of the V.

No longer fighting the addiction, I let him fuck me as I cry.

THIRTY-NINE

NAMELESS

She looks in a mirror and sees no reflection.
She's lost everything, gone without detection.

There's no fire in her soul.
No collateral
To hold against her

Because she no longer cares,
No longer sees
Just how beautiful they used to be.

They are faceless ghosts –
Vague memories
That ring with a banshee's shriek.
They are waveless coasts –
Broken ships
That sink with a lover's leap.
Into the sea.
The Dead Sea.
Where nothing floats
But a bitter need
To rise above the pain
With ecstacy.

And so she takes
And she takes
And she takes

Down on her knees
For Heaven's keys.

Only to burn in a lake of fire,
Too godsdamn tired
To swim to shore.

And so she takes
And she takes
And she takes some more

But each high gets shorter
And each fall gets longer
And each attempt to forget
Gets harder and harder

And so she takes
And she takes
and she takes some more

opening her mouth
to the devil's sweet allure
until there's nothing left
not even a shadow
of her pride or her fire or her stubborn need
to be anything other than down on her knees

and still she takes
she takes
she takes

she fucking takes
because she still feels the pain

and she'll do anything
fucking anything
to make it wane

FORTY

NAMELESS

"You want this?"

A whimper claws at my throat as I reach desperately for the V being held hostage in front of me. The lid of the vial's been removed, and the smell of pomegranates and chocolate tickles my nose – the only thing that can cut through the fog enwrapping me.

"Then beg me for it," Sadist says as Bear groans on the floor. I don't know what he did to him, but I don't care. I just want the medicine to my pain.

"Please," I say, scooting around on the bed to get on my knees. I tuck my legs beneath me as I lean forward, pressing my head to the mattress. "Please."

He scoffs, disgusted. "Pathetic. You really are broken."

I scoot forward, my hands searching for the vial I can almost taste.

I want it.

I need it.

"Please," I say again, not knowing what else to do. He hasn't given me another order. The panic is starting to set in. What if he refuses it to me? I can't go a night without it.

No.

No, no, no, no, no.

He can't take it from me!

I lunge forward to snatch it from him, but he backhands me across the face. Pain radiates up my jaw and across my eye, but all my focus is on the smell of V splattering onto the bed.

I scurry to the side, sniffing hard, my hands searching for the streaks of wet. Finding it having soaked into the sheets, I suck the fabric into my mouth and whimper.

Sadist laughs. "You're that desperate, whore?"

A stronger smell of it waves in front of me – what's left in the vial or perhaps another one entirely. I'm torn between reaching for it or continuing to suck on the tiny amount I can pull out of the cotton.

The high isn't enough, but it is something. What if he moves the vial away from me again when I try to reach for it? Then I'll have nothing.

"She's completely obedient," Bear says, still trying to save me. He's been washing me, shaving me – trying to bring a sense of normalcy to my life. He removed my binds after realizing I'm no longer a threat to the *thing* in my belly. I'm no longer a threat to anyone because I no longer fight. He's taken time to talk with me during the day, trying to remind me that I'm still alive despite the death of my soul.

A few times I have found myself wanting to ask about a boy with red hair and silent fingers, but all I ever say, if I say anything at all, is, "What time is it?" *How long until my next hit of V?*

I've kept Sunny's secret from everyone just like he told me to; I did not tell them about the V, so I don't know why I'm being punished. I don't know why he isn't here to give it to me.

I search the bed for another damp spot to suck on as Bear keeps trying to convince Sadist that I'll be of no joy to him. No entertainment.

But he just chuckles as he lifts my chin up by placing the open vial at my lips. My tongue darts out, dipping into the glass, lapping at the sides, trying to go as deep as I can in the small opening.

"What do you say, whore?" he purrs. "Would you let me fuck your eyes for this?"

I still, my pulse skipping a beat as my heart slams into my lungs, drawing them up sharp.

He pulls the vial away from me a fraction. I whimper, movement flooding back through my veins as I try to chase it with my lips.

His chuckle caresses my skin like an assassin's blade. He sweeps his thumb below my eye, across the bruise he gave me. I flinch, but the pain is nothing compared to the fear that I won't get tonight's fix.

A part of me wonders where Sunny is and tries to make sense of why Bear's here in his place – the old me slipping through the fog of my brain, attempting to solve the puzzle so I can prepare myself for any horror to come. But I don't want to think about it. I don't want to fight it anymore; I'm done being strong.

I just want the V.

So I nod into his palm as I tremble. "Yes."

He removes his hand from me and takes away the vial. I cry out over its loss, but I tell myself it's coming back. I just have to let him do this thing first. Once it's over, I can forget it under the taste of pomegranates and chocolate.

A zipper is pulled down not far from my face.

My eyes are already open; the habit still instinctive even though I can't see. Muscle memory causes me to blink every so often, but right now, I hold them open wide.

He pulls my head towards him, over the edge of the bed. His cock slides up my cheek.

Disgust curls in my belly.

My skin begins to itch, needing the V to calm it.

My hands pat the sheet, trying to find more patches to suck on while I wait for the rest of the dosage.

His dick trails over my cheekbone.

Then it pushes into my open eye socket, cupped by the muscles still there. It's a weird feeling, not quite on the level of pain but nowhere near pleasant. As he pushes in deeper, hitting the bone at the back, now the discomfort starts.

"You're a sick freak," he says as he pulls out and pushes back in, just the tip of his cock managing to bury itself in my eye. The truth of his words hammer into me as he picks up speed, his hands slipping around the back of my head.

Fight him off, Micha. He won't stop here.

Like a blackmailer, his demands will never end as long as their target is easy prey.

But I don't have the will to fight anymore.

I just don't.

He fucks me slowly at first, getting used to the feel of my eye socket rubbing against the head of his penis.

"Antonio will kill you," Bear says, still trying to save me.

A part of me thanks him for that, for being a 'friend' in a place that breeds hostility.

A bigger part hates him for trying to get between me and what I need to do to score some V.

This is the nicer route for me. Why can't he see that?

"He doesn't have to know though," Bear continues, his words winded and filled with pain. Whatever Sadist did to him must've been brutal. He sounds like he's speaking with multiple broken ribs and through a busted lip. "Leave her alone... and he never has to know what you did."

"What I did?" Sadist laughs. "I impregnated the bitch."

I grab a handful of sheet and bring it to my lips with

shaky fingers. There's barely anything on it, nothing really to suck, but I need whatever I can get.

My stomach burns with that sickness inside of me – that *thing* I'm trying so hard to forget.

I reach up and wrap my fingers around Sadist's cock, trying to jack him off while he jacks into me so I can finish him quickly and get my relief.

He laughs. "Look at this fucking bitch." He picks up his pace. He hits the back of my eye, slamming into the tender flesh and nerves, making my whole face throb.

But I endure it.

Chase the pain even.

Because it is better than the hole inside.

"She's going to tell Antonio exactly what I tell her to if she wants more V, and you're going to be the good guy" –he grunts– "of this little story. You just couldn't *bear* listening to her screams, so you got her addicted to shut her up."

"He'll kill me!"

"Nah. He'll just pass you over to Eduardo until the bitch gives birth."

I reach for his balls, massaging them like Varius always loved even as my stomach churns.

Frantic thrashing comes from the floor beside the bed, but he must be bound and tied because he never breaks free.

"Antonio won't risk culling his gene pool now that there is only three of us left, and he won't fuck her himself."

"I'll tell him the truth."

"He doesn't care about the truth. All he wants –" Sadist groans as he ejaculates inside my eye socket. The wet spurt of his cum fills it up before running down my cheek. I drop my hands from his body as I try to pull away, but his grip on my head just tightens. "– is someone to blame so he can feel in control. Because he knows there's nothing he can do to me." He pulls his dick down my face, rubbing through the trail of cum until he presses at the seal of my lips.

"Not when I'm the only one of us to make a hybrid."

My chin wobbling, I open my mouth just enough to show my submission. He pushes inside with a hiss of satisfaction. *It's okay, Micha. You can wash out your mouth with V. He's going to give it to you soon...*

I gag around him as he thrusts in deep.

"Suck me clean, bitch."

Tears mixing with the cum, I swirl my tongue around him. Cleaning him up like the good whore I have *chosen* to become.

"Fucking pathetic," he mutters as he pulls back, and he's right. I am fucking *pathetic*.

But I can't be anything else right now.

Can't be a fighter.

Can't be a Black.

Can't be the mafia queen to the Shadow Family.

I'm just so fucking tired.

"The V?" I ask, my voice as broken as I am.

He laughs, and then there's the sound of shattering glass on the hard floor beside the bed. "There you go, bitch."

I scramble off the bed as he moves back, presumably out of the room.

"Don't," Bear says as I get down on my hands and knees, sweeping my palms out, trying to find the elixir that can set me free.

A piece of glass cuts me deep, and I jerk my hand back on a sharp inhale. But I know where the V is now, and I inch towards it, so desperate to lap it up off the floor. I lower my head as Bear thrashes somewhere in front of me, trying to get free to stop me.

My heart rate kicks up, terrified he will manage, and so instead of going slowly and picking my way around any glass, I dip my head as fast as I can.

Glass cuts into my tongue, and I jerk back on a hiss. I reach up to pull out the piece embedded into my flesh. Then

I drop my head and start slurping up the spilled V.

Bear screams for Eduardo.

Fear hits me. Antonio doesn't want me addicted, so if the witch gets here, he'll pull the V from my veins and force me to be sober.

To feel all the things I don't want to feel.

So I drink faster, ignoring the pieces of glass that cut me and slip into my mouth.

And then I stop, realizing something even better.

There is another way out of this hel.

My hands scrambling on the floor, I search for a bigger piece of glass.

FORTY-ONE

NAMELESS

I knock into a piece with the edge of my hand, sending it clattering across the floor. My ears twitching, I scurry after it. When the sound stops, I slow down, inching forward so I don't send it flying once more. My fingers brush across the wood.

More wood.

More.

Where the fuck is it?

My heart rate increases as I think of Eduardo charging in at any moment and using his magic to take what V remains out of my veins. I can't go back to being a prisoner without it though. Can't survive.

My hand touches the cold glass of the broken vial, and I pick it up, running my fingers over it. It's the bottom half of the piece, a rounded base, splintered into jagged edges. A stab of pang resonates in my soul at the idea of never seeing those I love again.

Never seeing Dayne.

Or Lou.

Never given the chance to learn to love my nephew or niece despite my own pain.

And I think about Varius.

About how I'll never be able to kick his ass for what he's done to me. He took my eyes, so I will take his heart.

I hope this hurts like hel for him.

Rolling onto my back, I lay the smashed vial on the floor at the top of my head, the jagged pieces up. Bear screams at me to stop. I don't know how he's bound, but he can't reach me. Can't save me however much he wants to.

But he doesn't understand that this *is* saving me.

This is the only way free.

I climb to my feet, then shuffle back a bit, just enough so that when I fall, the base of my skull will land on the bit of glass. A few inches of penetration is all I need… If I destroy my brainstem, death will be instant. It's how they kill cows when they shoot them in the head. Eduardo can keep my heart going – hel, it'll keep going on its own for a bit, but my mind and soul will be gone. *I* will be gone, and the only way they'll be able to bring me back is through necromancy.

Eduardo will keep my body alive, my heart pumping, same as if I'm on a life support machine, and they'll use me as an incubator. They'll breed me, abuse me.

But *I* will be free.

With a peaceful weight in my chest, I fall back without hesitation. Time slows, and in this dragged out moment, I think about Dayne.

I think about Lou.

And I think about Varius.

Unbidden, one of my happiest moments come back to me.

A time before all the betrayal. Before the pain. When our love was young and full of hope.

I'm singing at a karaoke bar, belting out songs with a cracked voice. I'm way out of tune. The crowd is drunk, having bought drink after drink just to get through my performance. They all want to leave, but none of them will dare, too scared of disrespecting my fiance, the Boss of the Shadow Domain – the man I'm falling in love with.

Hopping down from the stage, I head over to him, my heart so full I can barely breathe. I never want this night to end. Never want to face the day of what the future is about to bring.

"Let's get out of here," I say.

"Are you sure?" He brought me here because it was a dream of mine as a kid – to sing karaoke, to be normal for once rather than a training assassin, and he wants to make sure I'm not just done because his brother, the reaper, looks like he wants to rip out my vocal cords so he doesn't have to endure any more of my 'singing.' I wish I could bring Rafiki here. Or just reenact this in our living room. Where she giggles and preens and smiles so bright, it matches the stars in the sky. I wish for so many things...

"Yes," I say with a smile so wide it hurts. It's a good pain though. A happy pain. Looking into his eyes, I murmur, "I could really demolish a burger right now."

His eyes light up, hearing the words within those words: "I like you." And those words stare back at me too, just more intense. "I love you."

And I feel it then, the depth of it, and the fear inside him too.

What it would mean to love me when he doesn't trust me.

Can't trust me because he doesn't know what that word means. Never learned it.

He has only ever known betrayal.

But he looks at me with such willingness to learn despite the fear of past experiences come to haunt him.

"I like burgers," he says.

"I love you."

"I love you, Micha Shadow."

But now that love is gone. Turned bitter from a broken heart and betrayals too deep to fix. He took my eyes after promising me he'd never hurt me again. He abandoned me here. How long has it been, and he still hasn't come for me? He still hasn't killed me, using up the blood bond until the magic of it takes my life as payment rather than our shared blood.

So I'm saving myself the only way I can.

Taking the only course left to me.

Time rushes forward again, but before I can hit the piece of glass and hope it cuts deep enough to actually destroy my brain stem rather than just hurt a fuckton, I'm tackled from the side.

I scream as my hope is ripped from me. I am pushed through the air by a massive body of fur. The ground slams into me, and the beast lands on top of me. Pain punches through my body, but the tears come from the agony in my soul.

I am never escaping this hel.

I scream and cry as the wolf pins me down, and another man places his hands on me, forcing his magic through my body to take out what V remains.

I beg for them to stop, to just let me have this. I promise them I'll be good and obedient and fuck them as much as they want if they just let me keep my sanity.

My protection against the pain.

But Eduardo makes my own body work against me. It uses up the V – sudden and quick, and I get a little high from the orgasm it pulls from me, but it isn't enough to sedate me. And then it is gone, and I remain.

I don't want to fucking remain.

I want to be gone.

I want to go *home.*

To her.

To Varius...

To that moment in the karaoke bar when everything was beautiful and perfect.

But instead I am here, carried back to the bed by a wolf twisted in form. Held down by a witch whose magic makes me feel sick.

"Shit," Sunny says after they manage to tie me down and he shifts into his human form. He sighs in annoyance even though I've stopped screaming, stopped fighting, once again consumed by unbearable grief. Just a broken shell stretched out on the bed, wishing for death. "You couldn't have killed him, Bear?" Sunny demands.

"Antonio would have killed me when he got back!" he protests, no longer from his position on the floor. Given the witch's snares are wrapped around something again, they must have set him free so he could work the magic of my binds; only the one who put them on can command them.

"I broke both of his arms and legs and tied him to the mast," he growls. His voice is still shaky though, still full of pain despite his anger. "He's only free because of Eduardo."

"What the fuck?" Sunny says, turning on the witch.

"Antonio isn't going to kill him when he's the only one who can breed hybrids." He talks with all the sootiness in the world shoved up his ass. "What do you think Tim would have done to me once he got free?"

"We could have blamed him for the V." He pauses. "We could still do?"

"And if Antonio doesn't care enough to kill him?" There is a second of silence as Eduardo's words weigh them down. "No. The risk is too great," he says. "Besides, he might not even be coming back. He's been gone for weeks. He could be dead..."

"Shit."

"Then we should kill Tim," Bear says.

"And face Antonio's wrath if he *does* come back?"

"Shit." Sunny again.

"So what do we do? We can't just live under his tyranny."

"He won't go that far. Not unless he knows Antonio's dead. Otherwise, even if he could stop him from using the portal to get back here, he will never be able to get off this ship," Sunny says at the same time Eduardo says,

"We pray Antonio comes back and is forced to stay now that the Shadow Domain has destroyed every place he can hide."

Their footsteps move away from me. A door opens. The hum of magic in the air dissipates, felt in its absence as I was too focused on screaming to realize its birth. A broken silence rune.

The door shuts, and the magic hums to life again. It seems they wish to save their ears from me now that I'm no longer docile on V.

Feeling so utterly helpless, I don't care if I'm only doing what they expect of me. I can't help but scream.

And cry.

And pray to Varius to please...

Please fucking kill me.

I can't survive anymore.

I don't want to.

Please... I'll forgive you for everything.

Just fucking kill me.

Bear brings me food, but he's forced to funnel it down my throat again. I've lost all desire to eat. He carries me to the bathroom for a shower and a shave and a brush of my teeth, trying to remind me that I'm still human. But I move like a puppet, like a doll with no purpose of my own. I don't

feel *clean* despite how much he cleans me. Pretties me.

The *thing* in my belly is a disease. I can feel it again, and I want it out.

I want it out.

I want it out.

I don't know how much time passes. Hours, days, weeks? Months? Years?

I don't sleep enough to tell the time – the nightmares feel like days anyway. I can't track the number of meals as the fog in my brain makes them roll together. There's just pain. And more pain. And more pain. It never stops.

I want it to stop.

"Please," I beg.

But no one ever listens.

It's only me and the pain.

The increasing agony.

The fire in my veins, like ants marching against my skin, burning bites injecting venom. Filling me. Consuming me. Until there's no part left that's *me*.

"Please…"

"Please…"

"I thought about this all night," Sadist says as he enters my room. I lift my head, feverish for his attention. He was the last one to give me V. Maybe he'll give it to me again.

"Please," I start to beg.

"Oh, I'll give it to you," he says as he moves towards the bed. There's two sets of footsteps. The unknown is making me anxious and sick. "But first you need to do what I want."

He stops beside my bed. I flinch, but I don't jerk away. He's offered me V. Whatever he does to me can't be worse than this pain, and it will be temporary. If I don't do it, then there won't be any end to my pain.

"Anything," I rasp.

He chuckles. "Release her. She's so fucking keen for this."

Someone stumbles into the bed – shoved perhaps.

"No," Bear says.

"Don't be an idiot. I can just break the bed to free her. I'm giving you a chance to get back on my good side. Don't you want that?"

"Antonio's never going to believe I'm the one responsible for all this."

Sadist laughs, then *tsks* multiple times. "All this fire you have because of her. It's gotten you hard, hasn't it? Having someone be so *dependent* on you again?"

Bear doesn't say anything, so I break the silence. "Do it for me. Please." If he wants dependency, I'll play the role to perfection. I have worn many masks during my life as an assassin. I can be whoever he needs me to be.

"*Cotealos*," he mutters, the word said in his voice the key to undoing the golden chains around my wrists.

"Now sit up and put this on," Sadist says.

As soon as I sit up, he throws something at my chest. I catch it on reflex, though my arms are weak and tingly from having been tied up all night.

All night.

Not nights... The pain of living without V has made time stretch unbearably. Panic runs rapid laps around my throat as I think about how terrible it'll be to survive a week like that. Every minute so agonizingly intense, it feels like a day. I couldn't survive. I won't. I need the potion to help me.

Frantic to do whatever I need to to get it, I feel the item in my hands. Flat leather lines lead to a large dick.

Having never worn a strap-on before, I struggle to put it on. It's hard to work out which straps are for the legs and which is for the waist, but eventually I manage it. I kneel up on the bed, waiting to see if Sadist will tell me I've done it wrong.

"Grab hold of it," he says, "and rub it up and down."

My hand responds immediately, and a spike of arousal pings between my thighs. Orgasms are tied to the magic of the V, and I am desperate for any kind of relief from the pain inside of me.

"Cup your breast with your other hand."

I obey instantly, rubbing my nipple until it's hard. I jerk when a mouth closes around my other breast and sucks on it, but I don't pull back. Don't dare. He bites down on me hard, and I whimper.

Lifting his head, he trails his half-severed tongue up my chest, then my neck, all the way up to my ear. His fingers wrap around my dildo, jerking me off. Each tug of his hand pulls on the plastic straps around my waist. I start to pant, ready for the release he's promising me.

"The V..." I murmur, but he grabs my throat with his free hand, silencing me.

"You're going to fuck Bear's ass, and then you're going to get him to fuck your pussy while you suck on this dildo. *Then* I'll give you the V."

I want to beg him to give me just a taste now, but I know he won't. The only way I'm going to get my high is if I do what he wants. So I nod, so desperate to begin.

He laughs, making me feel sick, but I beat it down. It's only temporary. Then I can leave all this pain and shame and self disgust behind.

Pulling away from me, he orders Bear on the bed. The man must resist because he gets slapped a couple of times and then tossed down. He might be able to take Sadist when he's in his werewolf form while the latter is not, but he's no match for him now.

There is a moment of hesitation as I recall all the kind things he's done for me.

He's been a friend.

The only one to care.

I know how devastating and painful rape is. How can I do this to someone who doesn't deserve it?

Because I need the V.

Hurting him is the only way to stop my own pain.

Reaching over to him, I find him on his hands and knees. I move behind him and grab his hip with my left hand while my right holds my dildo. I jerk it around, trying to find his hole.

Doing it without sight is frustrating, but I pull on all my training to focus. His hip is here. That mean his crack must be here. And then his hole…

The bed dips as more weight is added to it – Sadist in front of Bear perhaps, ready to have his cock sucked.

I rock my hips forward as Bear tenses, trying to refuse me. I don't tell him to relax. I know it won't help. Nothing will help reduce the pain and humiliation he's about to go through.

Don't do it, Micha.

You know how bad it feels.

But I can't think of anyone else right now.

I'm barely surviving.

Save yourself before you save another; that's what every emergency manual says…

My skin itching, my soul breaking, I push the dildo into Bear's tight, resisting ass. He cries out, but he's quickly muffled, his mouth filled with another man's cock.

There's resistance, and I remember my own pain. Being in his place. Getting my own ass ripped apart. A toy to use and discard.

Choking on my guilt, I grab hold of his hips and push in deeper. He tries to move off me, but I lean down and wrap my arms around his waist. I rut him like a dog, my face pressed to his back to hide my shame, my hips bucking awkwardly, not used to being on this side of things.

I slip out all the way sometimes and have to grab hold of

the dildo to push it back into his ass. The first time I touch any shit that's coating it, I gag, but I wipe my hand on his stomach and keep going. Eventually, I figure out the right rhythm, the right distance to pull out before pumping back in.

Now I'm sliding my clean hand down his stomach to his cock. He's starting to harden despite his whimpers of pain, and I jerk him roughly as I follow Sadist's commands. I have to get him hard enough to fuck me after this. That's what he said.

"Such a willing whore," Sadist grunts, breathless and full of pleasure.

I hate this.

I hate him.

I hate me.

The tears come, and I let them fall, knowing it'll get him harder. If he likes me, maybe he'll give me more V…

Sickened with myself, on how far I've fallen, I duck my head and focus on getting Bear hard enough to push inside me. At the moment, he's only at half-mast, nowhere near firm enough. Definitely not hard enough to come quickly once he's in me, and I don't want to have to ride him for long.

Sadist grunts.

A slap resonates in front of me.

"Swallow it," Sadist demands. "You want to get back on my good side, right? Want me to blame one of the others instead of you when Antonio gets back? Then keep your lips closed like a good fucking whore and *swallow.*"

I keep pumping into him as he does what he's been told, not sure when I should stop.

"That's it, let me see that throat work. Now clean me up, you fucking bitch."

A few more seconds pass – the only noise the slap of my hips and the slurp of Bear's mouth as he cries. Next thing, I am being pulled off him and the strap-on's removed.

"Go on; get him hard," Sadist snaps, a cruel note in his voice that gives me pause.

I still, a deer in headlights as the old me screams at me to run. But the fog is too thick. I don't know what direction to go in, so I stay frozen until it's too late.

"I guess you don't want –"

Panicking, I lunge forward. "I do, but I don't know how. I tried... touching him while I... was in his ass." My throat tightens with shame. "And you've taken the... the thing."

My stomach twists even more when Sadist laughs, loud and cruel.

"You think he's gay?" A chill runs across my skin. "No, you dumb bitch. Bear got run out of his pack because he raped a little girl."

"I didn't rape her," Bear says with such disgust that I believe him. This is just Sadist being an asshole, getting into my head and trying to turn me against the one 'friend' I have in here.

But then he says something that makes my blood run cold.

That makes my disgust almost push past my need for V.

"I loved her," Bear protests, "and she loved me."

I cry out as Sadist laughs, curling in on myself, wanting to be sick. I can't do this. I won't.

But the shaking tells me I will.

The pain in my heart that I can't bear to carry anymore.

Just thinking about what Bear's done has me wishing for a vial.

I need the pain to stop.

I *need* it to stop.

"I would never hurt a kid," he says, and I want to claw at my own skin. I want to break my hands to stop myself from doing what I know I will. "We loved each other."

"How old?" I demand, feeling my chest caving in.

I hate myself.

Don't do this.

Stop it, Micha.

You'll never come back from this.

I scratch at my thighs, feverish with addiction.

I need the high.

I need the escape.

I can feel the *thing* eating its way through me, can feel the absence of Rafiki.

Can feel my self-disgust and horror at what piece of shit I've become.

I can't cope with this.

I can't.

Sadist laughs. "What age do you think? There's a reason we call him teddy Bear."

FORTY-TWO

NAMELESS

Sobbing in disgust with myself, I push myself off Bear's cock, then crawl off the bed. I want to cut out my voice box for the things I've told him to think about to get him hard. I never hated the fact that I'm small or my chest is practically flat, but I hate them now. I hate *me*.

His cum runs down my legs, and I want to scrub myself clean.

But I know it doesn't matter how much I shower, I'll never come back from what I did.

Desperate to escape this shame, I crawl across the floor to Sadist as he laughs at me. I kneel in front of him, my feet tucked under my ass, my mouth open like the whore I am.

The smell of pomegranates and chocolate wafts in front of my nose, but it never reaches my lips. There's the sound of liquid being poured, and the sweet aroma grows stronger. A hand grabs the back of my head and yanks me forward. I don't resist. I go eagerly. A dick is pushed against my mouth, and realizing the V is on it, I suck him deep. As his cock hits the back of my throat, I wish he would choke me with it. That I'll die right here, right now. A terrible death for a terrible person.

I hate this monster I've become.

This dirty whore.

This broken, pathetic shell.

But my self-hatred isn't strong enough to make me stop.

My body wants the V, and so I take Sadist's cock deep into my throat. I swallow around him, moaning at the taste of pomegranates and chocolate to override the shit that was on the dildo. An explosion of arousal runs through me, and a tear slips free at the sweetness of it.

He grabs the back of my head and fucks me hard, and I slip a hand between my wet thighs as he scrapes himself across my teeth.

I want to hit the high as quickly as I can.

But he shoves forward so hard that I fall backwards. His cock slips out of me as I hit the ground, and he grabs my arms. I scream as I try to fight him, knowing what he's about to do. He's going to stop me from getting off. This is the only way he can get his release, and I know if I want mine, then I'm going to have to play his game.

I struggle against him, but he's stronger than me, and he quickly pins me down with my hands above my head. I cry out in pain and a desperate need, letting my tears fall. He likes seeing them streak down my cheeks. It gets him hard.

He grabs his cock and pushes it against my lips. I turn my head until he slaps me. Then I'm sucking him deep. It's too hard to pretend that I don't want this.

"You're such a greedy, little whore," he mocks as his cock slams deep down my throat. "You're a disgusting piece of shit that no one wants. I'm only fucking you because you're all that's available. But if there was even a pig here –" He grunts as he rams in ball deep, his stomach hitting my nose.

"Then I'd choose the pig."

Tears streak down my face, not an act any more. His words cut me deep, riding the coattails of my own shame. I struggle against him again, desperate to get myself off.

For the high of the V to rip away this pain.

But he keeps my arms pinned.

Laughing, he fucks my face harder. I twist against the floor, trying to buck him off. When that doesn't work, I spread my thighs in invitation, hoping Bear will fuck me again.

Choking on that thought, another part of me dies.

I deserve to stay here for the rest of my life. I deserve for Sadist to torture me.

"You're such a pathetic little whore. A bitch in heat. I bet you'd let an actual dog fuck you right now, wouldn't you?"

I flinch from the truth of his words.

Tears run down my cheeks.

Sobbing on his dick, I struggle to breathe. To live with myself. I need the high of the V. It's the only thing that'll stop the pain.

"I should get Eduardo to teleport one here," Sadist grunts, and I can see so easily what's in my future. Me on my hands and knees as some dog fucks me from the back. And when that isn't enough for his sick, twisted mind, he'll make me suck it off.

His cock rams into me as I start to hyperventilate, and I retch all down his length. He pulls out of me as chunks go flying. It sprays down my chin, and I turn my head on instinct to let it out.

He forces me onto my stomach, rolling my face into the pile of vomit.

"Eat it," he says, "and I'll fuck you."

I want to resist. To hold a little part of my dignity.

But the V pushes me to open my mouth.

Crying, I eat my vomit off the floor, the acidic smell

making me nauseous. I gag as it touches my tongue, and Sadist laughs. Moving around me, he grabs hold of my hips, lifts me onto my knees, then slams his cock into my ass.

I whimper in need, my palms pushing against the floor as I wriggle back against him. I can get off with him fucking my ass due to the V, and I'm desperate to come. I spit the vomit out of my mouth, but he pushes my face into the floor as he pulls out of me.

"Eat it all like the bitch you are," he snaps, and I know there's only one way for me to get my release.

Sobbing, I suck the vomit back into my mouth. I gag as the chunks of meat and pasta hit my tongue again. I try to chew, but that's making it worse, so instead I just straight up swallow. They went down the first time. Surely, they'll go down now without choking me. Though if they do end up in my lungs, that'll be no bad thing...

As humiliation paints me as a whore, Sadist lines his cock back up with my ass. He pushes in as I continue to eat. My stomach churns. The urge to be sick again gets stronger and stronger with every mouthful I choke down. My nose burns from the smell. My mind screams.

But at least Sadist is rutting into me, letting me chase that blissful release.

"Finish it, bitch."

I search the ground for more bits of vomit, sniffing my way to any chunks that remain.

He laughs behind me.

I nibble a piece off the floor. Fight back my urge to gag.

My orgasm is building. That's all that matters.

Soon I can escape this world.

I lick the acidic puddle off the floor, but that's finally too much for my stomach, and I throw it all back up.

He laughs as I push myself up on my hands, my chest heaving as twice-eaten spaghetti and meatballs hurls past my lips. Shoving my face down into the sick, he comes in me.

The pumping of his cock triggers the magic of the V, and I cry out as my own orgasm tears through me. The pain and disgust inside is washed away by the open floodgates of pleasure. I convulse on the floor, my body on cloud nine.

I moan as the high takes me away from this hel.

It is the only escape I have.

But it never lasts.

It never fucking lasts.

FORTY-THREE

HER

Holy shit. What have I done?

I lie curled on the floor, left where I orgasmed. The caked mess on my face tells me I threw up a lot last night, then slept in it. That's all I am. Vomit. Shit. A pile of disgust.

I retch, wanting to be sick again.

How could I have done that?

How could I have talked Bear through scenarios? To tell him what to imagine, then role play a minor to get him off? All to score some V...

Shit.

My hands start to shake.

I can't do this.

The drug is a poison. I can't take it anymore.

I won't ask for it again.

I have to stop.

Cut myself off.

Get clean.

My soul screams at the idea of suffering through this pregnancy without any help to take away the pain. But I can't do what I did again. Can't reduce myself to *that*.

Trembling, I roll onto my hands and knees, then heave.

My stomach is empty though.

I have nothing left inside me. No food. No soul. Just an empty black hole of shame.

Fuck.

I think about all the kids I've saved. Think about all the ones I've found families for. I gave them a new identity, an investment account for when they turned eighteen – started with half of the money I was paid to kill them. I took jobs that gave me a reputation as a heartless bitch all so I could do some good as an assassin. And what have I done?

I've failed every single one of them.

I'm no different to the monsters I've tried to save them from.

I stumble to the bathroom, my hands out in front of me, wanting to get clean before Bear tries to come in and do it himself. I don't want him touching me.

He shaved me…

Oh my gods.

All the times he's shaved me, and I was too out of it to connect the dots.

I fall against the bathroom sink and heave again as tears run free. I want to throw up, throw out everything inside of me. To purge myself of the disease I've welcomed into my body. The V is no longer in my system, pulled out by magic, but its effects remain. The knowledge of all the choices I made to get high.

Trembling against the sink, my knuckles clenched tight, I still can't help but want another dosage though. It'll stop the pain of my thoughts. It'll let me live with the monster I've become. It'll let me hide from myself…

But I can't.

I won't.

I *can't.*

Please don't make me, I beg my own body.

A body that isn't mine anymore.

I can't.

I can't!

Please...

Shaking with need, I force myself to turn on the tap. I splash water on my face. Scrub at the vomit, then at my top layer of skin, trying to wash it all away.

But it doesn't stop the craving.

It doesn't stop the burning in my veins or the knowledge that this pain can all go away, disappear, be forgotten for at least a little while if I just. Get. High.

If I just sell a little bit more of my soul.

But what part of my soul is even left?

Surely, it won't matter if that, too, is gone?

I already can't come back from what I've done. So why bother trying to resist? Why let myself keep hurting? After all, how much further can I fall?

Dropping my head under the tap, I try to rinse out my mouth and my thoughts. I spit out the water, but the bad taste, the infection in my soul remains.

I just need a little V...

No.

No!

Please don't.

Just a little taste.

Sagging to the floor, I bawl my eyes out, hating who I've become. I don't even want to be saved anymore. I don't ever want to see Dayne or Lou again. I don't want them to see *me.* I deserve to stay here. Die here. Be tortured until my final breath.

I sold my soul to V, so Hel is where I belong.

Varius, if you can feel this... Leave me to rot alone.

"Bitch, I don't think so." Dayne's voice snaps back at me, my subconscious trying to keep me alive as there's no way for him to actually speak to me. There aren't any telepaths on earth, and even if Varius managed to drag one through the portal, they'd have to know my mind well in order to pick me out among all the others on the planet.

"I'm busting my ass trying to get to you. You better not make me do all this for nothing."

My sob breaks, and I press my hand across my mouth.

"Bitch, do you know *how much sleep I've missed?"*

I crumble as I think about how grumpy Dayne is in the morning. I can hear his sass so clearly. See the annoyance in his eyes.

"So get your ass up and figure your shit out so I can catch up on my Zs."

Gods, I miss him so fucking much, but I don't want him here. Even in my mind, it feels so *wrong.* Like I'm tainting all the good memories.

He didn't sleep well when I first found him. Whatever had happened to him in that cage, he'd learned to always keep one eye open. But eventually, he started to sleep in my presence. Just naps at the start – though he'd always deny it. Then they would get longer. Deeper. Once, I made a loud noise, and he didn't even stir.

My chest constricts with the tears I cried that day. He went through hel as just a kid. *For years.* And I watched him heal from it.

But he didn't become the monster I did.

He didn't... He didn't do... what I did with Bear.

If he knew...

He'd want me to kill him.

Whatever happened between us after would be sorted *after.*

But Dayne would want him dead.

"Do it for me, princess?" he says.

I'll do anything for you.

"Atta girl."

With a last broken sob, I wipe my hand across my face as I take deep, shuddering breaths. My shaking starts to calm, then I push to my feet and turn towards the bathroom door. I lock it before I step into the shower.

It's a quick scrub this time – not an attempt to cleanse my soul. I'm just removing all the vomit from my face and neck and all the cum off my thighs. I hesitate for a second, thinking about cleaning my pussy of Bear's presence, but I don't trust myself to stop there.

Already, my body is responding to the mere closeness of my hand. The arousal is prickling at my skin, and sharp on its heels is the urge to find Sadist so I can score some more V.

Ripping both my hands away from my body, I press them against the wall of the shower and shudder out a breath. The urge is so fucking strong. The temptation to give in. Maybe if I seek him out, I can name the terms...

Maybe the price won't be as bad this time.

Clenching my teeth, I grope around for the tap, then turn down the heat. The sudden burst of cold water shocks me, and I breathe in raggedly as goosebumps spread across my skin.

I stand under the spray until I start to shiver. Until the urge fades enough to ignore it – *just.*

My pussy clenches, begging me to touch it, to experience a bit of that high just to tide me over. But I know it won't stop there. It *won't.*

And I owe it to Dayne... to all the kids to kill Bear first.

After... after, maybe...

Hating the weakness clawing so desperately at my skin, I turn off the shower and step out. Hoping there's still a towel on the railing, I grope around for it. It's still a bit damp from yesterday, but I pat myself down, ruffle the few inches of hair I have on my head, then wrap it around myself.

My throat closes as I realize this is the first time I have been 'clothed' in... I don't know how long. I've lost track of the time. It feels like I've been captive for years, but I touch my hair and know it has only been a month, maybe two. It takes hair a year to grow six inches on average. It was just below my ears when Rafiki... when I got attacked; Sau made me grow it out once I became engaged to her son so I could look more the part of a Boss' wife.

My heart twists with longing for my daughter.

She should be the one still in my womb.

I should be able to feel her kicking by now.

I waited so long to feel her move, and the only time...

I rip the towel off me, wishing it were my skin. Wishing I could dig into my belly just like Antonio did and tear out this unholy *thing* that's now inside of me.

My hands fisting in the cotton, I hold on to that rage, on to that desperate need for violence. Then I carry the towel over to the bed, drop it on the floor, and climb onto the mattress tucking my legs beneath my ass.

The door to my room opens not much later. Footsteps creep closer as Bear says, "Morning, angel."

There's a lift to his tone, a hop in his step; he thinks he's about to get his rocks off – and he will, but not in the way he wants.

Ducking my head, I shyly say, "Hello."

Like a little girl to her teacher on her first day of school. How many children did he have access to? How many did he *love*? How many parents did he shake hands with and tell them their little baby was *special?*

I keep my head down, focusing on my breathing. He isn't in his wolf form, so his nose isn't as sharp, but he'll still be able to sense the danger in the air if I think about how many ways I want to kill him.

And I need him to get closer. Need him to bring me my

breakfast and the utensils that come with it. Fork or spoon, it doesn't matter. I can kill him with either.

"I made a special breakfast for my special girl," he says.

With my face hidden, I could pass for a preteen with my flat chest and tiny stature, but he likes them younger than that. He's either imagining me as someone else, just like I got him to do last night, or he's decided beggars can't be choosers.

Either way, my stomach churns. I keep my face flat as he approaches the bed. The smell of syrup tickles my nose as he places a tray on my lap.

"It's pancakes in the shape of a bear's face," he says, like a father rewarding his little girl. "Blueberries for her eyes, and bacon for her mouth. And look at her hair. I did it just like yours with some whip cream and syrup. Do you like it, angel?"

My skin crawling, I nod. Pancakes and bacon means a butterknife and fork. Him making this, though, means he was most likely a father at some point.

I struggle to keep my face expressionless as I think about him hurting his own *special girl.*

"And I got you a present too." He sits down beside me and runs a hand across my face, pushing my wayward bangs out of my eyes. The sound of liquid shaking in a small vial has my heart jumping into my throat.

"If you're good, I'll let you have some."

I turn into his touch, my body needy, my pain desperate to be quieted. "I'll be a good girl just for you," I say even as my stomach churns in self-disgust. But fighting it is too damn hard when it's right in front of me.

He removes his palm from my face. There's the clatter of cutlery, then he's pushing a knife and fork into my hands. "Just eat all of your breakfast, okay?"

Where did he put the vial? I need to make sure I don't break it when I attack him.

I start to shake, start to second guess my plan.

"You can search his body after, Micha. Do this for me."

Anything for you, Dayne.

I promised I would protect him. I promised myself I'd be someone he would be proud of – a protector of those who couldn't protect themselves. We found a way to fight his demons together. We rose from the pain of his childhood *together.* I might crave the V with every part of my being, but I cannot fail him.

Not in this.

He means too much to me.

So I clutch the knife and fork in my hand and dig into my breakfast, making sure I make a mess of things. I want Bear to think I'm clumsy without my eyes. Helpless, even.

"Here, let me help you," he says.

Shit. I've played it too well. "I'm a big girl," I say, doing my best to sound like his preferred age range.

"Of course you are," he says, patting my head.

I drop a bit of syrup on my chest.

"Oops, you got some on you," he says. "Let me get that."

He trails his fingers across my skin, and I wonder how many times he's perfected this. How many pretty words he gave to *special girls* to get them comfortable. They wouldn't have known better. They would have just thought he was helping. They would've *trusted* him even as something in their back of their mind – a basic, instinctive fear bloomed. They would've trusted him. *Everyone* would've trusted him because that's how pedophiles work. Befriend the adults. Befriend the kids. Get everyone to think they're the good guys.

Then get them away somewhere private.

Make them believe that this is a *good* thing. A way to show I love you.

My skin prickling beneath his touch, I wait for him to stroke my left nipple, mapping his position in my mind. His arms are longer than mine, but his left one is twisted. He won't be able to move it fast enough to block me.

He pinches my bud with his right hand, and I explode into action, grabbing his thumb and wrenching his arm to the side. It *cracks*! He screams. His body will bend at the shoulder, an instinctive reaction to stop it from breaking. But he's too close to the edge of the bed, so he will wobble, trying to keep his balance – too inexperienced in fighting to know he should take the fall and use it to throw me off my attack.

He wobbles, and I lunge forward, pushing off my toes, my legs springing me towards his neck. I switch the way I'm holding the fork and shove it sideways into his throat, then wrench it free as fast as I can, letting the blood spurt free. The sudden drop in blood pressure will make him lose consciousness quickly. He falls off the bed. I go with him, still holding his thumb, using it as a way to *see* his body.

We hit the ground, and now I release his hand to cup the side of his face, mapping it. My thumb feathers his check, telling me where I need to aim, and I plunge the fork into his other eye, not wanting to risk stabbing my own hand.

His gurgle of pain cuts off. The fork doesn't go as deep as I want it to though, so I reach behind me and search for the tray. I grab it, twist around, and hammer it onto the top of the fork, forcing it deeper into his brain, killing him quickly. Now they'll need a necromancer to bring him back; a healer won't do shit.

I scream as I sag forward. My shame doesn't dissipate with his life though. His death doesn't fix what I did. The only thing that'll soothe that pain is the V.

No.

It's the only thing that will make life bearable.

Don't.

With numb arms, I search Bear's pockets.

You promised to get clean.

FORTY-FOUR

HIM

"Well, this is fucking depressing," Aleric says as he stares at the picture he's holding in his hands. "I thought you said you could draw? I was really rooting for you to survive this round."

The kid in front of him starts to cry as Vlad shows me down the stairs of his boss' house. "Aleric," Vlad says.

He sighs as he crumbles up the drawing. "I'm kind of in the middle of cooking here, boo."

"Dinner can wait."

"It took me forty-five minutes to prepare this –"

"It. Can. Wait."

He sighs even more exaggerated this time. "You're lucky you're my favourite kid," he says as he turns around to us. He tosses the crumbled pic over his shoulder. "Get back in your cage, Bella. I'll need to think of a tiebreaker between you and Blue anyway."

His eyes slide to mine. "You look like shit." He chuckles.

"And not a healthy shit either but one of those you get after eating at Ta–"

"You wanted to know about Mother and Caden," I cut in, not in the fucking mood for any of his shit. My jaw clenches at that, but he doesn't smirk at me like he normally would. His eyes are on his second as he sticks both of his hands in the pockets of his surfer shorts and rocks back on his heels.

"Am I killing him?" he asks joyfully.

"No," Vlad says as I stop on the stairs, only a couple steps from the bottom. The hairs on my neck rise. I don't know what I have just done to insult him, but if he's this volatile, perhaps this isn't the best time to strike a deal. I don't have much control of my magic, and I can't move fast enough to draw a knife before he's on me. None of my brothers know where I am either; I snuck out of the house after they fell asleep so I could have this meeting in private.

I am completely alone in the lion's den.

But Micha's pain is eating at me even through the walls I keep erecting, so I can't turn back now. Not when he could have the answers I need to save her.

"Pity." He inhales strongly, his smile one of ease. "You would've been a lovely meal. All that magic in your veins." He walks towards me, and I stand still, unflinching.

"Tell me everything you know about blood bonds, and I'll make sure Mother answers all your questions," I say.

"If I wanted lies from her, I would've asked her."

"What do you want then?" I have already told him all I know, but he refuses to accept my answers. So if he wants something I cannot give, then I'll have to revert to Plan B – figuring out a way to beat the information I want out of him.

Except, he's a masochist as well as a sadist, and he cares about no one but himself. Torturing him will be damn near impossible, but I'll figure out a way to break him. Even if I have to use Mother to do it.

There is not a single line I will not cross to save my wife.

"That cage Maddox made for the Shadow Domain," he casually says. "I want to go in it."

"Fine." I don't ask him why because I don't give a shit. All I care about right now is the intel inside his head. I've used up too much of the blood bond; every time I pulse, the uncontrollable burst of magic destroys the wall I put up between me and Micha; in the time it takes me to rebuild, I can feel so much of her pain. Even now, it lingers in the back of my throat, a heavy weight in my chest, and I'm terrified I'll use up just enough to not make it in time to save her. I need to figure out a way to extend it.

"While it's in the Shadow Domain," he adds on. "Pull me out every few days, but I want to be in there for a year – unless I decide I'm done with it."

My eyes narrow as curiosity starts to dig its claws in. I push it aside, however, staying focused on why I'm here. "Fine, but the book you read about blood bonds, I want it first."

"It's gone."

"Bullshit." Knowledge is power, and barely anything is known about blood bonds. He'd be able to name his price to anyone who wants to look at it – just like he has with me. Over and over again, as long as it stays in his possession.

He holds up both hands and shakes them in exasperation. "Okay, yeah, you got me. It's upstairs."

He vanishes in the blink of an eye.

Vlad reaches for me, but I step back. "Why did he ask you if I was to die?"

His jaw tics. "He thought you saved Micha but not Rudy."

My eyes narrow, but his hand is on me, and my thoughts are ripped away as we phase.

We land in a library with a tall ceiling, two floors high, but Aleric is nowhere to be found. The door opens before I can ask where he is, and he strolls in with a small leather book in his hand.

"This stays here," he says. I reach for it, but he pulls it back. "And you're to tell no one about it. I'll take a blood oath now."

Paranoia burns a brand into my brain, urging me to give it thought – a blood oath cannot be broken without severe consequences. I pull a folding knife from my pocket, then lift up my shirt. Cutting the palm is only done on TV and for initiation rituals that symbolize the giving of the hand, of one's service. Otherwise, it's a dumb place to cut as the wound gets agitated all the fucking time.

I look down at the flat of my stomach. Normally, I would choose the top of my forearm, but I don't want Khalid to know what I've done.

"With the gift of the gods," I say as I carve a V into my flesh, "I bind their blessing to my oath." Breaking it means I won't just be risking my life, I'll be risking the wrath of the gods. "I'll never mention the next book I touch to anyone other than the two vampires with me now."

"Or take it from this room," Aleric adds.

"Or take it from this room." I add an S after the V, then wipe my blade across my thigh, fold it, and slip it back into my pocket. Still holding my shirt up with one hand, I use the other to gather up a bit of blood and draw a silence rune over my initials.

The magic of the oath pulses through me – hot and cold, life and death, a blessing and a curse. "It is done."

Aleric tosses me the book, and I catch it. My eyes widen as my gaze flies back to his in a rage. "This is Caden's Book of Shadows," I say through clenched teeth.

"Hence why you can't fucking talk about it." He grins cheekily. "Sau will be pissed to know I have it."

"You stole it."

"What? No!" He slaps both his hands over his cheeks and turns to Vlad. "How could you let me stoop so low! Letting me take the pups from the school to force them to compete to live another day is one thing, but *stealing?* Dude! You're supposed to be my moral compass!" He turns to me as my jaw tics. One of these days, I'm going to kill him – once he stops being so fucking useful as an ally.

He smirks at me as he drops his hands. "What are you looking for anyway? I might be able to save you some time reading it."

He's fishing for information, wanting to see what else he can use against me. Ignoring him, I flip open my father's grimoire. Feelings of loss and discomfort settle in my belly as I stare at his name, signed in thick black ink across the first page.

Calen Shadow

He wrote this after he married my mother – the Shadow last name is always the one taken.

And he didn't abandon us because of me, because I failed to hit my ascension. Because he knew I wasn't his but was the firstborn of another man... He left because of *her.*

The emotions inside of me swirl, a cesspool of memories rising up to complicate them even more. He used to always have time for us. It didn't matter how many drawings or bugs we wanted to show him. Or at what hour we decided to wake him. He was always there – loving, laughing, and he never treated me any differently to his *real* sons.

Until he started to drink.

Until whatever Mother did to him cut too deep to bear; he isn't innocent for his actions, but neither is she.

My stomach clenches, wondering about the secret she's still keeping hidden. Is it in here? The reason father finally left? Was it merely the cost of creating the blood bond like she claims? Or was it something else? Something –

"Watch him while I go eat," Aleric says, and I push those

thoughts aside. "If he tries to leave with it or make copies, come get me. I could use a good hunt. The kids run *soooo* slow." He vanishes with a drawn-out sigh, but neither Vlad nor I pay him any mind.

I flip through the leather-bound book, searching for the information I need.

"How are we going to save him?" Vlad demands, his voice tight, his thick arms crossed over his chest.

Not them. *Him.* The man he can't help but care for.

I walk over to an armchair and collapse inside it, my head lowered to read. I skim the pages, flipping past spells and notes about magic and creatures of sacrifice, searching for something about blood bonds.

"I don't know yet," I say honestly. We've gone through four teleporters so far, and they've all said the same thing. Eduardo's safety spells aren't difficult to break, but he'll know as soon as we tamper with them. I need a witch who is stronger than he is, more clever, but Ryker, the Boss on the other side of the portal, refuses to kidnap anyone of status. It's too risky, and there isn't an amount I can pay or a threat I can make that will make it worth his while. He'd rather lose the portal entirely than draw the attention of the Elv've'Nor. Smuggling people to Earth and dealing in illegal human goods is only a fraction of his empire.

And I don't have the resources or knowledge to slaughter his soldiers and hold off any reinforcements until I find a powerful teleporter myself.

All we can do is watch the teleportation circles so we can grab Antonio or Eduardo if they try to use them. Neither of them have been seen though; the witch must be leaving the boat to get food and supplies, but he's using a circle we don't fucking know about.

If we break into his network, we'd be able to track all of them eventually, but the risk of him having more than one network is too great. He could just destroy the one we have access to, and then we won't have any way in at all.

So we're forced to wait.

But I can't wait any longer. He has my *wife.*

"But the book will help?" Vlad demands.

"Not Rudy," I say softly. My chest tightens as I look up at him. "Khalid says they haven't broken him yet."

"What are they doing to him?" His voice is tight, his control held only just. It's the first time he's asked, but I know he's been slipping down the same edge I've been for a while.

"Attempting to breed him."

"He's gay."

"They're giving him Ricks." The male equivalent of a V.

Vlad turns from me so I can't see the pain on his face, but I don't need to when his soul screams just like mine. I look back down at the book in my hands, searching for any way to stave off the payment of the blood bond. She's been gone for nine-and-a-half weeks. With how much I pulled on the magic to find her and how much of her emotions I have felt since... Khalid thinks we might only have four or five weeks left before it starts to kill her.

And so I read because I know in the pit of my soul that we will not save her before then.

We might not save her at all...

FORTY-FIVE

HIM

My eyes are going three rounds with my heart, beating the shit out of it, pinning it in a corner and not giving it any room to fight back. To defend itself. It can't even fucking *breathe.* My father's words are burrowing into my skull, hammering fist after fist into the pit of my soul, and I surge to my feet on the last page. As that last word delivers the knockout blow.

My whole body trembling, I flip the book upside down, spread it open, and shake it. Praying something falls out. Some last scrap of paper. A wayward note to tell me if the spell he detailed worked. Nothing.

"Aleric!" I shout as I shake the grimoire harder. But I've been through every page. I know there's nothing else tucked inside it. Twisting the book around, I run my fingers along the inside of the front, then back cover, seeing if there's a hidden pocket anywhere.

"What is it?" Vlad demands, his voice tight, but he does

not have the information I want, so I ignore him. I stride towards the door, though I'm not certain if he'll reappear before I get there or if he'll let me walk out of here just to see the blood bond bite me in the ass.

My feet grind to a halt, my brain finally pulling on their reins. Of course he'd let me deliberately break my oath and watch as the gods punish me. He's *Aleric.*

"What. Is. It?" Vlad demands again, his voice ice cold. He phases in front of me, his eyes turning a ruby red as the control on his rage slips.

My Craving surges forward, always lying in the pit of my stomach, a cancer spreading out. It wants to match his bloodthirst, and I take a step back, my nostrils flaring, my hands shaking. Vampires can feed on each other, and his pulse calls to me like a late night snack.

His eyes narrow. "You've not been feeding."

"How well did you know Caden?" I demand, changing the subject to something that actually matters. Vlad was around before the treaty Mother forced them all to sign; he might know something I can use.

His lips tighten, but his eyes shift back to their normal green. Not quite as radiant as Rudy's, but darker, like the heart of a forest whose roots are awash with blood. He holds on sharper to his control for me – and for him. The Craving is a breaking of the mind, an individual's reduction from man to beast, but it is also semi-contagious, able to spread like a mob's mentality. Like pollen through a forest, infecting an entire vamp nest or wolf pack with its madness. Temporarily, perhaps, but the damage would be done.

"He was ruthless, and there wasn't a line he wouldn't cross to protect the Shadow Family… or your mother." He looks away, wrestling with his rage. Given Caden killed Vlad's sister, I can guess the rest of his thoughts.

"What happened between the three of them?" I demand, finally curious, finally needing to know so I can make sense of the book of shadows in my hands. The one that ends on a spell that'll destroy the blood bond as if it never were.

He looks back at me, studying me. He knows I'm not asking just for midnight gossip. Breathing out heavily, his jaw tics as he says, "Caden loved your mother, but Aleric wanted her. I can't speak on her feelings –"

"But she never squirted with your father," Aleric cuts in as he saunters back into the library.

The urge to hit him is almost stronger than the Craving. I clench the grimoire tight as I hold it up. "Did he do it?"

Is that why he left? Why she's so ashamed to talk about it? He gave her everything, and all she had were regrets? Or did he do it when he came back?

Aleric shrugs a lazy shoulder, but his eyes are sharp and obsessive. "He was nauseatingly lovesick. Who knows?"

"You said you knew him well."

"Better than anyone," he says easily. "Including his wife and brother."

"Did he do it?" I demand again.

Can I replicate it from afar? Break the bond so we have more time to save Micha?

Aleric stares at me for a long moment before he says, "I think he might've tried."

"When?"

He smiles. "Come on now. Use that big brain of yours."

My eyes narrow, but I don't let my annoyance get in the way. "When he supposedly cursed her?" I glance down at the book in my hand. "Breaking the blood bond requires a lot of power." It could've pulled on hers, sapping her energy and making her think he'd cursed her. It could've pulled on his, killing him… or just making him seem dead.

"He never would've cursed her," he says simply. "Like I said, he was disgustingly obsessed with her well-being."

But that doesn't tell me if he succeeded. I couldn't feel Micha when she was in the Shadow Domain and I was here.

We're not fully bonded, so maybe that's why, or maybe –

My heart skids to a stop as my eyes snap to his. "Why do you want to go into the Plane of Monsters?" I ask. Even if what he thinks is true, that Caden didn't sacrifice himself to curse Mother, what can he possibly expect to find there? Either he was dead when she took him into her shadows, or he was close enough to it that the monsters would've made quick work of him.

Unless he failed. Unless the blood bond still runs through his veins, and Mother's blood has kept him safe all this time.

Aleric's grin widens, his dark-eyes growing wild. "He's like a cockroach. I'd bet Vlad's ballsack he's still alive."

"And you want to kill him," I breathe. Mother said he has a map of the Plane of Monsters. He knows the world. He could hunt Caden down and make sure he'll never be able to come home and save Sau from his 'attentions.'

Aleric breaks out in laughter. "Not at all. I want to bring him back." He scoffs. "Sau can't *choose* me if there's no one to choose between. Duh."

I stare at him in disbelief, then shake my head. If he wants to believe that Mother will *ever* be tempted to choose him, that's his delusion to bear. I need to focus on saving my wife.

"Do you know if he made another grimoire after this?" I demand, getting back onto the subject of what I came here for.

He shakes his head. "That was his last one, kiddo. There's no more notes other than what's in there."

Meaning there's no way to know if what he tried even worked. This book – *this hope* is just another dead end.

A fucking *dead. End.*

My hand trembles from the agony, but I clench my fist until my knuckles turn white. Not letting it consume me.

Not letting it break me.

Because there is still one way to save her.

The blood bond won't take her life if I give up mine.

So if the time comes where I use too much, it will not be her who dies.

FORTY-SIX

HIM

I step out of Aleric's house to find Khalid waiting for me by my car. His eyes are hard as he looks me over, no doubt checking to see if I'm hurt. Enoch is beside him, smelling as if he's been scolded; his hormones all over the place. Shame. Guilt. Embarrassment. Frustration. And worry.

"You should have woken me," Enoch says. He's my new bodyguard, the new reaper now that Leno's dead and Khalid has been forced to become secondborn.

"You should've known," Khalid corrects, his voice flat as he opens the door to the driver's seat. A silent demand for us all to get in so he can scold us in private. If the vampires think there is any discord amongst our ranks, they might think we're divided enough to attack.

Wincing, Enoch starts to reach for the passenger door, knowing this is unavoidable, but a quick glance from Khalid has him freezing. *"Shit,"* he thinks – his thoughts written all over his face.

He looks back at me. The reaper isn't to get in until I do. He's to keep an eye on my surroundings, ready to intercept any threat – which means waiting for me outside of the car, not in it.

He shouldn't be in this role.

Leno –

My throat tight, I look at Khalid. "He drives."

His lips tighten, but he nods at Enoch. After I slip into the backseat, Khalid mirrors me on the other side. Usually, I drive as I'm the weakest link. If we're attacked, the stronger ones should be free to defend us, but Enoch can drive with his telekinesis and still attack too, and I want to see the soul dolls.

"Show me Rudy," I say as Enoch peels off down the drive, back towards our house.

"He's alive."

"Show me."

Swirling his hand over his lap, he pulls a pool of shadows onto his thigh, then pulls Rudy's soul doll from it. It's in one piece; Eduardo stitched him back together with his magic.

Picking it up, Khalid closes his eyes as he listens to what is happening around our brother and sees what he does. I do not doubt that he keeps the darker stuff to himself, secreting the truth so it's only his pain to bear.

"There's been no change," he says after a few seconds, meaning Rudy's magic is still under wraps. For now. But if they break him, he will lose hold of the control he grips so tightly. His power isn't like normal. Most witches take the energy in their veins and manipulate it into what they want, but if a pregnant mother's hit with a violent spell, then their fetus, if they survive, is born with chaos magic.

Meaning, Rudy's seeps from his skin and feeds on the fears and nightmares of those around him. Then it runs back to him, its belly full with the equivalent of a grenade about to go off. It is a constant battle of wills to keep it from exploding, so if he loses his mind through Ricks or pain... it *will* erupt from him, affecting friends and foes alike.

But he will kill himself before then. We all know it.

"And Micha," I murmur.

"Varius –" he starts as he deposits Rudy's soul doll back into his shadows.

"*Show me.*"

He stares at me. His lips tighten into a line of fucking stubbornness. "No," he says. "It'll affect your judgement, and it's already clearly impaired as you went to *Aleric's* without any back-up –"

"I needed to talk to him in private," I say tightly.

"Privacy doesn't mean you go on your own. We could have waited outside – like we did."

"If he wanted to kill me, he would just do it at our house."

His eyes narrow. "How?"

I shrug. "I don't know, but he clearly has a fucking way inside." I think about the porno I found playing in Mother's room when I went back to check on Micha. About the lotion he has her put on every night. Certain words he's said here and there... There's just been this constant itch under my skin when it comes to him and our ward.

"The sky," Khalid says, and now it's so fucking obvious. The ward isn't a dome, it's a fence that reaches a hundred feet into the sky and digs down into the earth. He must phase up high, then fall to the ground. Or phase to it. He is actually crazy enough to try. *Shit.*

"I'll get the others to close it," he says as he digs out his phone.

"No," I say. Mother would want to help, and she can't use magic yet. The build-up in her blood is still too high. It's going to take months, perhaps even a year or so for it to dissipate back to normal levels. If she uses a large amount of power before then, she could develop loka, a magical cancer that is always terminal.

Plus, we'd need to tell Aleric so the idiot doesn't find out when he next decides to 'drop in for an unexpected visit.' As much as we'd all love to see him dead, his death would lead to too much of a power vacuum. When Micha and Rudy come home, I don't want them to be stepping into another war.

"Leave it in case we need a trap later," I say instead, and Khalid nods. He types out a text anyway, no doubt telling everyone about the hole in our security.

"You still shouldn't have left on your own," he says when he looks up. "It was foolish and stupid."

"You all have my number." If Antonio got spotted, they could've reached me. I would've convinced Aleric to take me there. But it's been months, and no one's fucking seen him.

Khalid's jaw tics. I know that isn't what he meant, but I don't care.

"You'd do anything for your girl," I say quietly. I don't admit I have forgotten her name. She's changed it recently anyway. Lou is teaching her how to summon eknor demons, and it's dangerous to use your birth name with them. So she decided she wanted a full change with her new life.

I'm pretty sure it starts with a K now though – or maybe an R?

I don't care enough to find out right now. "Now show me my wife."

He stares at me for a moment, then says, "Enoch?"

"Fuck," is muttered from the driver's seat, too soft for Khalid to hear. I only just pick it up with my hybrid senses. This is a test to see how he handles his new job as reaper – making decisions for the good of the Family.

My hands tighten, certain he will side with Khalid just because he's being trained by –

"Show him," he says, and I exhale sharply as I glance at him, then at Khalid.

My brother's face is a complete mask as he pulls on his shadows. "Wrong," he says, but he obeys the reaper's order.

"What else is new?" Enoch mutters as he takes a turn. "And it's not like you're doing a great job in your new role either. The Underboss is supposed to be *approachable* so the men feel like they can talk to you about any problems. But has anyone done that? No. Because you have the aura of a killer clown."

Khalid's mask doesn't shift an inch, but I know him well enough to know that stung. He takes his responsibilities all too seriously, and if my mind wasn't obsessed with getting Micha and Rudy back home, I would wonder what he was thinking of as a way to be more *approachable* to our men.

If Micha were here, would we have laughed about it?

The thought of laughter seems so foreign right now.

Closing his eyes, Khalid connects himself to my wife.

The seconds drag out in tense silence. All my hairs stand on end. My skin itches. Feeling foreign. I stare at his face, doing my best to decipher any subtle changes, but it is a mask like always.

Then his eyes finally open.

And he turns to me.

"She's –" he starts before the slam of the brakes cut him off. My head jerks forward to see Aleric's appeared in the middle of the road, with both his hands up. Khalid starts to pull on his magic anyway; I can feel it electrifying the air, but now Aleric's in the car with us.

"Antonio's been spotted in Mljet, Croatia," he says as he reaches across Khalid and grabs me. Then we're gone, my brothers left behind, though I do not doubt they'll be quick to follow. I caught Vlad's scent a second before we phased.

FORTY-SEVEN

NAMELESS

It's the breeze of a cave,
The crack of a whip,
The smallest silver lining
The downed horse's nip
To tell me it's alive
Able to carry on.

A fucking con.

The breeze comes from collapsing rock.
The crack not on air but your broken back.
The horse's nip is toothed decay,
A rotting carcass well on its way.

No. The shimmer, the glimmer, the pleasure is here.
Somewhere.

Somewhere.

Somewhere?

It has to be. It can't just be dark.
It can't just be me in this misery.

The silver, the bronze, the rusted old metal
The lining...

The line...

Where is the fucking line?

Feeling the breeze, I run towards the exit
Only to find crumbling rock.
Feeling the crack, I sigh in relief
Only to raggedly scream.
Feeling the nip, I grin at my last friend
Only to see death's marching end.

STOP!

It loves me.
It loves me.
Don't tell me the lies.

The drink isn't the solution.

I'm alive. I'm alive.

It's my friend.
It's my friend.

No.

It's helping me.

Why can't you see?
Why can't you see, you fucking bitch?
It's helping me!
You just want me to die.
You want me to suffer
A stick in your eye
A hole in your lover.

I hate you.

Fuck you.
Just fuck you.
Just fucking fuck you!

Where is the bottle?
Where is my drink?
Where is the drowning
Of my misery?

I don't know anyone by that name.
Stop talking to me!
I hate you.
Just go away.

What did you say? You fucking bitch?
I don't need you.
I don't want you.
You're not a friend.

Stop!
Just stop!

Where are you?
Why have you gone?
Why have you left me?

They always leave.
Everyone leaves.

Why have you left me?

Varius...
Rafiki...

Even me...

Only the bottle is your friend.
Only the bottle never leaves.

Mi...
Mi...
Who is Mi?

Does it matter?
Just drink.

Yes...
Drink
Drink to end the misery.

FORTY-EIGHT

NAMELESS

"Fuck! He'll kill me for this!" Sunny's words bounce off my brain, not heavy enough to penetrate the depths of the V-haze.

My orgasm is so close. I'm going to come on Bear's face, the fork I embedded into his eye, the only thing I could find to fuck. I'm facing backwards so his nose rubs the front of my pussy. My hands are wrapped around his chin as I ride him hard. The fork moves inside his brain with every jerk of my hips, and his insides squelch as they squeeze up out of his socket.

The potion itself gives me a high, but the intensity of the orgasm is what I'm after. That moment where nothing else exists but the glorious feeling of pleasure, no pain.

No pain.

A rough hand grabs me on the bicep and wrenches me off the fork handle. I scream as I reach for the corpse, trying to find my way back to it. I need that release.

He grabs my other arm and shakes me. "Stop!"

"Just fuck me," I beg, reaching between us to pull at his clothes. I don't need the fork if I have his cock in my hole.

"Shit. Tim! Get your fucking ass in here!"

He spins me around, trying to stop my groping hands. So I cup my own pussy. I don't need the fork. I don't need him. I just need the high.

As footsteps echo towards us, Sunny wraps both his arms around me, then grabs my wrists when that doesn't stop me. He jerks my arms behind my back, and I cry out.

The newcomer stops in front of me and snickers. "Let her go. I want to see her do whatever she was doing to Bear."

"Fuck off and get Terra."

"You just told me to get in here," Sadist drawls. "Also, she specializes in diseases. She isn't a healer." He laughs coldly. "Eduardo's due back with our Boss at any moment. You're so fucked."

Sunny's grip tightens on my hands. "Help me with this," he says, "and I'll tell you what happened to your brother."

Even through my desperate need to get off, I can feel the tension exploding in the room. It gives me pause, a warning blare going off somewhere beneath the rubble of my soul. I still in Sunny's grip, wondering if he's using me as a shield.

All this time, Sadist has taken delight in hurting anyone around him. Like I've chased the V, he's chased sadism, but there's always been a selfish, indifferent air to his actions. A transfer of pain from him to his victims. That's gone now.

It's been replaced by a feral need that feels too much like hope. A tight voice that quivers. A tension that suffocates.

"You don't know shit about him," he says. "He was gone long before you arrived."

"I met him right before I was picked up. He was looking for you."

"He's still alive?" he breathes.

"Yes."

"If you're lying to me –" He cuts himself off, his voice shaking.

"You'll kill me, I know."

"*No.* No, death will be too fucking *kind*," he hisses. "Tell me where you saw him and when."

"Help me with her –" Sunny pivots behind me, jerking me with him, keeping me in front. I'm absolutely a shield. I push back against his hips, my hands groping for his cock. I do not fear death; I fear living.

I fear the voices in my head.

The *choices* I've made.

I can feel Sadist's body heat right in front of me. Can feel the danger of his wrath. "Prove that you aren't lying."

Sunny talks low and fast. "He said you took his place in this program. And before that, you took the blows that were meant for him. You were always protecting him. He has a limp from where your dad beat him – and you gave yourself that same injury so when Antonio's pack caught you, they thought they had him."

"You could've found all this out –"

"How?"

There's a moment of silence, Sadist vibrating with energy in front of me. I can almost feel his utter terror to believe in something that will break him if it's false. Hope is such a terrible thing…

Tears burning my eyes, I try to get Sunny hard so I can escape this conversation, this world entirely, but he stays limp beneath my palm.

"Why have you never told me?" Sadist finally asks.

Sunny laughs hollowly. "Because you're a dick, and I'm an opportunist. Now help me with her because if Antonio comes back and finds out I'm the one who got her hooked on V, he'll kill me, and you'll never get your answers."

He curses.

The next second, he's down on his knees and lifting my

legs over his shoulders.

"What are you doing?" Sunny demands.

"She's addicted. Unless you want her riding whatever she was of Bear's, I suggest you help me calm her down."

His lips press against me. His tongue strokes between my pussy, and I arch against his face on a cry. Sunny's hands release my wrists, and I reach up behind me to grab a fistful of his hair with one hand, and the other, I slip into the fine strands of Sadist's. Sunny massages my breasts from behind, playing with my nipples. His lips and tongue run across my neck, then sucks on the base, and I scream.

Sheer pleasure cascades over me, rushing through me like a broken dam. As I convulse between the two of them, they continue to kiss me in two separate places, forcing me to ride the tremors until I can't feel anything other than this.

No pain.

No pain...

My legs drop to the ground. A hand grabs my chin, and a voice whispers in my ear, "If you want more V, you'll agree with whatever we say. Do you understand me?"

I nod on a sigh.

Anything at all...

They toss me down onto the bed, and I laze out like a cat, burrowing my head into the pillows with a sigh. But just as I'm about to drift off into sleep, a dark cloud storms in on the horizon.

I tense, my breath catching as the air electrifies with an alpha's presence. And he's *pissed.*

My mind screams with danger.

Take shelter.

But there's nowhere in here for me to hide.

"Antonio –" Sunny starts, a hint of panic pitching his tone. "We didn't know Bear was giving her V. He was the one taking care of her. We haven't been –" he cuts himself off, and I can almost hear his swallow of nerves, my senses on high alert.

Run.

Run!

Run!

I try to struggle to my feet, but I can't remember how to work my limbs. They feel so damn floaty, all the way up there on cloud nine.

"Check her," Antonio says, his voice a shock to my system. Terrible memories start to rise. *"Heal her."*

"She's coming with us."

A little girl, too small to survive outside the womb, is held in the palm of his hand.

No!

I stumble to my feet. Arms grab me. I scream and kick, desperate to escape the nightmares shouting inside my head.

I need more V.

I need more V!

"She's still carrying," Eduardo says as his hands push on my stomach, a warmth spreading inside me despite the chill of my marrow.

No! Don't remind me something's in there.

Get it out!

Get it out!

Get it out!

Screaming, I dig my nails into my stomach. They jerk my hands away. Antonio's presence burns like the devil's touch, a hot metal rod shoved straight into my heart.

"You *killed her.*" I sag forward, held up only by their hands, my body shaking, my heart aching. I suck in giant gulps of air as my lungs struggle to process its arrival. I start to hyperventilate. I can't breathe. My fractured mind shoves sharp shards of memories down my throat. Makes me choke on them. Makes me *bleed.*

"You killed her!" I yell, lifting my head, feeling my rage. Grabbing hold of that instead of my grief.

His voice appears right in front of me. "Who?" he says so casually, it's like a slap across my face.

I lunge for him, trying to bite whatever I can reach. The men hold me tighter – until Antonio slams his head into mine, then they release me, and I stumble back a few steps. Pain explodes through my skull. Large, callous hands lock around my wrists as I start to fall. My legs are numb, my entire body feeling foreign, but he holds me steady.

Pulls me close.

"Did you even have a name for her?" he murmurs with too much cruelty to bear.

I kick out, hitting one of his shins. Twisting me around, he shoves me forward. I stumble across the floor, then into a wall. My head aches from the sudden contact, a migraine of pain spreading down my face. He presses in close behind me, one hand pushing on the back of my head, the other twisting my right arm in pain.

My knees buckle as I sob in grief.

I call her Rafiki because it was the first name Varius offered, but we never agreed.

We never properly talked about it.

Just jokes and laughter.

We made *jokes*, and she died nameless.

Without ever knowing she *belonged.* That she was loved. Because of *him.*

I struggle against him, my fury renewed, but he just waits for me to tire myself out. It doesn't take long. I've been so used to being broken, feeling any other emotion is exhausting.

Collapsing against the wall, I cry myself dry.

His lips press against my left ear. Whispers so quietly, I almost miss it over my heaving sobs. "Well, I had names for mine."

FORTY-NINE

ANTONIO

June 23 1907, Jacksonville, Florida

"Evening, mister. Wanna warm me up tonight?"

I ignore the whore on the docks as I make my way to my Boss' office. If it was up to me, I'd take her some place quiet and kill her, but Oscar likes them hanging around. No better way to finish a meeting than by sticking his dick in a couple of whores. He also thinks they'll act as a look-out if the cops arrive – and failing that, they will be a distraction, giving us time to get away while they get carted off – sometimes to be arrested, other times to be fucked in a train or gangbang in exchange for being let go with just a warning.

This particular whore has been picked up half a dozen times from here, but she keeps coming back because sailors are an easy score. Most aren't married, and those that are – well, their missuses don't travel with them.

"Oh, come on, big daddy, I'll make it worth your while." She lifts her red skirt up slowly, revealing her ankle, then her knee. She trails her own hand along her skin. "You can help me just like this…"

My jaw tightens. Filth like her should be cleaned from the city. If only they'd all been burned in the fire of 1901, but they weren't the focus of that attack. We were.

After we took a few key streets of Jacksonville, Florida, from the Blood Fangs, they decided to try to burn us out by sacrificing the whole damn city. Their Boss is a genuine psychopath. This gang war isn't business or retaliation for him like it is for us or the Shadow Domain. It's pure, simple pleasure.

"Like what you see?" the whore purrs as she swishes the red fabric back and forth across her leg.

"No." I stride past her, leaving her spitting curses. But a whore like her can never give me what I need.

Slipping a hand into my pocket, I pull out my gold watch and flip it open. I don't look at the time though; I know I'm ten minutes early. Instead, my eyes fasten onto the painting on the other side. The one of a wide-eyed girl with the biggest, goofiest smile.

"Look what I found! Isn't he just the cutest?"

I turn around, expecting her to have brought back some stray cat like she has in the past. My heart jumps sixteen feet into the air, and I damn near follow it. "Godsdammit, Siome!" I shout. "That is an alligator!"

"It's actually a crocodile –"

"That's worse!"

"You mean better!" she squeals. Holding the hatchling up to her face, she kisses him on the nose. "He's so pretty. Can we keep him?"

"No."

"Why not?"

"Because when he grows up, he'll eat you."

"Ah." She nods sagely. "And you don't like it when other males get to eat me."

She laughs as I choke on my next breath.

Dear gods, my little helfire is going to be the death of me.

I snap the pocket watch closed. Thinking about her right now is dangerous. I need to keep my head cleared for this meeting. We're about to hit the Shadow Domain in only a few hours.

Marching towards the office at the docks, I slip inside and nod at the man at the door. He isn't a wolf like me, but he's loyal to the cause. He lost his older brother to the Blood Fangs, then his parents to the witches. He will give his life for us – a price he will undoubtedly pay. Everyone dies in this war.

But not her.

She's safe out west. In a stable pack. In a well-established territory. She's even mated to some fucker now, and he can give her the peace I cannot.

Forcing her from my mind, I make my way into the back room. It's already filled with capos – all women par one, but none of them greet me. I am just a lowly soldier. Oscar's perfect killing machine, his favorite hitman. Which makes them scared of me. They know I have the skill to kill them and take their title, and I have the favoritism of the Boss. After all, one cannot rise in rank if all the rungs are filled.

But I've never been interested in politics.

I'm pissed off enough with the world the way it is. I don't need to be involved with people actively trying to make it worse. I might take orders from Oscar, but he knows better than to try to use me for his own personal gain.

I fight for the innocents trapped in this war. For people like Siome. Not him.

My eyes narrow as I clock movement towards me. All those around me move away, able to smell my irritation. They know how fast I can shift into my wolf form. What takes them minutes takes me only seconds, and I can handle the pain enough to fight back even while I change.

The woman walking towards me, however, only hesitates a half-step before she continues. Her dark hair is cut to her shoulders, and she wears pants instead of the dresses of the whores out on the docks. But she's still a whore – always tossing herself at me, as if I'd be happy to take any scraps.

Because that's all every woman is compared to Siome.

Fucking scraps.

"I hear we're hitting a drug den," she says.

I don't look at her, knowing I will get told what I need to soon enough. The meeting's to start in three minutes, and Oscar is never late.

"Maybe we can grab a couple Ricks and Vs," she says as she sidles closer to me.

Now I do look at her.

My eyes flash dangerously, and she sucks in a breath as she takes a step back. Fear paints the air sickly sweet, and one of the other capos call her name as Oscar steps into the room. Taking the out she was given, the whore scurries off.

My irritation doesn't wane though, and the space around me doesn't fill. All through the meeting, I'm left alone. My arms crossed, I listen to the plan Oscar gives us.

While everyone storms the east side of the warehouse, I'm to go in through the west. Working alone is how I work best – no one to babysit; no one to try to keep safe. Then we're to destroy the warehouse and any product inside. The drugs might be worth millions, but taking them would cause more trouble than they're worth.

As long as we scorch it, our war stays with the Shadow Domain. But if we start dealing the Ricks and Vs ourselves, we will be targeted by every dealer of it in the world. The Mattos twins, the two geniuses who make the potions, are notoriously strict about who they sell to and who is allowed to distribute for them. There's a list of detailed requirements their partners must adhere to, and one of those is to kill any unauthorized traders.

So if we try to sell even a single vial, we'll instantly put a multi-billion dollar bounty on our heads and create enemies on every continent.

The Mattos twins are not ones for mercy.

We move out, a dozen of us stalking through the city in our human forms. Oscar only joins us as far as the whores on the docks though. That is where he stops; he hasn't got his own hands bloody in a long time.

We continue through the cloud-covered night, weaving our way through quiet streets until we reach the outskirts of the city, where humans are few. They might not know about our existence, but they know danger haunts these woods. They know better than to be out this late alone.

Slipping into the cover of the trees, we strip out of our clothes, then shift. Pain cuts through our skin – a curse of the gods, the consequence of some ancient sin. Grunts and growls rip through the group, and even I'm not quiet as the intensity increases, but at least mine doesn't last long. Shaking out my red fur, I push to my feet, towering over them. Most of our soldiers are female due to the make-up of our pack – one alpha male, a few betas, and the rest women, but werewolf males are still bigger. Stronger.

My eyes slip to the whore in the middle of her change, and terror permeates the air. They are all too aware that I could kill them one by one. I move too fast, when they don't shift fast enough.

But capo openings just cause strife within our Family. So I turn my gaze to the woods around us and breathe in deep, checking for any Bloods or Shades, standing watch while they finish.

Then we race through the trees as one, heading towards the secret outpost Oscar marked on a map. It's hidden by magic, but it's been scent-marked by a couple of our guys, and we turn our heads side to side, pinpointing its direction.

I veer off when we get close, and as the rest of them start

to target the east side, working to destroy the invisibility and protection ward by overloading it with their attacks, I wait on the western side. The air shimmers in front of me, the witches' pale-blue shield taking a hammering. It starts to weaken.

My fur stands on end as adrenaline rushes through me. I could probably push through the ward without dying right now, but I'm only resistant to magic, not immune.

If I calculate it wrong, I'm dead.

And so I wait.

It fizzes out in a few minutes. A wooden hut pops into view. As the sound of fighting dances through the trees, I streak towards the building in a blur of red fur. We only have ten, maybe fifteen minutes before more reinforcements arrive. They'll have a witch in there who knows how to scry, and they would have sent out a cry for help as soon we started attacking the ward.

Launching myself into the air, I crash through a window rather than the door. Rolling to my feet, I dart to the side and slice through the chest of the man I have taken by surprise. They've only left one guard for me, and I whip my head around, breathing in the smells to track where I need to go next.

But the whole place stinks of sex, Vs, and Ricks. We must've just interrupted an orgy – the dealers too tempted by their own product. If we don't kill them for their mistake, Delun Shadow will, so perhaps they haven't requested back-up at all. Perhaps they are dumb enough to think in their drug-induced state that they have what it takes to fend us off. To be the heroes and hide this mess from their Boss.

My cock twitches as the drugs in the air hook their claws into me. Ricks are the only way I've been able to get off in the eighty-two years since I chased Siome away. It still feels disgusting to get that release every few years, but at least with a Rick, the dick isn't 'mine.' It's a thing of magic with its own shape... And yet, I still kill the women after. Still feel the disgust too strongly. Like I'm cheating on her even though it's been decades since I've even seen her outside of the painting in my watch.

Shaking my head, I fight the effects of the drugs, but they've filled the place up like a fucking opium den. It's only a matter of time until I succumb. If they were having an orgy, then they have whores, and if any of them are wolves in heat and on V, then it will trigger a primal instinct I'll struggle to fight. There is a reason most packs are made up of women. Too many males cause too much trouble too easily.

Heading deeper into the house, I kill any witch I come across, biting off their heads or stabbing my claws through their hearts. I move quickly and efficiently, feeling the timer ticking down on my control.

I barge into a room, and my cock jumps to attention. Beneath the smoky haze of the drugs filling the place, I spot a woman I would know anywhere.

Her scent calls to me, fills me, demands I make her mine.

I dig my claws into the door frame on either side of me, my muscles rippling as I struggle to control the urges of the Ricks so potent in the air.

She lies naked on a bed with one hand between her legs. Multiple bottles of V lie around her – a few full, more of them empty. The smell of her pussy is all wrong, too twisted by the potions' own scents. Too filled with other men's cum.

A pack member screams from outside, but I ignore their cry for help.

All my attention is on my childhood sweetheart.

The woman I thought I'd saved.

Siome.

Shifting back into my human form, I stumble towards her.

She turns to look at me, but her eyes are all wrong. The

beautiful bright red delights are now dull and empty. Full of all the pain she was never supposed to experience. There's no recognition there, no big smile to greet me. There's just pure desperation. "Come fuck me," she purrs.

I flinch away even as my cock demands me forward. I don't want her like this though. Where she doesn't even know who I am.

My eyes fall to the glass bottles tossed beside her. To the addiction that's dug into her veins.

"I need to get you out of here."

"No," she cries, still riding her fingers. "Let me stay, big daddy. Let me stay, and I'll fuck you real good."

Ignoring the throbbing of my cock, I thank the gods she's not in heat. I pick up the bottles she has lined up on the bed, then throw them at the wall. They smash into pieces, and she screams like I've hit her.

"Stop!" she shrieks. "I've been good! I've sucked off all your friends. They fuck me whenever they want! Why are you doing this to me!"

She sits up as I peel off my shirt. She scrambles towards the wall and tries to lick the dripping liquid, but I grab her arm and pull her back.

"Siome, it's me! I need to get you out of here."

"No!"

I force my shirt on her, then lift her up and throw her over my shoulder.

"Get off me!" she screams as she pummels her fists into my back.

She bites me. Kicks me. Starts to cry.

Her tears have always stabbed like knives, and hearing them after eighty-two years of nothing is fucking lethal, but I push through the pain as I stumble out of the house.

"The V!" she screams. "At least go back for the V!"

FIFTY

HER

I sag down the wall as soon as he releases me. The fact he named his children weighs me down like a cinderblock around my feet. He's a monster. And yet even he is a better parent than me.

My heart breaking, I rasp, "I need some V."

"Why?" The word is short, clipped, a simple demand, but the heft of it is too much. An anchor to those cinderblocks.

A sob ruptures from me as I lean my head against the wall. "It *hurts*."

"What does?"

I slam my fist against my chest – once, twice, my mouth twisted in pain, unable to speak. I drop my hand to my belly, wishing I could feel her again.

Terrified I'll feel something else, I rip my hand away.

My tears come faster. I can't do this. I don't want to talk. I don't want to think. I don't want to *feel*.

"Tell me."

My throat closes. This is worse than anything Sadist has forced me to do. Worse than what I did to Bear. I flinch, hating the comparison, but that request just asked me to violate me and my morals. These questions? This incessant demand that I confront my own guilt? My *loss.*

I *can't.*

Then she'll really be gone, and I'll just be left with the truth of the monster in my belly. I know she's dead. I know he killed her, but these questions will lead to the first step of healing. To letting her go.

And *I can't.*

She's my baby.

She's my baby.

I can't heal and leave her behind.

Cradling my belly in my arms, I scream on broken sobs.

June 26 1907, St. Augustine, Florida – Antonio

I have fallen asleep to the screams of men dying. I have pulled shrieks from the mouths of many, cutting them into pieces, torturing them without a care. I have ignored the cries of pups as I slaughtered their parents. But hearing her whimpers, her moans of pain as she thrashes in bed –

I cannot bear it.

"Siome, *please!*" I beg as I hold her, wrapping my arms and legs around her. She fights me as I try to raise a bottle to her lips. "You need to drink something!" She needs to eat too. She's a bag of bones, wasting away, refusing anything that isn't V. I don't know how long it's been since she's had a proper meal, don't know how long she's suffered in that witch's den, but it's been three days since I rescued her, and she hasn't eaten a damn thing.

"So give me V!" she shouts. Then she jerks her head and bites me in the wrist, her canines digging deep. I clench my teeth in pain, but I don't try to shove her off. At least blood is something. It has to be better than nothing.

She releases me quickly enough on her own anyways, screaming for me to let her go. To let her run back to the men who "really love me." Who "actually care."

I want to go back and kill them all over again. I want to raise them from the dead and take my time.

But I'm terrified if I leave her, she'll find a way to kill herself – or leave to find more V. The Shadow Domain has hundreds, if not thousands, of drug dens over their territory, and the Mattos twins have suppliers all over the world. If she can't get it in St. Augustine, she'll just keep moving until she can.

A fist bangs on my door. "Antonio –" My Boss shouts over the screams of my only treasure. I can smell his alpha scent, the power he's trying to push out to bring me to heel.

My head whips in his direction, shifting into that of my wolf. A feral snarl rips from my throat, shaking the walls, and his fear permeates the place even through the closed door.

He might be an alpha, but he knows I can kill him. That the only reason I haven't is because I haven't had a reason to. But for her, I will. I'll kill them all and damn every other innocent caught in the bloodbath afterwards.

I'm never leaving her again. Never trusting her safety to someone else. I trusted the gods, and look what they have done to her.

Because of me.

Because I was too greedy and selfish, keeping a piece of her with me, keeping her light shining in the darkness I had wrapped around my shoulders.

"You know what will happen if you stay with her," Oscar says, trying for authoritative but sounding too damn scared. "The gods will see this as an act of defiance. They could kill us all. Let someone else –"

I shift back into my human form so I can speak. "Let. Them. *Come*."

I hold Siome close as she shrieks herself hoarse. I keep trying to coax her to drink the water; she keeps trying to demand I give her V.

That's the only thing she wants.

She used to only ever want me.

"Siome, please," I murmur in her ear. "Come back to me."

"Go away! I hate you! I *hate* you!"

I release her, my chest cracking open to leave my heart bare to the crows, but I'm not giving up. I'll never give up on her. Stepping quickly from the room, I go to grab a vial of V I have hidden at the back of a kitchen cupboard.

Disgust twists my stomach as my fingers wrap around the small bottle of glass. Every two to four years, I am reduced to my primal urges, caught by the scent of a bitch in heat that I can't refuse. So I take a Rick to make it more bearable to be inside someone who isn't Siome, and I force the poor substitute to take a V.

But I'm always sickened with myself as soon as it's over, so I kill them. Slowly. So they know they're being punished for their sins and mine.

I slip the vial into my pocket, then head back into my bedroom. She's on the bed, her fingers inside her. She did it as soon as I released her, trying to chase a poor man's high. Tears fall down her cheeks. Frustration pants from her lips.

Feeling the hole in my heart spread, I dig into my pocket and pull out the V. As soon as I pop the cork, she freezes. Then her head snaps to me, and she scrambles off the bed to crawl across the floor, where she kneels at my feet.

"I'll do anything you want, big daddy," she says, and I flinch.

"Just close your eyes, little helfire," I murmur, my tongue feeling thick in my mouth.

She obeys in an instant. Then I walk over to the bed and

pick up the bottle I was trying to get her to drink. Coming back to her, I kneel in front of her.

I hold the vial beneath her nose. She starts to open her eyes, but I tell her to close them. She does so immediately.

A slave to a master. Her to the poison of the V.

Keeping the vial under her nose, letting her 'taste' it as she breathes in deep, I pour the bottle of water into her mouth. She tenses, uncertain that what she's drinking is the potion she wants, but she can smell the V so strongly, and the fog in her brain keeps her dumb.

"I need more," she says, and I give her more water to drink.

It kills me that I'm deceiving her though, using a placebo against her. I've never lied to her before – even when I sent her away with another man, I was so fucking clear that it would break me. That I would trade the world to keep her if I could.

"So why aren't you?" she demands.

"You know I'm sun-touched." That I'm cursed by the gods to only live a life of misery. Every wolf is supposed to suffer as punishment for a past sin – that is why our change is one of pure agony. The fact that I can bear it means I must pay the price by suffering in all else. If I don't, the gods will kill her and anyone else that brings me joy.

"I don't care! I want you, you idiot!" she shoves me in the chest, her red eyes spitting with rage. With pain. "Don't you want me?"

"Of course I do." I ball my hands at my sides, knowing that if I reach for her, I'll grab her and never let her go. "I'll always want you."

"So take me." Tears burn her eyes.

Burn mine. "No."

She rears back as if I hit her. Her lower lips wobbles. Fuck. If she cries, that's it. I'm not going to be able to let her go. But instead, she lifts her chin. My little helfire, my little stubborn ball of flame. "Fine. Then I'm going to marry Jack. And I'll – I'll carry his eight pups, and I'll – I'll love him –"

"You'll never love him," I cut in on a low growl, shoving my hands into my pockets as the rest of me vibrates with a need to hold her.

"I will!"

"You might lie with him, Siome, and you might carry his eight pups –"

Her face cracks, breaking my fucking heart.

"– but your love is mine. It will always be mine."

"So then take it," she whispers, so much agony in that plea. "Please."

"I can't." Lifting my head, I look towards the group of men on the horses. They are ready to carry her away from me. To a territory out west, where she will be free from all this violence.

From the touch of my curse that has already taken three of my four siblings.

I cannot bear it if it takes her too.

Looking at Jack, a man I owe my life, I wave him over. He hesitates, then he nudges his roan horse in our direction. Vance, Siome's brother, comes with him.

In the last few seconds I have with her, I memorize her face so I can paint it – once I learn how.

"Smile for me, little helfire," I murmur. "Just one last time."

"Go to hel."

Turning on her heels, she runs from me.

And it takes everything I have to let her go.

A vial of V is placed at my lips, and I lurch to the side, my hands reaching for it. But the air moves, and then it's gone, and a frustrated cry escapes me. "Please..." I scramble around so my back's to the wall, trying to figure out where he is.

"Tell me why it hurts," he says, his voice beating down on my pathetic body as he stands over me. Not far.

I reach for his legs, willing to beg.

He steps away. My hands clench on air.

Collapsing to the ground, I rest my head on the hard floor. "Please…"

"You want it? Tell me."

Her memories rise, and I start to tremble.

A little girl I'll never get to hold.

Who I never *got* to hold because they took her from me.

They took her and put a parasite in her place.

"Please… I can't…" Not without the V.

With a sob, I reach a hand between my thighs, trying to mimic the high, the relief of pain that the drug can give me. I don't want to remember what I have done or lost or left behind. I just want to escape the agony of my soul. I want it all to stop.

Antonio grabs my wrist and pulls my fingers out of my pussy. Crying, I try to tear myself away from him, but he holds me easily in an iron grip.

"Tell me," he demands again.

"I can't," I sob. I hate myself. I hate him. "Please." I curl in on myself. "Just give me a taste. One drop, and I'll talk."

I'll do anything to forget this pain.

He crouches down in front of me, the smell of chocolate and pomegranates so close I can almost taste it. I reach for it, but he swats my arm away, then places the vial under my nose. I lift my chin and open my mouth, trembling as I wait.

The liquid hits my tongue, and I sigh, feeling its effects wash over me.

It's not enough though.

I can still feel that hole in my stomach.

"I need more."

"Why?"

My face scrunches up in pain. I don't want to remember this. I don't want to remember *her*.

No, I do.

I don't want to ever forget her.

Oh my gods. What kind of mother am I, that I'd want to forget my own child? Maybe it's better that she's gone.

The tears only come harder.

"Please. I need more…"

"Then talk."

Sobbing pathetically, I try to find the words I don't want to speak. I tell myself all I have to do is tell him, and the pain will stop. But my lips tighten. My teeth clench.

Some silent, forgotten part of me is telling me to resist; it sees this path as a threat. If I open up about this, what other secrets will he pull from me? What other people I love will he hurt?

He is the enemy.

He is the enemy.

He is the enemy.

I shake my head, trembling so hard, I'm finding it hard to breathe.

"I never got to hold my children," he murmurs, his face now lowered to mine. He's crouched in front of me, well within my reach. My hands clench with the need to search him for the V, but his words slam into me, crushing me still with their weight. With their solidarity. An understanding. An experience shared that means I'm not alone.

And gods, I don't want to be alone anymore.

"Sau's monsters ate them," he says slowly, "as well as the lower half of my mate. I held her in my arms as I begged the gods to intervene." He's quiet for a moment, but his words keep repeating inside of me. Screaming that he knows. He *understands* my grief. "I even begged Sau. I pleaded with her to save the love of my life."

My chin wobbles; I know the ending of this story.

But it isn't fair.

I want it to be different. I want *mine* to be different.

"Stop," I beg, not wanting to hear the truth.

"Not speaking of it doesn't change what happened," he says. "They are still gone. I will never hear Siome's laughter again. I will never see her eyes light up as she smiles at me, and I will never hold our children. Never see how they take after their mother, how they carry on the best parts of her."

I sag forward, my hands hitting the floor again as I cry.

I press my hand to my stomach, feeling Rafiki's absence, the death of her love and laughter and all the things she could have been.

Would she have taken Varius' eyes or mine? Would she have had his hair? His dry sense of humor? Would she have held herself back, so fucking terrified to love, to be used for her position, to be killed for her genes? Or would we have figured out a way to make the world safe for her? Would she have driven us mad, feeling safe enough to dash out in the middle of the night to rendezvous with some boy? Or girl? Or just a bunch of friends?

How many of her lovers would Varius have killed? Or at least scared the living daylights out of? How many bodies would I have helped him bury? Would she have caught us? Told us off for being 'so traditional and controlling and ugh, *parents*?'

My lips wobble as I think about all those milestones we will never have.

"I lost my entire family that day," he continues, pulling me from my grief and tugging me into his. Where it's a bit more bearable... "My mate, my three pups, and my brother-in-law, the last of her line."

"How did you..." I start, only to flounder into silence.

"Continue on?" he says. Not 'survived.' Not '*healed*.' The fact that he didn't use either of those words makes me feel like he really does understand. There is no *surviving* this. It has broken me. There is no way this can scab over and be forgotten. It will scar across my heart, my soul forever. But I can carry on... I can drag myself forward on broken legs.

His voice hardens, but I'm not scared of him anymore. He's showing me that there is something to feel other than grief. "Because I am making her killer suffer like I am."

I latch onto his words like an addict, trading one poison for another. A soul-numbing hatred. A righteous fury.

"And I will get her back."

My throat closes, his hope burning into me, branding me, changing the essence of who I am.

"So if you help me, Micha" –there is so much *honesty* in his words, so much understanding of what I am feeling– "then when I venture into the Underworld to get Siome, I will bring your girl back too."

My lips tremble as my hands ease from the tight fists they were in, no longer desperate to reach for the V. I still want it, but I want his words more.

He nails it home with a murmured, "Don't you want her to know her name?"

FIFTY-ONE

ANTONIO

June 29 1907, St. Augustine, Florida

"Go to hel!" Siome screams as she tries to shove past me, but I grab her shoulders and push her back into the middle of the living room. I can't let her leave the house. I know she's just going to try to score some V; the placebos I have been using are starting to lose affect – a placebo tolerance built up by her drug-obsessed mind.

"Siome –" I try again as she tries to dart around me, but I'm too quick, back in her way. Back in her face.

"Fuck you!" she screams. Her eyes flash wildly. Her pain is breaking my fucking heart. She shoves me in the chest with both hands. "You can't keep me as a prisoner!" She lifts her chin. "Help! Someone help!"

"I am helping!"

"You're hurting me!" She slaps me in the face.

My head whips to the side automatically, reducing the energy of her blow. I turn back to look at her in shock.

Her lips tremble, a moment of doubt, but then she shoves down her guilt. "You made me do that," she says. "It was your fault."

The agony I feel for her escapes on a twisted rasp. I will her to see the horror of her addiction. I let her see the pain in my eyes – something that once upon a time she couldn't bear to see. I only ever had to sigh in despair for her to come running to my side.

"I smelled your tears all the way across town, Mymecia Pyiformis," she says as she stops at the trunk of the tree I'm sitting in. She places her hands on her hips as she breathes hard, having just run from who knows where. "And what did I tell you about crying alone?"

"I'm not crying." I shake my head as I push away the thoughts of her leaving me. Jack will keep her safe.

"It's not a bad thing to cry, you know. I do it all the time, and I'm not weak"

"I know." A smile pulls at my lips. Bittersweet with the knowledge that moments like this are going to be gone soon. "What's Mymecia pyiformis?" I ask to push aside the pain.

She climbs up into the tree, dragging her skirt along the bark in a very unladylike manner, but I love her so much for it. I scoot down the branch so she can sit closer to the trunk, where it's safer. She looks at me and arches an eyebrow. She's told me too many times that it's ridiculous that I'm the one who sits further along the branch given I'm heavier, but I don't care. I don't want her falling from this height.

Besides, she knows I'm upset. She won't fight me on it this time. I bite back another smile as she begrudgingly sits between me and the trunk of the tree.

She presses a kiss to my cheek, then grins. "Only the best ant ever," she says as she places a hand on my thigh. "Their common name is the bulldog ant, and they're aggressive and mean, which fits you as perfectly as your cock fits in my pu–"

"Siome!"

She laughs as she throws her arms around me so wildly she knocks me off balance. I curse as we both fall out of the tree. I hold her tight to my chest, using my body to protect her from the ground.

Still, she screams – at me.

Jumping to her feet, her dark skirts swishing around, she berates me for having taken the impact. I groan, and her eyes widen as she quickly starts to fuss over me, a smile at my lips as I stare at her beautiful face under the blue sky.

But today, there is none of that care in her dull red eyes.

All there is is a demand for V.

"Please, little helfire," I beg. "Just let me help you."

"You can help by going to hel!"

She throws a punch at me this time, but I grab her wrist and pull her towards me, wrapping her in my arms. I hold her as she screams. As she fights.

"Siome, *please*!"

"Fuck off!" she yells. She starts to shift in my arms, and panic hits me as I'm all too aware of the fight she is about to force on me. I don't want to hurt her.

But I can't let her leave either.

She shrieks in agony as her bones break and her tendons tear. Her skin rips beneath my fingers. Sharp shards of bone break through, cutting up my arms and chest.

Stepping back, I release her in fear of fucking up her change, of hurting her permanently. I watch on in horror, wondering if the girl I knew is still in there at all. She used to follow me around like my own little shadow. She loved me when I couldn't even love myself. She was the only one who wasn't afraid of my curse. Even my own parents hated me for the misery I brought them – but never her.

Never my little helfire who defied even the gods – being my friend when I wasn't supposed to have any. Being the only light in a world I was supposed to walk in darkness.

I can't leave her enslaved to the V.

With a heavy heart, I strip out of my clothes, then start to shift into my wolf form so I can fight the woman I love. So I can try to protect her from herself.

I drop to my knees as my senses become enhanced – my ears elongating, the network of nerves in my nose growing. I dig my claws into the wooden floor, a low growl ripping through my throat as the skin breaks all along my back.

But despite the pain of my shift, the real agony is inside. Because I'm fucking reminded that I'm cursed. That once I help her, once she's no longer broken and the sight of her no longer kills me to see, I'm going to have to leave her once more.

I slam a fist into the ground, splintering the planks of wood. I want to rip the world to pieces. I want to go to war with the gods just so I can keep her.

But I am not a fool.

They've taken my entire family from me already, and I fucking know that Siome is being punished because of *me*. Because I kept a part of her with me all this time, using her memory to get through the bane of my existence.

I howl in pain as that knowledge rips through me.

She screams in agony as her shift still continues.

I'm going to have to let her go.

But I don't know if I can.

Don't know if I'm strong enough...

Leaving her the first time nearly broke me.

Her screams turn into snarls, her werewolf form nearly complete. Her beautiful red fur haunts me in my dreams. A rusty red that enhances the brilliance of her ruby eyes. But it is her scent that has me freezing.

Stilling.

Feeling like my soul's just been knocked out of my body.

My beautiful little helfire is in heat.

FIFTY-TWO

ANTONIO

Micha's fists vibrate from how hard she clenches them, and I'm hit with the memory of Siome's rage. She told me to go to hel so many times. Cursed me, hated me. Then pushed me to be better.

To change the world to make it safe for her. For us.

For the little pups she carried. *And look how bad I failed.*

"Bring her *back*?" Micha snarls, her words twisted with all of her pain – but still so minuscule compared to what's inside of me. "You expect me to kiss your feet and thank you for this?" She lunges at me and grabs my shirt. Her empty eye sockets narrow as she trembles. "You killed her!"

"No," I say, wrapping both my hands around hers, and push down my memories of Siome. I stand, dragging her to her feet. "*Sau* killed her. I was just the gun she used to pull the trigger."

"She was a baby!"

"A fetus," I reply flippantly. "Incapable of feeling pain

until twenty-four weeks."

"*I* felt it!" she screams, her pulse beating so damn hard at the base of her neck.

"And I felt the death of my *mate*," I say. "You cry over a clump of cells that could not feel, while I mourn a mother who understood her babies had been murdered and she was dying. Who I couldn't even comfort by telling her they were okay, and I would raise them in her absence. Sau killed her but only after she knew that pain.

"Yet, you only wonder how I could do such a thing as eat a baby?" My words vibrate through my chest, choking the air from my lungs. Spat with such venom, with such fucking *agony* that I'm struggling to control it. "I ask you how you can kill an adult and claim it's any different. If you take that same kid, and I kill him eighteen years later, would you see me as a monster then or just a soldier?"

I lift my head from her ear, but my grip on her body does not loosen. My fingers are tight, white-knuckled, the rage in my chest burning out from my soul. "What innocence we put on babies as if they are special," I sneer. "When dogs have more personality. Cows and pigs and all the animals we eat and beat and don't give a damn about."

"It's different," she says.

"Is it? Every living creature feels pain. A baby doesn't even know to fear death. So what is it about them? Their potential? Our own hope that they can be better than us?" I demand as I'm assaulted by the memory of my three pups.

They lie curled up in their placenta, their bodies bloody and ripped apart. I think about the life I could have had with them. The yipping laughter, the little tongue kisses that all pups do. Siome and I would've taught them how to hunt, to chase, to fucking *live*. Oh, yes, they had potential.

But so did Siome.

And I'm tired of defending why her loss hurts more.

She was my everything. My past, my present, my future.

My reason for living. My reason for dying when the time comes. She is my everything, and she is *gone*, and that hole she's left behind, filled only with the phantom chill of her loss, is all I have to remember her by.

So many lost moments. Lost dreams. Lost laughter and love and light, all made more bitter by the experience of once having had them.

I never had kids.

The ones with my last name aren't mine. I was never able to bring myself to touch Mary – the wolf I took years after Siome died. Only taken once I believed Sau dead and her line gone. But Mary and I had only entered a pact for the good of the pack. She fucked who she wanted, and when she got pregnant, I gave her kids my name to uphold the illusion of solidarity to keep the witches and vampires from thinking us weak.

Because I lost the chance for kids when I lost Siome.

My throat closing, I shake my head. My thoughts always run too much when I smell fucking V.

I stare into Micha's eye sockets, feeling as empty as them in my soul. Her whore of a mother-in-law carved out all I was, all I promised Siome to be, and she filled it with *poison*, turning me into someone I don't even recognize, someone Siome would be ashamed to see.

"So you ask me how I could eat your baby," I say, needing to get out the fucking words, needing to get through to this bitch in my arms so I can ween her off her addiction for my own fucking sanity – the memories she's dragging into the light too fucking bright. "It's because your family made me eat my wife."

June 29 1907, St. Augustine, Florida – Antonio

Siome jumps to her feet and kicks me in the chest. Her

claws rake across my skin, and I stagger back so they don't cut too deep. As my back slams into the door, she lunges for me, her arms outstretched. I catch her on muscle memory – as I've done so many times before.

Her knees thud into the wood behind me, cracking it and splintering the frame. For the slightest of seconds, with my hands on her ass and her legs around my waist and her face so close to mine, I feel like my love's come home. My cock is swollen from the scent of her being in heat, and the feel of her body against mine is making it hard to think clearly.

But then the door swings open from the impact. It throws me off balance, and I lurch forward to stay upright, holding her tighter to keep her from falling off me.

Her teeth sink into my shoulder. Not a love nip. A full-on bite that tears through muscle and has her teeth nicking bone.

My head whips to the side, and I snap at the air around her elongated ear as I straighten. She growls low, and so do I. I know she can smell it. The pheromones I'm giving off – those of an alpha even if I'll never take the title.

And I know she can feel it. The urge to obey even in her anger. Her need to mate with the strongest wolf around.

The smell of her arousal increases.

There is a second of hesitation

Of resistance.

And then we're exploding into action, our bodies a slave to our needs. Her teeth release me. Her hands grab my cock. She licks her way up my neck, and my hands squeeze her ass. I try to reach between us to see if she's wet enough, but she lifts her hips up and spears herself on me before I can.

I stumble forward on a growl, aiming for the sofa.

I collapse onto it with her beneath me, my knees weak, my cock aching.

She feels so fucking *good*, and I want to take her like the animals we are, but I don't want to hurt her.

She snarls her frustration when I refuse to move, my body trembling as I struggle for control. She snaps her teeth in the air around my face. Shoves at my chest. Pulls at my hips. Even pokes me in the bite wound she gave me.

I bare my teeth, letting her know she's gone too far, and she whimpers low before she starts to lick me. Her tongue is rough, not as pleasant as she thinks it is, but I don't care. Because I saw it for a moment – that old her. My stubborn little helfire.

"Ugh! You are such a Mymecia pyiformis!" She pushes down on my wrists as I grip her hips, keeping her from sinking down onto my cock. It's the first time she's gone into heat, and she's too desperate to think clearly. I'd be lost too if it wasn't for the stud of Artemis' silver I've pierced my ear with, an attempt to use the pain to clear the fog in my brain.

"I'm not going to hurt you," I growl, my voice raspy, my whole body tense, feeling like it's going to explode at any moment. My muscles shake as the head of my cock pushes into her virgin pussy. Holy fuck, I have died and gone to Elysium – the paradise of the Underworld.

"It's supposed to hurt the first time," she snaps, wriggling her hips, trying to get the release she needs.

"No, it's not."

"Mary said –"

"Talk about anyone else right now," I bite out through clenched teeth, "and I'll kill them." I lower her down another inch.

She pants, and she whimpers. Her hands claw at me. Her nails dig into my skin, raking lines down my hairy chest.

My eyes fasten onto her face. On the half-lidded rubies begging me to fill her with my cum. On the parted lips I'm so desperate to taste again. On the flush of her cheeks. Then my gaze drops to her pussy as she sits on my lap and takes me another fucking inch.

My arms tremble so damn hard as I fight myself from yanking her down onto my cock and fucking her until she can't even recall her name.

But the first time doesn't have to hurt if I take it slow. If I get her ready and put her need above my own. The taste of her pussy is already all over my face, and I lick my lips in an attempt to ease my own feral need. It doesn't help. I want her hard and fast and deep.

Gods, I want my cock swelling inside her as her own muscles lock around me, knotting us together.

"Don't move," I rasp as I reach up to touch my earring. I pinch it between my fingers, letting the pain push through the mindless heat.

But Siome doesn't fucking listen.

She just sits her ass down, taking in every inch of my cock. And if I thought I'd died and gone to paradise before – surely this is hel.

Because I can't stop myself from rolling her beneath me and fucking her like a beast.

She growls, the same frustration she had during our first time bleeding out past her lips. But just like then, I refuse to hurt her. I haven't done any foreplay; she can't possibly be ready for this.

So I pin her arms above her head, and I take her slow. My teeth nuzzle her neck. I lick the side of her face. She snarls at me, wanting me to move faster, fuck her harder, but I am taking the time to relearn her body. Over eighty years we have been apart, and I'm going to erase every other male she's been with.

The memories of the drug den come back to me, but I push them away. They don't belong here. Whatever male she has fucked doesn't matter. They only used her, degraded her. And I will remind her that she is loved. That someone wants her for who she is.

How can they ever compete with that?

So I take my time relearning the feel of her pussy, the scent of her heat, the feel of her body against mine. I rebuild those memories so they impregnate on my brain, never to be forgotten, there for the days when she is not.

The pain grows in my heart, the knowledge that this can't last if I wish to protect her from my curse.

But I push that away too.

In this moment, she is mine, and that is all that matters.

I love you, little helfire.

Come back to me.

Her frustration turns into crying whimpers. An edging that threatens to spill my seed. But I keep moving slowly. Keep learning every inch of her as she takes every inch of me.

She starts to shiver beneath me. Her eyes close. Her lips part on frantic pants. She's so close, and I stop to enjoy the feel of her pussy clenching around me. Stop to inhale the delicious scent of her heat.

She growls.

Snaps her teeth as she opens her eyes to glare at me.

She tries to wiggle her hips, but I hold her still in my hands, pinned between me and the sofa. Looking into her eyes, I lift myself up. Most of my weight is on my knees, and my stomach clenches tight as it holds the rest.

She gasps as my cock leaves her, ready for when it comes back to fill her.

But I don't push in.

I just let the head of my cock rest between her lips.

She howls. Her hands swat at mine. She tries to tug me off her. Then tries to yank me down on top of her. She kicks her feet as I kneel between her legs and just watch her as she falls apart.

She always hated being edged.

It was always my favorite part.

My hands shaking, I hold myself away from her for a full

minute.

Then I sink in with a groan.

She howls. I growl.

And we both come apart at the seams.

My cock swells inside her.

Her pussy locks around it, holding me deep.

And as my cum fills her, I bury my head in the crook of her shoulder and hold her tight in my arms.

We stay like that for a long moment, the silence lying thick around us. Until I hear her nose twitching. The giant inhales as she finally catches scent of the V I have hidden in my kitchen cupboards.

My heart breaking, I push myself off her, then roll to the floor and shift. She sits up, her head swinging back and forth as she tries to pinpoint where it's coming from. I've hidden it under piles of dried fish, but her nose has always been sharp.

"You don't need it," I say as I face her.

She doesn't even look at me as she surges to her feet. I shove her back down, and she almost swings for me, but then she clocks that I'm in my human form, and there is *some* part inside her that doesn't actually want to see me dead despite the bite she gave me. She growls as she flips over the back of the sofa, deciding to go around me instead of through. I dart around it and stand in the doorway to the kitchen.

"Siome, *please*! Just stop. You could be pregnant with our pups."

She growls again, telling me to piss off. She needs the V. For whatever fucking reason, she wants to check out of this reality. I'm not enough to keep her in it.

"Then live for them! Don't give a fuck about me, but you live for them!" I press my hand to her belly, where our pups might already be growing, and I will her to be the fierce protector she once was. The one who defied the gods and ignored me if she thought listening would mean those she loved got hurt.

My stubborn little helfire.

Growling, she slaps my hand away, then drops to the floor to shift. She screams out her agony, and I barely hold in mine. Gasping through the pain, she staggers to her feet as soon as she's able. I want to tell her to sit down and rest, but she wipes a hand between her thighs, scooping up my cum, and slaps it on my chest.

"You want me to think about the future with you? *Now!*" She shrieks as she shoves me back, and I stumble through the cracked splinters of the door. "You don't get that right! You don't get that fucking right anymore! You *left* me! You passed me off to Jack, and you *left* me!"

"You know I couldn't –" I clench my teeth as I struggle to keep my voice level. She came from a broken home. She hates it when I yell. "The curse –"

"There is no curse!" she shouts.

My eyes widen as I stare at her. My mouth drops open in disbelief. "How can you say that? I lost my entire family."

"Over ninety years!" She throws up her hands. "At war! You are at *war!*" She jabs me in the chest. "Name one single wolf in this fucking pack who hasn't lost anyone!"

I open my mouth, then snap my teeth shut again.

Her eyes fill with so much pain, pain I know I caused. Not the drug. Not the V that's been giving her an escape. *Me.* She took it to run from the pain of me.

Fuck, little helfire, I never wanted to hurt you. I stare at her, my throat too swollen to speak.

"You were supposed to ride after me." The words fall out of her mouth like a crumbling cliff into the sea. She starts to tremble as she stares at me, at all the hope she once put at my feet. "You were supposed to *come for me!*"

I flinch at the agony in her eyes. In her voice.

"I waited for you for over half a century –"

My throat tightens. Curse or not... "You deserved a better life."

"I deserved *you!* I wanted *you!* But you never came!" She clenches her fists as her lip wobbles. "You *never came!*"

I stare at her, wanting to mention the curse again. Tell her that I was doing what was best for her, but I cannot. Because I want so badly to believe that I can keep her this time. That once I fix her, I don't have to send her on her way again.

But I can't let myself think of that either. Because the gods have taken everything from me.

I *am* sun-touched.

I am supposed to live a life of misery.

Aren't I?

She sniffles as she sees the warring decision in my eyes.

"You want to know why I don't want to get better?" she asks softly – a bitter pain to her words, a defeated sigh from someone who knows they'll never win. "Because I know if I do, you're just going to leave." She swallows hard as tears flash behind her ruby-red eyes. "And I'd rather have you like this than not have you at all."

Breaking on a cry, I try to reach for her, but she shoves past me to get to the V.

FIFTY-THREE

NAMELESS

I try to pull away from him, not wanting to hear what he is saying anymore. I just want the mindlessness of the V. But his grip only tightens.

"Are you going to fail her like her father did?" he asks. "Or are you going to do something to get her back?"

My knees buckle, and I would've collapsed to the floor if not for his strength. He holds me up as I tremble, my heart hurting too fucking much. I want to believe in him. I want to risk hoping for a miracle, an impossibility, but I'm so godsdamned afraid of losing her all over again.

Of preparing for her return, only to stand on the tarmac as the plane crashes.

My stomach clenches. I can't handle the thought of this right now. "Please... I need more V," I say through my tears.

My desperation.

My terror to hope.

But I can't...

I can't do this.

Not when the grief is too harsh.

And the loss is too recent.

And the hole inside of me is dragging me down. Down to a darkness that only the V can penetrate.

"No," Antonio says, and I break apart in his arms. I need it.

"*Please...*"

"The V isn't going to stop the pain."

I flinch.

"You'll feel it a hundred times more when the high ends."

I shake my head, but his words drill into me. Fill up my soul and suffocate me with their honesty. I've already felt the effects of those crashes. It's why I have been chasing a constant high. But if I can't even have hope in the V, then how can I ever handle life's misery?

"The only way the pain stops is if you face it."

I cry out, sobbing hard now. Shaking in utter refusal. I can't face her loss. Can't face the idea of living without her. Of *healing* and moving on. Of *abandoning* her while I live my life, and she doesn't.

Hers has stopped. Mine should too.

"But I can help you," Antonio says. "I have been where you are, felt that grief that destroys all you are. But I have not forgotten those I love. I have not left them behind."

Each word he says pounds into me. Makes me feel as if I'm not alone. I'm drowning in this grief, raging stormy seas with no sight of land, and here he comes with a boat and a lifeline.

I just have to make the choice of whether to grab it.

Or sink to the bottom of the sea.

My throat tightens as hope and despair war inside me. I struggle to breathe. To think.

"She needs you to be her mother."

His words crash over me like a tsunami, shoving me

down, tossing me head over heels and heels over head until I can't tell which way is up anymore. Can't tell which way to swim.

Do I cling to the past, where my baby's death swirls like Charybdis' mouth?

Or do I drag my exhausted limbs to a sand-patch island? Where death might come slower but inevitably? Starved to death with no food to eat – agonizing moments felt in their greed? Where the land itself might get washed away when the next storm rages, killing everything that remains even as I try to build a castle – fucking ruins that crumble around me as I scream into an uncaring sea?

My throat swells as the waves crash, carrying me down.

Down.

Down.

I shake my head.

I *can't.*

This hope is too terrible of a thing.

"I'm *going* to get Siome back," Antonio says, his voice so strong in its certainty. "You have seen what I can do. Do you think I'll fail?"

I flinch as I remember how easily he took her from me. He fought his way through a whole yard of monsters called forth from Sau's shadows. He moves fast enough to dodge a bullet. Too fast to properly see. And his strength...

His willingness to do whatever it takes to get her back...

Cross whatever line.

Sau would do anything for her children, and yet even she failed to keep her grandchild safe. I failed. Dayne failed. Varius failed. And all the Shadow boys and Blood Fangs' members he took to kill Antonio out at the crocodile park – they all failed too.

I remember how easily he fought Sau the first time he broke into the Shadow House. How he ripped her apart faster than she could heal...

He heard the impossible – heard that he wasn't strong enough to trek into the Underworld, and so he made himself stronger. He was struck by grief just like me, but instead of crumbling, he shoved more sticks into his foundation to keep him going.

He didn't leave them behind though. He didn't *move* on.

He figured out a way to bring her back, and it is not hope that drives him.

It is determination.

Dedication.

Love for a mate who's been dead now for decades.

It is fucking *certainty*.

My limbs shaking, I reach my hands out to the lifeline he's tossed me and clutch my fingers in his shirt. There is no strength in my grip, but there is power in my words.

"Save her," I plea. *Save me.*

Give me a reason to fight this misery.

A purpose to carry on.

His hands move to cover mine just like they did before. "I will if you give me something in return."

My breath catches in my lungs. My brain screams at me in warning – that this is a trap, that this is what he wanted all this time, and he's just going to use me, but the haze is too strong for it to properly penetrate.

Though even if I heard it truly... He is offering me a way to get my daughter back. How can I refuse him?

Swallowing hard, I wet my lips. "What do you want?"

"Tell me who gave you the V."

FIFTY-FOUR

ANTONIO

I already know the answer, but I want her to tell me. I want her to take that first step in trusting me so I can get her off the V.

Siome needed to believe in something other than herself before she could take that first step towards recovery, so I will be Micha's higher power.

I will be her safe corner.

Her savior.

The omniscient god she trusts without question.

Then I will use her to end the Shadow bloodline just like Sau did Siome's.

She makes a noise of pain, not wanting to spill the secret of her dealer, still hoping he'll be able to sneak her a dose behind my back.

The men tense beside me. They're still here, having stood in silence all this time. They know better than to leave and make me have to hunt them down.

"Eduardo," I say.

"I wouldn't –" the sniveling coward starts to say, begging for his life already.

"Take a bit of the V out of her."

"No!" She jerks on my shirt, trying to grab my attention. "Please, don't," she pleads as she faces me. Her head keeps jerking towards the witch though, able to hear his footsteps as he walks towards her. "Please."

"Give me a name."

"It was Bear," she says, blurting out the words.

But I know it fucking wasn't.

Eduardo told me it was Tim when he teleported me in, but the fucker would blame anything on him. He wants him gone. But though Timothy often pushes his luck with me, he never crosses the line. He'd beat her face but not her belly. He'd piss and shit on her and degrade her in every way he could imagine, but he wouldn't risk giving her V, wouldn't risk terminating the pregnancy he knows I want. It doesn't matter how defective the fetus is. As long as it survives, it will give me power when I eat it. As long as he doesn't cross that line, he knows I don't give a shit about what he does.

But Digby (Sunny) is too fucking dumb for his own good. He knows the only way out of Eduardo's experiments is by getting her pregnant with a hybrid, and he can't do that if she's already carrying. Given Eduardo blamed Timothy for this mess, I know they were working together to set him up as the patsy – probably because Tim's been torturing them in my absence.

But when I came into the room, Digby blamed Stephen instead, which means he has aligned himself with Tim now, cutting Eduardo out, always swapping teams to be on the winning side.

I glance at Stephen's corpse. A pedophile who got what he deserved. He has all his clothes on, but the smell of syrup still lingers in the air. A child's breakfast. Micha must have learned what he was, and that level of sadism has Timothy's name all over it. Meaning all of these fuckers were in on it at one point or another, and all of them will pay.

"Why did Stephen – *Bear*," I say, using the name she knows, "give you the V?" I signal for Eduardo to wait. He stops beside Micha, his body drenched in sweat. He played his hand and lied to me, telling me it was Tim. He knows if she doesn't tell me the same thing, he's fucked.

I brought him in to make hybrids, but he's failed at that, having only made chimeras. They are stronger and faster than a normal wolf, but I don't need them to fight a war anymore, having lost most of my pack to the other two gangs and the police they used like puppets. His use to me has dropped. His teleportation network will stay up even after he's dead, and I can find a merc to replace him easily enough.

"He wanted..." She swallows, pain and disgust twisting her face. Oh, she knows what Stephen was, alright. I do not doubt that he wanted her to role play for him, but he was a coward through and through. He never would've disobeyed me. So I lift my hand to her chin and feather my thumb across her mouth.

"Lie to me," I murmur, "and I will leave your daughter where she is." She shudders as tears fall down her cheeks. "Tell me the truth, and I will bring her home."

Her lips wobble.

The last of her fight leaves, too beaten down by her hope that I can save her child.

"I gave her it," Timothy says, stepping forward, his words strong.

Digby's head snaps to him in shock. Eduardo's mouth drops open.

"I wanted to break her. The fighting was getting boring, and she just wouldn't *shut up*."

"Is that true?" I ask her.

"Of course –" Timothy cuts himself off when I look at him.

She trembles in my grip. Wets her lips. "Yes."

"You've just lost your daughter."

"No!" she screams as she starts thrashing in my hands. "I'm sorry! I'm sorry! I lied! He told me I had to agree with him. But he didn't do it. Sunny did. Sunny –"

I throw her at the bed as Timothy lunges for me. The fool was hoping I'd be too slow with her in my arms. She hits the mattress and bounces off it. Eduardo darts back, out of the way as a glint of silver arcs through the air, aiming for my heart. I pivot to the side. Timothy twists the knife to cut at me again. Digby –Sunny as she calls him– rushes at me from the other side, with a knife of his own, and Eduardo, the coward, waits to see whose side he will take.

Perhaps if he joined them now, they could get in a few good shots. I might have a natural resistance to magic, but he could still blind me with a flash that fills the room. Still disorientate me with an ear-bleeding noise. Then again, he never learned combat magic outside of the basic red ball of energy.

A pathetic fool.

I dodge out of the way of Timothy's attack. Grabbing Digby's knife arm, I kick Tim in the chest. As he flies back unconscious, I yank Digby to me. My body shifts into that of my wolf from the waist up. He screams. My mouth closes over his head. My teeth crunch through his skull, and the knife he holds drops to the floor. Fucking pathetic.

I take another bite, consuming the left side of his face, eating his life and his power.

Tossing him at Eduardo, I shift back into my human form. "Strip him," I say before my attention to Micha, who kneels on the bed, sobbing and begging for forgiveness.

"Please," she cries. "Give me another chance. I won't lie to you again. I promise. Just *please*. I want my little girl."

I walk over to her as she shakes.

"Please... Please... I'll do anything."

I grab her face, pulling her up to her knees, then release her. "Give birth to the pup inside you."

She flinches. Pain rips across her snot-covered face, but she doesn't deny me.

"And help me kill the Shadow line."

Her throat works hard as she caves in on herself, warring with the choice to help me get her daughter back at the cost of the rest of the people she loves.

"Just them?" she asks eventually. "Not the whole gang?"

She doesn't give me the names of those she wants saved, doesn't trust me enough. Yet. But she will give them to me eventually. I don't have any need for them. My goal isn't to hurt her; it's to hurt Varius through her, but she will tell me who they are simply because I will become her god.

Because she will give me all her hopes and dreams.

She will turn to me with all her prayers.

And I will give them to her.

I will turn her into a dog who crawls at my heels.

The perfect little sleeping agent once I let Varius "save" her and take her home. She'll lie in wait until I'm ready for the next part of my plan.

Because I know now what they've tried to hide from me. What Varius tried hard to portray in our initial video call. And he succeeded too, had me believing he didn't give a shit about her.

I thought he was callous enough to have given up on her in this life, planning to just collect her in the next. After all, I am not a god. If I kill her, she won't die permanently. The true death can only come from the gods, a godslayer, or one of the families that stop the dead from escaping the three underworlds. So she will come back to him, her soul pulled to his as soon as she's reborn.

And I hate them for that. Envy them. Why should they

get to have something I cannot?

Only witches can create blood bonds. It defies the wishes of the gods. It isn't right. It isn't *natural.*

My hands clench as I stare at her, waiting for her answer even though it doesn't really matter.

Because in the end, I will kill her regardless of what she does for me. It is impossible to bring back her baby anyway, so she will probably thank me for ending her grief.

"I'll do it," Micha says, her words so broken and quiet. "Just bring her back."

"As long as you obey me," I say. Dismissing her, I turn to Eduardo. Timothy groans against the wall, finally regaining consciousness. The silver knife he tried to stab me with lies close beside him. I don't bother to kick it away from him. If he tries again, it's no energy to stop him.

Shifting fully into my wolf, I drop onto all fours and start eating the rest of Digby's corpse. His bones crunch beneath my teeth. His flesh tears. His blood sprays free. And his power seeps through me, a hot burn that flushes through my skin.

Timothy lifts his head as his eyes open, and I catch his stare as I swallow Digby's heart. His ugly face pales, and he pushes to his feet. I growl low, a warning, but he doesn't stop. Howling, he picks up the knife and lunges for me.

"What'd you do to my brother?" he screams.

I lunge forward, jumping over Digby's corpse, grab hold of his arm with the knife and snap it at the shoulder. He screams, the blade drops. I catch it out of the air and stab it into his chest. Shifting back into human form, I throw his body at Eduardo. "Keep him alive for his sperm. I don't care what else you do to him." I glance at Digby's and Stephen's bodies. "And put those two on ice. I'll finish them when I'm back."

"You're leaving again?" Eduardo asks, his voice shaky.

I turn to face him fully. He's already tried to kill me once with his teleportation circles. To send something through them, thousands upon thousands of threads snake out from the destination circle and latch onto the traveler. If any of those threads cross, the person's body will be reshaped. If any of them break, they'll lose whatever part of their body that was attached to it.

And if they all are corrupted in order to tear apart in the middle, the person will be killed.

If Eduardo had tried that when I first met him, he would have succeeded in killing me. But by the time he'd grown the balls, I'd grown too strong, and my resistance to magic allowed me to step out between the circles. Oh, I had taken damage – a lot, and I'd ended up in the middle of a random family's home and had to kill them to leave no witnesses, but I survived.

I killed all of his precious little experiments –he has an unhealthy attachment to them– then nearly killed him. He's never gone against me since.

Perhaps he needs another reminder of what I can do.

His eyes widen, and he damn well trips over his words. "I'm only asking because I need a bit of time to recuperate." He's used a lot of magic recently.

"How long?"

"A week – three or four days," he hurriedly corrects.

My jaw tightens.

I'm so close to being able to head into the Underworld and bring Siome home. When I sought out a way how to, I was told by ancient scholars it was impossible for a mere wolf to venture into the deep as Hades' domain will poison all that lives. An Earth human does not have enough magic in their veins to spend more than a minute or so there. A demigod could spend a couple months, and it will take me at least three weeks to travel through all the check points, longer still to get an audience with Hades and Persephone.

Refusing to give up on Siome though, I found a way to

increase my magic. My family has always eaten our dead as a way to gain a bit of their power. So I expanded the Death Hunt Family and bred all the women until I found those who could birth hybrids. Then I ate their babies, taking their power as mine. Another two or three fetuses, and I will be able to spend six weeks in the afterlife before it kills me.

But first, I have to make it through the Lesser Eleusinian Mysteries. That will cleanse my blood-stained soul so I can enter the Greater Mysteries, where I will learn how to split my soul from my body without it killing me. Then I'll just need to call forth a keres, a reaper of the dead, and bribe my way to Hades' throne room.

The Lesser Mysteries open in the spring of next year, giving me only months to find the rest of the bribes. I have been growing my collection of cheesy, one-off romances for Hades, a lover of books, for the past few years. I have just been to Blódyrió, where I commissioned a special music box for one of Cerberus' heads. I have four more "gifts" left to sort: two for his other heads; one for Charon, the ferryman who'll take me across the river splitting the living from the dead; and Persephone.

I can feel the pressure of my deadline, but three more days will not matter. Besides, I can use the time to research who holds the recipe for Byzantine fire – a green mythical fire that spreads on water. Persephone likes explosives, and I am certain she will love it.

"Three days," I say, and Eduardo bows his head. There is a sickly smell coming from him, and I do not doubt he needs more time to fully recover, but I don't like him that much. If he dies, he dies.

Turning from the room, I head down the hall, then up the stairs to the second floor. The yacht rocks in the waves but barely enough to notice due to its size. Everyone on board rotates being captain, steering us away from any storms – though mostly, they just leave it to drift. There's an app that will tell them if they're in the way of another boat, but with the size of the ocean, they'll only see someone every month or so.

I head towards Rudy's room. There isn't a ward outside his door. There aren't any guards to stop him from leaving. There's simply an explosive collar around the necks of the girl and dog he tried so desperately to save. He gets to see them every so often to remember why he does what he's told. If he even tries to get down to the lower level or to reach out to Micha at all, they will detonate.

He is far enough away from her to not hear her though. If he could, I don't trust him not to break. When people are put into impossible corners, you never know which way they'll go. But if he can't see her pain, he will tell himself what he needs to in order to justify his decision.

Just like I did when I sent Siome away, believing I was doing the right thing. Instead, I lost eighty-six years with her. Lost the chance to have a family. And I destroyed her life. My choice led her to the dark depths of V, and it took over a year to bring her out.

A year of her promising to get clean, only to relapse over and over again. One day, I'd leave to go get food as I'd done many times before, only to come back and find her gone. Find her in some alley getting railed just to score. It didn't matter how many people I killed in warning. How many examples I made. Neither an addict nor a dealer has much thought to the consequences of their actions.

My chest tight, I hug the memory of her, then let her go.

But I would take decades of the bad just to have her back in my arms.

Opening Rudy's room, I step inside.

He's being fucked by one of the female wolves. She's riding him as he lies on his back in bed. She's cupping her own breasts, and the place smells of smoky vetiver with an underlying base of tobacco. The Ricks they're using increase sperm count and allow the taker to ejaculate multiple times in a row.

"Have any of you succeeded?" I ask as I walk over to the bed. She turns her head, her ass still bouncing up and down. There is a pillow over Rudy's head. I don't know which one of them put it there.

"No," she says.

"Leave us."

She gets off him instantly, then grabs her robe off the floor. Given our kind is comfortable naked and her purpose here is to breed, that seems out of place, so I ask her the question with my eyes.

She ducks her head. "He feels too innocent."

I'm taken by surprise, but I don't say anything, and she leaves, closing the door behind us. Rudy sits up, letting the pillow fall into his lap, hiding his pierced erection. His eyes are haggard, but they still hold a sharp intelligence.

Another surprise.

While I was on Blódyrió, I heard rumors about someone targeting teleporters. Hushed whispers in taverns warning witches not to go out alone. My gut told me that was Varius searching for a way to sneak onboard so he could save his wife. I thought Rudy was too much of an embarrassment for him to bother with as he was a Shadow who couldn't kill. He was a traitor who'd given up his Boss' wife, his *brother's* wife in order to save some random child and mutt. Pathetic.

But looking into Rudy's eyes, knowing the suffering he's gone through –Timothy not caring about the gender of his victims, and Eduardo excited to dissect his powers– I'm not so sure if the reason he was never seen on a mission before was because he was too weak to join his brothers.

There is a strength within him, and his eyes look too damn old. Like he has seen too much misery.

"How are they?" he asks, mouthing the words. I learned to read lips a long time ago, when I watched Siome from the shadows, not wanting to infect her with my curse.

But I'm not here to talk to him.

I'm here to cut off a bit of him to send to Sau. I need her angry at me, shaking with fury as she vows to kill me herself. Because to get to the River of Styx, which splits the living world from the dead, I need to catch a ride with a reaper of death. But keres only come to collect those who've been brutally killed on their path of vengeance.

So Sau will be that someone.

It's the only reason I've allowed her to live. Once I kill all of her kids, I will beat her to death inside a binding circle, temporarily tying our souls together. Then I will use her to catch a ride to the Underworld. She took my mate from me. It is only fitting that she be the sacrifice that lets me get her back.

Stepping up to Rudy, I shift the nails of my right hand into five lethal claws.

FIFTY-FIVE

HER

It's been hours since I have been raped. Despite logically knowing that that is a good thing, I'm starting to freak out. What new, twisted thing is Sadist going to come up with after being denied his toy for so long? I can't handle the anticipation, the horrible thoughts of my imagination. Will he get me to dig up Bear's corpse and fuck it? Will he figure out a way to get me to Rudy and then force us to –

"No!" I clutch my head, starting to shake. I slam my palm against my temple, wanting to stop the thoughts. Stop the pain.

But only V can give me relief.

"Please," I beg to an empty room, and I have never felt more alone. Despite wishing for privacy, now that I have it, I hate it. Where is someone to beg for some V?

Where is someone to *help* me?

"I need it," I cry as I crawl across the bed. I go over the edge and hit the floor. I spread my hands out, feeling for the damp patches of blood, hoping to find where they all stood and thus any vials of V they might've dropped.

I search for what feels like hours, the minutes of my life ticking away. My hands hit a pool of stickiness, and I nearly weep. But there's no vials nearby. I almost scream. My body trembling, I check the entire place, each wall, each corner, the space beneath the bed and bedside table and other bits of furniture.

Then my hand knocks into a small glass bottle. It rolls across the floor, taking my breath along with it. Swallowing hard, I hurry after it, trying to figure out where it's gone.

My fingers graze it. I pick it up tenderly, my heart racing. *Stop.*

You could lose her if you take this.

Antonio wants me to carry the pup in my belly to term. Then he'll bring my daughter back. All I have to do is not take the V.

My hands shake from the impossible choice.

I'm not strong enough.

You are.

Do it for her.

She left me.

Why should I think about her at all?

I flinch, feeling sick with myself. What sort of thoughts are they? What sort of mother – what sort of monster am I?

You can still be good.

I shake my head. *I'm too filled with poison.*

There's no point trying to be better when all that'll be is a lie. *This* is who I am. A terrible person. A terrible mother.

I uncork the bottle of V, and I raise it to my lips.

July 1 1907, St. Augustine, Florida – Antonio

Shit!

Dropping the bag of fish I've just come back with from the market, I pivot and sprint away from my house, leaving the front door open. I'm well within Death Hunt territory, and no one would be dumb enough to rob me, but I don't even care if they do. Siome's presence isn't in the house. I can't smell the musk of her fur or the sandalwood and citrus of the soap I bathe her with. I left her asleep in my bed. She was never a morning person. I thought I would have time to sneak out to get her something to eat; I'd damn well run out of food and hadn't eaten anything myself for days.

I barge into Oscar's house. He's fucking some whore he picked up off the street –I don't know what his obsession with prostitutes is when, as alpha, he has a whole pack of willing women– but he tosses her aside as I enter.

"What –"

"Did you fucking take her!" I yell as I fight the urge to shift. I know he wants her gone, wants me back. But if I attack him, it'll be seen as a play for alpha, and I don't have any interest in the role.

"Who –"

"Don't –"

"Alright." He grabs hold of the whore as she tries to run out. I might not've attacked him, but I've disrespected him in his own home, and now he needs to make sure there's no witnesses if he wants to keep his throne. The alternative would be to punish me, but he knows that's damn well not going to happen – not without my permission, but I'll give it if he helps me find Siome.

"I won't tell anyone," the whore whimpers.

He breaks her neck and drops her at his feet. Normally, he would've soothed her, given her some false hope before he killed her, but he knows I'm not in the mood to wait for that little play of mercy.

"I haven't taken her," he says as he turns his back on me, showing me that he isn't afraid, that I can trust him. He opens up his bedside table and pulls out a pendant that can cloak us. "The gods want you miserable, and this is the most miserable I've seen you," he says. He turns and holds up the pendant. "When you find her, bring her to dinner. She needs to meet the pack."

"She's not staying," I say. Despite how much I want to keep her, despite how much I want to believe her that being sun-touched is just a superstition told to keep those like me in line, I cannot take the risk. If Artemis punishes me for defying her by killing Siome herself, she'll never be reborn.

"I know, but she's going to go crazy with just you for company, and the pack's getting curious."

"Give me the pendant," I growl.

"Your word she comes to dinner or I'll make you fight me for alpha."

"You won't win."

"No, but I'll smile in my grave knowing you're fucking miserable." He flashes me a cheeky smile.

"If I find her and get her clean –"

"Good enough." He tosses me the pendant, and as it sails through the air, I drop to the ground and shift. I rise fully in my wolf form and grab the pendant before it hits the floor.

"Shit, you're getting fast," Oscar mutters, but I'm already gone, racing through town, my nose in the air, searching for the trail of my mate.

Those two words burn a whole in my chest. *My mate.*

I dreamed of claiming her one day.

Of making her mine.

Foolish dreams that could never come to pass. So when the yearning got too big, I sent her away out west.

I don't know if I made the right decision. Don't know if she would have died if she'd stayed, just like everyone else I cared about. But I will do whatever it takes to keep her safe, even from herself.

I track her to the edge of Shadow Domain territory. The

wards around their main street keep out all but witches; even the pendant won't get me through. But the branching streets are outside the wards so they can still deal to non-witches. The desperate wolfs and vamps like Siome.

"No cash, no product," I hear a man say, his thick voice carrying on the wind. She's with him; I can smell her, and I veer off in their direction.

"I can give you Sahara Storm," she says, her voice shaky. My street name rolls off her tongue like a curse. Sahara for the reddish-gold color of my fur. Storm for the wreckage I leave behind. I have a large bounty on my head from both the Blood Fangs and the Shadow Domain, and hearing her use me to score hits me like a hot poker to the chest.

The man laughs. "He will not care about trash like you."

A low growl builds in my belly. I turn the corner and see them. Neither of them can see or sense me due to the magic of the pendant, but Siome still stiffens and turns to look behind her.

"I swear –" she starts to say, but he shoves her back. She stumbles out into the street, out of my path, and I barrel past her and into him. He stumbles back into the house. My teeth rip into his throat. He doesn't even have the chance to scream. Siome does, though, shrieking in fear even though she knows it's me, and hearing her fear twists the hot poker deeper into my heart. Doesn't she know I'll never hurt her?

I lift my bloody jaws just in time to see her run away from me. Noise deeper in the house warns me of another witch coming my way, but I leave him to chase after her. I shift into my human form beneath the cover of the pendant.

"Leave me alone!" she screams as she peels off down the street. There isn't a lot of people out in this seedy part of town at the moment, only addicts and homeless hiding in corners, so I wait until she passes a side street, then tackle her to the ground, twisting in the air so I hit the earth first. I roll her into the shadows of the smaller lane, stopping as I lie on top of her.

"Siome, stop!" I hiss as I remove the pendant from my neck so she can see me. My face doesn't bring her the calm it used to though. Doesn't make her smile. Doesn't make her hollow eyes light up in joy.

She lifts her head and tries to bite me, the feralness in her eyes breaking my heart.

"You don't need the V!" I say. "Come on, helfire. You've been so good. You've been getting clean."

"Fuck you!"

She screams, and I'm forced to place my hand over her mouth so we don't draw unwanted attention.

"Please, Siome. Come back to me."

"You want to know why I don't want to get clean?"

"Because I know if I do, you're just going to leave."

Her words from days ago still haunt me, cutting deep. I want to give her what she wants. I want to offer her the world. There is nothing I wouldn't do for her.

But giving us a chance could kill her.

So I do the next "best" thing. The thing that makes me feel sick to my stomach, but it's what I know she needs – the poor man's version of V.

Pinning her down, I kiss her and press my thigh between the folds of her skirt. "Let me help you without the V," I say as she thrashes beneath me. I grab her hips and lift them up, making her rub her pussy against me. She gasps against my mouth. Her hands stop scratching to start pulling my hair. Despite my desire to stop, my cock starts to thicken as she kisses me back.

I want us to make love because she loves me, not because she's using my body for some basic pleasure. But in the end, I will gladly take whatever crumbs she gives me.

"Fuck me here," she groans.

"Not in the street." She isn't some whore. She deserves to have a bed. Privacy.

"Yes," she pants. "Don't make me wait."

Cursing internally, I stand and help her up. I look around to see if there's anything we can hide behind. She pulls me towards a wall and starts to lift her skirts. My cock twitches.

"You're not a whore," I say, fighting the desire to bury myself inside her right here, right now, where everyone can see. Just like she wants.

She pouts. "What if I want you to make me your whore for the night?"

My hands fist as I fight the memories of all the whores who've asked me something similar over the years. She isn't a disgusting piece of filth like them. Their faces don't belong here between us.

She reaches for my pants – a baggy set that's able to stay with me as I shift. A dark color to hide the blood from my torn and broken bones that then heal.

I grab her wrist to stop her, then kiss her to distract her from whining. As much as she wants it, I don't want to take her here. Pulling her towards the closest door, I break it in. A man jumps up from the sofa and turns towards me with a shout, but I shut him up by punching him in the jaw. He reels back a step, then crumbles to the ground, knocked out. I dig into my pocket and pull out some cash, throwing it on the floor as I shout, "If anyone's home, get out!"

Siome rubs herself against me. She kisses my neck. I lift her up as the house stays silent. Her legs wrap around my waist, and I carry her until I find a bedroom.

I fuck her on his bed. Me on top, facing the door, ready to jump up and fight if he decides to come in once he regains consciousness. But he never comes in, and I come in her as she screams.

She collapses back onto the mattress, and I shudder on top of her, my cock pulsing deep inside her pussy. She sighs as she closes her eyes, riding out the pleasure of her orgasm, basking in her addiction. My eyes on her face, I wonder how long I can keep doing this. I stopped her from getting V today, but how long can I keep her clean? I thought she was getting better, but she's just going to keep seeking it out.

My throat tightens as I brush a tendril of hair off her face as she starts to drift off into sleep. She never was a morning person.

I press a tender kiss to her lips. She sighs against me.

"Stay with me," she murmurs, already half-asleep. "Just promise to stay and I'll quit the V. I promise…"

My throat closing, I hold her in my arms. I can't give her that promise, but I leave my cock in her as she dreams.

Present day, Somewhere adrift in the ocean – Micha

Just as the glass of the potion touches my lips, someone rips it away from me. I cry out, then jerk back as something else is pressed to my mouth. The smell of chocolate is soon followed by the taste of it on my tongue. A salt-crusted bit of sweetness. So familiar, yet so alien in this hel.

"Where did you get the V?" Antonio demands.

My tear ducts burn at the thought of him taking it away from me. Maybe if I'm honest with him, he won't punish me? "I found it. Someone must of dropped it. Please don't take it from me. I need it."

"You don't."

"I do."

He grabs my right hand and places it between my legs. A shock of thrill rushes through me.

"You have the power to do it yourself, Micha. Don't let it control you."

I bite my lip. I'm not as strong as the V.

"You need to stay clean if you want your daughter back," he says, his voice soothing. "You want her back, don't you?"

My lips tremble as I nod.

"Then don't let it control you."

He releases his hand from me, but I can almost feel his fingers still on me. Guiding me. I rub a finger between my pussy lips. I think about him watching me, and I swallow nervously. Is he going to hit me? Hurt me to get himself off?

"I need the V," I say, my hand stilling. "Just a couple drops."

"Why?"

A frustrated noise escapes my lips, but he gave me some when I answered him earlier. Perhaps he will do that again.

"I'm scared you're going to hurt me." I push the words out, yank them out of my throat even as they dig their claws in in an attempt to stay silent. Telling him my fears is just giving him ammunition... isn't it?

"I won't hurt you as long as you obey me."

I believe him; the honesty in his words resonate inside my soul. "But Sadist –"

"Will never touch you again. I made sure of it."

"You saved me?" My mouth opens in surprise. Another piece of chocolate is popped into it.

"Yes," he says as I chew.

"Why?"

"Because you're carrying something very important to me."

My throat works hard as I lift my hand to my stomach. "The cancer?" I can't bring myself to call it a baby.

"Yes."

"I hate it. I want it out."

"But then your daughter will die, and you want her to live, don't you?"

A small cry escapes me. "Yes."

Another piece of chocolate is offered me. It reminds me of the V. The smell entwines with my memories, and I feel as if he's giving me what I want. What I need.

"I will bring her back to you. I will give you whatever

you ask of me as long as you do what I say."

I nod. "I will." I just want her home.

"Then no more V."

I flinch, but I don't beg again. I just drop my hand to my pussy and try to take the poor man's version like he showed me. I slide my fingers between my lips. Shuffle my legs so I can get into a better position to ride them. As he stands silently in front of me, I kneel at his feet and chase the high of the V.

My fingers slip inside myself. One. Two. Three at a time. I rub my clit on the palm of my hand. I can feel his presence like a god's touch, an omnipotent force that's protecting me. So much power and danger just out of reach.

My breath quickens as I become intoxicated from being the focus of a man so dominant. Desire rushes through my veins. I roll my hips, curling my fingers to hit the G-spot that's only a few inches inside, but the pleasure is coming from him. From knowing his eyes are on me. From his body being in front of me, protecting mine.

With a cry, I orgasm on my fingers and chase the high of that release. I shudder and shake as the pleasure rushes through me, erasing the pain and fear I've been trying so hard to outrun.

"See?" Antonio murmurs as I collapse onto the ground at his feet. "You don't need V to stop the pain." His fingers brush a piece of hair from my face. "You just need me."

Yes... I think as I close my eyes. *I just need him.*

My savior...

He's the only one who cares about me and Rafiki.

The only one who deserves my loyalty.

FIFTY-SIX

HIM

I feel it. The moment she gives up.

The moment she damn near breaks.

I'm deep in the caves under the island of Mljet, Croatia, searching for the portal that leads to Blódyrió. Antonio was spotted in the area this morning, but no one knows if he was coming or going. The Kacic brothers, the vamps whose territory we're in – century old pirates that once fought the Holy Roman Empire, never opened the portal after it was closed by the archangels. They never even knew it was here. The cave system itself is a fucking maze full of dead ends and tight spaces that you just have to squeeze through and trust you won't get stuck.

I've never been claustrophobic, but with hundreds of tons of rock over my head and it pressing in on all sides, with the air muggy and suffocating, the space we're in feels like it's fucking shrinking.

And now I can feel my wife needing me while I'm stuck

down here.

My magic crawls beneath my skin, wanting out, and a pale pink glow emits from Stormie's fingers.

I inhale sharply, trying to get my nerves under control. If I pulse here, everyone is dead. There isn't enough space for Stormie to trap me in a bubble on my own. She might be able to throw up a wall between us, but we don't know if my magic can seep through rock.

"Khalid," I say, turning to my brother. "Check Micha. I think Antonio's back on the boat."

There is a collective sigh. No one here's been having an easy time – except for Maddox, who shapeshifted into a rat, and if we don't have to continue down this way, no one's going to protest.

Khalid holds his hand out, palm up, while he murmurs an incantation. Her soul doll rises out of the shadows that swirl there. As they disappear, he clutches the green stone in his hand, and his magic hums in the air, a buzz on all our skins in the tight space.

There is a long stretch of silence. Then he sends her doll back into his shadows. "He's there," he says.

"Thank gods," Enoch mutters.

Ignoring him, I turn to Maddox. He's sitting up on the ground, inside the small tunnel we were about to squeeze through. His whiskers flick with the movements of his nose. "Figure out what he was doing on Blódyrió," I say. "But recon only. Don't get caught, and never use your own face."

"And may there be no blood moon," Stormie adds with a shiver.

He squeaks, then runs off.

My stomach tightens. I wish I wasn't sending him alone, but when it comes to gathering intel, he's the best brother to do it. Besides, he knows why he's really going, what his real mission is. And he accepted that danger...

The tightness in my stomach spreads to my chest. If I

lose Maddox because of my actions too...

He volunteered...

He's just a child though, a baby. It's my job to look after him.

I want to call him back, tell him the mission is off. But I don't. Because I want my wife back. And I know he would not listen anyway. Despite his choice at the school, I know he loves Micha.

Then again, maybe he's agreed to do this simply because he's more suicidal after I killed Krypto. *Fuck.* That guilt is even more suffocating than this damn cave. I did it to end his suffering, but it doesn't make it any easier to live with. I loved that dog, and the sound of the gun going off keeps me up at night.

Wanting to get out of here, I glance at the others. "Let's go."

We head back out of the cave. If Aleric was with us, this would go a lot faster, but he stayed on the surface to talk to the Kacic brothers. Their friendship goes back centuries, and they don't often get the chance to catch up. He was never going to follow us into Blódyrió anyway.

Ezriel isn't here with us either. He's scouting the rest of the island in case the portal has nothing to do with why the Boss of the Death Hunt was here, and Mother is back in St. Augustine, running the Family while we're away. It should be Khalid's job now that he's the Underboss, but he refused to stay at home. He thinks I'll do something stupid in his absence and doesn't trust Enoch to keep me in line.

But what he calls 'stupid', I call logical. I should've done it a long time ago. Because I'm fucking *done* with sitting back and waiting for crumbs to fall into my lap while my wife fucking *suffers.*

I'm getting to Micha. *Today.*

As the light of the world finally pierces the dark gloom of the caves, the sound of crashing waves on rock comes with it. We stop underneath a shimmering hole in the ceiling, a light-blue shield that's holding back the weight of the sea. It's about seven feet off the ground and three feet at its widest point. The secret entrance to this place requires us to swim. There was a reason this portal was forgotten. Going in and out of it is a pain; carrying anything with you is almost impossible.

Dayne climbs up the wall of the cave first, takes a deep breath beneath the water, then disappears through. Khalid follows, then Enoch, leaving Stormie and I alone.

"You're getting more control of your powers," she says as she starts to climb ahead of me.

'More' control but not enough to actually use. All I can do is push back the pulsing for a little bit. My frustration tics in the pulse at my temple. She hears my silence and understands me enough to end her attempt at a pep talk.

As much as it might seem like it to the others, we're not back at square one. I don't need her to try to "lift my spirits" by focusing on what's positive because this hel ends today.

I linger in the cave for only a moment, doing what needs to be done while no one is watching. Then I use my hybrid speed to make up the difference in time so the ex-reaper's not suspicious with how long I took to breach.

I tread water in a narrow, low-roofed tunnel for a second before swimming towards the bright sunshine. The cavern opens up to a wide grotto that's empty of everyone but us despite it being a tourist attraction; this is where Odysseus, the ancient Greek hero, washed ashore in the *Odyssey*. The legend got a few things wrong. Calypso didn't hold him for twelve years here because she'd fallen in love with him. Nor was she a nymph. She was a succubus, and she kept him as a sex slave until he was able to make her cum sixty-nine times.

I look around at the golden cliffside and turquoise water, knowing Rudy would've loved it here. He loves the water, the peacefulness of it even though drowning and being eaten by sea creatures are common fears he's assaulted with all the damn time. He even has a boat, a thirty-eight-foot monohull called *Whale Endowed* that he takes out once or twice a year; he'd take it out more if he could, but he stays around St. Augustine for us. In case we need him. When he's back though, I'll have to make sure he has more time to go for a sail. He deserves to have some peace.

My chest tight, I swim to the others.

"Now what?" Dayne demands as soon as we're back on land, Ezriel having met back up with us. His voice is tight, his control on the verge of erupting. Feeling the eyes and ears of the thick woods around us –paranoia perhaps, but not wanting to take any chances– he covers us in a shield, giving us privacy on an island full of tourists.

"We go home?" Enoch asks. "Wait for Maddox to get back and tell us what he's found?"

"We've been doing nothing for months!" Dayne shouts, then clenches his fists as he reins his frustration back in. "Micha needs us *now*."

"I know –"

"Do you? Because you don't seem to give a –"

"Our brother is there too!" Enoch yells.

"Enough," I cut in.

The two of them clench their jaws and cross their arms. I look at Khalid. "Is there anything different that'll help us?" I know he won't tell me what my wife's going through, but he won't hide any intel that I need to make a plan.

"Eduardo is struggling with his magic," he says, but I already knew that. I've been keeping tabs on how much he's used, how much he could possibly have left in the bank, and I know he has to be running on near empty. That's why I'm only now putting this plan into action. I needed him out of the game.

"And Antonio's killed one of the chimeras," Khalid adds.

I blink, not having expected that. "Why?"

His lips tighten. Then he says, "They got her addicted to V."

"What?" Dayne steps forward, and I shift in front of him. He normally isn't stupid enough to try to beat out answers from the reaper – ex-reaper, but his emotions are volatile right now. He thinks we've hit another dead end.

He glances at me, his eyes darkening. Then he takes a step back with a hard exhale. I look back at Khalid.

"Abort the child." I don't call it hers, can't call it fucking hers. Because then it would be *mine*. Regardless of whether or not I'm the father, anything she decides to keep will be mine too. I will accept all pieces of her. I will be the peace she fucking deserves. But first I have to bring her home, and she'll never need to know it was Khalid and I who aborted the thing in her womb.

"What?" Enoch this time, but he's more confused than outraged.

"Antonio killed one of his men for giving her V. He's feeling the stress of whatever deadline he has. We kill it now, he'll blame it on the potion or Eduardo, and that will sow more discord in his ranks."

"And how does that fucking help *her*?" Dayne demands.

I look him in the eye. "He won't trust them to watch her. He might take her with him when he leaves." Now that she's stopped fighting, and he can't trust his own men around her. Maybe. But it's enough to hope.

His eyes widen. "Then we can grab her."

I doubt it'll be that simple, but it'll give us a much better chance than what we have now. Khalid pulls her doll out of his shadows. Murmuring beneath his breath, he shapes the air around it, using it like a phantom hand as he uses his actual hand to pluck a pin of green energy out of the air. It's a tether of his soul, and it won't just connect him to the doll. It'll connect the doll to him.

What if Micha's so far gone that she's attached herself to Antonio? He's just gone back and killed one of her abusers. That's a situation ripe for turning her to his side. If Micha fights Khalid, she could save the fetus and kill him.

My stomach tightens, but I push that fear aside. She has been tortured for nearly three months, and she won't know it's him doing it if she's in a V-haze. She won't know there's anything to fight...

But what if I lose him too?

My brothers used to feel invincible to me. I used to think we could take on the world together. Now their existence feels so fragile. That guarantee is gone. I've lost two already, within months of each other.

I could lose Maddox on his mission.

Khalid could die.

Stop.

Worrying won't do anything but waste time. I need to tell them the rest of my plan so we can bring my wife and brother home. Locking down my fears, I look at Ezriel. "You said you found out where the Lesser Eleusinian Mysteries are now held?"

He nods. "Orpheus Cave."

"Wait, where we just were?" Enoch says, and his twin slaps him upside the head, ruffling the edge of his mohawk, which has been cut into the shape of a gecko. "That was Odysseus' Cave, dumbass."

"They sound the fucking same!"

"One has an R in it!"

"*You're* going to *has* my fist –" His mouth slams shut as Dayne touches him on the side of the head.

"You were saying?" he asks as he looks at me. I pulled out my phone as soon as they started bickering to text Vlad and Aleric. I hit send, letting them know we need a lift.

"Antonio won't risk the place being tampered with when he needs it to go into the Underworld. He'll have something or someone watching it. So if we just let ourselves be seen in the area –"

"He'll go check it out," Dayne finishes as he lets Enoch go. Then he shakes his head of dark hair. "I don't think he'd bring her with him for that."

"No," I say. "It's two plans. The miscarriage is for if this one fails."

"So what's this one?"

"We set up an ambush to kill him and Eduardo."

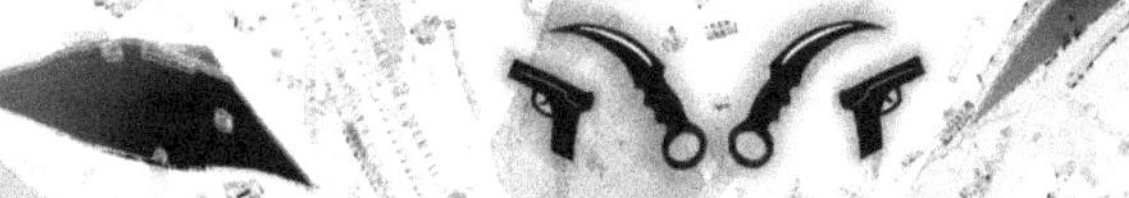

Aleric never replied back, so Vlad ferries us in multiple hops one by one on his own. He's never been to the area the cave's in though, so the first time he goes, taking Enoch, he can only phase the distance he can see for the last couple miles. The new reaper is still on his knees and groaning by the time the rest of us got there two hours later.

"Oh my gods, you're such a baby," Ezriel says, and I turn away from them, sorrow piercing my lungs at the thought of the baby I've lost.

Dayne looks at me, and I can see the pain on his face too.

"This needs to work," he says, his voice tight and low. "If she's broken –"

"I know," I say, glancing at Khalid as he pulls out Rudy's soul doll this time, checking in on our brother. If his chaos magic spins out of control, Micha will die too.

I look back at Dayne, and he nods with a small jerk; he's ready to do what I asked him to – as suicidal as it might be.

When we went to the school to save her the first time, I had one plan. Now I have three. One of them has to work.

"Spread out," I say, "and look for the cave."

We're not looking for the one on Google maps. There's another one hidden deeper in the rocky shrubland. The sun beats down on us, and the heat of its rays bounce back up off the dry ground, making us sweat. But it isn't the killer temperature that's bothering me. It's the lack of any human heartbeats other than ours. Are we in the right area? Is he not watching it at all? Are we wasting time on a foolish –

I stop, my head jerking all the way around to look behind me. I can smell a wolf, and it's one I fucking know.

"Antonio," I hiss. He's tried to hide his scent, cloaked it with magic. If I was a regular witch and Eduardo wasn't so weak right now, perhaps he would've succeeded. He doesn't want us to know where the cave is; he's come in quiet and is most likely getting Eduardo to simply double up whatever cloaking spells he has on it.

Then he's going to be gone again.

Then this plan will fail.

"He's here!" I shout to my brothers. We need to catch him before he can disappear. According to all the research Ezriel's done, only those who have gone through the Lesser Mysteries will know where the location for the Greater ones will be. This is the only choke point in his plan to get into the Underworld. If we miss him now, we will have to wait until February or March, when he actually needs to be here.

That's months away.

Months of her being tortured more.

Being broken *more*.

No!

Vlad phases in front of me, almost as desperate to get to Rudy as I am to my wife. I don't tell him that he isn't strong enough to take Antonio on his own. If he dies, he'll still buy me a few seconds, and I'm callous enough to take it.

I'm fast with my hybrid speed, streaking away from my brothers and Dayne, but I still don't know how to phase. Don't even know if I can. A hybrid's abilities isn't always a mix of their parents'.

By the time I spot the fucker I want to kill, he's already inside a teleportation circle. I don't know where Vlad is or if he's dead or alive, but the wolf clearly isn't concerned with being attacked by him. He smiles at me, even lifts a hand to wave. Then he's gone, along with Eduardo, and the damn hope that was building in my chest.

But I don't stop racing towards the spot where they were. In fact, I dig into everything I am and try to sprint faster.

Because the circle is still aglow, still has a bit of power for another couple seconds. It's wild and dangerous, just the flickering lights of what one needs to safely travel between the circles, but it is enough.

If I get there in time.

Only a few more feet...

"Varius!" Khalid shouts from behind me. He opens up the ground in front of me, covering it in shadows. I leap over them, hoping like hel I can clear the distance. If I touch it, I'll be sucked down into the Plane of Monsters – safe but away from her and then she'll be alone until she dies, killed by the blood bond I asked her to start with me. Because Khalid will take me home, lock me up, and throw away the key. My heart will break. All reasons for existing will go, and I'll have to tell Bambi that I failed her mother as much as I failed her.

My throat closing, I pray I can cross the gap. But it's growing. Stretching. Following my actual shadow as it races across the ground under me. Half a second. Half a fucking second is all it might take to kill my plan.

But when I hit the ground, the shadows are gone, sucked away, and I know Dayne's grabbed Khalid, with both his hands on his head.

"Run!" he shouts. "I can't hold him for –" He bites his words off, struggling to hold my brother. The ex-reaper. The one who knows me so damn well as to think I would try something this stupid.

But it isn't stupid.

Because everything I want is on the other side of that

teleportation circle. Staying out here, away from her, is the stupid choice.

Who chooses hel when there's a chance of heaven?

I can't do anything to save her from out here, so I will chance my luck from inside.

I run towards the teleportation circle, to the light glow that's fading too fast, the final tendrils of the spell starting to disappear.

I barrel into the circle.

The power grabs hold of me.

I scream as thousands of fine golden threads, sharp like barbed wire, latch onto my body. It isn't supposed to work like this. I am supposed to be studied by the witch as the circle is made or included during the incantation ritual so the magic knows to take me and how to take me and how to deposit me as I was.

So it's tearing me apart, trying to figure out what to do with me. Ripping off pieces of my body and trying to fling it into the ether, but I push out all my grief, all my hope and pain. All my love for the woman at the other end of this journey, and I feed the magic inside of me.

Let it out. Let it *pulse* without Stormie here to contain it.

Smoke-like shadows pour from me. They shoot out like a thousand arrows, a thousand lassos, a thousand tar-lined vines – all weaving onto the golden threads.

Black consuming color.

My power consuming his.

Holding me together when the circle would rip me apart.

A stupid risk, one I wasn't sure would work, if you asked Khalid.

But what is love if not risking everything you are just to see them one more time? What is hope without a leap of faith? My wife is that hope, and I will leap into the fucking ether for her.

I scream as the pain rips me apart. Tearing at every atom

of my body. But my power ties it all back together, battling it fiercely, refusing to let it take me. The black threads keep wrapping around the gold. Crawling across the strands until no color remains.

And then I am gone from that world, that plane between the circles, that nothingness where hope fought to survive, and I'm back on my feet. Then down on my knees, my legs giving out as I crash to the floor inside another circle.

A teleportation destination circle.

I lift my head to look at my surroundings, praying I'm on a boat. Eduardo screams as he looks at me. He starts to form a ball of red energy as Antonio shifts fully into his werewolf form.

"I'm a hybrid," I rasp past all the agony that's pulling at my brain to knock me out. "And I'm fertile."

My vision narrows. My body collapses as it convulses. I hoped I would have the strength to at least slip into my shadows upon arrival, but there is nothing left inside of me.

Just pain.

And more pain.

I think I might be bleeding internally.

I don't even know if I have all the parts I left with.

But I have my eyes. I see Antonio signal for Eduardo to stand down, and that is enough.

That means he's going to keep me alive.

And that hope I jumped into the circle with.

That leap of faith to see my wife.

It ignites brighter inside of me even as the world dims.

Dims.

Gone.

Perhaps I am stupid for her.

But hope is such a beautiful thing.

HER

I stand under the spray of the shower, trembling from the hope blossoming inside my belly. It's only been a few hours since Antonio saved me and gave me a purpose for living again. But I feel like it's a new day. A new year. A new *me*. I feel so different.

So hopeful.

He's going to get my baby back.

I grope around for the shampoo bottle, then cradle it in my arms like I used to do with Lou. I rock it back and forth, humming a melody I remember my own mother singing to me. Tears run down my face.

But they're happy tears this time. Full of love. I'm going to hold my baby girl for the first time because of *him*. He's going to save her like he's saved me.

There's a thought tickling inside my head, but I run from it fast. Throw up walls left and right to keep it away from me. *He* saved me. He will not hurt me...

Not as long as I obey him, and I will. Because he will give me what no one else can. Not my husband –pain lances through me– not the gods –anger fills me now– not even me. Feelings of shame and filth wage war across my heart, leaving a blood, muddy field death-stomped in their wake.

The tears aren't happy anymore.

I drop the bottle of shampoo, and it splatters open at my feet. Leaking out. Disappearing down the drain. My child gone, ripped away from me.

I'm such a failure.

Am I even worth being saved?

Being given the chance to be a mother again?

What if I fuck it up? What if she's better off dead?

I can't even protect a bottle of shampoo…

A sob rips out of me, and my body curls inwards.

"Antonio!" I scream, needing him here. Praying for my savior, putting my faith in him like he told me too. "Please!"

He comes to me.

Instantly appearing in the shower beside me, he gathers me in his arms and holds me, asks me why it hurts.

Bubbled snot runs down my face, only to be washed away by the hot spray. By his presence here taking away the pain. He's naked with me, and I take comfort in the closeness of his body.

I press a hand to my belly. "What if she hates me?" I sob. "I'm so dirty and disgusting and weak."

"So be strong for her. It will take me a while to bring her back; you have time to learn. But look at you."

I take in my pathetic state and wince. The craving for V claws at my stomach.

"You turned to me instead of V," he says, knocking the breath from my lungs. "That was your second step to being strong. The first was having a shower. I'm proud of you."

His hand slips between my legs, and heat slams into me, so much hotter than the spray raining down on my head and shoulders, filling the place with steam. I stand frozen as his finger rubs between my pussy lips. Not going in but going up to my clit. He presses on it, and I shudder against him.

"What are you doing?" I ask, my breath a hitch in my lungs. I look up at him and see his golden eyes staring down at me, burning with an intense heat.

"Rewarding you," Antonio says. "For being a good girl by taking a shower, you get my fingers inside you." I cry out as he slips a finger deep into my pussy. My hands clutch at his muscled shoulders, holding on to him as my back arches, pushing my breasts against his chest. A golden dusting of hair clings to him and tickles me.

"For praying to me like a good girl, they get to move." He pulls out slowly, then pushes back in. Another cry escapes me. I fall to the floor, my legs giving out, and he crouches down in front of me.

"Every time you're good, I'll reward you." He curls his fingers inside of me, and I clutch at his hand as I lift my hips, riding him to his bottom knuckles. I don't need any V when I have him. All I need is him. He will save me. Provide for me. Care for me just like he promised.

My lips part. The urge to suck his dick and pleasure him as he's pleasuring me is nearly overwhelming. I'm getting so wet. So turned on. He's even better than the V.

"Every time you're not…"

I scream as pain pierces my lower abdomen. It's pure fucking agony, increased by the fear of confusion and the unknown. My hand feels wet with something too sticky to be water, and I pull it out from between my thighs, my heart racing so far it lodges in my throat. I can't breathe. Can't comprehend. Can't think.

Antonio vanishes, his absence leaving me cold. Sitting on the floor of the shower, unable to see, I place my hand back between my legs. There's more stickiness. More pain. More fear.

How long have I been bleeding? I've been in the shower for hours, sitting under the spray, just trying to get clean. I picked up a shampoo bottle at one point, but I got distracted rocking it back and forth like a baby. I never cleaned myself, couldn't do that step of touching myself all over.

Touching me like Bear did…

I sob.

Press a hand to my mouth.

Taste the blood coating my fingers.

Jerking my hand away, I press it back between my legs, trying to stop the flow. But the floor of the shower is all wet with something that isn't water or soap, the thickness of it too great. The consistency of it all wrong.

There's so much of it too. All down my legs. All around me. Clotted clumps that tell me I'm losing the thing inside me. And I have no love for it, no desire to carry it to term, but if I lose it, I lose Rafiki.

And I can't lose her again.

Can't bear it.

"No," I rasp, grabbing at the clumps with my free hand, trying to stop them from going down the shower drain. Can I put them back? Can I squeeze my legs hard enough to stop more from leaking out? Can I save it? There has to be a way to save it.

Because if I lose it, I lose Rafiki.

And I *can't.*

Panicking, I stumble to my feet and out of the shower, not bothering to turn it off or even shut the door behind me. I grope around the cabinets for a hand towel. Wad it up and press it between my thighs. Hoping it helps. *Needing* it to help.

Eduardo said the fetus was okay only a few hours ago. So how is this happening? Why is this happening!

Rudy.

My breath catches. Rudy is doing this. He's punishing me for trying to save my child. He's just like his mother, a heartless bitch. Antonio was right. The Shadow family only cares about themselves. They're evil and cruel. They don't care about the innocent lives they hurt. Even the kindest of them could do this to a child... To a grieving mother.

I just want my baby back. What is so wrong with siding with Antonio when he's the only one who'll save her? Sau started this. He told me that. Everything that is happening is because of *her*. Because she decided to kill his innocent wife and pups. Like mother, like son. She should have to pay for what she did to him. What she did to me!

She killed my baby!

She deserves to die. Antonio deserves to win. He's just trying to save his mate. My child.

Why can't Rudy see that?

He told me the truth.

What's wrong with the truth?

Sau killed Rafiki.

She should have to pay.

Why can't they see that what they're doing is wrong!

I hate them.

I waddle out of the ensuite and into my room, clenching the towel tight between my thighs.

I hate them all.

I make it to the door.

They're killing my little girl.

Ruining the only chance I have to get her back.

I just want her back.

I want her back.

"Stop," I beg. I don't know if Rudy can hear me, if his magic reads minds and fears subconsciously, or if he hears all one's nightmares and fears and picks and chooses who he hurts. But if there's a chance he can hear me, I will beg until my voice box bleeds.

I can't lose her again.

Hope is such a terrible fucking thing.

Yanking on the door handle, I step out into the hall. I need to find Eduardo and get him to heal me before Antonio finds out.

I don't know which direction to go though. I'm too afraid to call for him and risk the werewolf hearing me.

He will punish me for this.

It's my body.

My fault.

I'm nothing but a failure.

A disease.

"Stop..."

I collapse to the floor as another cramp knocks me down. The towel falls away. There's so much copper in the air. So many tears on my face.

"Please..."

Defeated and hopeless, I pray to the one person who has been there for me.

"Antonio... make him stop..."

Almost instantly, his voice cuts through the dark.

"Can you save it?" he demands, his voice rough and full of anger.

I flinch, pressed up against the wall, terrified of what he will do to Rafiki because of me.

"I'm sorry," I rasp, begging him to believe me.

Two hands press against my stomach. A warm feeling grows from them, like the feel of an old lightbulb being held up to my skin, an inch away.

"No," Eduardo says, the word shaky. A tremor of fear that ties us together. "He's gone."

"You said it was fine."

"I thought –" He blunders. "He was!"

"You thought or it was?"

"He was!"

"You're exhausted," he says, his voice low and lethal. "Or maybe you just lied to me?"

"No! I –" The healer cuts himself off on a whimper. "I might not have checked the heartbeat. But I checked he was there," he blurts. "I didn't –" His words are smacked out of his mouth.

"Fix her and start her ovulation again. I want her bred this evening."

"I'm too –"

"Has your use to me ended, witch?" he murmurs.

A heavy weight smacks the air. A terrible silence. "No," Eduardo wheezes. His hands are back on my belly. The heat that flows from him this time is a lot warmer. I whimper in discomfort, but my attention is on the man lording over me.

"Please... My baby girl..." I say as to Antonio, pushing the words out through the clog of tears. "Don't leave her..."

"Who was her father?"

I tense, my heart rate increasing. There's a memory in the fog of my brain. "What?"

"Her father. You told me it was Aleric Zadar." His voice softens dangerously. "Did you lie to me."

My shoulders shake as I'm hit with an earthquake of fear. "I'm sorry. I'm so sorry. Please –"

"Who is it?"

His name lodges in my throat. I sob against the wall as Eduardo continues to heal me. But he can't fix the hole in my chest. Can't fix the chasm created by the choice I'm about to make.

"Varius'..." I sob, pushing his name out even as it wants to choke me, grabbing hold of my tonsils so I can't speak. "But please don't leave her because of who her father is," I beg. "You promised me you'd get her back. *Please*... You can kill him." My throat closes even tighter, wanting to stop the words from escaping. But I can't hold them in. Can't protect him if it means losing her. "*I* can kill him. He doesn't have to have anything to do with her at all. You can still end the Shadow line. I won't even give her his name. *Please*... Just bring her back to me."

Don't judge her for Sau's sins.

Let me have my girl.

The air moves, and Antonio squats down in front of me. His voice brushes the air right in my face, a tender caress, a god's attention. "Birth me a hybrid," he says, "and I will let her live."

Sobbing, I reach for him. "Thank you." My fingers grip his shirt tight, holding on to the only lifeline I have. "Thank you... Thank you..."

Who needs hope when you have a man who cares?

FIFTY-EIGHT

HIM

Someone is on me.

I'm on my back in a bed, every nerve feeling splintered and fried from my jump through the teleportation circles. The touch of their body, their movement against my hips is making me sick from the increasing pain. My eyes roll back in my head. My atoms weep. I almost lose consciousness again despite having just regained it.

I fight through the darkness, though, dragging my body kicking and screaming into the world of awareness. Because a woman's body is riding mine, and I don't know if it'll be worse to find out if she's a stranger.

Or my wife.

Her pussy grips my hard cock as she slides up and down my length. Her hands are on my chest, her fingers flat, and just from that, I know it's *her*.

I shudder from the force of my warring emotions, the battlefield shaking underneath steel-toed feet. I'm relieved to feel her against me, to be beside her after months of being apart, but the fact that she's gone straight to doing what Antonio wants breaks my fucking heart. She used to be such a fighter.

I'd hoped that once she realized I was here, she'd get a bit of that back. She would know that I had never given up on her. She'd understand that I had come here just so she wouldn't be alone. And that would break through to her. Remind her that she is loved. That she has a life outside of this hel. A family who wants her home.

But her movements are frantic as well as robotic. What remains of her mind isn't the Micha I know.

Fighting through the pain of my body and that truth, I open my eyes just as her pussy squeezes the tip of my cock. It jerks inside of her, remembering all too well what solace I found in her when buried to the hilt. Or when I had my tongue deep between her pussy lips.

But then I see the other person in the room.

Antonio is standing in front of the door, his eyes on her. His cock hard. His arms crossed.

"Sorry she doesn't feel as tight as you remember," he says mockingly. She turns her head to him, so clearly desperate for his attention even as he insults her. "My boys got a little excited." He smiles cruelly. "And she likes riding my cock almost as much as your whore of a mother did."

I jerk up in bed, trying to get to him, but my shoulders barely come off the mattress before I drop back with a yell. Burning agony shoots up my arms, and I look over at my left one to see a dozen modified nails holding me down. There must be a thick piece of wood beneath the mattress.

I pant heavily as the pain in my arms throb like a mother fucker. He's pierced both of my palms too so I can't use my shadows. I expected him to cut them off when I leaped through the teleportation circle, so I try to tell myself this is a better outcome, but it's fucking hard to do at the moment.

"You want to show him how well you take me, Micha?"

She blushes as she nods. "Please."

My heart is stabbed through with its own set of nails. Disbelief. Shock. Horror. Fucking terror that I came to her too late.

"Micha," I rasp, but she doesn't even acknowledge I've spoken. She just rides my cock rhythmically as she reaches a hand towards Antonio.

He starts to strip off his clothes piece by piece. With each bit he drops to the floor, my heart races harder. He pops a Rick, and his cock changes, becoming tongue-like but long and fat and splitting an inch at the tip.

This can't be happening. My little monster... wanting the monster who killed our child.

"Micha!" I yell, trying to get through to her. "He killed our daughter. He –"

"No!" she screams as she slaps me on the chest with both hands. Then she reaches up to hit me in the face. "Your bitch of a mother killed her! She set me up as a patsy!"

"He –"

"*She* blamed me for tearing the ward down."

"He did that!"

"*He* didn't blame me! He didn't *lie* about me! He's just trying to save his mate because *Sau* killed her and their babies. Three of them, Varius! She killed all three of them and then forced him to eat them!"

She smacks me again. No longer fucking me. No longer able to focus on anything other than her grief and the lies he's fed her.

"And I screamed for her! I begged her to help me, but she never came! She didn't even wait for me to get down to the basement. I bet she wanted either Antonio to kill me or her monsters to, but he didn't!" Her mouth drops open as if she has just now come to this conclusion. I want to be optimistic that that means he's only just started digging his claws into her and rewriting her memories with his lies.

But that optimism only feels like foolishness.

Early stages or not, she is clearly convinced of his purity.

"He saved me!" she shouts. "He saved me. He only hurt me because he didn't know me. But you already knew me then, and what did *you* do!"

My guilt strikes me mute.

"You tortured me! You raped me! I don't have my eyes because of you! I don't have my magic because of you! I couldn't save myself because of *you!* I couldn't –" Her voice cracks, killing me, especially so because I know what she's about to say. "Couldn't save *her.*"

Her face twists up like she's about to cry. I try to say something, but Antonio cuts in to comfort her before I can.

"Pull on your fury, Micha. Not your pain. Your pain does nothing but make you weak."

She swallows hard as she turns her head towards him. He walks over, and I try to rise again. Try to intercept him before he can get to her, but the nails are too fucking deep. At least one of them has gone through bone, and I'm forced to lie here and watch him touch her.

He cups her cheek, and she leans into him.

"Your grief doesn't make you weak, Micha," I say, but her attention isn't on me.

It's on him.

"You want him to be hurt for what he's done to you?"

She nods, and he slips his hand into her short black hair. "Then suck my cock while you make him come."

I roar, struggling against the nails. The smell of my blood seeping down my arms pulls at the heart of my Craving. I haven't fed since Aleric broke my jaw and forced me to that first day she was taken. I try to fight the hunger, recalling how I hurt her, how I scarred her the last time I let it take me in her presence.

Remember how she cut my mark from her willingly.

Fear how it might push her further into his arms if I let it out now.

But she's leaning over to suck his Rick-changed cock as her pussy starts bouncing on mine again. She kisses his tip, then licks her way down it as she holds on to his hip with her hand. His tongue-like dick "kisses" her, and she moans as she fucks me harder. Her cries become muffled as she takes him deeper.

Deeper.

Until I can see the bulge at her throat as she swallows around his tip. His fingers tighten in her hair, but he doesn't guide her where he wants her. She does that all herself. She bobs up and down his dick, sucking him off, and the agony of watching them is barely matched by the pain running up my arms and chest. With everything hurting, I'm struggling to stay in control.

She moans around his cock, and the primal beast inside me rises closer to the surface. Then all I am pinpoints into two basic instincts as the Craving rips free:

Hunger.

And sex.

With a roar, I jerk my hips up into her. Her lips pop off his cock as she shouts in pleasure and surprise. Pride rips through me as her pussy squeezes me. I want to wrap my arms around her tight little body and fuck her hard and fast, so I start straining against the nails.

The pain is intense, but my hunger for her is more so. Antonio fists her hair and guides her mouth back on him. I roar in fury.

That's my fucking wife!

She places her hands on my chest, her fingers flat, and that simple action calms me a little, piercing through the utter mindlessness of the Craving.

But it doesn't stop me from trying to tear free and take her just for myself.

He pulls her down hard onto his cock. Her nose presses into his muscled stomach. She moans around his dick as she squeezes mine. Her pussy feels so godsdamn fucking *good* that I come too.

"Don't swallow," he commands, angering me enough to push me off the high of my orgasm. "Kiss him and let him taste who you belong to."

Micha pops off both our cocks as she crawls up me with puffed out cheeks. I growl, wanting her bouncing her tight little pussy back on me, but she ignores me, only listening to *him*.

I strain against the nails, ripping them through my flesh and bone. My left arm gets free, the one furthest away from the fucker I'm going to kill, but her lips are on me now, and she's spitting his cum into my mouth. It tastes of cocoa with a tinge of salt.

I try to spit it out, but her tongue is inside me, sweeping it around my mouth, and I am consumed with the need to kiss her. To make love to her. To sink my fangs into her neck and make her mine.

My fingers are useless on my left arm. The nails have ripped through too much, but I wrap my whole arm around her, pinning her to my chest. I turn my head and nudge hers to the side. Then I lean up and bite her at the base of her throat.

She cries out as her hands press down on my shoulders. I suckle her skin, drink down her blood as it squirts into me. Growling, I hold her tighter, the pain of my injuries ignored under the pleasure of her body.

Of the taste of her.

Of marking her as fucking *mine*.

As the haze of the Craving starts to wane now that it's been fed, I pull my fangs out of her neck and bite my tongue hard enough to bleed. I press it against her wounds, pushing my blood into her. The payment for the bond between us.

She cries out against me as it snaps into place, tying us together in a way he can never touch. I lick her neck, giving her more. I pray she can feel all my love for her now, that it makes her come back to me.

But instead of falling into my arms, she shoves away and stumbles to her feet. Tears streak down her face.

"I hate you!" she screams as she runs from the room, and I can feel the truth of that so damn hard.

The blood bond *hurts*.

I try to sit up to go after her, but my body crumbles from exhaustion. My right arm's still pinned to the bed, and the crash from the Craving hits like a fucking truck. I fight it as much as I can, but my eyes close, and all I'm left with is the nightmare of having lost my wife.

FIFTY-NINE

ANTONIO

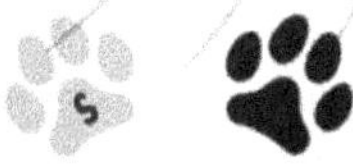

May 30 1893, Cornelius, North Carolina

She presses herself up against me as soon as we enter a private room of the whore house. She wears only her skirts, her breasts free to dangle and grab. I have no interest in them though. Or her. It's just been three years since I've been touched, and the primal part of me will no longer be ignored.

Especially not when I just got news from Jack that Siome is dating some fucker with a ranch. I am happy for her. I truly am. She deserves all the good things in life, the love and laughter of a good family. I'm just miserable for myself.

So I got drunk and came here. The matron knows what I'm really after though. She's been paid well to clean up after me. She also knows that if this place didn't have the Death Hunt stamp on it, I'd kill all of them for being dirty fucking whores.

Instead, I'm just going to kill this one. It's still cheating on Siome; it's still fucking *wrong*, but it eases some of my guilt. Allows me to get hard enough to actually use her for the release I need.

She murmurs something in my ear as she reaches her hand into my pants. I've already taken a Rick, so the dick she grabs isn't mine.

I'm not interested in foreplay though. I don't care about her getting any pleasure from this. She sold her body and I purchased it. So I shove her up against the wall, turn her around, and hike up her skirts. She tries to face me again, to tell me perhaps to slow down, she isn't wet enough, but I punch her in the face, breaking her nose. She screams as her knees buckle. I hit her again, this time in the jaw, and she stops on a dazed whimper even as she hits the ground. I reach down and grab a fistful of her golden hair, then drag her just far enough to lay her out. Right in front of the door. She isn't fit to have a fucking bed.

This isn't romantic.

This isn't *pleasurable.*

It's just a fucking animalistic drive.

I turn her over onto her stomach. She moans in pain as blood seeps into the wooden boards. I hike up her skirts and throw them over her head, then pull my cock out of my pants, slip on a condom, and lie down on top of her. Not caring which hole it goes in, I push in wherever it lies.

She yelps, her ass clenching, her torso jumping off the floor. I wrap a hand around her head, pressing her skirts into her face as I muffle her cries.

Her ass is squeezing my cock, trying to stop me from going in any further, but with a jerk of my hips, I ram in balls deep. She screams against her skirts and my hand, and I close my eyes as I fuck her, trying not to think of Siome with another man.

I want her to be happy.

I *need* her to be happy even if it isn't with me.

I just want her –

That's fucking it.

I just *want her.*

And I can't have her.

Because of the godsdamn curse from Artemis, Grecian Goddess of the Moon and Hunt. I'm sun touched. Supposed to live a life of misery so she doesn't.

And I can deal with that. As long as she is happy, I can take the torture of her absence. As long as she is fucking happy.

This new man better take care of her, or I swear to the gods, swear to death itself, that I will kill him and anyone he fucking knows. Including Jack, the man I owe a thousand times over for taking her away from me and watching out for her all these years.

Because they might think they're not at fault, but they knew him and allowed him to live long enough to hurt my mate. I don't give a shit how little they knew him. Not when it comes to her. The whole world will burn for failing her. And then I will kill myself too because I'd be the biggest failure of them all.

I squeeze my eyes tight as I rut the whore, imagining her easy laughter, her quick smile. Her fearlessness in the face of my grumpiness and misery. Not even my parents ever looked at me like I was worth knowing. No one like that deserves the only life I'd be able to give them – an infection of pain and sorrow.

She deserves the world.

She will get the world.

Or I swear to everything I am that I will burn it down.

I come in the whore beneath me, a physical release that gives me nothing. Fucking them never makes me feel any better; it just helps with the urges for the next few months or years. The ones that are so ingrained within our kind – a pack, a society, a *home* in the touch of another. Werewolves are not meant to be alone; being touch-starved can literally drive us to the Craving. So I seek a whore out every few months or years when needs must be met in order to ease that hunger.

It doesn't help with the self-loathing though.

The guilt.

No, that expands, exploding out in an instant. Jumping to my feet, I kick her in the stomach. She curls up and wraps her arms around her head. I kick her again, breaking her bones. I stomp on her, beat her, and my dick's not even soft yet. She tries to defend herself for the first few seconds, but soon she lies still, her body moving wherever I kick it, like a rag doll. My rage continues to rain down on her broken and bleeding body, and with it, a howl erupts.

I cheated on Siome.

Hearing about this will hurt her.

How the *fuck* can I claim to protect her, to give her the world when I do shit that I know will make her hurt?

Shifting into my wolf, I give in to the hunger, the rage. And I slaughter everyone in this whore house until all that's left is my guilt and misery.

Present day, Somewhere adrift in the ocean – Antonio

My cock is wet form the Shadow whore's mouth, and it makes me want to tear the fucking thing off and choke her with it. She isn't my fucking mate. I shouldn't have touched her. I promised Siome "till death do us part" – *our* deaths, not just hers, and I fucking failed her. This will hurt her if she finds out. I knew it would, and yet, I still did it just to hurt *him*.

Varius fucking Shadow.

Furious with myself, I grab his hand. I'm not worried he pulled an arm free from the nails. There's a witch's snare looped around his neck and two more around his ankles. Power alone doesn't mean anything when it comes to those golden chains.

Besides, he's passed out from the effects of the Craving, so I have time to bite off his fingers and swallow them down before he wakes, make sure he can't use any magic he has.

I don't know what he's capable of, had always thought him to be a witch without magic. So it's better to be safe than sorry. Shifting just my teeth into those of my wolf, I bite off his fingers. I don't bother with his other hand. I want him to know the consequences of his actions. I want him to break. To *suffer*. I haven't kept him just to breed him and then let him loose when it suits my plan, letting him "escape" back home with Micha. He's here to pay for his mother's sins.

Thinking of my own crimes, of the wetness of my cock, my fury ignites through every inch of my skin. I use a bit of the sheet to wipe off her slobber and traces of my cum. Then I stalk from the room, knowing I need to kill her to make this right. It's the only acceptable way to apologize to my mate.

I failed her.

I was *weak*.

But I will make it right.

I don't need Micha alive anymore. I have three other female wolves on the boat that I know can make hybrids. Rudy hasn't managed to get any of them pregnant, so I'll give him to Eduardo to play with and dissect, then pawn his women off on Varius.

Getting Sau will be harder when the time comes but not impossible. I'll just go with my original plan of torturing her sons so badly that she comes to me.

So that confirms it. Micha will no longer breathe. She'll no longer be alive to insult my mate's memory.

My clenched jaw radiating my fury, I track her down to

her room. The shower's running. She's trying to get clean. I can hear her crying beneath the spray. She hates his touch as much as I hate hers.

I wrench open the bathroom door, and she turns to me. "Antonio. I –"

I cut off her words with a punch to her face. I don't want to kill her slowly by cutting off her air. I want to beat out my guilt and shame. I want to hurt her for helping me hurt Siome.

She stumbles back into the shower and hits her head.

"I'm sorry!" she blurts. "I'm –"

I hit her again, then grab and haul her out of the shower.

"I did what you want!" She cries as she lifts her arms to block her head. So I hit her in the stomach, causing her to curl in. "Stop, please! I'm sorry."

I kick down on her knee, breaking it with a hard *snap*! She screams as she collapses to the ground, but still she tries to face me. Down on her knees, her hands together as if in prayer. "I'll do anything to make this right. I just want Rafiki back. Please! I'll do anything to get her back!"

My foot freezes an inch from breaking open her face.

My heart beats too damn fast.

Skips a beat.

Skips all of them, I'm fucking sure.

Because the world doesn't feel right anymore.

My peripherals are closing in.

The noise of the shower's fading behind the buzzing in my ears.

"What did you call her?" I rasp, my entire body shaking as I set my foot down beside her and haul her back upright.

Her head lolls, so much blood pouring from her nose, lip, and temple. "My baby?" she croaks. "I call her Rafiki." Her face twists in pain, and I remember her saying she never really named her. So it's just a nickname.

A nickname...

My hands fucking *shake.*

"Please just let me help you get her back..." She sobs in my grip, so much pain on her face. So much mother's love and worry. "I'll do anything."

Rafiki...

Rafiki...

Raphello

Fiana

Kimmy

The names of the three pups I shared with Siome...

February 14 1917, St. Augustine, Florida

"Do you think we'll recognize each other if we meet in the next life?" Siome asks as we cuddle on the front porch, waiting for the sunrise. My hand is on her belly as she lies against my side, curled up on the couch I bought just for her to drag me out of bed too damn fucking early every day. But though I yawn, I cherish every moment I get to spend with her. Not even utter exhaustion can make me want to sleep in when she's the alternative.

Especially since, although she might have convinced me that being sun-touched doesn't mean I'm cursed, we are still in the middle of a war with the Shadow Domain and the Blood Fangs. Though, in a couple days, I'm asking them to meet me behind the old library in town, a place of peace talks that all three of our gangs have honored since this war began. Despite how quick I've been to turn to violence, I am excited for what can come from this parlay.

My fingers dance across Siome's belly. I'm excited for the future family we are about to have.

When we found out she was pregnant – after years of struggle, she asked me to leave the Death Hunt for her. But with my desired skill set and past sins, it was too dangerous for us to live without a pack. Both our enemies and allies alike would hunt us – wanting us for different reasons but wanting us all the same.

She screams in frustration as she stands in our kitchen. "There's always an excuse with you!"

"It's not an excuse. Siome, I want to. I just –"

"Can't. Yeah, I know! And so what? You're just going to send me away again? And our three pups? To save us?"

"You know that's the best –"

"That's not the best! You're the best. Us staying together is the best! They need their father!"

My heart twists all the way up my fucking throat. I want to raise them with her. Be there for her. Fall asleep to her every night and wake up a few hours later to soothe our babies so she can sleep. But I can't.

"A war is no place to raise a family," I try.

"So stop it!" She says it like it's so fucking obvious, and for a moment, I just stare at her in disbelief.

Then I shake my head. "I can't just stop a two-thousand year war!"

"Why not?"

"Well, for one, I'm not even alpha!"

"So become it. Oscar is too conservative. He doesn't look to the future."

"Siome –"

"You talk about burning the world down if it fails me," she cuts in, her red eyes blazing. "But what good is all that talk when you can't even figure out how to change one small corner of it to protect me?" She grabs my hand and places it on her stomach. "To protect us?"

I huff out a breath.

But her eyes soften. She knows she's got me.

When I promised her the world, I fucking meant it.

"Okay," I say, and her grin breaks out completely. "But you're helping me figure out a way to stop this war. That's *going to be a lot of sleepless nights."*

She shrugs a shoulder. "I'm about to be a mom. I'll be up anyway."

Gods, I love this woman and her optimism. Gathering her in my arms, I show her just how much.

It's crazy to think that in one month we've come this far. I took the position of alpha and convinced all my capos to agree to peace talks. We're all so tired of this damn war. We all have kids we wish to raise in peace. Who we wish to see grow up.

My fingers dance across Siome's stomach once more as I stare at the lighting sky. In another few months, by the time our pups are born, who knows what the world will be like?

"Hmm?" she says, prodding me in the side and turning her face up to mine.

Remembering her question: *Do you think we'll recognize each other in the after life*, I say, "We won't have to. I forbid you from dying."

She laughs, but I'm fucking serious. I won't survive it if she dies.

Snuggling up tighter against me, she lifts my arm from her belly and kisses it. Then she beams up at me, her red eyes burning with so much mischief. "I'd recognize your grumpy ass anywhere, anytime."

"No, you wouldn't. The gods don't let us come back with our memories."

"I know. But I'd just have to look for the guy who gets jealous of alligators."

My eyes narrow. "It was a croc." And it was way too close to her face. She kissed it.

"See?" She pokes my frown. "Instant ID for Mr. Grumpy."

I fight the smile for a second before giving in. Squeezing her tight, I kiss the top of her head. "And I'll just have to look for the lady who infuriates me the most."

"Hey!"

She turns to face me, and I pull her all the way onto my lap with a cheeky smile. She's so predictable. She straddles me. I kiss her. We strip.

But then she stops me.

Pulls back. "You know, a good girl like me shouldn't be having sex out of wedlock," she says, fighting back a grin.

"I'm already mated to you."

"Yeah, but my soul could burn for all eternity if we don't get married."

"It's a silly ritual when compared to –"

"*Mymecia pyiformis.*" She places her hands on her hips and huffs out a breath. My eyes dart to her tits, and she reaches forward to twist my nipple between her fingers.

"Ow!"

"You better ask me to marry you *right now.* Because I'm tired of waiting for you, and I'm fucking horny."

"If you're happy to curse without damning your soul, you should be happy to have –"

I yelp as she tickles me. She grins as she attacks me further, her little fingers destroying my sides until she gets me to yield.

"Fine! Siome Jackson, will you marry me and put me out of my misery?"

She lights up, and silly human tradition or not, I'd marry her a thousand times if she keeps looking at me like that.

"No," she says.

My mouth drops open. "What do you mean no?"

She shrugs. "I feel like that was a lackluster proposal."

"You put me on the spot!"

"Well." She sniffs. "Do better."

Rolling her beneath me, I *do* better all right, and she is Better.

I get her to scream until she begs me to fuck her and marry her and do anything else I please.

Curling up with her in my arms, I realize we forgot to

watch the sunrise. But that's okay because we can watch it together tomorrow.

And the day after that.

And the day after that.

Because this parlay is going to lead to a peace treaty. I can feel it in my soul.

Surely, they are as tired of war as we are?

Present day, Somewhere adrift in the ocean – Antonio

My mind reels as I look at the woman in my grip.

It can't be...

But it *could*.

Siome's been dead for over a hundred years. She would have had time to be reborn. To come back to me... She never was one for waiting.

I shake my head, trying to clear my thoughts.

But she looks a bit like her. If her black hair was longer. If her eyes were red...

And she's been such a pain in the ass since I met her. First at the Shadow House when I tried to grab Khalid's girl. She made it so I didn't have time to check for the back-up stash of alexandrite I knew they had.

Then when I went to kill her that second time. I wanted to grab Sau, but she fought back harder than I thought. She was supposed to be a quick done deal.

And then here – killing all my breeding chimeras one by one. The successful ones are infertile, so I let them go, no longer needing them because of her fucking husband having destroyed the foundations of the Death Hunt.

My throat tightens.

And the similarity in the V. I came back to find her just like I found Siome – the Fates perhaps needing to smack me in the face with a four by four because I didn't get all the previous clues. Even her name overlaps. Siome – ends with a 'me' sound. Micha starts with it.

One cycle to the next.

"Oh my gods."

Gathering her up in my arms, my heart bursting with love and grief, with shame and guilt for all I've done to her, I carry her out of the room, racing for Eduardo's quarters. He'll heal her. I don't care if it kills him. He'll *heal* her.

"I'm sorry," I say as she clings to me, her head so bloody and bruised. "Fuck, little helfire. I'm so sorry."

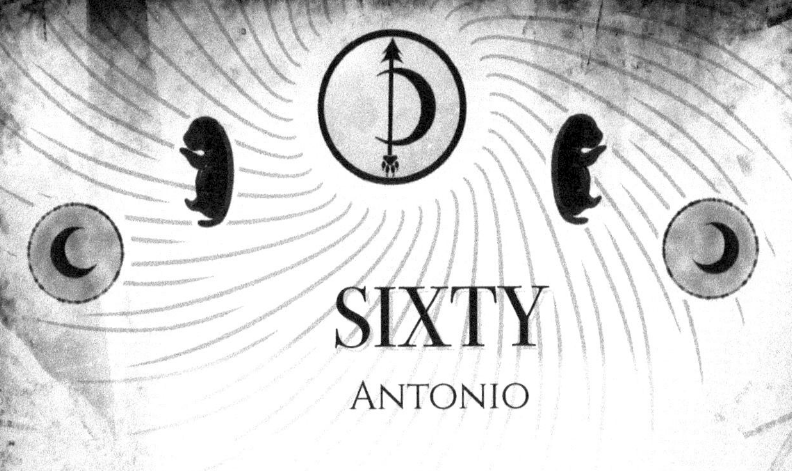

SIXTY

ANTONIO

I barge into Eduardo's lab. He has Timothy strapped to a table, his dick hooked up to a pumping machine, jerking him off and collecting his seed. Normally, the witch would have his subject opened up in some horrific experiment or another too, but he's used too much magic recently. I can smell the onset of loka building up in his blood. He'll die a terrible, agonizing death if he uses much more, so he's only been carving shallow cuts into the chimera's skin.

He turns to me as I enter with Micha in my arms. "Heal her."

"I ca–" He cuts himself off. Either he dies trying, or he dies now. Micha's injuries aren't fatal; he has nothing to barter with.

"Put her down," he says.

"Not here." I don't want her touching the filth of his lab. She isn't the same as Timothy. She isn't even the same as me. She's so much fucking more. Better. Purer.

He follows me out and to my room. He's normally not allowed inside it, but I don't want my mate anywhere else. I lay her down gently on my bed. The blood crusted on her face stands out sharply even amongst the swollen bruises. She moans, and I grab her hand to comfort her.

How could I have been so stupid as to not have seen the signs? She has Siome's fire, her stubbornness, and her fierce protective nature of those she loves.

Siome jumped into my fight with Declan Shadow to save me. Despite that choice ending in her death, I know she wouldn't hesitate to do it again. She loved her pups, as did I, but we loved each other more.

Eduardo steps up to study her face – the injuries I put there in my idiocy. "I'll grab some healing –"

"If I wanted a wand or potions, I would have grabbed them," I growl. I don't want mediocre. I want the absolute best for her.

"I've used a lot, and her injuries aren't ser–"

"Heal her," I snap. They're fucking serious to me. I laid my hands on her. I fucking *hurt* her. And I'm so fucking close to killing him for taking his time.

His lips tighten. He nods. But there's a flash of defiance in his eyes. If he thinks he's going to die anyway, he could kill her. Or permanently disfigure her. Give her a chronic pain or a lifelong illness.

"If you hurt her," I say slowly, "death will be a blessing. And when it comes, I will drag you back from the dead to start it all over again."

He gulps.

Resting his hands on her, he calls on his magic. White light bathes her, reducing the swelling in her cheeks and stitching up her split lip and busted skin. The bruises fade, and she opens her eyeless sockets. The sight rams into me. Suffocating me. I kiss her hand, then rise to my feet. "Get out." I hiss at Eduardo before gathering her in my arms. He leaves, and she tenses against me.

"I'm so sorry, Micha. I'm so fucking sorry. I know better now. I'll never hurt you again."

"Why did you hit me?"

I wince. My heart screams.

"Did I not please you? I'm so sorry for –"

"You don't need to apologize." I kiss the top of her head and squeeze her tight. "You never need to apologize."

She trembles in my arms. Silence. Then, "Why did you ask me about my daughter's name?"

My chest tightens. She doesn't remember what she lost. What *we* lost. When people are resurrected, they don't get their old memories.

I want to tell her about all she's lost – not just them but *us*. All the memories. All the laughter and joy. And the pain. So much pain as we fought to stay together. As we cleared hurdle after hurdle, spurred on only by each other. We were each other's strengths, each other's change, each other's push to be better.

She was my life, and I was hers, but now I am the only one who remembers.

Trying to get her to recall her past life could fracture her mind; there is a reason the gods wipe them clean.

But all that means is I'll just have to get her to fall in love with me again. My heart pinches at the thought of courting her all over again. A bittersweet opportunity.

"You – Siome," I say, knowing I need to keep the two of them separate. As much as she's the same woman to me, she does not remember that life. I don't want to confuse her, make her panic if she doesn't think she is who I know she is. "Siome and I had three pups. A boy and two girls on the way. We named them Raphello, Fiana, and Kimmy."

I don't explain further. I want to see if she gets it, if her soul just *knows* and can put the pieces together. It takes her a fraction of a second. She gasps, and I know she knows.

"Their names make up Rafiki," she says.

She remembers them. Subconsciously. In her heart and soul. She remembers them.

I squeeze her tight. Kiss the crown of her head. I could cry with how happy I am to have her back in my arms. But I don't because I can't linger here despite how much I want to. Varius has only recently hit his ascension, and given he is strong enough to have walked through the teleportation circle on his own and survived, I know he's strong enough to pulse. Eduardo is too weak to contain him, which means I need to go see Terra.

She's been creating a disease to target the Shadow line. I can get her to tweak it so it isn't as deadly. So it'll keep him alive but too weak to use his magic. I would prefer if he was lucid for all his torturing, but this is the only choice I have. I might be strong enough to resist his magic should he pulse, but I don't know if Micha is.

And I will still take pleasure in torturing him.

"I need to go," I say.

"Will you be back soon?"

The fact that she wants me here warms my heart. But she should be more angry with me. I don't like how much I've broken her. The guilt rams into me, just like it did when I learned I was the reason she took the V the first time. I need to build her back up. Make her comfortable enough to yell at me again. Gods, I've missed hearing her yell at me, hearing all that fire and spirit and *beauty.*

"I'll be back before bed."

"Will you eat with me?"

I smile. Siome always pushed for what she wanted. "As you wish." Kissing her on her head one last time, I leave her in my bed.

She looks too small in it. Too broken.

For now.

But she is a fighter.

And when I build her back up, we'll destroy the Shadow family together for what they did to her.

When I step into Varius' room, I am barely able to stop myself from killing him. He is blood bonded to my fucking mate. I might've stolen her from him in this life, but he will have all the lifetimes with her I will not.

My shoulders tight but my hands loose, not clenched into the fists I want them to be, I stride over to him. He is awake and wary and pleasantly pale. The big scary boss half of the US is terrified of, struck down like a little lamb. Soon he'll be butchered like one too.

"Well, don't you just feel like a fool?" I mock as I stand in front of him. "Gave yourself up only for her to leave you for a better man."

"She won't leave me," he says. "I have a part of her you'll never have."

My eyes narrow. "I already have it." I had it *first.*

But I will not have it last. She will end up with him in the next life.

And that *infuriates* me.

Pulling out the needle I picked up from Terra on the way over, I hold it up. "I was around for the war between Terra Harrison and Cara Jervis. The humans called it the Spanish flu." His eyes dart to the needle, then back to me. There is a flicker of fear there, a knowledge that he can train as much as he wants, but he can't learn to fight a fucking disease.

"A fifth of the world's population killed off because of a lover's tat. In just four months, the disease they made took the lives of twenty-one million people. Not the young or the old either but the healthy." I shake my head. Then smile. "How *crazy* do we get over the people we love, huh? All the terrible things in the world because of it." I pop the lid off the needle. Take a step forward.

He laughs, and there isn't a single trace of fear in his eyes. "Even if you kill me, you won't have her in this life." Just utter fucking conviction.

I grab the arm he yanked free earlier, pressing my fingers over the piece of metal nailed through his wrist. He grits his teeth, his jaw tight, his nostrils flaring. Sweat beads across his brow as he struggles to stay conscious despite the pain. Jabbing the needle into the swollen, tender area around the nail, I look him in the eyes and say, "I already have her."

I push the disease into him, and I take delight in the light tremors running down his arm. The fear he's trying to hide.

"This won't kill you," I assure him. "You don't deserve to go that quick, but you'll run a fever, and you'll shit yourself in this bed. Every part of you will ache, from your toes to your wayward thoughts, and the entire time you will know that *your wife* is riding my cock and shouting my name."

He smiles wolfishly. Leans forward. "But she will still be *my* wife."

My jaw tics.

I break the needle in his arm.

He laughs even as he falls back, sweat already starting to break out across his skin. Terra's disease is working quickly. "Go ahead and torture me. Whatever you do to me, she'll be able to feel through the blood bond. And my brothers won't even have to save her then. You'll lose her all on your own." He chuckles. "Just like you did Siome."

My hand shifts into that of my wolf, and I lift my arm to rake my claws across his chest. But I stop myself before I cut him open and rip out his fucking heart. Death will not be that easy for him.

My jaw clenched, I drop my hand and storm from the room. He might've won this round, but I'll figure out a way to make her hate him. A hatred so deep that it sears itself into her very soul so she loathes him across all the lifetimes they might have together.

I will not get her in the next life but neither will fucking he.

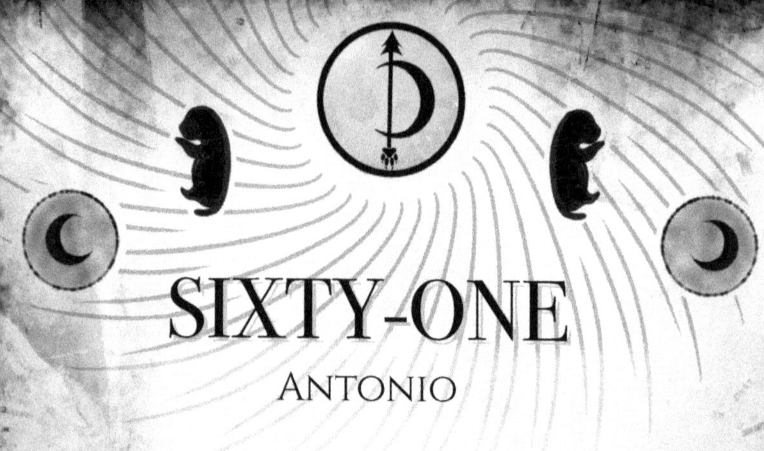

SIXTY-ONE

ANTONIO

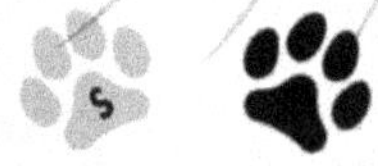

I had to wait three fucking weeks for Eduardo to feel well enough to do a transplant. I wanted to push him to do it earlier, but the operation is too risky at the best of times. If he's struggling with his own illness, he could accidentally kill her.

But today is the day I give my mate back her eyes. It won't change what I did to her, but it's a start to fixing my sins.

And it'll bring her closer to me while pushing Varius out of her orbit. Although she hasn't wanted to see him at all, she keeps asking about my plans to bring back Rafiki. *Their* child.

And she's pregnant with another one of his fucking kids. I wanted it aborted, but Eduardo warned me that if he did, her next pregnancy would be extremely risky. Magic got into her womb somehow, making it practically radioactive. He tells me he can't heal her. He doesn't know if it's from the V –there haven't been enough studies– but Siome had a hard time getting pregnant too after she became an addict. Ironic if it's the cause, though, considering they have a line for increasing pregnancy. Either way, I'm fucking pissed. I can smell it in her womb every time I hold her.

Growing like a demon.

Claiming her like her fucker of a husband has, refusing to let go.

He's still holding out despite his daily torture. I asked her if she could feel what I did to him, and she said no, so all the gloves came off. I haven't told her she's pregnant though; I know she isn't ready to hear that news, and so I've been taking it all out on him. Skinning him. Hammering more nails into his skin. Making him eat bits of himself – muscle cut from his thigh, his left testicle, his right eye.

But physical pain isn't breaking him. He's still laughing, knowing that the more I do, the more I worry that Micha will go back to him.

She's in my bed every night, but we haven't made love yet. Haven't even kissed. She still seems too fragile despite getting stronger and more confident every day. She asked me this morning if she could help me kill Sau when the time came, and that's made me hopeful that she is looking to our future.

But every time I mention Varius, a bit too much rage flits across her face. He still has too much hold on her. Too much control over a woman who should be all mine. And I don't want there to be any trace of that inside her when we make love for the first time. I want her solely focused on *me*, the man she loves. The one who loves her, who hasn't stopped loving her for nearly two hundreds years.

So tonight I'll be setting up a video camera in Rudy's room and letting Varius watch what I do to him. He hasn't once asked about his brother, so perhaps he will not care, but I want to torture Rudy anyway. Cut off another piece of him –his tongue this time rather than his ear– and send it to his mother.

Just like Aleric used to do all those years ago. Except I don't want to kill him and ship him all at once. I want to drag it out and make it *hurt.*

He is a Shadow, and all Shadows deserve to be wiped out after Sau killed off all of Siome's line. It matters not that she is reincarnated; she lost her entire family because of that head bitch. And I lost all of mine.

But for now, I just need to grab Jenny Ann – one of the three breeding women still on the boat. Her eyes are red. The other two women's aren't. So when she opens her door, I punch her in the face. Move in to choke her out quickly, then carry her to Eduardo's lab over my shoulder.

As much as I don't want Micha passed out on his table, there's nowhere else to do the operation. So I lead her to it when the time comes, after Eduardo digs out Jenny's eyes without an anesthetic spell because he doesn't have much magic to spare.

"Will you be here when it's over?" she asks.

"I'll be there the whole time," I reply. And she climbs up on the table.

It takes him four hours to undo the spell he used to heal her after I scooped out her eyes. Anytime one is broken, it triggers an explosion of energy, so he has to concentrate hard in order to unravel it and control it, to stop it from going inside of her and frying her brain.

Then it takes another three for him to connect all of the nerves to her new sets of eyes. Each passing minute feels so godsdamn slow.

And then finally, he is done. He steps back with a wipe of his brow. He wakes her up, and I step forward as she opens her eyes so I'm the first thing she sees.

She sucks in a breath as I stare into her new red orbs. He modified them a bit, changed them so they don't quite look like Jenny Ann's. They don't look like Siome's either, and I can't stop the flicker of pain in my chest at the knowledge that I will never see those specific beauties again.

Pushing that thought aside, I smile at her. "How does everything look?" I ask.

She blinks, then keeps her eyes shut. "It's too bright."

"Hold on." I pick her up and carry her out of here. Back to my rooms. Our rooms. I close the curtains to block out the majority of the sunlight. "Open them now," I say.

She cracks them open in the gloom of the room, but our kind can easily see in the half-light. She sucks in a breath, then starts to cry. With a jolt of worry, I hurry to her and gather her in my arms.

"What's wrong?" I ask, terrified Eduardo messed them up somehow.

"I can *see* again. I never thought I would see again after the fucker chose to take my eyes," she babbles against my chest. Her fingers dig tight into my shirt. "Thank you." She starts to cry with joy. "Oh my gods, thank you."

And that's when I get the idea – how best to break Varius and make her solely mine.

SIXTY-TWO

VARIUS

I don't know how many days have passed; each one has been blurring into the next. It's too much of a struggle to keep track through the sickness. My body is drenched in sweat, and I'm lying in my diarrhea just like he promised I would be. But I'm too out of it to care. Too dehydrated and aching all over. It's like I've been hit by every strain of the flu at once, and I don't know how the magic inside of me hasn't killed me yet.

Hasn't seen my weakness and striked.

Perhaps because it's sick too...

I wouldn't put it past a witch as badass as Terra fucking Harrison to make a disease that could target magic itself.

Not that I would allow myself to pulse and hurt my wife. Or Rudy...

Tears burn at the memories of him being dissected on screen. I want to cry. I want to scream into the void and have the noise itself wrap around this ship and drag it into the sea. I'm going to fucking kill Eduardo for healing him, healing me so we can be tortured over and over again. And I'm going to kill Antonio for everything he's done to them.

Maybe not in this life though…

I feel so weak.

Too weak to help anyone.

I came here hoping to let Micha know she was still loved, that we hadn't given up on her. And to find a way to escape with her from the inside, but I haven't seen her outside that first time. I've been trying to push my feelings of love and no regrets down the bond – even after all of this, I do not wish I'd stayed away. She needs to know that she is loved. That I love her enough to have followed her here just so she wouldn't be alone. But all I've felt from her is hatred.

And love for another man.

And then, slowly, nothing at all. We need to exchange more blood for the bond to slip back into place.

Agony twists through me, deeper than the aches and pains of the disease. Because what if she wants to reject the blood bond entirely now? What if she does give that part of herself to Antonio, lost to his madness and brainwashing?

The panic hits hard.

I try to control it.

Somehow manage it as the hours pass.

I just need to get her away from here, away from him. Then I can help her through her trauma. And I don't even care if she leaves me then, if she wipes her hands of all this and walks away with just Dayne and Lou. The gods know she cannot be blamed for it, for seeking out a life of peace and healing. It's all I want for her – to be happy. Not this twisted version of Stockholm syndrome and a broken shell so desperate to please her enemy to stop the pain. I want her happy. I want her safe.

I need to find a way to escape…

There's another pain deep in my chest, a reality I don't

want to face, so I shove it down and try to concentrate. I didn't just jump into the teleportation circle without a plan. Dayne tattooed me with a tracking rune, the same as he gave my wife. It's under my right armpit, hidden in the hair, an unlikely place for Antonio to see. So he can feel where I am, and he won't stop coming for Micha.

But the issue remains of how he – and the rest of my brothers can get here. Before I can come up with any sort of plan to help them though, the door to my room opens, and Antonio walks in.

My stomach twists in fear about whatever new horror is about to happen even as my rage ignites. I have given up struggling against the nails. More of them have been added anyway, and both my arms are pinned down again. I need to save my energy to do things that actually matter. I have so little left in the bank...

"Today is your lucky day," Antonio says. "I could use you back on the outside. It isn't mandatory." He cocks his head to the side and shrugs. "I will find another way to release Terra's disease on your family, but I'd like it if you carried it to them. It'll be such a fitting end, don't you think?" He grins like the wolf he is. "Not that it will be enough to kill them. It'll just weaken them enough that I can get to them one by one even without the help of a Family behind me."

He stops in the middle of the room this time instead of coming to my bedside to torture me. But that doesn't make me feel any better. It makes me feel a thousand times worse. I know he has something planned. I can take the physical torture. I deserve it after everything I've done to my wife. But the emotional shit he attacks me with...

My thoughts go back to Rudy, of seeing him vivisected and raped on screen, and he doesn't even have the luxury of dissociating. He has to stay completely aware so he can stay completely in control of his chaos magic, or everyone on this boat will die.

Including me. Micha. The dog he's trying so hard to protect, every life mattering to him. Everyone.

My heart breaks for him, wishing I'd been more open about how much he means to me in the time we had.

"But first, you're going to make a decision," he continues. "To get your freedom, all you have to do is give me an answer."

"My answer is... fuck you."

The fact he smiles chills my feverish skin. "You'll want to think this through better than that," Antonio says. "But the rules are simple. You will have two choices. One will die. The other will live."

My heart beats rapidly, my brain sluggish but still able to understand. One choice will be Rudy. The other Micha.

He's no doubt using this as a way to show her that I'll always hurt her. That when it comes to my family, I will choose them over and over, just like I did with Khalid. It's not true, but in this instance, logically, I have to choose her to be the one to die. Because I know he won't hurt her. I can see his obsession of her clear on his fucking face. Choosing her will only hurt her emotionally, but it'll mean they'll both still be alive. Because if I choose Rudy, he *will* kill him.

"I'm not playing your fucking games." My voice cracks, splinters, shatters all apart, but I don't care. I can't do this. I won't do this to her. To him. To fucking me. I can't survive knowing the decision was mine.

"Oh, you will," Antonio says. "Because I won't just be letting you out. I'll be letting you leave with her."

I surge forward before I remember the nails embedded all down my arms. They remind me with gut-wrenching agony, and I collapse back in bed, panting hard. "You're a liar."

"Not in this. I think it'll be fun to watch you suffer." He grins. Shifting his right index finger into a claw, he carves an A into his arm and says, "With the gift of the gods, I bind their blessing to my oath."

My stomach drops in horror. He's making a fucking blood oath. He's giving me an actual way to escape with my wife. I'll be infected, a carrier for a disease that will cripple my family, but he doesn't know we have Cara Jervis. She can undo whatever Terra makes – maybe. Hopefully. The two were evenly matched when they went to war and killed millions of people when their disease magic took on a mind of its own. And I'm certain he's hoping to use her as a mole, a sleeper agent perhaps, so confident she will choose to help him from inside – and that I won't tell my brothers, won't tell the reaper because I'll be too desperate to save her. Too hopeful that I can.

My stomach twists at the cruelty of his plan. And the knowledge that I will damn well choose... I just need to make sure that even if I choose her and he fails to kill her, that the blood oath will still demand he lets us go.

"I'll let you and Micha Shadow –" My last name is hissed out between his teeth. I hope it fucking hurts him to know that she's still mine – at least in that. "– leave this yacht in the condition you are now in" –he carves a G next to the A– "after you choose who will die." He smears the blood from his cuts into a silence rune over his initials.

My heart is racing hard. He didn't make it part of the blood oath that one would have to die. I just need to choose. And picking her will make her hate me, but it'll save him and get her out of here alive. Then Rudy will be free to let his chaos magic out, and we will all reunite at home. I try not to smile. But Antonio doesn't know what shitstorm he's about to release on himself. Rudy's secrets have always stayed within the family.

"K," I say, keeping my tone flat, my thoughts hidden. But I know that reply will piss him off, especially after he's been so theatric. I know because I've been on the receiving end of it enough times with fucking Aleric. Genuine annoyance seeps into me at the mere thought of him, which just goes to show how terrible of a person he is that even when utterly drained and tortured, I can still find it in me to hope he gets run over by a bus that then reverses.

Antonio's lips tighten. But he doesn't react other than that. Instead, he merely says, "So tell me who you choose to die." He looks towards the door. "Rudy," he says as Eduardo wheels him in. He's strapped to what looks like a dentist's chair that's been modified to be even more terrifying, with multiple tools of torture attached to movable arms. Our eyes meet as Eduardo walks out again, and my baby brother still tries to smile at me, tearing my heart from my chest.

"Or Dayne."

My head whips to him in horror, wondering when the hel Antonio caught him but able to imagine it all too easily. He was able to feel me through the tattoo he gave me. Fuck the odds, he would've come for her the first chance he got.

Antonio smiles at me, wide and feral. But my attention is pulled from him as another chair, so much like the first, is wheeled in.

Dayne's head hangs limp, bloody, and still. But I can still sense him breathing. He's alive.

For now.

My stomach drops.

Churns.

Wants to come back up.

"Choose," Antonio says, "and I'll let you leave with your wife."

SIXTY-THREE

VARIUS

I want to tear free of my binds and rip out his fucking throat. Even if I managed to pull the nails out though, the three witch's snares would keep me thoroughly restrained.

I am helpless.

I am weak.

And I have to make an impossible choice.

All my life, I have been forced to make them. Kill Talon or hear him out? Send Maddox in to almost certain death or risk never seeing my wife? Torture the woman I'm in love with or lose Khalid, the only brother I truly trust, forever? Listen to the woman who raised me, who protected me all my life, or the one I've only known for a few months? Focus on saving Micha or Rudy? Stop to try to save Leno or run for my wife? Kill a grieving dog or force Krypto to keep on living? Eyes? Or ears?

I've not always made the right choice.

But this isn't *right*.

Neither of these choices are right.

Rudy is like a fucking son to me, and this whole time I have been focusing on Micha. I can't end it with him dying because I chose her friend – *my* friend over him. I won't. I don't care how much he'd make that choice himself.

He is my *son*, and I cannot leave him to die.

Nor can I choose Dayne, the only man my wife needs to recover. She doesn't love me anymore. She hates me with every fiber of her soul, and no doubt will run away as soon as she's free. So she needs Dayne. *I* need him to watch out for her when I am gone from this world – giving up my life so she can continue to live without being forced to complete the blood bond. Without being forced to tie herself to a man she hates.

"Choose," Antonio says, his tone light and mocking.

I look at Rudy, tears in my one remaining eye, the other in my stomach – or perhaps having already passed through to the sheets. He looks at me and gives a little nod. *Choose me. I'm ready.*

I know he's suicidal. I've walked in on him trying to kill himself multiple times. He's only here because he loves us, because he knows how big of a hole his death will bring to the family. But he isn't happy as much as he smiles. He has chaos magic inside him, and it's tearing him apart. So if I choose him, maybe he won't die.

I shake my head, my whole heart bleeding. *I can't.*

He smiles at me. A bit sad but entirely without judgment. Without blame. *You can. I'm ready.*

I'm ready.

I'm ready.

Well, I'm fucking not!

I'm not ready to lose another brother.

I thought Rudy the most infallible of us with his magic. With his self sacrifice to stay alive and be our emotional support. We need him with his love of the little things in life. His rosy glasses. His time out to stop and smile. We need his comfort. His humor. His warmth. We need all that he is. *I* need him.

I can't lose him.

"I need you," I rasp.

He looks at me softly. "Not if you have her."

But I might not have her. I might have lost her for good given all the things I've done, and I fucking understand it. I failed to save her. I took her magic. She thinks I made the choice to take her fucking eyes. To hurt her again despite my promises.

So she believes Antonio. Believes him to be her savior. The one who hasn't lied to her because she isn't of the right mind to see his words for the lies they are.

What if I choose? What if I give up on my *son*, and she just leaves?

Pure agony rushes through me. I can handle her walking away from me to be happy somewhere else. But I can't do it while also losing Rudy. Can't stomach it. Can't handle it. I start to hyperventilate. Can't hold back the tears.

"Aw, look at the big man cry," Antonio mocks.

I ignore him, keeping my eye on Rudy. A silent question. *Can you control your magic?*

Pain flashes in his eyes. He shakes his head.

And I break.

Chaos magic isn't like regular magic; it doesn't wait to be commanded. It's wild and unpredictable, and it will latch on to every one of our fears, bringing them to life. If he tries to use even a little, to poke a hole in his tight control, the magic will burst free.

And my greatest fear is losing them all. Micha, Rudy, all my other brothers, my mother, Dayne, Lou, and Stefaan. Everyone I care about, everyone my wife cares about could be killed in an instant, wiped from this world by Rudy's magic.

I can try to focus on a different fear of mine, pull up the line-dancing goats that I've conditioned myself into being afraid of just for him. But I know Dayne's greatest fear is losing Micha. Antonio's too. And I don't want to know what horrible things Eduardo can come up with. Or Terra – one of the strongest disease witches in the last two hundred years.

And then there's Rudy's fear.

The whole world gone. His body rotting with decay. But he's still alive, left to wander alone in perpetual pain. Left to scream into a void that will never answer back.

Perhaps he is not strong enough to make that reality true for the whole Seven Planes or even this world. But he is strong enough to take out an entire city. Entire islands that might be nearby. Or kill off all the fish and other creatures in the sea around us, causing a devastating effect for the world. It's why he doesn't come with us on missions. Why he's so godsdamn careful with his magic.

With chaos magic comes chaos.

Comes death.

He tries to smile at me again. *I'm ready.*

But I'm not.

Gods fucking dammit. I'm *not.*

Dayne groans, finally coming to, and my attention pulls to him.

His shoulders jerk as he tugs on his binds. He isn't nailed down like I am, just chained. He even still has his hands – though they're tied together so he can't use them.

"Fuck!" It's a sudden shout full of fear. He knows where he is. His head snaps up, his eyes wild with a remembered panic, a childhood of trauma and terror-filled pain. I'm sure he's looking for Eduardo, but they land on me and freeze. I can sense his heart beat running wild. The Craving lunges in my belly, wanting him to run. Wanting me to chase. My teeth start to ache, but I fight it back. If I make the choice when I'm mindless...

"Shit," Dayne says. "I'm sorry." Sorry for getting caught. Sorry for ending up here. He's the only one who could feel where I was through the tattoo. Now my brothers have no hope in saving us. In saving Micha. He's doomed us all, and a part of me wants to punish him for that, to let him feel the consequences of his mistake by picking him.

But he wouldn't be here if it wasn't for me.

None of them would be.

If anyone should die, it should be me.

"Kill me," I say.

"So you can get her in the next life?" the werewolf scoffs. "No."

"Choosing won't stop the blood bond!"

"It will because we both know who you'll choose. And then she will come to hate you."

I shake my head. He's fucking delusional. "When she learns you were behind it –"

"I would've done nothing but proven to her that *you* will always hurt her when given the chance. You will put your own selfish needs above hers."

"You will hurt her if you kill him!"

"I will be all she needs." He says it so flippantly, so damn confidently. He truly believes it. He doesn't know her at all. A life with him will destroy her in so many ways. *As if a life with me already hasn't,* a mocking voice says.

"The blood bond isn't completed!" I shout desperately. "If I die, I'll never see her again." Never be able to hurt her even by accident.

"You're lying."

"I'm not –"

"A pathetic attempt from a dying man. Now *choose.*"

"I'm not lying! If you kill me –"

"I want you to *suffer,*" he cuts in. "I want you to wake up every day, wondering what you could've done differently.

What you could have *possibly* decided to do that would've changed what happened. I have spent over a *hundred years* living with the choices I made. The guilt that led to my mate and pups dying. She wasn't supposed to be there. She was supposed to stay back. Sau was supposed to be an easy kill, so I threw her at my wife, fucking *damning* her because I thought she could handle her.

"I saved your mother from being killed by my pack for what she did, willing to let bygones be bygones if she just *healed my mate.*" He shakes with his emotions. So much fucking rage and fury and pain and grief flickering across his face.

"But she refused, and so you will suffer for her sins. She took *everything* from me. Death will not be so easy for you."

I stare at him, trembling with my own rage. With the fear that I'll lose my son or my wife's best friend – *my* best friend who I have actually come to trust over these last few months.

Then Dayne cuts in. "You *really* need to go to therapy, dude."

Rudy's mouth breaks out into a grin. Mine falls open in shock.

"If you think killing me is going to push Micha into your arms, you don't know her at all."

"She's already in my arms." I pick up on how quick he is to get jealous. Wonder how I can use it.

Dayne shrugs as well as he can in his chains. "Eh. She always did have a terrible taste in men." He glances at me, that same smile on his face Rudy has, that same willingness to die for her. "You know her first crush was on the mean kid in *Karate Kid?* Like *hello?* Blond villains are never hot." He points his head at Antonio as if the point is made.

Seething, the wolf looks at me. "You have one minute to choose," he demands. "Or she'll stay here with me forever."

SIXTY-FOUR

HIM

"Thirty seconds," I drawl as I pull out the needle that I got from Terra. "This is a nasty little disease. It targets the magic in one's blood, eating it until it's gone, and do you know what that does to a witch?" The magic is a part of them, woven into every atom of their being. "His death will not be quick," I say. "Or pleasant."

It gives me great pleasure to see the pain on Varius' face as he struggles to give me an answer. I might have Siome back, but his family is the reason I lost her in the first place. I used to think a child shouldn't be punished for the sins of their parents, but then I held my mate in my arms as she died, and I changed my fucking mind – at least when it comes to the Shadow family.

They're all as vile as the disease I'm holding.

"Nine seconds...

"Eight.

"Seven."

He screams, so much delightful pain in that sound. His mother took my mate from me, and he thought he could take her again. But once I tell her he picked her best friend to die – regardless of who he actually chooses, she'll hate him forever. Siome always could hold a grudge, especially against those who hurt the people she loved.

"Three.

"Two."

"Rudy!" Varius shouts, then screams again, so much pure agony erupting from his soul.

I smile as I step up to his brother. I wish I could drag this out more, but Terra told me Rudy's magic was becoming unstable. She's been taking blood samples from him every week to keep an eye on his chaos magic. If I don't kill him today, he could take out this entire ship. Enemies and allies alike.

I stab the needle into Rudy's neck.

Varius screams, raw rage and terror ripping out of his lungs. He will blame himself for his brother's death, but in truth, this was never about him having a choice. I merely want him to suffer. Rudy would've died either way – either as a choice or as a punishment for Varius having chosen Dayne. But Dayne would've lived because my mate likes him, and I would never hurt her.

"Have fun watching him die," I say. "He will ooze from every orifice, but it won't be blood that comes out. He'll be melting from the inside, the disease destroying every organ and bone, every tendon and muscle he has, and all that *goo* will slosh out of his mouth and ears and eyes."

Varius struggles to get free so fiercely that he manages to rip both his arms off the bed. The nails are embedded in his skin, into his bone.

I look over at Eduardo. "Heal him. I don't want him dying anytime soon."

The witch pales as he looks at me.

"He's tied down with witch's snares. Stop being a pussy and get over there."

Eduardo gulps, but he does as he's told.

I turn to Dayne. "Thank you for playing along." I speak loud enough for Varius to hear me even over his screams, knowing this will destroy him even more. He chose to save a traitor, and because of his decision, his brother is melting from the inside out. "Your acting was fantastic," I say.

He smiles back at me. "I learned from the best."

I undo his binds. He hops off the chair. "Where is she?"

Micha told me how much he mattered to her a couple weeks ago, that he and her sister were the two she wanted to save from the Shadow Domain. So I tracked him down, then brought him here as a surprise. I'm looking forward to seeing her eyes light up like they used to.

Her sister is being harder to get to, but I will save her in time. I will be Micha's god in every prayer she directs at me. "In our room." I turn for the door to lead him to her.

Rudy convulses with a gurgle of blood pouring down his lips. Varius cries, and I stop for a moment just to enjoy it.

"That's some serious shit," Dayne says. "Is it infectious?"

"No. It'd be too dangerous then."

"So it's safe for me to get a closer look?"

I smile, able to see why Micha likes him. Gallows humor is something we always shared. As much as I want to trust him simply because she does though, I keep my senses well tuned to him. If he even tries to sign a spell into existence, I will have to bind his hands.

Then I will work on convincing him he wants to stay here, just like I did Micha. What my mate wants, she'll get.

I nod at Rudy. "Be my guest."

He steps up to him, moving around to the side of his chair. "Fascinating," he murmurs as he places both his hands on Rudy's head, one on each side, and tilts it up so he can get a better look.

"I'm going to kill you!" Varius screams. He's trying to rip the witch's snare off his neck, but nothing can break that golden chain.

Eduardo jumps back nervously. "What if he gets free –"

"He can't," I say. His fear is so fucking annoying. But I don't need him for much longer. After I find the recipe for Greek fire –still wanting to venture into the Underworld so I can check Micha is really Siome. Though I know she is deep in my soul, I would never be able to forgive myself if I got duped by a Shadow whore– I will be taking Micha into Blódyrió and never coming back. There, we will make a life together. Or I will kill her if she isn't Siome.

But I know she is.

I can feel it in my bones.

Can see it in so many aspects of her now that I know to look.

"Come on," I tell Dayne. "Micha is –

My eyes widen as the chain at Varius' neck shatters, as does the two around his feet. He scrambles up and lunges for me. Eduardo screams. I start to shift –

Only to find I can't.

"Help me!" Dayne screams. "I can't move!"

Rudy's magic is breaking free. Terra warned me she did not know how chaos magic would react to hers.

Cursing, I pivot out of the way.

But my legs are nightmarishly heavy. I move too slow.

He rams into me, shoving me off balance. As I fall to the floor, he snaps off one of the metal torture instruments that is attached to Rudy's chair. Eduardo screams once more like a little bitch, then throws up a ward around him.

Only to have it instantly flicker out.

Scrambling for the door, he tries to run, but his feet sink into the ground. Then the wood solidifies around his ankles. Blood seeps up and out of the floorboard, and he falls to his hands. They sink in too, up to his wrists. More blood. More pain. The floor looks like it's rippling towards me.

Cursing, I roll away from both it and Varius, then jump to my feet – and get kicked in the chest. I stagger back, my feet moving as if they're encased in lead blocks. I need to kill Rudy. Free Dayne from his grip.

I try to shift again, but Artemis' gift doesn't come.

Knowing I can't move fast enough to keep dodging with my limbs affected by Rudy's magic, I let Varius come to me. He'll try to stab me with the weapon he has – a metal rod with a pair of pincers at the end, meaning I can get away with focusing on only one thing, and I don't need to hold out long, I don't think – No. I *hope*.

Chaos magic is a different breed. The shot I gave Varius was of the same disease though, just a much weaker strain, so we know it eats magic. It was created from Micha's blood after all.

He jabs the weapon into my side. I knew I wasn't fast enough to block it, so I didn't bother. I left myself open in the place I wanted him to hit. Then I grab his wrist and wrench him to me. I smash my head into his, and his eye goes glazed for just a moment.

Eduardo screams as a monstrous spider appears behind him. Human faces line its bulbous back, their mouths open as they shriek in horror. I try to not get distracted by it, but a massive dong swings from underneath it, large enough to drag on the floor. It mounts Eduardo, its dick sharp enough to pierce through his clothes. I don't think it cares about finding a hole. Wrapping its front legs around him, it pins him down as it fucks him hard and fast. The faces shriek. So does Eduardo, and Dayne yells, a deep roar of pain.

I don't know what Rudy's magic is doing to him, but I don't want him to die. It'll devastate my mate.

But I can't help him until I deal with Varius first.

I try once more to shift.

And this time, my werewolf form ripples up my left arm.

Rudy's magic is weakening as he dies.

Varius is fighting as hard as he can, but he's suffering from blood loss, months of torture, and the disease in his blood. He isn't thinking as straight or moving as fast as he otherwise would be. I slice my claws towards him, holding him with my human hand, locking him to me.

He jumps up with both feet and kicks me in the chest. I stumble back, releasing him, and my claws rip through the air. He lands on his back. I trip over something behind me, but as I stumble, I yank out the metal rod he shoved into me and then shift completely into my werewolf form.

The spider starts to shrivel up. Rudy's not far from death. But before it dies, it bites off the top of Eduardo's head. His brain's now exposed to the air, but he doesn't die; the chaos magic has wrapped itself around him tightly. The spider's dick is still inside him, and he screams in utter agony.

Dayne's legs give out, and he collapses to the ground, blood pouring out of his eyes and lips. But it's pinker than it should be, almost the color of brain matter, and I wonder if Terra didn't screw me over. If the disease is infectious after all. Then again, chaos magic is called so for a reason.

But with its effect on me greatly reduced, Varius doesn't stand a chance, not in his condition.

Grabbing him off the floor with a burst of speed he can't match, I slam him into a wall. His head cracks, and I hit him again until his eye rolls back and he falls limp. Dropping him to the floor, I run over to Dayne. Check his pulse.

Nothing.

Closing my eyes briefly, I curse.

Maybe I can hide his body from her. She doesn't have to know he's dead until I venture into the Underworld and get him back –

"Antonio?" Micha shouts from down the hall, her voice alarmed yet courageous. She must've heard all the fighting and run down here from our bedroom. Varius' room is one of the furthest away from ours as with them being blood bonded, I didn't want him close enough to affect her. There isn't much known about how the bond works, even inside witch communities, but I seem to have made the right call. Terror squeezes my lungs at the thought of her being close enough to be affected by Rudy's magic.

I run for the door to see her quicker and make sure she's okay. I catch her right as she's about to enter. Standing inside the door, I gather her in my arms. "I'm so sorry," I say. "Rudy killed Dayne."

"What?" Her voice is high-pitched with shock. "Dayne? How did he get here? I don't – I don't understand?"

"I brought him here to see you," I murmur. "I wanted it to be a surprise, but he wanted to help me torture the Shadow brothers first for what they did to you. They killed him."

She pulls back, shaking her head. "No! No! That isn't true."

"I would never lie to you, love."

"No!" She screams in my arms, soul-wrenching, heart-breaking. I want nothing more than to gather her up and take her away from all this pain, but I gave my blood oath, and so I will honor it.

I lead her into the room, and she runs to Dayne. She sits beside him, then lies across his chest, holding him to her in her grief. But she no longer cries. Now she shakes with rage.

Walking over to Varius, I kick him in the stomach, then haul him to his feet. His eye is glazed, but he tries to focus it on me.

"I gave you a blood oath," I say. I turn to look at my mate to ask her the question I have to. "Do you wish to go with him?"

"No," she says, her eyes flashing with Siome's fire as she climbs to her feet. "I want to kill him." Her voice drips with a cobra's venom. "I need to hurt him like he's hurt me. He needs to *pay.*"

Smiling at my reincarnated mate, I say, "Tell me how you want him."

SIXTY-FIVE

VARIUS

They drag me into a different room and strap me down to a chair. As soon as they do, I know I'm going to die in it. Despite the lack of chains and nails holding me down now, I recognize the set-up. My arms are lashed to the arms of the wooden chair, and my fingers are individually wrapped with shoelaces. This is how I restrained my wife when I tortured her, certain she was working with Antonio.

The irony isn't lost on me.

I thought she deserved to die then for hurting me, for taking my trust and stomping on it, for hurting Mother and kidnapping Khalid. For kissing the enemy in my own damn home. I wanted to punish her just for that.

Now she's well aligned with the enemy.

And yet... I don't want to punish her for it.

I still want to save her.

I should have wanted to save her all those months ago. Perhaps we wouldn't be here then.

My eye tears up as I think about the two I've just lost. I feel like I have been hit by a fucking roller coaster, then dragged all along its tracks. Antonio's mention of Dayne being a traitor, of seeing them be buddy buddy made me so fucking angry and sick. But then I saw him place his hands on my brother's head, and I was hit with shock.

And pain.

Micha needed him. He couldn't die.

I tried to tell him not to do it with the wild look in my eye. Even if the disease wasn't infectious, trying to control that amount of chaos magic for his first time would kill him. Stormie nearly killed herself when she helped Rudy when she was younger. She's only alive because Mother got to her in time.

But Dayne just looked at me with a silent reply of his own. "*You get her out of here. You get her home*"

I don't see how I can though. She doesn't want to leave with me, and I can't kidnap her. I can control my shadows a bit now, but if I suck her into the Plane of Monsters, without a cage to hide in, she'll be ripped apart.

"You're going to pay for what you've done to me," she snarls as she stands in front of me with a knife as long as her forearm. I almost expected her to have a hammer and a screw. I would deserve it.

"I love you," I say, staring up at her with all that truth in my eye. I might not be able to get her out in this life, but I will come back for her in the next.

I will never give up on her.

Her anger wavers. For a moment, I see the old her. The her I knew and who loved me. But then her rage comes back and she slices me with a thousand strikes. Shallow cuts all across my body, including my arms and hands.

"I love you," I say again as my head lolls. I struggle to keep my eye on her. I need her to know that I do not blame her for what he's turned her into. If she ever comes to her senses, I do not want her to be haunted by my screams.

"I love you."

"Shut up!"

She stabs me in the head, piercing right through my skull and into my brain.

The lights are going out. I see all the moments we shared.

The karaoke nights.

The dinner dates eating burgers.

Her smiling at me as I painted her.

I die with that smile in my mind.

And one final thought.

I will find you in the next life.

Whatever fucking deal I have to make with whatever god, I will find her.

And I will pull her back to me.

SIXTY-SIX

HER

Turning to Antonio, I place my bloody hand on his chest and breathe, "Fuck me right here."

I have too many emotions inside me. So much joy and rage and pain. And I need him to fill me. I need him to show me he loves me. That he will give me all the protection and safety my husband could not.

He yanks me to him, his hands on my ass, lifting me up as his mouth comes down. I part my lips; his tongue invades me. I kiss him back as fiercely as he's kissing me, the last two months' build-up exploding in a blinding heat.

Reaching between us, I yank at his cotton shirt, tugging it up. I can't get it off him unless he puts me down though. He squeezes my ass, then lowers me to the floor. I step back and to the side. He lifts his shirt, and my jaw drops as my eyes roam over the muscled cut of his chest. Grabbing his hips, I tug him towards me and kiss my way across his skin.

Up.

Up.

Up.

I suck a nipple into my mouth, and he groans.

He slides his hands all across my body, touching me as if he knows me but is learning me at the same time. He cups and pinches, lingers and strokes. We strip off our clothes, our mouths still glued together, then we rub naked against each other. But he's moving too slow, and I want him now.

I want to feel the closeness of his knot. I want to feel it expand inside me. Reaching between us, I grab his cock. It's thick and hard in my hand. He grunts, lifting me into the air. I wrap my legs around him, then slide down his cock.

He breathes harshly as he presses me up against a wall. I cling on as he fucks me hard, jerking my hips as much as I can, trying to get him off quickly so I can feel that knot.

That closeness.

That connection he can't stop.

I run my fingers through his hair, panting and crying out. The urge to take some V is clawing at my stomach though. If I take some, it'll feel even better. We'll feel even closer.

My mouth moves as I start to beg for some, but he turns my face to the side as he kisses my neck, and my eyes land on Varius. Then move to the vial of V on the table beside his bed.

"The bed," I rasp as my orgasm builds. Antonio kisses me on the lips as he carries me, his cock jerking against the walls of my pussy with every step. He lays me down on the bed. I arch my back as he fucks me fast, using the motion to secretly look at the bottle of V. I raise my arms, hiding my reach under thrashes of desire.

Thinking better of it, I pull back. Wrapping my arms around the back of his head, I clutch at his hair, moaning and crying out as I kiss him hard. I need to distract him. Wait for him to be on the verge of coming so he won't be as quick to stop me.

He groans against my mouth. His tongue sweeps around inside me. His hands tighten on my hips as he slams in deep and hard. I clench around him. My arms lift back up, one aiming for the bedside table, seeing the unstoppable arousal on his face. His knot starts to swell, and I wrap my fingers around the vial of V...

I cry out as his hand grabs mine.

"No," he grunts as his knot nestles thick inside me.

"You've taken a Rick," I whine. Then my red eyes widen as I peer around his shoulder, and he jerks his head to look behind him to see what I've seen. He starts to roll, trying to put me between them, but Varius lands on his back before he can, his eyes even redder than mine.

The Craving has grabbed hold of him completely – Sau's safe-guard having kicked in even though his curse's broken.

The three of us fall off the side of the bed, and as Antonio releases me to fight off my husband, I take the vial of V.

And smash it into the werewolf's right eye.

This is the moment I have been waiting for for fucking *months*.

He screams as I crunch the glass into his socket, blinding him. With the shards inside him, even if he shifts, he won't be able to heal himself. Fur spouts across his neck, only a section of him changing – just enough to stop Varius from sinking his fangs into his throat.

Calling on my fire, I push it down my arms, letting it burn me to get to him. Normally, he would have time to run away, but he can't leave me because of his knot.

Check.

And fucking.

Mate.

"Tell Siome I said she could have you," I snarl as my fire starts to singe his flesh. "You killed my baby!"

Howling, he shifts his lower body, and I scream in utter agony as his cock grows inside of me, the size of it tearing apart my pussy. My fire dies beneath the onslaught of pain, what remains of my control on it slipping. Varius roars in anger as he slices his new claws down Antonio's back. The werewolf starts to shift his top half, but I push my fire back through my arms, stopping him. He can't shift the part of him that's on fire. It'll harm him permanently.

He looks at me, so much pain in his gold eyes. So many feelings of betrayal. He thought I was his fucking long lost love. And maybe I am. We are not reborn with our previous memories. But even still, I want him to *burn* for everything he's done to me.

Seeing the anger twisting my face, he mirrors it with his own.

Varius jumps onto his back and wraps his arms around the alpha's neck, choking him, but Antonio shifts one arm into that of his wolf and slices his claws across Varius' face. My husband lets go on instinct. A primal beast under the effect of the Craving.

Antonio rolls, his cock still stuck inside of me, and I go with him as he regains his feet. He grabs hold of my waist. His claws dig into my skin – now both arms changed. My fire flickers across his chest, but I keep it burning – until he yanks me off his knot.

He tears off most of his own dick, but he also rips out a chunk of my insides.

I scream.

Varius roars as he jumps off the werewolf's back to get to me.

But Antonio throws me so hard across the room that I go through the wall and well into the next one, my intestines hanging out of me, flapping in the air. I hit the ground with a gasp, my body convulsing from the pain. I'm going into shock.

A keres, a reaper of death –long billowing hair, a scythe with dozens of souls trapped inside its blade trying to get free– flickers into existence. Her kind hugs the outer planes of Purgatory, and she's shaping her world around me so she can reach inside me and take my soul.

Varius screams as he tries to get to me, but Antonio, now fully in his wolf form, though his chest is heavily burned, intercepts him, and the two of them crash through the other room.

My eyes flicker to the reaper.

She steps closer to me on bare feet, the world rippling out from her like she's walking across a lake. Every ripple turns a bit more of this world into hers, changing nothing other than the fact that she can rip my soul from my body.

She smiles, a wide spread of small, sharp teeth, all points of pain and pleasure.

"Not long now, dearie," she coos as she reaches a hand towards me.

Her eyes bug wide as a child appears on the other side of me. A demon of some sort with red skin and little horns on her head above a smile so crazy, it matches the madness of her eyes. She jumps over me, a set of wings spreading out, and her barbed tail whips out, wrapping around the keres' scythe. She yanks it out of the reaper's hand. Tosses it into the air.

Then grabs it and slices it across the keres' neck, cutting off her head.

My mouth falls open, blood trickling out of it. I have no idea what this creature is. A drazic perhaps, but they don't have wings. So maybe she's just a keres hunter... There is so much unknown about the planes of Purgatory.

"Micha!"

My head tries to turn at the sound of Maddox's voice, but there's no more energy left inside of me. The demon child thing turns back to me. She shakes her head on the vertical axis as she smiles wide. Her pigtails swish. A forked tongue flicks out to lick the lowered scythe.

"Pah." She spits to the side. "Tastes like chocolate."

She drops the weapon, her little button nose wrinkling in disgust. Then she dances towards me like a ballerina, the tutu she's wearing finally making "sense" – the only sense I can catch at the moment. Her shirt is way too big for her though, and it billows as she moves. The words: *Wanna be my bitch?* is scrawled across it, above two dog collars: one black, one pink and spikey.

She stops beside me. Bends down with her hands on her hips. "Helicopters go nom nom nom. Goats go vroom vroom vroom."

She vanishes, as does the plane of Purgatory, and I find a bottle of healing potion being pressed to my lips.

Maddox is talking to me, telling me to stay with him as he squats down beside me, naked and covered in blood. He points a wand between my legs, then up to my stomach.

I stare at him, so fucking happy he's still alive.

I've known he's been inside Varius' brain for the last two months – that he went in as the egg of a tapeworm. Khalid contacted me through my soul doll not long after Varius stepped through the teleportation circle. He gambled with his brother's life, not knowing what I'd do.

But I've wanted to kill Antonio since he took my baby from me. I lost my way a little, fell a bit too deep into the person I was pretending to be, almost died under the need for V – but I struggled forward every fucking step.

So Khalid told me it'd take two months for Maddox to mature enough to be able to use his magic again. Meaning, I had two months to get Antonio to lower his guard so we could attack.

But now that's failing.

And he's killing my husband.

My eyes fly over Maddox's shoulder as I gulp down the liquid. A scream builds in my throat as I watch the two of them fight. Varius is completely consumed by the Craving, so he's moving purely on instinct. He's not thinking. He's not *planning*. He has the power and speed to almost match Antonio now, and his wounds are bleeding less, but he can't get the upper hand. He's being torn apart piece by piece – a slash here, a bite there. Slowly but surely, he's going to die.

"Help him," I beg, knowing I need more than one potion and a few flicks of a wand to get back into the fight.

"You're the prio–"

I scream as Antonio punches my husband in the chest. Safeguard spell or not, he won't survive having his heart ripped out. I try to push to my feet, but my legs won't move. Maddox curses as he abandons me to pull on his shadows. Priority doesn't mean shit if we're all going to die.

He has Aleric inside his cage in the Shadow Domain, and he knows our only hope is if he gets him out. *Now.*

Varius roars as he headbutts Antonio in the face. The wolf staggers back, and his arm jerks free, but instead of blood and bits falling out, nothing does. Black smoke-like magic swirls in the hole, then solidifies, and flesh is there once more.

My mouth drops open, but I push my questions aside. There's no time to wonder about whatever new magic he has. I struggle to my feet, ignoring the pain of my injuries, but I'm not leaving my husband to die after he walked into hel to save me.

Not leaving him to kill Antonio when that right is *mine.*

As Maddox starts to pull the cage out of his shadows, I rush forward. Bending low, I scoop up the knife I used to torture Varius. If I can heat it up until it's molten and leave a chunk inside Antonio, he won't be able to heal it until it's out.

I've already taken his eye and damaged a good part of his chest. He can't keep this up forever.

The damage I've already taken says neither can we.

But I'm already dead inside. He's already killed me. He

took my baby and Dayne, and if he takes Varius, there'll be nothing left. So I jump into the fray, not caring that I am joining a battle between two sups way more powerful than me.

SIXTY-SEVEN

HER

With every minute that passes, Varius is getting weaker and weaker. He's alive because of the dark magic his mother tied to his soul when she cursed him, but it's still based on his vampire side. If he doesn't feed soon, he will die. If he takes the time to feed though, Antonio will cut him down all the same.

I'm not fast enough to fight the blur of bodies. I can't risk letting my fire outside of myself because I won't be able to control it at all then. All I can do is wait for Varius to press him hard enough against a wall that I can dart in and strike, burning a clump of the knife into his flesh to stop him from being able to shift and thus heal that part of himself.

Varius takes the hits for me whenever I do that though, protecting me from Antonio's claws and bites. But he's not losing chunks of himself like he was before – that smokey substance that filled his chest seems to be everywhere inside him now, and he shifts between smoke and flesh whenever he's about to get hurt.

Still, he is tiring.

And when he collapses, Sau's spell on him running out unless he can feed, Maddox and I will be alone, and neither of us are strong enough to fight him off.

"Where's Aleric?" I shout, risking a glance towards the youngest Shadow brother. The cage is fucking empty.

"I don't know!" he says. "There's no blood in it, so he wasn't eaten."

Unless they took him away and ate him elsewhere.

But I don't have time to argue with him. I barely have time to dart into the openings when I see them. Every time Varius gets him in a hold or pushes him against a wall, the next second, Antonio is free and going on the offensive. But the burn on his chest has killed a lot of his speed, and he's using a lot of energy shifting the parts of himself that he still can, going back between human and wolf to heal most of the damage he gains.

With two punches, an elbow, and a kick, Antonio sends Varius stumbling back a few steps. Not far. He hasn't even bought enough time for himself to turn all the way around if he wanted to. But he's bought more than enough to lunge for me because I'm way too damn close.

Way too optimistic in my ability to defend myself alone.

But just as his teeth are about to snap across my face, a large body with black smokey eyes barrels into him from the side.

My heart leaps out of my chest.

Dayne!

He's alive, and we know each other's moves. I don't have to be as fast as I do with Varius because Dayne and I work like two streams merging into one. I dart forward, expecting him to get Antonio to turn sideways like he usually would, force him to open himself up for an attack from me in order to block one from Dayne. But he doesn't. He fights with the same animalistic, mindless ferocity as Varius, and I end up stumbling to a stop with a claw piercing my shoulder. The knife I'm holding falls from my grip.

The world flickers as the planes of Purgatory tease me with their proximity.

Knowing I'm going to die anyway, I look at Dayne.

But instead of finding comfort, I see that it's not him at all.

It's a husk filled with the shadows that swirl around my husband.

Antonio yanks me to him, and I'm just about to give myself up to my fire when Varius lunges past me.

And another blur joins him.

Aleric has finally fucking arrived, and he's wielding two monstrous blades – the front legs of an echidna perhaps (the same monster that lives in the Shadow's kitchen counter) and then worked down to be his size.

With a movement too quick for me to track, he slices off the arm that's holding me. I only know when I stumble back in surprise, not having expected the sudden release. Maddox catches me and pulls me back even further. He removes the claws in my shoulder, then points the wand at me again.

"He's going to go get Sau in a moment," he says. "She'll make sure you're healed properly."

The internal bleeding in my belly tells me I might not have that long.

"What's he done to Dayne?" I ask, wanting to hope that he's still alive. That the smoke trailing out of his eyes does not mean he's *gone*. It just means Varius is healing him in his own way.

Maddox's voice softens. "He can turn people into husks," he says. "It doesn't seem to be reversible once it's in deep."

"But is he still alive?" Can we find a cure eventually?

"They don't seem to be," he says, and my heart shudders, wanting to break. But I do not have that luxury.

Because even with Aleric helping with his knives, we're not going to win. Varius is slowing down. Starting to get cut as the smokey blackness isn't trading places with his flesh anymore.

His timer on his curse is running out.

If he doesn't feed, I'm going to lose him.

I stumble forward just as Aleric vanishes.

And doesn't reappear.

"What the fuck!" Maddox shouts. But Aleric was never one to hang around on the losing side.

Antonio pivots and slices his arm across Varius' face. He shifted his half-severed arm, healing the open wound so it no longer bleeds. He's weakened, but not weakened enough.

He turns to me. "Dayne" jumps on his back and bites him. He doesn't have any powers in his husk form. He's just a mindless zombie. Antonio pays him little mind. I call on my fire, and his eyes widen. He pivots and dives for the window. My mouth drops open first in shock, then utter rage. He's trying to leave. To fight another day. A tactical retreat.

"No!"

He crashes through the glass, taking Dayne with him. I run to the ledge, wanting to jump after him, but someone grabs me and hauls me back.

"Wait," Sau says.

She barely finishes speaking before Aleric appears back in the room, having brought Antonio with him.

But no Dayne.

The wolf falls to his knees, defeated, one blade through his stomach. Aleric raises the other one to cut off his head.

"He's mine," I hiss as I walk forward.

"Pretty sure he's Antonio," he says with a cheeky smile. He cocks his head, his smile drops. Then he vanishes to who knows where.

The wolf lunges, and Sau shoves me to the side to take

the hit. I remember how easily he tore her to pieces. He isn't as fast, and he's more wounded due to me and Aleric, but that trauma must still be imprinted in her mind. And yet, she did not hesitate.

He tackles her to the ground. Shadows open up beneath her, sucking her down. She can't bring out her monsters, but she can sure as hel take him to them. His teeth dig into her neck, then rip free. A fountain of blood shoots up high. Her shadows die, and with severed feet and hands – those parts that touched the ground, he lunges for the window.

And I lunge for his back, refusing to let him go. I'll kill him even if it kills me.

I land on top of him. He tumbles through the window. Wrapping my arms around his neck, I push out my fire.

And together, we fall into the sea.

I gasp as the impact of the waves knocks into me. Water fills my mouth. I hold my breath as we go under. I let go of him instinctively.

I try to swim to the surface, but my arms won't work. The fire I pulled on to burn him also burned me. I start to sink, going down, my eyes closed tight but still able to see all the sharks circling me. Imagining the worst. An end of torn limbs and eaten misery.

After all that's happened... how funny would it be if this is how I go?

I imagine Dayne's body floating beside me, beckoning me.

Perhaps there are worse ways to die...

Hands grab me as my head grows heavy and my lungs burn. They pull me to the surface as I struggle to keep my mouth closed. They push my head above the water, and I gasp, sucking in a huge gulp of air. A wave comes, hitting me in the face.

Varius turns me in his arms. "I've got you," he says. "It's over. We're going home."

"No!" I rasp. "Where's Antonio?"

I need to see his body. I need to make sure he's gone.

"He's gone."

"He might not be!"

"Your fire can't be put out," he says.

Normally, no. But I don't have control of it anymore, and the ocean is such a vast amount of water...

"Where is he? I need to find him!" I turn my head, trying to spot him through the waves.

"Let him go, Micha," he says, so much pain in his voice. "If he comes back, we'll deal with it then, but for now let's just go home."

He tugs on my chin, and I let him pull my face towards his. As he looks at me, I feel so utterly *empty* when I should be feeling safe and alive and full or hope. Or at least happy that the nightmare is over.

But I don't.

Because I need to see his body. I need to cut off his head and rip out his heart and bury him in fucking cement inside a containment circle so I can know for sure he's dead.

Otherwise, I can't trust that he won't come back.

"Come on," Varius says, ducking his head to press a kiss to my forehead. "Let's go bury our daughter."

I rear back to look at him. My throat burns at the idea of seeing her one last time. Of being there when she's sent off into the ether. Of having that closure. "You haven't taken her into your shadows already?" I rasp, barely letting myself believe it. It's been months...

His eyes grow wet as he looks at me. "I was waiting for you; we should tell her goodbye together."

Closing my eyes, I finally tell him to take me home.

SIXTY-EIGHT

HER

Perhaps I will regret it later that I don't hunt Sadist and Eduardo down myself. But right now, I am content to let the others have that honor for what they did to Rudy.

All I want is to see Rafiki.

To hold her for the first time.

After Sau heals us (she shifted her arteries around inside her body in the split second it took for Antonio to bite her, then healed herself), Aleric phases the two of us home. He drops us off at the edge of the ward before he disappears back to the boat. As we walk through the shimmering blue shield surrounding the Shadow House, dripping water from our clothes, a flood of emotions hits me all at once.

Relief mixed with dread mixed with disbelief.

Is it really over?

Am I really safe?

Is he really dead?

I feel like I've gotten to the happy parts of a trauma-filled romance, only to notice there is still a good chunk of the book left. Like something is going to happen in those final pages.

My stomach churns as I walk along with him in silence.

I want to tell him "I'm sorry" for what I did to him, but every time I think about those two words, my thoughts are consumed by Grubs saying them. By the feel of his hands on my body. His dick inside my pussy.

Then my throat tightens, and I can't get anything out.

"I love you," Varius murmurs, and I turn to him with pain in my eyes. To tell me that after I stabbed him in the head, after I said all those nasty things while I tortured him, after I made him believe I fell in love with another man, and then forced him to watch me fuck him...

My throat is an overworked dam, the water building up in my eyes, about to flood out.

He looks at me and hears my silence. But he does not push me into saying anything back. Does not attack me for being mute despite all he has done for me. The responding words are trapped in my throat or perhaps deeper inside of me.

In the soul of a girl I'm just not anymore...

No.

No, regardless of all the other emotions of uncertainty swirling around inside of me, I know that one to be true.

I reach for his hand. Let our pinkies brush – not ready for any more contact than that.

"I love you too," I murmur, my voice cracking with all the feeling I'm struggling to express.

Through the blood bond, I can feel his desire to gather me in his arms and just hold me, but he doesn't. He simply continues walking, and I follow.

I glance at him as we move along the tree-lined path, under green, overreaching branches that smell like fucking freedom. I inhale deeply, breathing in the scent around me, slowly letting myself believe that everything is over. There is no smell of the sea.

"You walked into hel for me," I say just as the house comes into view. The lack of flowers hits me hard, and I stop short as my heart drops.

"Hel was being out here without you," he says, his voice so raw and broken; I can feel his pain in the landscape itself, though.

It isn't scarred from war or a muddy brown field. But it's missing the field of flowers that used to spread out from there to here and all the way down to the lake. He doesn't need to tell me Leno is dead. The grass itself weeps. The land itself mourns.

"How?" I ask, my voice shaky.

"He got ripped apart by some of the chimeras at the school. Three of them are in the garage, but the main one was Timothy."

Fucking *Sadist*.

My hands ball into fists. "We should go back for him to make sure he doesn't escape."

"He can't. Once I attacked, Khalid got the teleporters to destroy Eduardo's teleportation circles."

"You have teleporters now?" I ask in surprise. Khalid didn't give me the whole rundown – just what I needed.

"No."

He doesn't explain, and I don't care enough to push. We continue on, our footsteps heavy, our hearts even heavier.

"I never got to hold her," I say softly.

A part of me wants him to tell me he hasn't either, but the rest of me hopes he held her every night he could.

"There is not much left to hold," he says sadly.

My throat tightens. We walk up the porch, where a small section of flowers lie. They bloom one by one as I sweep my gaze across them. My ears strain to hear the sound of a dog somewhere, but the house lies silent when we enter.

I don't have the heart to ask about Krypto. Not right now. Not today.

A set of footsteps pound down the hall. "Micha!" Lou shouts as she flings herself at me. I tense, and Varius moves in front of me, catching my sister without a word. She starts to protest, but he murmurs something to her, and she stops.

Quiets.

He sets her down, and she places her hands behind her back as she looks at me. But despite her attempt to settle my nerves, that just pushes her stomach out, and my eyes latch on to her bump. She gets to have a baby while mine is lying dead upstairs.

I fucking hate her.

I *hate* her.

Moving past her, I head for the stairs. She calls my name, so much hurt in her voice. Varius lingers to talk to her. Just for a moment. Just a sentence, maybe two, then he's back by my side.

My throat tightens as I glance at him, wondering if he's judging me. She's my own fucking sister, and I can't bear to look at her.

But there's nothing negative that comes down our bond. Just love.

The same love he pushed into me when I tortured him. When he believed I was going to kill him.

When I did kill him in order to give Maddox a way out, for his Craving to activate, and so I could distract Antonio.

So many reasons...

But it doesn't justify what I did to him.

It doesn't make it okay.

"I'm sorry," I want to say.

But Grubs' memories shove into me, making me mute.

"I love you," Varius murmurs, and I realize he can feel my guilt, my sorrow, no words needed between us.

My chest tight, overwhelmed by everything he means to

me, I say, "I love you too."

His bedroom door looms large in front of us.

Taking a deep breath, I twist the handle and step inside.

He leads me to his bedside table, where she lies on a torn piece of shirt. Nothing more than a smeared blob of red, and I drop to my knees on a silent cry.

I want to scream for all the injustice.

I want to resurrect Antonio so he can keep telling me lies about how he can bring her back.

I want to believe them.

I want to believe them so fucking hard.

But I know she's never coming home.

Reaching out a shaky hand, I pick up the slip of fabric and cradle her to my chest. My husband kneels beside me.

The silence thickens the air around us, cocooning us in a shared grief. I shake as he cries. I scream inside but feel too hollow to let it out.

The world still spins, but I feel as if it's stopped inside of me.

"I was thinking…" Varius says softly, breaking through to me, his voice rough with tears. "That we could tattoo her ashes on us."

I lift my head in shock. "You're not going to take her into your shadows?" It's their Family custom.

"She's your child too," he murmurs, looking into my eyes. I sob, sagging forward, and now my tears come freely. I nod rapidly, with my whole heart. His hand touches me, asking permission, and I lean into him as I struggle to breathe. He moves to wrap his arms around me, then cradles me tight to his chest as I hold our little girl.

"She needs a name," I say between my sobs, so damn desperate to give her that at least.

"I've been calling her Bambi."

I choke on a cry. "I call her Rafiki."

Which means that conversation wasn't a joke. She's had

a name all this time.
　　She knew she was loved.
　　Bambi Rafiki Shadow.

SIXTY-NINE

HER

I breathe out harshly as I twiddle my wand in my hand. We're both freshly showered and clothed, dressed in funeral finery. Varius lowers Bambi inside the metal pot we placed in middle of his room. His family has come back from the super yacht already, but we haven't invited any of them up to join us.

We want this to be a private affair.

Just us three.

The family that never was.

Varius comes to stand beside me, his eyes heavy and full of grief. "Are you ready?" he asks.

I nod, then grab his hand, pulling on his magic so both of us will fuel the fire that cremates our little girl. Inhaling, I lift the beautifully carved wand, aiming it into the pot. The air hums with my magic, like a raincloud about to break, and I shudder as the feeling of control comes back to me like an old lover.

Varius squeezes my hand gently, and I pull on more of his magic before adding it to mine, causing it to twirl in my veins, to dance and merge and mix. Then with a flick of my wrist, I send my fire racing through the wand. The flames carved along its length light up with purple energy. I can't see the ethereal fire I was born with anymore; my new eyes don't have the magic-imbued piercings that allowed me to see them. But I can see the metal pot glowing hot, and I can smell the cotton burning, and I can feel the familiar magic calling to my soul.

Like an old friend.

The lover who got away.

A childhood home.

Cherished memories of nostalgia.

For a moment, it gets hard to breathe. But I don't just draw Varius' magic from him, I draw his strength.

And I send him mine.

We grieve on our feet, but in truth, we are down on our knees as our little girl burns.

Tears run down his cheeks. Mine stay dry, and that hurts me. Makes me feel inadequate, like a bad mother. But I just don't have the energy to cry. I don't have that part of my soul right now; it's too smothered by my grief.

When she turns into ash, I swish the wand and put out the flames. We stand in heavy silence.

"Do you want to go first?" Varius eventually asks.

My throat tight, I nod. I tell him what I want tattooed on me, and he gets everything ready, having the strength to do what I cannot – taking the next step in saying goodbye. He sits me down at his desk, not the bed – not that fucking torture device, and mixes her ashes with the different inks as I pull down the top of my dress.

With the tattoo gun ready, he begins to draw over my

heart. A little purple flame with a baboon stretching out in its shadow.

"When did you learn how to draw?" I ask, wanting this moment to have something more than just pain. I recall the painting in his office and all the other pieces he has in his art studio.

"When Caden left. I found it meditative." He pauses for a moment, then adds, "I have a few pieces of you."

My throat closes as I think about him painting while I was being fucking tortured. But then I think about how he walked into hel for me and called it heaven just because I was there.

"I'd like to see them one day," I say stiffly.

He nods, and we lapse back into silence.

It isn't comfortable.

It isn't easy.

And I worry that what I did in order to kill Antonio has scarred across us too heavily.

"I love you," he murmurs, and I swallow hard.

"I love you too."

With my tattoo done, we swap position. He doesn't take off his black dress shirt, just unbuttons it enough so I can see his chest. He lifts my hand and places it a smidge above his heart. "Here," he murmurs. "I placed her here."

My throat tightens. Doing my best, I draw a blood smear onto his skin, with little footprints going through it.

"You know," I say, trying to inject some levity into my voice. "I would've trained her well enough to know not to leave this much evidence behind."

He laughs, but it feels a bit hollow.

"And if I didn't, Khalid would have."

His next chuckle feels more genuine.

"Her first toy would've been a blade," Varius says with a shake of his head.

"And Maddox would've paid for ballet lessons." He really

enjoys watching their plays. He admires them for their craft and skill and their ability to tell a story without words.

"Leno would've given her a bag full of dirt."

I look up at him curiously despite the hole growing in my chest.

"He could connect to it," he says. "So he'd always be with her."

I force out a smile. "I bet he would've taught her to jump in all the muddy puddles."

He grins, tears in his eyes. "He would've made puddles for her to jump in, the fucker. Right after we battled her for hours to get her dressed just to be an absolute *asshole*."

A sad, choking laugh escapes me. It feels both good and terrible to feel joy right now. Her uncles would've loved her so hard. "You think Enoch would've shaved her head? Give her a gehawk?"

"A what?"

"Like a gecko mixed with a mohawk. A gehawk."

"A mogecko would make more sense," Varius replies in all seriousness. "Replace the animal with another animal."

I smile as I shake my head. "A mogecko then."

"No. It only looks good to you because you're shorter than him. If you view it from above, it looks like he's being T-bagged by a monkey with massive balls."

I half-cough, half-wheeze. "No it doesn't. Really?"

He grins. "I'll take a picture for you."

I shake my head, my chest hurting with all the would've beens. We lapse into silence for a bit before I build up the courage to ask, "And Rudy?" My heart pounds in my throat as I wonder if I have pushed too far. But he deserves to be remembered here too. He would have loved her the most.

Varius looks away and doesn't say anything.

My lips trembling, I focus back on the tattoo. I just about finish with it when he murmurs, "He would've given her so many damn goats."

I jerk my hand away from him as I laugh loud and hard. I can't stop the bubble of noise exploding out of my lips. A bit manic. A lot of pain. But also full of love and joy and that tentative hope that hints at one day being okay.

Bambi Rafiki Shadow would've *loved* goats.

"I bet she would've asked for a goat instead of a pony," I wheeze out, and Varius scowls, which only makes me laugh harder.

"I would've got her one," he grumbles.

"Maddox would've taught it ballet."

He shudders. "I don't know if that's better or worse than line dancing."

"Maybe the tango."

"Stop."

"Oh! Oh, let's teach them disco. Or belly dancing!"

"No."

"She could get waltz lessons and have you do father and goat –"

"No more goats."

I laugh, and he smiles.

And for a moment, for one little, tiny moment, the world doesn't feel so cruel.

It took our little girl – *Antonio* took our little girl. But she still lives in us.

Dropping my head, I swallow the rest of my laughter as I finish off his tattoo. A final footprint to say goodbye. My hands shake as I lay the tattoo gun down.

Varius stands, then offers me his hand. I hesitate for a moment before I take it. He leads me into the bathroom. To the mirror where we stand and look at the ash-filled tattoos on our chests.

My heart burns.

My soul screams.

My eyes latch onto the last mementoes we have of her.

They're not perfect.

But neither are we.

I'm sorry for how brutal it's about to get.
But the hardest part of trauma
is facing ourselves after.

SEVENTY

Him

I slam into Maddox, wrapping him in a hug as soon as I come down the stairs and see him standing in the living room with our other brothers, mother, and the three women who are now a big part of this family. I didn't know if he had survived inside my brain until I saw him in the fight.

From the teleportation circle to the disease Antonio gave me, I feared he'd died. I could not tell Khalid about my plan beforehand, knowing he'd try to stop us, so he didn't get the opportunity to study Maddox's tapeworm egg form, which meant he couldn't make a soul doll of it. Couldn't check in to see if he was alive. The fact he's returned is a relief to us all.

"Oh... big guy's actually allowing hugs," Enoch teases as he and his twin join in too. When Ez pulls out his phone to snap a group selfie, I start to pull away, but Khalid shoves me back into it. He doesn't join in himself, unlike Mother, but he keeps his hand on my shoulder.

"Are you okay?" I ask.

"Well, I didn't get laid for two months, so not going to lie, this is giving me a hard-on –"

As one, we all groan and shove him away from us. He laughs. Then he quiets. "It was pretty fucking terrible," he says. He looks me in the eye, lets me see the honesty. "But I'd do it again."

I nod at him, my throat too tight to speak. He would've been aware the entire time, locked in to a form that couldn't move. Completely in the dark and cut off from everything that was happening.

"How is she?" he asks. Micha hasn't come downstairs with me. Her sister moves closer to us, needing to know.

"Tired." My heart aches, the tattoo on my chest seeming to burn. "We just cremated our daughter."

Mother pulls me into her arms, and I stiffen against her. I want to ask her how she managed it. How she kept having kids even though she knew she might have to say goodbye to each one. But that wouldn't be fair. She stopped having them until after the treaty. She changed the world she lived in so her kids could have a better life.

And finally understanding that, her sacrifice and pain, all the anger I've been holding on to, blaming her for making me paranoid enough to hurt my wife, eases from my chest. She fought to change the world for us. She's only ever tried to protect us. It's just... she's still human. She still has faults. Still makes mistakes.

"I'm sorry," I murmur as I finally hug her back. "I never should've tried to sell you to Aleric."

"You did what now?" Ezriel asks.

"Say again?" Enoch demands.

"Bruh, not cool," Maddox says.

"I know. I'm sorry."

"And I'm sorry for being so secretive in my dealings. I should have come to you – or at least the reaper, with any concerns." She sighs as she pulls back. "You think I would've learned from that given how many times secrets have hurt me." She looks around the room. Straightens her shoulders and lifts her chin. "Aleric is his father."

"What the fuck!?" Ezriel shouts.

"I'm going to kill him," Enoch says.

Khalid simply heads for the door, and Mother darts in front of him with a shake of her head.

"Bruh, that explains so much about Varius."

"What does that mean?" I ask, turning on Maddox. He holds up his hands in surrender, then uses one to give the 'coo-coo' sign at his temple.

My eye narrows, but the tension in the room dissipates, even though all the questions from my brothers remain. *Did he rape her? What happened? Is Maddox also his?* Out of all of us, he actually seems like Aleric's kid. As if he called *me* fucking coo-coo.

But now it isn't the time for any questions.

It is time to take Rudy into our shadows. It's the reason we're all still up. The reason I'm not currently in bed with my wife, holding her in my arms.

As if they can read my mind, the mood shifts, becomes somber. Then everyone looks to Mother. I assume she has him in her shadows inside Maddox's cage, modified to not let anything even reach between the bars.

She nods. Swallows. Then heads for the front door. There is a collective inhale of trepidation. Of hesitation. Then one by one, we walk outside, off the front porch, and through the blooming row of flowers.

We already held a passing for Krypto and Leno, taking them both into our shadows, and now, within only a few months, we have to do another.

Tears burn my eyes. I want to drop to my knees and scream. To rage against an uncaring world "watched over" by uncaring gods. Maddox turns to me and throws his arms around my waist. When he'd shifted into a tapeworm egg in the cave on Mljet, having pretended to go through the portal to Blódyrió so Khalid wouldn't question his absence, he was so determined to not lose another brother. And I failed him.

"I'm sorry," I croak into his hair as I hug him back. My chest swells with all the pain I hold inside. It feels like it's going to burst, to explode. To kill me with the shrapnel that will pierce every inch of my soul.

"It's not your fault," he says. But he doesn't know the choice I made.

I try to pull back –why should I be able to find comfort when Rudy is dead because of me?– but Maddox clings to me tighter. "I need this," he murmurs. "Please."

Closing my eyes, swallowing hard, I hug him back until he's ready to let go.

When he finally pulls away from me, his eyes are wet, but there's a fierce determination there. "You owe me for the tapeworm bullshit," he says.

"Of course."

He shakes his head. "You really don't, but I'm calling it in anyway. Therapy, bruh. You're going to fucking therapy."

"I don't –"

"Tough."

I close my mouth. After all he's done for me, I can give him this. I'll just need to find someone I trust all my secrets to.

"I might as well put my psych degree to use, you know?" he says, an attempt to laugh making his throat tight.

I blink. "*You* want to be my therapist?"

"Who else could it be? You'd legit scare them all off." He pauses. "Or bury them somewhere." He shrugs confidently. "You ain't gonna do that to me."

Unable to argue with that, I breathe out. "Alright."

He nods, and together, we rejoin the rest of our family. Mother has already pulled Rudy from her shadows, and he lies face-up on the grass.

"Fuck, he almost looks at peace," Maddox says.

"He always was so annoyingly optimistic," Enoch says, a smile breaking his voice.

Ezriel groans. "Honestly, he's probably kicking it up right now. A goodie two-shoes like him?"

"In the Elysian Fields, no doubt." Enoch nods.

I'd like to think so. That's he's being rewarded for all the pain he's suffered. That's he finally able to be at peace, away from the nightmares of his magic and the cruelty of this life.

"I bet he's being swarmed by a thousand puppies."

"Just one," Khalid murmurs, and my chest tightens.

He would've found Krypto. And Leno.

I can't find it in me to say anything though, to voice all the love I have for him. I want to be able to say something as he goes, but my throat is just too damn tight.

I love you.

A small hand slips into mine, and I turn my head to look at my little monster. She's pulled herself out of bed to face a crowd she isn't ready for just for me. "I love you," I whisper.

She squeezes me, and I curl the only remaining finger on that hand around hers, having lost the others permanently to Antonio's teeth.

"He is gone but never forgotten," I finally manage to say as I take a deep breath and pull on my shadows with my other hand. It takes a lot of concentration for me to hold them, even more so to make them form under Rudy rather than wherever they wish.

My brothers and Mother pull on their shadows much easier, having had years in which to perfect their craft. In the silence that rings through the night, Maddox starts to sing. Beautifully and clearly, and for a second, we all freeze.

"You little shit," Micha says, voicing what we're clearly all thinking. All this time, he's sang like a cat being dragged against a chalkboard.

He grins as he winks at her, but he doesn't falter in his singing. And one by one, we join him, and Enoch even pulls a guitar out of his shadows.

"The sun is only rising,
The dew's not even burned,
The colors are all enticing,
But, Mama, I'm ready to come home.

Oh, my days.

Coming home.

I sit by a lake in the mountains
Throwing in coins to cross the black
I dance in the arms of my lover
Feeling her chill across my back.

The Devil's come a'knocking
And I'm opening up my door
Offering her a beer
Then grabbing up my coat

And though I untie my shoes
The laces are still used.

Oh, my days.

Oh, my days.

Oh, Mama,

I'm coming home.

The moon is finally rising,

The dew's turning cold,
The colors are all shaded,
Thank you, Mama,

Thank you, Mama,

For welcoming

Me home.

Oh, my days.

Oh, my days,

I'm

Finally

Home."

Swirling our shadows around him, we all take him home together.

SEVENTY-ONE

HIM

Despite the suffering in my chest, the world moves on. It doesn't stop for me to get my bearings, to figure out how to live in a world that doesn't feel right anymore. Doesn't feel *safe*.

I still have a Family to run. Still have responsibilities. But I'm double guessing almost every choice I make, wondering if it'll somehow cause me to lose my wife or brothers. In my panic, I've forbidden Lou from summoning demons, but I doubt she's actually going to listen –she might seem sweet, but she has a stubborn streak so long it could wrap around the Earth three times– so now I'm stressing I'm going to wake up to find her gone, kidnapped by the Prince of Pride and taken to Halzaja so he can be her baby's daddy. Then I'm going to have to figure out how to get her back before Micha realizes.

Or perhaps Micha would be okay with that.

She seems too okay with everything now. Outside of her

first day back, she seems like she always did. Laughing with her sister. Helping her with her pregnancy. Acting as if she didn't just suffer a nightmare most can't even dream of, and that's making me even more stressed.

Because I suffered two months at Antonio's hands, and perhaps he didn't make her eat her own eye or testicle, but he hurt her just as deeply. And he did it for longer.

I understand, thanks to Maddox and our sessions, that we all heal differently. But how can she even hope to heal if she can't even admit that what she endured was traumatic?

Exhausted and terrified of losing her to something I can't fight, can't beat this time, I flop down onto Maddox's couch as he sits in an adjacent chair.

I run my left hand through my hair, then get annoyed at the missing fingers and use my other one.

"I can't sleep with her, Maddox," I say.

"Is she ready for –"

"Not like that." Though she seems to be. She's pushing me all the time, touching me, kissing me, trying to get me hard, but I'm not ready for it yet.

"I mean actually sleep." I tug on my hair. It's getting long. It needs to be trimmed. I shaved the beard I grew while in captivity, but I haven't tackled my hair yet. "I just watch her all night."

Maddox surges to his feet; it seems I've finally broken his mask of professionalism. "It's been six fucking days!" he yells. "Do you know how bad it is to not sleep for one night, let alone nearly a week!?" He turns his head towards the closed door. "Ma –"

Lunging off the sofa, I tackle him to the ground. I place my hand over his mouth as I lie on top of him. "I don't want her magic," I hiss.

I don't want any healing magic working on me at all unless it's absolutely necessary. I can still feel the warmth of Eduardo's touch crawling through my body, infecting me, *owning* me, and my fingers tighten over Maddox's mouth. His eyes widen, and he shifts into his shadows, running from me before I can crush his jaw.

"Shit," I curse and roll onto my back, my hand clenching into a fist. If he was a second slower, his face would be splattered all over the floor. I press both my palms into my eyes, sleep pulling at me at the same time as it screams for me to stay away.

With sleep comes the nightmares.

Her with Antonio.

Me with another.

Both of us raped in different ways.

And then comes Bambi.

Sometimes, she's grown and stuck in the same Hel we were.

Other times, she's just a baby, and Eduardo –

I rip my hands away from my eyes, allowing the light to come streaming back and push away the darkness. "I'm sorry. But that's why I can't sleep. I'll hurt her." Maybe even kill her by accident.

"You were awake when you just attacked me," he mutters beneath his breath. I still hear him though, thanks to my hybrid senses.

"I'm more controlled with her."

"Good to know." He sits back in his chair. "But maybe you shouldn't be –"

"No." I push to my feet. If he thinks I'll risk her life just to get some shut eye, then this session –

"Not with her." He darts in front of me, holding his hands up to get me to stay. "Here. I was going to say, maybe you shouldn't be so wound up. You might not hurt her at all. When you're asleep, you're not exactly a ninja."

I stare at him for a moment. Exhaling, I head back to the couch.

"Take the bed," he says as he flips off the light. "It's not like you haven't fucked in it already," he mutters.

"Oh my gods, I remember that!" comes a high-pitched voice from on his desk. Marrabelle, the five-inch tall woman he keeps as a pet, has moved out of his fish tank and now has full range of the room. Thankfully, he has also started giving her clothes – doll clothes that he's modified to fit her.

"Marrabelle, love, remember what I said about you being quiet?"

"You don't like it because it makes you feel like you're not doing a good job?" she says with a nod. "Oooh –" she says with a moan.

"No!" he cuts in quickly, blushing hard as his eyes dart to me. I do *not* meet his gaze. I don't even want to lie down on his bed now.

But the idea of being able to sleep without harming the woman I love is too much to resist. I collapse down on top of it, trying not to think about what's happened *in* it.

"Are you not going to take off all your clothes first?" the little woman asks, her voice one of disappointment.

"Hey." Maddox scoffs. "I'm right here."

"I wish you weren't," I mutter.

"Right. You heard him, Maddox. Out. Mama's gonna –"

He grabs her and tosses her into a drawer, that he then shuts firmly.

I glance at him finally. "Did you put a silence rune on that?" I can't hear her at all.

He shrugs a shoulder. "She has enough air in there for weeks. Besides, it's my underwear drawer, so she'll –"

"Maddox?"

"Yeah?" he asks, a grin stretched across his mouth.

"Shut up and let me sleep."

"Of course, bruh. I'll be here when you wake."

My chest tightens. I haven't told him all that happened to me onboard Antonio's yacht, but he still understands that I can't stomach being alone... That the world doesn't feel safe enough to sleep in.

That the sleep itself isn't safe…

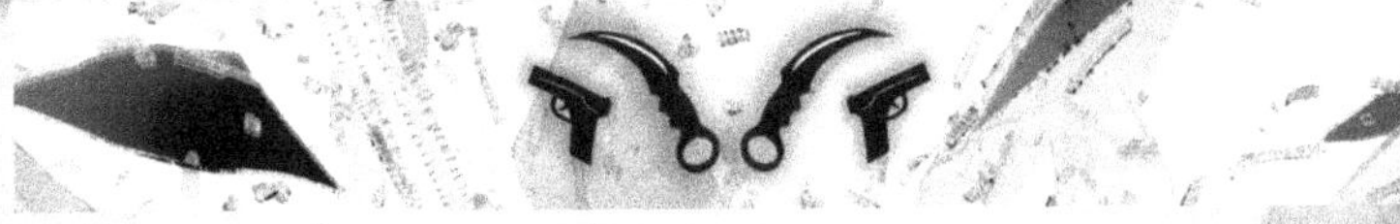

Someone is on me.

I'm being waterboarded with Ricks, the smell of tobacco and cedar permeating through the rag covering my face. I cough hard as I struggle to breathe. I jerk my head side to side, trying to throw them off.

But the sickness in my veins has made me weak. Every toss of my head sends sharp pains through my brain. The migraine is making it hard to think.

But I don't need to think to know this is wrong.

That I don't want this.

None of these women are my wife.

The rag is removed, and I turn my head, coughing and sputtering and trying to breathe.

And all this time, some whore is riding my cock. Another is humping my foot, forcing it inside her. The third places the rag back over my face and pours more Ricks across it.

I jerk awake, throwing the covers off and jumping to my feet, my fangs already bared.

"Easy, tiger." Maddox switches the light on, and I turn my head to the side as I close my eyes.

My heart rate starts to slow.

"Want to talk about it?"

I collapse back onto the bed, perching on the edge of it, breathing hard, my body drenched in sweat.

I shake my head.

So we just sit there in silence until I calm down enough to breathe. It felt so fucking real. I know I will eventually have to talk about it, have to address it, but I'm not ready right now.

I stand. "What time is it?"

He glances at his phone. "Three twenty-nine."

I drag a hand over my face. "I slept for over four hours, and still feel like shit."

"Because four hours is not enough sleep, especially if you're catching up for six days. You should lay back down."

"I need to see Micha."

"She's with Lou and Kiyana."

"Who?"

"Khalid's girl. She's changed her name now that she's learning how to summon demons." A name is power where an eknor is concerned, so if the demons learn the name of the person who's summoned them, they can break out of the containment circle.

I frown. "Wasn't that what it was before?"

Maddox shrugs. "No idea, bruh. Khalid always calls her *kira,* and none of us wanted to 'disrespect' her enough to ask what it actually was."

Because Khalid is fucking mental whenever it comes to her being 'insulted.' It's the same reason I never asked. "At least it's close," I say. Might be easier to remember.

Then my eyes widen as the rest of his words settle in my brain. "Lou's not supposed to be anywhere near a fucking summoning circle," I snap as I run for the door.

"Chill, bruh. Nothing's going –"

But he can't guarantee nothing will happen! And if a demon does try to take her back to Halzaja, Micha will try to stop them. Then I'll lose her all over again. I race down the hall and slide around the banister before taking the stairs down to the basement. I push open the door, terrified I'm going to find an empty room, and don't breathe again until I see her.

She's sitting on the floor, smiling at her sister, but there's a hollowness in her red eyes. A tension to her shoulders. It's not good for her to keep everything bottled up, but any time I try to suggest she talks to Maddox too, she tells me she's fine. She looks fine. She sounds fine. But inside? She has to be struggling. I hear her whimpers in her sleep.

"Varius," Lou says, not even having the good graces to look ashamed. In fact, she fucking smiles at me, but I'll deal with her later. Striding across the room, I head for Micha. She jumps to her feet, a wall up around her, a fear in the back of her flat eyes, and I stop. As much as she pushes for sex, she won't even let me hold her.

I'd be tempted to give in if I thought she'd cuddle after. But I know she won't. For all her talk about being fine, she's just not.

Forcing myself to calm, I look at Lou, then at the floor. There's no summoning circle, and I feel like a fucking fool.

Maybe Maddox is right, and I need to chill out.

Or maybe I just need some more fucking sleep.

SEVENTY-TWO

HIM

I'm sitting in Maddox's room again, my guilt clawing at me. Micha is acting like she's fine, but beneath her act, I know she's struggling with adjusting back to the normal world. She's hurting because of me. Because I failed her.

"I should've saved her sooner," I say.

"How?"

"I could've stopped Eduardo from leaving with her at the school."

"How?" This time, he doesn't even let me answer. He just leans forward and says, "You've had months to think about it, and you still don't have an answer, do you?" He shakes his head. "There was nothing you could've done."

"I –"

"No," he cuts in, but if I'm being honest, I didn't have any other thoughts lined up besides that one word anyway. "You ordered Mother and Rudy to find her, knowing they were the only ones capable of going alone. *They* failed. I was the only one who could've pulled the demon free, and *I* fucked up. I should've closed the summoning circle."

"Lou could've done it. It's her expertise –"

"And the Prince of Pride would've just kidnapped her once she let him out of the circle. Then he would've either killed her or dragged her back to his world once he found out she was pregnant."

"She said she could've figured out a better working –"

"She's lying because of her own guilt. You know that. She's *sixteen*. The demon is who knows how old. As smart as she is when it comes to summoning circles, she can't compete with his experience. He would've found a way to take her. And Micha doesn't want her in this life."

"*She's* my life."

Maddox's eyes soften as he looks at me. His empathy is through the fucking roof. It has to be to know how to torture someone psychologically in a way that will actually break them. He steps into their shoes as easily as if they're his own. He understands them – all their fear and love and desire.

But he can't understand this.

He can't fucking understand that I could feel her dying with every passing day. That I felt her agony, and I couldn't do anything to stop it.

Leaning forward, I drop my head into my hands and say, "I should've been able to do something to help my wife."

"You did. You never gave up on her. You went into hel for her, and you brought her home."

"She saved herself. She played him like a fucking badass."

"She would've died without you. She almost did die." He frowns, looking off into the distance. Then he shakes his head. "She's here because of you."

"I should've got to her sooner."

"You got to her when you could. You did nothing wrong."

"I could've stepped through the teleportation circle at the

school," I say. Like I did at Orpheus' cave.

"Then you'd both be dead. You needed me and Aleric. You got fucking *Aleric* to go into a cage on the Plane of Monsters for two months. That's a fucking huge thing you did."

"It's not. He wanted to go in there for a year." But I guess he found what he was looking for while he was in Maddox's shadow because he hasn't asked to go back.

"What? Why?" He shakes his head immediately as he holds up a hand, back to being my therapist rather than my curious brother. "Regardless of his reasons, you found out he wanted something and traded what you needed to with the devil himself. You did *everything* you could've done for her, Varius."

"I should've done more."

"You couldn't have."

I frown, and he sighs. "I'm going to give you a game to play."

"A game?"

"Yes. It's something people do for fun."

My eyes narrow. Mother *said* he wasn't Aleric's, but I don't know how much I believe her.

"It'll help you." He smiles. "Trust me." His smile tells me I shouldn't, but how much damage can he do with a game?

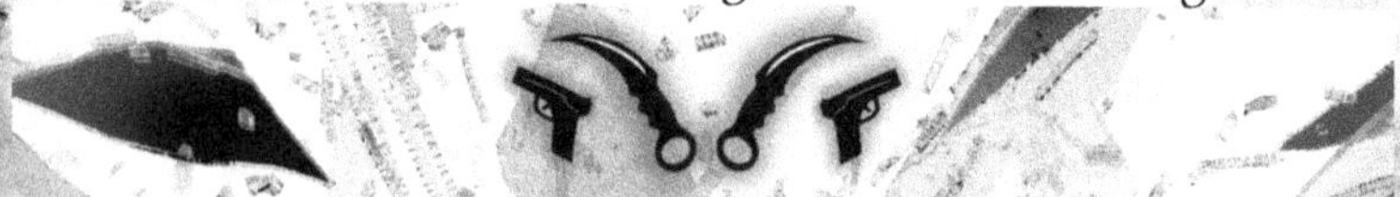

I storm into his room a few days later and throw my fucking laptop at him. "The game is stupid!" I roar. "Every time I jump, a pterodactyl comes out of the sky and fucking grabs me! And if I manage to dodge it, then I land on a bomb! And when I try to diffuse it, it sets off a timer, so I try to run away, only to get hit by a car! Which, if I take the time to try to dodge, the fucking bomb explodes and I'm in the radius! Which, by the way, takes up the whole map! It's impossible to outrun! So I have to choose how to die – car or bomb. It's unwinnable! There isn't a lake to jump in or cover to take! Every fucking thing I try, it just kills me! This is a really fucking, stupid, fucking, dumb, fucking game!"

My chest heaves with all my anger. I want to throttle him for being an absolute *little shit.*

"Did you try –"

"I have tried *everything!*" I yell.

"How many times?"

"Fucking hours! You are the *worst* therapist!" I storm over to grab my laptop just so I can throw it at him again. "I bet you couldn't even do it!"

"No, I couldn't," he says as he ducks under the flying computer. "I could get past the bomb; there is a little pixel of the screen that's safe, and you can get past another thirty levels that are just as hard. But you can never get to the end because it's impossible to win."

My mouth drops open. He admitted it! "Then why give me it? Why make me play it, thinking there was a way to finish?"

"Because you needed to know that sometimes the world sucks, that there is no right choice." He smiles, but it's not his normal cocky grin. It's one too knowledgeable for his years. "And when you played, did you blame yourself for making the wrong choices? Or did you blame the game?"

I stare at him, annoyed to all hel. "I blamed the game," I admit through clenched teeth.

"Exactly. Because it was the game's fault. All we can do is control ourselves," he explains. He flashes a sly grin I do not like. "But if you don't see that yet, you should play the game some –"

"Fuck you," I snap. "I'm going to bed. That's the only reason I come here."

He laughs, and I flop down onto his bed.

The nightmares still come... but the weight in my chest

lifts just a little.

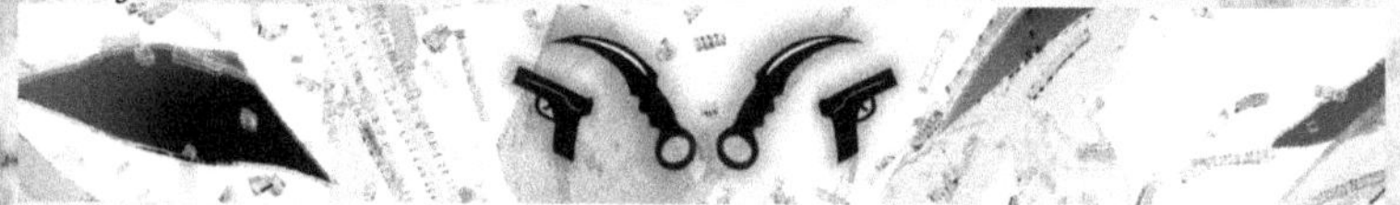

My talking sessions with Maddox get shorter even as the length of time I spend in his room gets longer. Ten minutes to chat; four hours to sleep.

I'm slowly starting to feel more human as the days pass, but the nightmares stop me from feeling refreshed. I still haven't managed to talk to Maddox about what I see when I sleep. What I remember... But we talk about other things. The guilt I have in taking so long to save her. In failing Leno and Krypto and Rudy.

I rise from Maddox's bed two and a half weeks later, my head filled with another nightmare. "Where is she?"

"Downstairs with her sister."

I head down to see her so I can ask if she wants to go to the portal with me in an hour, which is why I've cut my nap short today. We're getting a new shipment of alexandrite, so I want to be there myself when it arrives. The stuff is not just fucking expensive, but it's rare as all hel, and I don't even trust my allies to keep their fingers to themselves.

The memory of my nightmares clings to me as I walk though, whispering dark secrets, filling my thoughts with things I would rather not remember. I need to focus on the incoming shipment, on my duties as Boss. I shake my head to try to free myself of them, but then I realize there is something wrong. The pull to my wife isn't leading me in this direction.

Yanking the door to the basement open, I try not to panic when I only see Lou. "Where's Micha?" I demand.

She jumps to her feet, her eyes widening. "Um, in the bathroom."

My stomach drops. I push out with my senses, searching the heartbeats in the house, not wanting to use up the little amount of blood we have left in the bond in case I need it to find her; we haven't exchanged any more blood since I fed from her on the super yacht. I can't even feel her emotions anymore, not unless I really concentrate, and there's only a couple more times I can do that before it's gone. So I search for her with my senses.

But her heartbeat isn't here.

"Where is my wife?" I ask again, and her face pales.

She takes a step back, and I try to control my rage so my Craving doesn't break free. The last time I fed was when Maddox forced his blood in me to save my life, and it has become a constant hunger. I'm going to have to feed soon. I know it, but I want it to be with Micha, and she isn't ready.

"Shit," Lou says. "She just wanted some fresh air. She said she'd be back before you woke –"

"Where is she?"

She swallows. "I don't know."

I turn for the door, pulling on the blood bond to lead me to her. The urge to reach her isn't strong, which means she isn't far. And when I search to see what she's feeling –

My heart breaks as I close my eyes for a single step. I know where she is even without the blood bond leading me to her.

"Don't be mad at her!" Lou shouts after me as I climb the stairs.

"I'm not," I say.

I'm just terrified.

Because I know she's snuck out to get high.

SEVENTY-THREE

HER

I went into Dayne's room today for the first time since I lost him. Found the card he'd left me. He hadn't left me a note like a normal person. No, he'd left me a fucking card. A 'sorry for your loss' card. The fucker had bought me his own fucking good-bye card, and he'd *written* in it.

I traced his hand-written message with my finger, the last thing I had of his soul, and I cried.

Don't cry for me.

I died doing something I loved: protecting you.

I love you, and I'll be waiting for you in the Underworld with a whole host of books I've stolen from Hades' library. I'll even let you read me one of those porn books you love so much and spank me whenever I laugh. You think that'll make Varius spank me too? ;)

Okay, look, not going to lie, some things happened between us in your absence. Not like that, porn-brain. But I've come around to him. He's alright. He clearly loves you.

Not as much as me, obviously. And when he's stressed, he doesn't look as handsome either. I can pull off the 'two hours of sleep, forgotten beard scruff, and haggard eyes' look so much better than him.

I love you, Micha. Forever and always.

Death can't stop that.

PS: Delete my search history. Actually, just burn my whole computer.

Then I came here, to Ezriel's office, the one Talon used to occupy as he managed the distribution of Ricks and Vs.

I *needed* to come here.

Because Dayne tore apart my heart.

And Varius hates me.

He thinks I'm disgusting.

Ugly.

Wrong.

A *disease.*

He can't bring himself to touch me.

He won't even hold me.

Or sleep with me.

Or even just actually *sleep* with me.

Because he doesn't trust me anymore.

Fuck.

I don't know why he hasn't thrown me out of the house.

Stop thinking about him.

Take another vial of V.

The temptation of that is almost impossible to ignore, but I only have an hour before I need to be back at the Shadow house. I don't want Varius to be able to smell the V on me and think even less of me than he already does.

Shame hits me so fucking hard. I *am* as dirty as he thinks I am though. I willingly fucked Grubs and Bear and Antonio and Sadist. I rode Bear's corpse. Told him what to imagine about a *child*.

Pushing up from the office chair, I yank open the top left drawer of Ezriel's desk. I grab another bottle of V. My hands shake as I try to fight the memories. The knowledge of what I've done.

"Fuck you, Dayne," I rasp as all my self-hatred slams into me. I was fine before I found that fucking card. I managed to move away from the boat and all that happened there. I managed to move away from his *loss*, from the hole in my heart. From all the grief.

From Antonio.

I was fine.

I *am* fine.

Because Antonio is dead, and I'm alive, and I'm going to fucking *move on*.

I might manage to grieve Dayne and Rafiki one day, but I'm never going to grieve me. Because he didn't break me. *I* broke *him*.

"*Micha...*" Dayne murmurs, his voice in my head, as if even his ghost thinks his words alone can break me.

My throat tightens as I uncork the vial of V. "He didn't turn me into a fucking victim," I say to an empty room, an empty hole, an empty shell of a woman. "So don't *Micha* me. I survived all his shit, and I killed him."

He stares at me in the guilt of my mind.

"I played my character to perfection. I got him to lower his guard, and *I killed him*." I'm not a victim. He didn't break me. I'm not going to fucking give him the satisfaction of giving me trauma. "It was just a job. An act to get my target, and I always get my target."

I always got it with Dayne.

"I always got it with you."

But he isn't here anymore.

Just a ghost in my head.

A fucking *good bye* on a card.

Tears burn my throat and eyes, but I shove them back.

I will not cry one more fucking tear.

I am *done.*

Antonio is done hurting me.

He *can't* hurt me anymore. He's dead.

He's fucking dead, and I'm done giving him any more parts of me.

I killed him.

I killed him.

"I killed him!" I throw the bottle of V at the opposite wall, my entire body shaking from a scream that's building deep inside of me.

I killed them all.

One by one, I cut them down, and now it's only me who remains.

I'm not a victim.

I'm not a fucking victim.

"Fuck you, Dayne, for leaving me."

I yank open the drawer again. Grab another bottle of V and raise it to my lips.

The door of the office bursts open. I try to tip the glass back further, but with a blur of movement, Varius grabs it from my hand and tosses it to the floor beside me. He picks me up before it can smash near my feet, then sits me on the desk and steps back.

"Fuck you!" I scream. Why'd he have to step back? I just want his arms around me. I want him to fuck me. I want him to replace the V. I want him to fucking *care.*

"This isn't how you cope, Micha," he says.

"What the fuck do *you* know about coping?" I snap. "You don't talk! You don't touch me. You pretend like nothing happened!"

"I have been trying to get you to go to therapy! I don't touch you because –"

"I don't need therapy!" *I need you! I want* you*! I want*

my fucking husband, who I gave up so much of myself to save.

"Then why are you here?"

"What, you want me to kill myself?"

He rears back, then shakes his head. "No. Of course not. Fucking hel, Micha."

My throat clogs as the tears build up behind my eyes.

"I meant here in this office, taking V, not still *here*. The fact that's where your thoughts went first –"

He takes a step towards me, then stops. "You need help."

I shove him back. "I don't need fucking therapy." I don't need to talk about what happened. I need to forget it. I want to just forget it and move on. I have lost so many months to that helhole. To *him*. And I just want my life back. I want *me* back. How can I fucking get that if I have to confront all I did? If I have to relive it and share it and explain why the fuck I *did* it?

"Talk to me," he says. "Why do you want the V?"

I stiffen, hearing Antonio's words.

But I see my husband's face, and I try. "It's just a fun drug," I say.

"Micha –"

"I don't know why you're making a big fucking deal out of this!" I yell, unable to stomach Varius asking me like Antonio did. Trying to *heal* me like Antonio did. "You sell millions of dollars of this shit a year. Everyone else takes it."

"*We* don't," he says. "My capos don't. You –"

"Stop trying to control me!"

"I'm not! I'm trying to help you!"

"Then fuck me."

"Micha –"

I grab at his pants, but he steps back. Because I disgust him. Because he looks at me, and he sees the monster I am. *Little monster.* He called it all that time ago. He looked into my soul and knew it was *rotten.*

I am rotten.

I am a fucking disease.

No wonder he doesn't want to touch me.

"Just leave me alone," I say.

"Come home with me."

"I don't want to." I don't want to go back to the house that didn't protect me. Where I lost my daughter. Where Dayne's room sits painfully empty. Where the flowers are all gone minus the ones at the front, a reminder that Leno died because of me. Where there's no dog barking. Where it sounds even more silent for a mute man's absence.

I brush at my eyes, but I'm not crying.

Because I'm fucking done being weak.

"Okay," he says, offering me his hand. "Then let's just go for a drive."

"I don't want to be in a car with a fucking hypocrite," I snap.

"How am I a hypocrite?"

"You come in here, and you judge me for ignoring shit and for healing in a way you don't approve of –"

"Giving in to an addiction isn't healing."

"And you've ignored everything too!" I shout over him.

"I'm not ignoring any–"

"I raped you!" I scream as I hop off the desk and shove him backwards. "*I* raped *you!* Say it!"

"Micha!" He takes a step back.

"Say it!" *Admit it. Don't pretend it didn't happen, so when you say you love me, I can believe you actually do.*

"You didn't –" he starts.

"Why won't you say it?"

"Because you're my wife!" he roars. "And the thought of you –" He cuts himself off, his chest heaving, his nostrils flaring. He clenches his fists in an effort to control himself, and I *hate* that he still has that ability. That he can think about me, about how much I need him to be *safe* and *loving* and *good* while I'm such a fucking disease to him. I can't control the pain inside of me. I can't stop it from bleeding out into a rage-fueled attack on those I love.

I just need the fucking V.

I spin towards the desk, but he wraps both his arms around me and hauls me to his chest.

"Just let me have some," I say, a desperate whisper, a heart-felt plea. I try to pull apart his hands, but he doesn't let go of me.

"We can get through this." I don't know who he's trying to convince, but that anger I'm trying so hard to bury raises its ugly head.

I claw at his hands, try to stomp on his feet. "You're ignoring it as much as me!" I shout.

"No, I'm –"

"Then say it! Fucking *say it!*"

Fucking see me as the monster I am instead of just acting like I'm not. Fucking *see me.* Fucking *see me and let me know that I'm not a monster.*

Because I know I am.

And I need him to tell me I'm not.

I sag in his arms, breathing hard.

"I raped you because I needed to play along. To let him think I would do anything he asked, and you didn't matter. But I know the reasons don't change how much it hurts." My lips wobble. My eyes burn. "I know because you hurt me to save Khalid, and it didn't fucking *matter.*

"So don't fucking say you *understand.* I understand that you wanted to save Khalid. But you hurt me. So I know I hurt you." I shake with all the pain. All the guilt and shame and self-disgust. I hurt him, and I don't know how to fix it. I don't know how to confront that part of me to even say sorry because *sorry* reminds me of Grubs, and I can't –

He doesn't say anything for a long time. Too long, and his arms start to feel constricting. Like a prison. His silence like rejection.

I struggle free so I can wipe at my tearless eyes, my back to him. "I would die for you," I mutter. And he won't even talk for me.

Grabbing my elbow, he turns me around and tilts my chin up. I look into his single eye as he looks into my red ones. Both so wrong...

"I don't want you to die for me, Micha," he says softly. "I want you to live for me. I want you to fucking *live*."

"I'm aliv–"

"But you're not living." He leans his forehead down to mine. His eyes close as he shudders against me. His thumbs brush across my skin, and I can almost feel his pain echoing through me. "I just want you to *live*."

My body trembling, I close my eyes and fight back the tears. I don't need therapy because I don't need to face any of this. I just need to move on.

But how can I deny him when I can see his pain?

When he holds me like this and makes me feel less of the monster I am?

"I'll... I'll go to *one* session," I whisper, my voice thick, my throat tight. If he wants to believe in me... maybe that'll be enough to save me.

SEVENTY-FOUR

HER

"I don't need fucking therapy," I say as I flump into the chair across Maddox's desk that he has set up in his room. "I'm fine." There's nothing wrong with me. I survived. I fucking did it. No one will understand what I went through, so talking about it won't fix a damn thing. *I* already fixed it when I killed Antonio and all his chimeras. *I* did that. No therapy fucking needed. "I don't need to be here," I say.

Maddox nods, his agreement taking me by surprise. The rush of relief I was expecting to feel doesn't come though. I feel even more irritable and confused. Like he failed me. Like I've yet again been left on my own, abandoned to save myself even though I'm the one who pushed him away.

Fuck this.

I shove to my feet, wanting to get out of here. I don't like this at all.

I was fine before I came into this room. I'll be fine again as soon as I leave.

Maddox starts to stand too. "It's understandable to be too scared to confront your enemy right now. I'll tell Varius you aren't –"

"I'm not scared," I snap. "And I killed the enemy."

"You killed Antonio's body. You didn't kill his soul. You are keeping that alive inside you."

I rear back as if he'd slapped me. My teeth clench tight as my throat burns. I hate that analogy. Hate the truth of it.

Hate how Antonio still feels so godsdamn *alive.*

How his touch lingers in my soul, entwined.

Like I'm still *protecting* him.

Unable to let him go.

My hands shake as I try to find the words – any words to convince him that's not true.

"But it's okay, Micha," Maddox says as he straightens, his tone light and without judgement despite being able to see right through me. He can see *me.* The shame, the sickness still clawing at my veins. I know he can. I can feel his eyes on my soul, and yet, he doesn't look at me like I'm *wrong.* He doesn't look at me how I look at myself, with these damn eyes that aren't mine.

"I shall just go then," he says, "but I'll be back when you are ready."

Tears burn my eyes. I don't want him to go. I want to be the one who walks away. Not the one who's left behind. Not the one who's the fucking *victim.* Who's forced to seek him out later on my hands and knees. Begging like some whore. Like Sadist used to force me to do.

The memories of that fucker's demands claw at my brain. Ripping it to rotten shreds until blood and bits run down my throat, making me mute. Suffocating me so I can't get my mouth to speak or my legs to walk. I just stand frozen, panicking that he's going to leave.

That he's going to make me a victim.

Except he doesn't take a step. He just stands there behind

his desk, waiting.

Patient.

My throat burns as bad as my eyes now.

My legs giving out, I collapse back into my chair, feeling like I've sprinted a mile.

I still don't want to be here. I just don't have the strength to go.

I tense, waiting for him to talk, to take my presence as consent when it fucking isn't.

But he doesn't. He just sits back down and waits.

And waits.

The silence is thick with unsaid words.

But there's no pushing.

There are no demands.

I can feel Varius' growing concern as the hours pass and his attempt to tamper it so I can't feel it. I can almost feel him pacing in our bedroom. Waiting. Hoping I'm okay.

But I *am* okay.

I am.

He wants to come in and see how I am.

I don't push any comfort down our bond. I don't have it in me to take care of him. I hate that he's making me feel like I have to take care of him when *he* should be taking care of *me.*

His feelings disappear, the wall between us thick again, and I hate their absence too.

I just hate everything.

I hate *me.*

I hate what they did to me on that godsforsaken boat.

They were such terrible things.

No.

No, it's better to just hide it. To bury it deep and move on.

I'm fine.

"I'm fine."

"What about you do you think is fine?" he asks.

"Taking V is fine."

"It is."

I stare at him in shock. Then the words are blurting out. "So give me some. Write me a prescription or something so I can get Varius off my fucking back."

"V is fine in regulation and when you're not an addict."

"I'm not addicted. I haven't taken any in months."

"So why do you want some now? If everything is fine?"

I clench my teeth, not liking his questions. I shrug one shoulder. "It's just fun," I lie.

"Is it fun to be beholden to a craving?"

"It's not 'holding' me. I'm not a fucking victim to it."

"But you want it without knowing why?"

"I know why?"

"So why then?"

My nostrils flare in frustration. I want it to stop the pain.

But if I tell him that, he's going to think I know I'm not fine.

But I am.

I just wanted to have some fun.

"Because everyone's so fucking uptight around me," I snap. "I'm not broken."

"I know."

I'm brought up short again, surprised at his agreement. "Well," I sputter. "Varius fucking doesn't. He hasn't once fucked me."

"Do you want him to?"

I flounder.

I hate him for making me actually think about the words I'm saying. I just want to be angry. I want to feel something other than the crippling, fucking pain I felt on that boat. I want to know that I'm free, that I'm safe to be angry, and they're not letting me.

They're not letting me heal the way I need to.

Ignoring it isn't healing.
Fuck you.
Attacking everyone who cares about you isn't healing.
Fuck you!
My own damn voice should be on my side.
I hate this.
It's this room.
It's suffocating me.
I stand abruptly.
"I told you I don't need fucking therapy. I just wanted to have a bit of fun. That's it. Taking V isn't a big fucking deal. You guys are all being dramatic."

"Do you think you can have fun without the V?"
I flinch, then turn on my heels.
I'm not running away.
I'm just yanking open the door and striding out.
I storm through the house, hating how shaken I have become in only a few minutes. My body is trembling. My heart is aching. I'm hurting so godsdamn much, and I don't want to be. I'm out. I survived. I killed him. Why can't I *move on*?
I should be able to move on. Fuck!
I pick up a vase on a stand in the hallway and launch it at the other wall. My stomach drops as soon as the ceramic leaves my fingers. That was a flower Leno coaxed to life. I can't kill it.
It smashes into pieces, and a cry rips from my throat.
You're hurting everyone around you.
I don't know how to stop.
Hurrying over to the fragmented pieces, I pick up the plant. It feels so heavy in my hands despite barely weighing anything at all.
A flurry of footsteps come up the stairs, and the door to Varius' room opens. He didn't come to me earlier, didn't want to rush me, but he strides over to me now and stops

just short of folding me in his arms.

"What the fuck is wrong with you!?" Enoch shouts as he reaches the top of the stairs and sees the mess on the floor. Leno loved this plant. He loved all of his plants, and he's not here to grow any more. I'm destroying a part of him. A part of all of them.

I want to say, "I'm sorry," but I can't. The words trap in my throat. Grubs' voice whispers in my ear, making me hate that damn fucking phrase, and my legs shake with a need to run. Varius steps in front of me as his brother marches down the hall.

"She didn't mean to," my husband says.

"She threw it across the fucking hall! How is that a damn accident? Leno is *dead!*"

Varius flinches. I flinch. Enoch's face twists in pain, his anger draining out. "He's dead," he says softly, "and she's breaking what little remains."

I open my mouth to try to apologize once more, hating myself as much as he does, but I still can't get the words out.

I'm not fine.

I'm fine.

Placing the plant back on the ground, I run past the two of them and down the stairs. I just need some fresh air. This whole house is fucking suffocating. That's all.

I just need some air.

I don't go out the front door though. Don't go past Leno's blooming flowers. He's dead because of me, because I wasn't strong enough to stop Antonio from taking me. Because I didn't immediately go hide in the basement like I was supposed to, too much pride making me stupid enough to think I could help fight. I should've gone down there and helped strengthen the ward. I would've been safe. *We* would have been safe. And all the brothers who died trying to save me would still be here. Krypto would be too.

Fighting back a sob, I yank open the back door and run. A momentary thought flashes through my brain to jump into the pool and drown myself, but I know Varius will just fish me out. I can sense him right behind me, worried. Concerned. And that's just pissing me off.

I'm not broken.

I don't need to be chased after.

Watched over.

I'm fine.

I'm fine.

I'm fucking fine!

Running through the trees, I relish in the slap of the branches across my skin. I want to cut all of Antonio's touch off me. Let the poison seep out. Let him die.

"You're keeping him alive inside you."

I know.

I know, and I don't want to. But I don't know how to get him off me.

I could never get them off me...

My chest heaving, I slam into a tree and clutch at the trunk as the memories assault me. I can feel them touching me all over again. Putting their hands on me. Their mouths. Their cocks. Violating me. Ruining me. Making me feel like a stranger inside my own skin. I want to feel like me again. I want to be *whole.*

Feeling Varius come up behind me, I spin on my feet and throw myself at him. He tries to grab me to pull me into a hug, but I drop to my knees and pull at the front of his pants, my movements desperate, my hands shaking.

"Varius hasn't fucked me."

"Do you want him to?"

No.

I don't want him to touch me at all. Just the thought of this is making me sick.

But I want to prove to myself that I'm okay.

"Micha –" He grabs my hands, and I struggle against him. Knowing he'll let me go if I hurt myself, I twist my arms the wrong way, prepared to break my wrists. At least that pain would be bearable.

Cursing, he releases me. "Don't use me as a substitute for the V."

Ignoring him, I pull his cock out and suck the tip into my mouth. He stiffens as he starts to grow beneath my tongue. His hands move to my shoulders. His fingers dig into my skin. Before, his grip would have scared me – the blatant show of violence.

But now it causes unwanted arousal – my body recalling all the pain I got when I was *there*. With *them*. Taking the V.

My stomach churns. My self loathing strengthens. How can any parallel to that time give me pleasure? But I can't deny the heat pooling in my pussy. I reach a hand between my legs and slip a finger inside myself.

"Micha, stop," he hisses. But his hands don't shove me off, and his cock is growing hard. If he really didn't want this, he would stop me. He isn't even trying to get away. He's just trying to refuse me. He's just trying to deny me something I want.

It gets him off, doesn't it?

Telling me no. Taking away my control. Making me just his pathetic little bitch. Tears burn my eyes as their faces flash in front of me. Their cocks. Their orders. The pain and humiliation.

My teeth ache with the urge to snap down. Rip his cock off. Set myself free. But I squeeze my eyes shut.

I'm okay.

I'm okay.

I'm already free.

They can't hurt me.

But the urge doesn't go away. I'm going to –

"Get off me!" His roar of anger makes my pulse jerk inside my veins. I pull back, terrified of the punishment that's coming, but I've moved too slow, and his fist is already slamming down on my head. Pain explodes down my face and neck, knocking me to the ground.

He kicks me, and I curl up instinctively. All my strength gone. Reduced to a weak, pathetic victim. I want some V.

Need the V.

His foot pulls back again.

But then it stomps onto the ground rather than me. He stumbles back as he grunts, his hands on his head.

"Run," he bites out as a black, inky substance pours from his fingers, running down his legs, then moving towards me.

I scramble back, my heart racing as the smoke-like fog thickens. But then I stop.

If he kills me, will my pain end?

Or will I just suffer some more in the afterlife?

"Run!" he roars.

"Varius!" At the sound of Stormie's shout, I jump to my feet. She must have been following us. She must have seen what happened. How *weak* I am. How pathetic.

I stumble away from them, horror painted on my face. I look at her, wondering what she sees.

But she doesn't look at me.

Her attention on my husband, she throws up a pink ball around him. I look at him as he screams my name.

My head throbs from the weight of his fist.

"I'm s–" he starts.

The bubble goes up, but I'm already running away.

"I'm sorry, princess," Grubs grunts as he grabs my hips and rams into me like an animal. "Daddy couldn't wait. I kept thinking about how good you feel, and I just had to get back to you. You understand, don't you? You forgive me?"

I'm okay...

I'm okay...

I'm not fucking okay.

SEVENTY-FIVE

HIM

I can't breathe.

My heart is beating too fucking fast to stay in its lane. It's blitzing all over the place, ramming into my lungs, going off the rails, causing the air bags to fucking explode in my face.

I claw at my chest, then clutch at my head as the horrors I have been trying so hard to keep down explode out of me just like my magic.

The smoke billows, filling Stormie's bubble, and I can see Dayne's husk fighting Antonio, guided by magic I can't yet control. A desperate attempt to save my wife. Or perhaps it was him. His soul. His last need to protect the woman he loved.

I try to grab on to him. To use him as an anchor.

But he's shoved aside as the three female werewolves I was forced to fuck grab hold of me, their claws digging into my skin, their teeth sinking into my neck. I fought back as well as I could, but with my arms nailed down, my legs and neck strapped to chains, and the sickness flush inside my veins, I failed. Every day I fucking failed. Every hour. Every godsdamn minute. When Antonio wasn't torturing me, they were.

And if they weren't, then Eduardo was.

Shoving things into me *down there.*

And not into my ass.

Needles, pens, catheters. I had to throw out all the metal pens in my office. And then I practically destroyed it, taking out all my rage and pain on objects that couldn't fight back. On things that couldn't stop me.

The smell of tobacco and cedar fills my nose, suffocating me with its poison as Stormie traps me in her bubble and in my nightmares.

"I fucked your wife this way," Eduardo says as he holds up a needle. He pushes the end, and dark-blue liquid shoots out, smelling like blackberry and oak. A different Rick that increases the intensity of an orgasm. Heightens the shame.

A pleasure I don't want to feel.

But I keep wanting to chase.

I struggle futilely. He laughs before grabbing my dick. He sucks it into his mouth, swirls it around with his tongue to get me hard – not because he's gay but because it's a play for power. Power when I am helpless. Strapped down like a dog in a cage. Fish in a fucking barrel.

But I don't get hard, and he gets annoyed.

So he jams the needle into my urethra.

I get hard before he even injects me, the feeling new and foreign and good even though I don't want it to be.

He takes his time fucking me. The women have already had their turn, but one comes back to fuck my feet. She knows better than to sit on my face. I tore off one of their lips a couple days ago. Wanted to feed and drain her dry, but I wanted Micha to be the first person I sank my fangs into more.

"Are you fucking sure? Look at him!" Stormie's words brush against the edges of my brain, against the nightmare as it twists and turns into more memories I want to keep buried and forgotten or limited to just my dreams.

"Do it."

My heart jerks at that voice. That calm control. That safe space.

I can't get my breathing under control or my magic. Or my fucking thoughts.

But I hear that voice, and I turn to it.

"Find my hand," he says. "It's on the outside of Stormie's bubble."

I look, but all I can see is the black smoke and shadows filling every gap in the air, plunging me into darkness. Into all that pain suffered on that ship.

One of the wolves is riding me again. I can feel her pussy sliding up and down my dick. Can feel the shame and urge to cut the damn thing off.

To remove it so my body might feel like mine again.

So this control becomes mine again.

"Come on, Vay Vay, find my hand."

I tremble as I hear his words. Hear the love in it, the old stupid nickname. I see Rudy signing it at me for the first time and laughing, and my heart twists in my chest.

Beats back a bit of the nightmares with its own misery.

Even my rape can't withstand the agony of losing my boy.

Tears run down both my cheeks as I see him struggling to breathe. Strapped to a chair in front of me, filled with a disease so much stronger than the one I was infected with, and yet, he still manages to smile. To let the last thing I see of him not be a face of pain and fear. He fucking smiled at me as he was dying.

Dropping to my knees, I start to cry.

"Find my hand," Maddox says.

I don't want to move.

I don't want to fight this anymore.

I stop even trying to breathe.

I'm giving in. Letting it kill me as I'm sure it will. No heart can withstand beating this fast.

But Maddox is insistent, and just to get the little shit to shut up, I crawl to him along a curved surface, the bottom of Stormie's bubble. I can see a bit more here, a few flickers of light as the smoke weaves and spins around me.

"You see it?"

I catch sight of a calloused hand pressed up against the pink.

"Can you see it tapping?"

There's a feeling of movement, but I can't quite see, so I push the smoke aside with my magic. Just enough for his hand to be clear. It taps against the bubble.

"How many fingers do you see?"

I instantly think five, only to be caught off guard when I count them.

One.

Two.

Three.

Four.

Five.

Six.

Six.

That's not right.

Why is my brother so fucking weird?

That thought jars me. My thoughts.

A bit more of the smoke clears.

"Can you hear what it's saying?" he says.

Most people might think hands don't speak, but I learned sign language just so I could teach Rudy. I know all the words they can say, the laughter and joy and happiness they can shout from the rooftops.

My heart beat skitters to a stop as I hear it.

He's saying my name in the tap Rudy used to give at my door.

"Varius!" Rudy calls for me on my wedding night just as I am about to make love to my wife. I yank open the door to our room in annoyance as Micha locks herself in the ensuite and moans louder than she usually does, making sure I can hear her. I want to throttle him.

I don't. I don't. I just want him back.

"You can't just marry me off! Maddox said you were marrying me off? To Lou! I demand an explanation. Post haste! Look how much you're making me panic! I'm talking like an idiot! I –"

"You knew you would have to marry one day," I cut in.

"But she doesn't even know sign language!"

"You have six years before you wed. She can learn in that time."

"What would we even talk about? I'm almost double her age."

"Twenty-six to her sixteen is hardly double –"

"Fucking close enough."

"– and by the time she's of age, you'll be thirty-two. Half plus seven. You're fine."

"Well, what if I'm gay?"

A half-sob, half-laugh breaks out past my lips. He said that as if he really thought I didn't know. Everyone in the family knows. We knew since he was five. Though, in truth, he knew we knew, but whenever he got annoyed, whatever he thought, he signed.

"Would you rather marry Vlad?" I ask in exasperation, wanting to get back to my wife.

I wish I spent more time with him. I never even asked about him and Vlad. I didn't care then. I didn't know if his feelings were serious. I should've asked. I should've taken the fucking time to ask.

And now I can't.

Because he's gone.

And I'm never going to hear his hands again.

Strong arms wrap around me as I sit on the ground and shake. The smoke is gone. The bubble is gone. I feel so damn exhausted.

So empty and hollow.

"That's it. Just breathe. Feel the ground. Smell the air."

I feel him. Notice the sickly smell of my sweat.

Ground myself in his arms around me.

Ground myself and remember why I lost control in the first place.

"I hit her," I rasp. "Where is she?"

I need to find her. To apologize and explain.

"Just take a moment. You've had a panic attack."

I shove him off me.

"Good rest," he says dryly as I pull on the blood bond to find her. She's heading back to the fucking warehouse.

I slip my phone out of my pocket and dial the manager there. He's to let her in, then lock her in the office after he takes out all the V.

She's pissed as all hel when I arrive, but at least she isn't high. I open the door, then dodge the book she throws at my face.

"I'm surprised there's a book in here," I say. Ezriel isn't big on reading physical copies.

The words take her off guard, just like Maddox's fingers did to me, but instead of being annoyed I distracted her from her rage, her face twists in pain, and she sits down heavily in Ezriel's chair. My throat tightens as I turn to the book on the floor. Squatting down, I pick it up and fix its crumbled pages. Talon might have turned traitor and set up my girl to take the blame, but he was still my brother.

I walk slowly over to her, collecting my thoughts, then

place the book on the desk.

I start to tell her I'm sorry before I recall how she reacted to that phrase. The panic in her eyes, the self-disgust. I want to ask her to exchange more blood for the blood bond so I can feel what she's feeling and better navigate this difficult conversation, but I don't want to push her.

If she doesn't want to be tied to me... If she doesn't want to bond with me anymore... I want that to be her choice.

And besides, my emotions are so fucking crazy right now that combining them with hers and making us both feel everything would be relationship suicide.

So I look her in the eyes and do my best to read her despite the impassable walls she has up.

The first step to reaching her, though, is bringing my own walls down.

So I take a moment to figure out what to say, and when I finally speak, I don't say sorry. "You were right, Micha. I've been avoiding facing what happened on that yacht, and it was wrong of me to think that what I was doing was better than what you were." I purse my lips. As much as I believe that though, the only thing that matters is – "It is not on me to judge how you cope."

She glances away, her eyes wet.

"But I would like for you to talk to me. We've struggled with that a bit, huh?" I say, trying to add a bit of humor.

"I *talked* to you," she says, rounding on me in anger. "I told you I was innocent, and you didn't believe me."

"You're right. *I've* struggled with that. Sor– I shouldn't have blamed you."

Her lips tremble, but she clenches her jaw.

"I shouldn't have hit you either."

She looks at me, her eyes so full of pain. Of knowledge of what she did. "You told me to stop. I should've stopped."

It's my turn to look away. Take a deep breath and gather myself. "Even still, I should have been discussing this with

Maddox. Therapy doesn't really work if you don't talk about your issues."

"Don't blame yourself," she snaps. "Blame –"

"I'm not going to blame you –"

"You should."

"Perhaps," I concede. "But I'm not going to."

"Why not?"

"Because you'll just use it as another way to tell yourself you're a monster."

She flinches, and I thank the gods I talked to Maddox about her, trying to understand what she is going through. He's kept all her secrets to himself, but he's just helped me see what her new walls mean.

"So you see, you're not the only one making mistakes. But that's what they are, little monster. *Mistakes.* Those do not define us. How we deal with them is what does."

She swallows, but she doesn't look at me.

"I haven't touched you," I say, recalling our argument from yesterday before she cut me off, "because I don't think you're ready –"

"I am –"

I shake my head. "You want a poor man's version of V, and I want to be more than that to you."

"If that's all I wanted, I could sleep with anyone here."

I growl, a primitive noise I can't stop. "Good luck fucking trying." Marching over to the door, I yank it open. The men and women lingering around in curiosity scramble to look busy, but I want them to hear this, so I raise my voice. "If anyone here even fucking *looks* at my wife like they want to fuck her, I will kill them and every friend and family they have."

She hurries over to me and slams the door shut before rounding on me, forcing me back. "You're such a fucking neanderthal!" she shouts, her cheeks flushed.

I grin as I look down at her, my jealousy settling a little

as we feel, almost, like we did before. "Only ever with you," I say softly.

She glances away, and my smile drops. But we still feel better than we did before, so I'll take it.

"There's another reason I haven't touched you too," I say, getting us back on track even though I'd much rather be on said track, tied down as a train barrels towards my face.

I look up towards the ceiling, only to focus quickly back on my wife, using her presence to ground me. To keep the nightmares from rising too brutally.

"They used me as... a thing." I swallow. "I don't want to feel like that ever again, and I especially... don't want to feel like that with my wife."

She bows forward on a sob, and I move to gather her in my arms, but she darts to the side, away from the wall and back towards the desk.

"How can you love me?" she cries as she stumbles back, putting distance between us with more than just her feet.

I step forward, determined to close it. "Because you're my little monster."

"I'm just a *monster.*"

"No, you're not."

"You don't know what I did!"

"No, but Khalid does."

She flinches. Her eyes widen. Panic carves deep into her face. Shame. Guilt. Self-disgust.

"He never once thought you were worth leaving. And he's a very good judge of character on that front because that was his job for a very long time. Deciding who to kill because they became too much of a monster. And knowing who was still worth saving."

She's backed up against the desk, and I take that final step towards her. I lift my hand to her face and brush away her tears as she cries.

"I love you, Micha Shadow, because you are worth loving

and because I am in love with every part of you. The fire. The courage. The ability to do things that are *bad* for the greater *good*. I love Rudy for his ability to stay good despite all the bad, to never waver in his damn annoying morals, but I love you for knowing that sometimes, you cannot win by playing by the rules." I tilt her chin up and look her in the eyes. The redness bothers me, knowing she lost them because of me – even if I didn't choose them, and I miss the color they were. The defiant brown. The honeyed laughter.

But they are her, and that is enough.

I press a kiss to her forehead, feel her shudder against me. "I love you for being you." Lowering my head, my heart pounding in every vein and artery inside me, making me feel like I'm about to burst out of my skin, I press my lips to hers.

She trembles, and so do I.

She doesn't move, and neither do I.

We just stand here, our lips touching and nothing else. Tears streak down our cheeks.

But the gap between us has been closed.

Now we can finally start to heal.

SEVENTY-SIX

HER

Varius no longer sleeps in Maddox's room.

He sleeps in ours while I watch him.

I thought he didn't trust me, but in truth, he doesn't trust himself, and he didn't want to put his stuff on my shoulders. Not because he thinks I'm weak, but because he still sees his trauma as a burden – just like I do.

So I can't join him in the bed. I have to sit in a chair across the room, or he can't drift off. He moves too violently while he sleeps, kicking and lashing out. I want to wake him, but the times I tried just made it worse. Instead, I've learned to talk to him. He never seems to wake up knowing what I've said, but my voice seems to soothe him enough to calm.

At first, I only read books out loud. Fantasy or sci-fi with no smut at all. Then I started to talk about easy things like Lou being annoying because she wants to drop out of art school so she can become a demon summoner for the SCU.

The fucking *SCU.* The secret agency that governs sups on Earth and has a prison underwater that makes Alcatraz look like it's guarded by a rent-a-fence that got pushed down ages ago by a bunch of kids. Then I bring up the idea of moving out of this house. List the pros and cons. Pros being away from the place where so much of my trauma is rooted. Cons being away from his family. I know we both need them.

Even if I haven't been to see Maddox in a therapist role since that first time three weeks ago, I like seeing him every day as a friend. I like hearing the twins bitch about random things to each other. I like seeing Khalid with – whatever his girl's name is. Not *kira* but something close. Fuck.

I make a note to ask Lou what it is the next time I see her; for some reason, I don't think Varius remembers either.

And then I talk about my dad. About how I'm avoiding his calls because I'm not the strong assassin he could be proud of. I'm the weakling he always told me I was when he tried to toughen me up so I wouldn't be an embarrassment.

"When I see him again, I just want us to be on equal footing," I murmur. I tried so hard to gain his approval when I was a kid, and although I gave that up in my teens, for some stupid reason, I'm back to wanting it.

Almost needing it.

I don't know why, but I'm sure Maddox would have an answer. Annoyed with that, I stand. "I don't need therapy, but I do need to fucking pee."

I feel like I have been peeing every fifteen minutes these last few days, and there's this weird fluttering in my belly. Given it started when I began talking to Varius rather than reading to him, I thought it was just butterflies. But now it feels like I'm passing gas all the fucking time, so maybe I should see Sau. My intestines didn't exactly get the VIP treatment while I was away.

I snort. Then ache. *Dayne would've laughed at that.*

Avoiding looking at myself in the mirror, I think about his card with a bittersweet pain. Black font with a smiling purple flame on it and the words: *I'd ask you to cremate me, but I'm already smoking hot.*

Another flutter passes through my stomach, and I frown as I wash up. That felt like something moved.

Then it hits me.

Panic.

Terror.

Crippling nausea.

I try to shout for Varius, but my mouth is too dry. My throat is too tight. I yank my shirt up in front of the sink and look down at my stomach. Is that a bump? I look in the mirror, then turn to get a better angle.

It can't be a bump.

I haven't had sex in –

I don't know.

I don't know.

I lost track of the time in there.

Too many days merged together.

"Varius," I croak, barely loud enough for even me to hear.

I lean against the sink, trembling.

My stomach twists so tight, I throw up. My skin is flush. My head is warm. My body doesn't feel like mine.

It's *theirs.*

I want it out.

I want it out!

I want it out!

If I can feel it kicking, that means it's older than Bambi, and the thought of that is ripping my soul apart. It can't be older than her. I would've noticed. Sau would've noticed when she healed me on the yacht. She would've told me so she could check up –

My skin runs cold. She's been checking up on me every week. A brush of the fingers here when she passes me a cup, a hand on my back there as she moves past in the hall.

"You *bitch*," I hiss. She's taken my choice away. Just like Antonio did. She's been using me as an incubator to get her damn grandkids.

Fear tightens around my neck as I wonder if it's even Varius'. I try to remember if Eduardo managed to rape me while Antonio was gone or if Antonio did it while I slept. Or maybe it is Sadist's. Some Vs keep sperm tucked away to be used later; others allow you to get pregnant while you're already pregnant.

So maybe it's Bear's.

I'm sick at that thought, throwing up in the sink. The smell of it reminds me of too many nights with Sadist, and I heave again. Panic claws its way across my mind. I can't have conceived another monster. Another thing. And not on that night where I pretended to be a child to get a pedophile off just to score some V.

And even as I hate it, my body still craves the potion that smells of pomegranates and chocolate.

What is wrong with me?

Why can't I stop even knowing what harm it brings?

What *pain*?

I have to get it out of me.

I need to get it out.

Get it out.

Get it out.

Get it out!

Dragging myself along the edge of the sink, I reach for the cabinet to the right of it. I open the door and quickly find the knife Varius keeps in here. He has them stashed everywhere around the house. Guns too. And wands now.

But a wand isn't going to help me. I'm not a healer, don't know much about the human body.

But I know this *thing* needs a womb, and I don't want it in me anymore. I lost the chance for kids when I lost Bambi.

I can't go through this again. Can't let some *fucking disease* experience all the milestones she should have had

I step into the bathtub and tear off my shirt. My hands shake, so I take a deep breath, readying myself for the pain. I'm not going to have long before the shock kicks in and makes me pass out, but it will only take half a second to cut my belly open if I don't hesitate. Then another second to push my hand inside, grab it, and rip it out.

Tears clog my throat as I think about Antonio doing this to me. I force the memories to rise, visualize where he hit me to rip Bambi away.

Fuck.

I don't want to do this.

I don't want to do this alone.

I want Dayne here.

He would've helped me. He would've made this safe and bearable, and he would've been there for me after as I fell apart on his shoulder.

I press a hand to my stomach, feeling the damn thing kick.

What if it's Varius' though?

What if it's a new start?

I tremble.

Fight back the urge to sob. To think about that.

Because that would be worse than it being Bear's.

I don't want just any baby of ours. I want *Bambi*, and this isn't her.

I can't be a mother to this thing.

I *can't.*

If it's Bear's, at least I'll be happy killing it. But if it's his...

It can't be.

It *can't.*

Moving in a panic, I slice a line across my belly, drop the knife, and then push my hand inside. The agony is fucking insane. My heart rate is screaming at me. My blood pressure is dropping. I'm losing consciousness faster than I expected.

I dig my hand around, trying to remember where *he* hit me. Where he pulled out all my hopes and dreams.

And then I find it.

The thing kicks against me as if it's trying to get me to stop. As if it's fighting for its life.

Tears in my eyes, I grab hold of the sac and start to rip it out.

I'm sorry.

I'm sorry.

I just can't be a mother to you.

I wake up to the smell of blood.

The Craving hits me hard, demanding and needy, and I stumble out of bed as my fangs ache with a desire to feed. It starts to take over me, but I know that smell. I know that person, and so I fight it back.

My wife is hurt.

She needs me.

I shout for Mother as I race into the bathroom, following my nose and heart and the wild panic inside of me. That's a lot of blood I can smell.

I bang into the door, smashing it in even though a simple twist of the knob would've done. Seeing her in the bathtub, passed out and pale, I scream for Mother again as I turn to grab the healing wand out of one of the cupboards.

The door to my room opens before I can even get it out. Mother enters, her heartbeat high from cardio, having taken the stairs multiple at a time. Her stress factors are low. She's in full healer mode. "Don't get in my way," she says.

She kneels down beside the tub, and I sag against the sink. The smell of vomit assaults my nose, and I turn to clean it up, to do something helpful, regardless of how small of a help it is.

"Tell me she's going to be okay," I croak as I spill water across the sink.

"What's going –" I turn towards Maddox as he and my other brothers come skidding into the room, crowding the bathroom door. Lou tries to push through, but my youngest brother pivots on his feet and tackles her back past Enoch and Khalid.

"You don't need to see this," I hear him murmur.

"That's my sister!" she screeches.

"Calm down," he says. "She needs to concentrate."

"Sau!" I snap. Or perhaps it's more of a plea. A ripping of the soul out through my teeth.

"Khalid," she says, not answering me. "Come here. I need your blood. Enoch, call Aleric."

Enoch doesn't even groan this time. He just pulls out his phone and steps back to call him. Khalid moves forward and holds out his arm.

"*How is she?*" I demand, even though I already know it's serious. Otherwise, she wouldn't be calling the person she hates the most.

She picks up the knife Micha used to cut herself and slashes it sideways across Khalid's palm. She makes another cut on Micha's shoulder. Knowing what to do without being told, he presses his hand to her wound, and Mother uses her magic to tie their blood vessels together. Thankfully, he's a universal donor; if he wasn't, she'd have to use her magic to constantly fight Micha's rejection of his blood, and she's already low on energy.

Too close to developing loka.

But I can't think about that right now. Can't weigh the risk of losing my mother to save my wife.

"I can't lose her," I rasp as I lean against the bathroom sink, my heart falling down the drain.

"Even at the risk of the child?" she asks. "He's yours."

A boy.

My boy.

I want to scream. Love and guilt, hope and shame, joy and grief – they all battle it out inside of me at hearing the news from the first time. That I'm a father, and I have a son.

But I had a wife first. *My* wife.

"She lives," I rasp.

"She won't be able to conceive another," she says. "There has been too much damage this past year, and even I can't fix it."

Those words slam into me. Shove me against a wall, and shake me. I clench my fists as the rage pummels into me. Then I spit out my answer – the only fucking answer there will ever be.

"I don't care if you have to sacrifice the child in a fucking ritual, Mother. She *lives*."

Gods, just let her live.

SEVENTY-SEVEN

HER

I come to with my eyes still closed, wanting to scream and cry and rage against an uncaring, unfair world.

I cut that *thing* out of me, braved the agony of it, and yet Antonio is still fucking here inside of me. He haunted my dreams while I was under, telling me Varius would let me die, that he'd save his heir, that I'd just tried to kill his child, so why the fuck would he want me to survive?

A woman's only purpose is to breed...

I spent fucking hours flitting in and out of consciousness, perpetually being stuck in my nightmares, thinking I would not wake up... Yet now I have, and I don't know which is worse. Which I would've rather have come true.

"Micha." Varius' voice makes me want to cry. I know he must have been the one to find me. I did it in our fucking bathroom after all. Why didn't I have the good grace to do it elsewhere?

Because I panicked.

Because I'm not fucking okay.

No, I am.

Now that that thing is out of me, I'm okay.

I have to be.

Otherwise, there's no point in continuing on. Because if that didn't fix me, then what else possibly can?

"Therapy, bitch."

I ignore Dayne's voice. He's dead, so it's not like he can talk.

My mouth pops open.

"Micha?"

Laughter erupts from me.

I can't help it.

It just comes out loud and crazed and deep from my soul. He can't talk. He can't *talk.* Oh my gods, that's terrible. And he suggested *therapy.*

"Micha!" Varius says, concerned for my sanity. "Maddox, do something."

"She's laughing, bruh. Let her get it out."

"She just ki–" He clamps his mouth shut, but I already heard the words, the accusation, and now I know that thing inside me was *ours.* Varius' and mine, not Bear's or Sadist's or Antonio's... *Ours.* And I just killed it. Somberness hits me like a fucking truck. As quick as it started, the laughing stops, but I feel so utterly drained.

"I wasn't laughing because of that," I say as I open my eyes and sit up. Everyone in the house but Sau is sitting around me. She must have used a lot of magic to save me. The build-up of magic in her system isn't going down like it should be. Combined with her curse... I might've just killed her too.

My heart twists with guilt. "How's Sau?"

"Resting," Varius says, but the way the other brothers are sitting rigid on the chairs they pulled up to my bedside tell me she isn't good.

I look at Enoch, wondering if he'll kill me for being a threat to his family. His face is an utter mask as he looks at me, and a shiver runs down my spine. For a moment, he looked too much like Khalid. A reaper through and through.

"How do you fe–"

"Did you know it was Varius' kid when you did it?"

The men all shove to their feet as Sau's voice wafts from the door. The twins go to help her stand, seeing her leaning against the door frame. Khalid and Maddox move in front of Varius as he turns on her in barely-controlled anger.

"Stop," he snaps. "She doesn't need to hear this."

Her fierce green eyes bore into mine. I shake my head. I didn't know. "You will never have another child," she says. "That was his only heir."

"Get her out," Varius snarls, his words low and lethal. My mouth falls open as I stare at her. I gasp for air as the grief in my chest starts to suffocate me.

I didn't know. But...

"I can't be a mother," I whisper.

"I'm not judging you." She stares deep into all the twisted parts of me. *Sees* me. "There was a time I couldn't either."

"Enoch –" Varius snaps.

"No," I cut in, my voice raspy. I need to hear what she has to say. I'm floundering in that fucking sea I was adrift in for months, and her eyes are so damn *calm*.

He turns to me, studies me, but my eyes stay on Sau.

"When I came out of the Plane of Monsters and found out the last of my children was dead, I refused to have any more until I brought peace to this city. I aborted three of them, and I would have helped you abort yours too if I had known where your head was." Her lips tighten with self blame. "I thought you would be vocal enough to ask, so I assumed you were just avoiding it until you were ready. I kept the check-ups quick, thinking you wanted it because it was Varius'. But I shouldn't have assumed. I'm s–"

"Not that phrase," Varius cuts in, and my heart flips over. He's been paying attention enough to know that I can't bear to hear those damn two words. Fucking hel, what did I do to deserve him?

I finally turn to him to find him already looking at me with so much love in his eyes. Not an ounce of accusation lies within them even though I just killed his son, his only chance for an heir. I reach a shaky hand out for him, and he practically falls forward to grab it, and I hate myself even more for what I've done.

What I would've done again. Even knowing it was ours… I can't bare the thought of leaving Bambi behind. Of moving on with another child while she should've been my first.

"I apologize," Sau says. "If I'd known, I would've given you an abortion. Though I would have also told you that the amount of damage you suffered under Antonio means you would have struggled to carry to term again. Now, you will never conceive." Her eyes soften. "But your son is a fighter."

"He lives?" I ask as Varius tenses ever so subtly, his hand almost squeezing mine. He's holding back his own desires and questions so this choice can be mine alone.

"For now. I do not know if he will survive. He's twenty weeks and needs constant care. Louise is with him now."

I shudder, my throat tightening. I don't look at Varius. *Can't.* I know what I'm going to say will hurt him, but… "I can't be a mother."

"You don't have to be. He'll have us. But if you are ever ready, then we can figure it out. Communication might not be my strong point. I've been making decisions all on my own for a long time. But learn from my mistakes, Micha. You are not alone." She smiles at me. "You're my daughter."

I swallow down the emotions clogging my throat. Varius squeezes my hand, then raises it to his lips.

"Yeah, sis, you're family," Maddox says. "And we don't leave family."

"Except for Talon," Enoch cuts in. His twin hits him on the shoulder. "Fucking hel," Ezriel says with a shake of his head. "Read the fucking room."

"Sor-arwawar. It just slipped out." I stare at him, a smile pulling at my lips at his 'correction' despite the pain in my chest. Dayne would have said something similar –gallows humor being one of his favorites– and the last remnant of his soul buries into mine.

Swallowing hard, I look at Sau. "Thank you for saving me," I say.

"Then don't waste it." She turns to leave. "Go to fucking therapy."

It takes me a while to feel emotionally strong enough to bare my soul to Maddox, but seven weeks later, I'm in his room, on his couch. Varius hasn't been to see his son –I still can't think of it as mine– because he's 'given his loyalty' to me, but I know how much he wants to see him. I might have given the kid up, but it isn't fair to force him to do the same.

"So what do we talk about?" I ask.

"Whatever you want."

"I don't want to talk."

"Okay then."

He doesn't say a word for over half an hour. I blow out a breath, getting bored and irritated with how patient he's being. "You're really not going to say anything?"

"Not if you don't want me to."

"Then why am I here?"

"You tell me."

"You said you could fix me."

"Therapy isn't magic. The only person who can fix you is you."

I start to open my mouth to say this is stupid as I rise to

my feet, but he cuts in.

"But what do you think needs fixing?"

"What do I think —" I clench my teeth together. I don't know why I'm feeling so combative with him. I like him. He makes me laugh, and he reminds me of Dayne.

"Does the anger you have bother you?"

It bothers me that he can read my mind. "No," I snap.

A flicker of a smile twists his lips and lights up his eyes. "Because it's understandable that you're angry."

I glare at him. "No, it's not."

"It is." He's completely serious now. "Because you were punished for being defiant. So you are testing us to see how we will punish you. You're still in survivor mode, banging against the parameters of your cage to see where it's faulty." He leans forward. "But you are safe here, Micha. You can let that part of you go."

I glance away, unable to handle what he's saying because what if I let go, and there's nothing that remains? Then all I'll be is a victim.

My throat works hard as the silence stretches between us. But his patience eventually gives me the chance to give voice to my fears.

"I don't want to be a victim," I say. "And if I let myself believe it's over, that's all I'll ever be."

"You're not a victim, Micha. You're a survivor."

"A survivor?" I rasp in disbelief, my head whipping to him, sudden fury building in my chest. "A *survivor!*" I yell, my rage spitting free. At him, at the world. At fucking *me*. I beat a hand against my chest. "*What part of me* survived, *Maddox?*"

I jump to my feet, incapable of sitting still. "I can't even look at my *reflection*! I can't eat. I can't breathe. I cut open my fucking stomach because I couldn't —"

I cut myself off, not wanting to think about what I've done. Or why I did it.

Because he's right. I'm not strong enough to face it.

I'm not capable of fighting this enemy.

I'm not who I used to be.

I'm weak.

I'm scared.

I'm fucking *terrified* that Antonio is still out there, and he will come for me.

He will come for me, and I won't be strong enough to face him.

To fight him.

To stop myself from giving in if he offers me V.

I love Varius.

I love the Shadow brothers, and my sister. But I can't seem to stop myself from hurting them.

So maybe I am better off with him.

Maybe they should've left me to rot on that yacht for eternity.

I slam my fist against my chest again, wanting it to stop beating. Wanting it to just *cease*.

"I'm nothing but a broken shell!" I say. My words crack and splinter apart like the rest of me. "So you tell me… you fucking tell me what part of me – what part of me…" My words are choking me, killing me. I'm so weak, even they are breaking me down. "*Fucking survived!*" I finally manage to spit out. Then I collapse back onto the sofa, sobbing too hard to speak.

And I hate that. I hate me. I hate that I can't run from that truth anymore. Can't bury it under smiles and laughter and a masked face that pretends it's not screaming all the fucking time.

I hate myself.

I hate my tears.

And I *hate* that I am keeping Antonio alive inside of me. But I don't even believe he's gone. I want to see his body. I need to see his body. But I can't. I can't put that fear to rest.

He will always haunt me. I'm never going to get better. I'm never going to *want* to get better because I need to be on edge. I need to be watching every fucking shadow and be ready to fight. I can't take the time to heal. I *can't.*

Maddox rises slowly from his chair. I tense, so damn tuned for danger. He walks back and forth, and despite my tears, I clock him. Always aware. Fully prepared to explode into action if someone moves in a way that threatens me.

My tears start to slow as I focus on him more and more. It doesn't matter that he hasn't moved in my direction. He could cover the distance easily now that he's standing.

"You still have your heart, Micha," he says firmly, making said heart pound. It bangs like a drum, giving me another thing to focus on other than the fear. "You still have your utter need to defend those you love." He stops now, and I stare at him fully, no longer looking at him through side eyes of unease. A few tears still trickle down my cheeks, but the rest of them are caught in the dam at my throat. My pulse skitters, waiting for his next words, holding on to them like a lifeline to keep myself afloat in the sea of pain and bitterness rolling around inside of me.

"You have your compassion and your love of those you trust." His voice softens as his eyes bore into mine. "They broke the outside of you, yes."

My lips waver, feeling that loss, that black hole that's consuming me.

"But they couldn't touch your *core*. You were too strong for them because you *are* a survivor, Micha."

I tremble as I stare at him. Looking into his eyes, I try to pull his opinion of me into my soul. Fill up that black hole. But the words feel too hollow. Just silly wishes born from rose-colored glasses. *"I don't want you to die for me, Micha. I want you to live for me. I want you to fucking live."*

How can Maddox claim I'm a survivor if I'm not even living? Sorrowful tears roll down my cheeks.

"You are still you," Maddox says. "If you take a vase and you drop it, what's it called?"

I flounder, not sure what he means.

"A broken vase," he says. "It's still a *vase* despite its new shape. You take a bottle and you break it over some guy's head, and it changes from being safe to drink from to being a weapon because of its jagged edges, but it's still a *bottle*. The core of it is still the same. The destruction of it does not change what it is. And you, Micha, are still a fighter. That is why you're here, fighting to work through this. You are still a protector of children –"

I shove to my feet, clawing at my shoulders, ripping off lines of skin. "I'm not!" I scream. The memories of what I did with Bear slam into me. I drop to my knees, still tearing at my flesh to get it off me. To get him off me. To get to the sickness of my soul so I can rip it out too. He thinks my only sin when it comes to kids is cutting out that *parasite* while Varius slept. But he doesn't know all I've done. He wouldn't be saying this if he *knew*. "I *hurt them*," I rasp, the words tumbling out.

"You traded yourself for that little girl."

I shake my head as I start to hyperventilate. He doesn't understand. He doesn't fucking understand!

"You could have killed yourself in my cage so Antonio could never get to you."

I stare at him, wanting to confess my sins, but I can't. The words lodge in my throat. The shame. The self-disgust. Bear didn't violate me that day. *I* violated me.

"But you didn't. You accepted Rudy's –" He falters on a hard swallow. His eyes flick away from mine for a second, moisture painting them with an unbearable pain. But then he looks back at me, lets me see the truth of his words. "You accepted his trade because you still wanted to protect her. You're a protector, Micha. That has not changed."

"I'm a pedophile!" I scream. I might not have actually

hurt a kid, but I was able to think of it. I was able to *role play* it to get high. "You don't know what I've done! You don't know who I've hurt! So don't sit there and tell me – don't *tell me* that I'm not – that I *survived!* Because they broke me. They fucking – they fucking *destroyed* who I was. And I let them. I let them just so I could get high. I did that! That was all *me."*

I stumble back as he stares at me. And I finally see it. The horror, the disbelief, the inability to know what to say. All this time I thought he saw me, but he only ever saw the mask I was putting up.

I shake my head, my heart grieving. It hurts too much just thinking about what I did. I need some V. I need to stop the pain. Stumbling towards the door, I yank it open to find Varius. This session is over. I can't do it anymore.

"Micha –"

"Just stop!" I run out, my skin itching, my mind infested with fire ants and boiling tar.

I pick up the pace as I hurry down the hall. By the time I reach the stairs, I'm flat out running, so desperate to escape my own skin. My own mistakes. My own misery and self-betrayal.

How can he call me a protector of children when I did *that?*

When I killed Varius' child too?

Tears streaking down my cheeks, I start to run towards Varius' room. He appears in front of me before I can take more than a few steps. Gathering me up in his arms, he lifts me, and I wrap my legs around him as I bawl my eyes out on his shoulder. He doesn't take me to our room though. Not to a bed. Not to those memories I'm trying to escape.

He carries me outside so the wind will stroke my face, and the fresh air will fill my lungs, grounding me in a world so different to the prison I knew. He's trying to stop the memories by overriding my brain with different smells, *present* smells.

He sits down on the ground in the middle of the woods, with me on his lap. "You're safe here, monster," he murmurs as he runs his fingers over my body. "Feel my hands. They will never hurt you." He reaches down and digs one hand into the dirt, then lifts the earth to my face, which still lies buried against his shoulder. "Smell the woods. This is home."

I squeeze him harder, starting to hyperventilate as my heart runs wild. But I can feel his safety. I can smell the roots of home.

"And take this knife," he says, removing one of my hands from around his back and pressing a blade into it. "This moment is yours, Micha. *I'm* yours."

I grip it hard, finding solace in its presence, in the gift of it coming from him. He lifts it to his neck.

"I'm yours to stop, monster. You have absolute control over this."

My hand trembles. Fear swamps me at the thought of cutting him open by mistake. The fucking idiot shouldn't have given me a knife right now. I could hurt him.

"You're still you, Micha. You still want to protect those you love."

My lips wobble as that truth hits me. But that just makes me cry harder. Because that confirms it was *me* doing those things. Not a shell. Not someone too broken to know right from wrong. It was me. It was all me.

Tears rush down my cheeks.

"Please," I beg, crying into his shoulder, "make it stop."

"I don't know how," he says, his words twisted in pain, in a desire to know how to help me.

"It's simple." It's so fucking simple. "Give me some V." The words tumble out of my mouth. The shame hits right on their curtails, but I don't draw them back. My hands shake as I say, "You can take a Rick and stop all your pain too." The nightmares that keep him from sleeping when I do still.

"We can do it together."

His eye closes briefly, a mask falling over his face. But he won't deny me in this. I have a knife to his throat. I'll make him get me some V.

I need it.

It'll help more than therapy.

If he loves me, he'll get it.

And I know he loves me. I can use that. Use him. I just need the V.

"Micha," he murmurs as he opens his eye, and I look into it looking into me.

I see his disappointment at what I've asked. But I also see his willingness. His need to help me in some way when I'm this broken.

Fuck.

I can't do this. I can't use him like this. I'm tainting even the purity between us. He walked into hel for me and called it heaven purely because I was there.

And I'm repaying him by doing this.

I'm nothing but a monster. He should've left me in hel.

Cupping my face with his dirty hands, Varius rubs the earthy scent over my skin, grounding me in the scent of home. "Will you let me touch you without the V?" he asks.

"It won't be enough –"

"We could strengthen the blood bond," Varius says softly. "Then it will be."

I tremble, wanting to deny him. I don't want to use the bond. Don't want to infect it with my disease.

But I need the pain to stop.

It's consuming me.

Breaking me.

And there's not much left to break. Just splinters of a soul dead and gone. Why couldn't they have left me be? I was fine until they pushed me into therapy.

The hollowness of my womb mocks me. The fact that it

was Varius' child.

I'm a terrible mother.

A terrible person.

But at least I did it while it was still a fetus, incapable of feeling pain.

Instead of letting it grow. Be born. Then hurting it with all my addiction. My sickness. My bad decisions and trauma packed brain, where there's no room for nurturing and love.

"Just make it stop," I beg. I don't care if it's a poor man's version of V. I just need it all to stop.

"I will try, little monster," Varius murmurs as he slips one hand between our bodies. Under my waistband. My panties. Until he's stroking between my lips.

I tense, feeling fear rather than the pleasure I expected. His other hand feathers its thumb across my cheek. "Smell the earth," he murmurs. "You're not on that ship."

I inhale deeply, clinging to the aroma I never smelled out at sea. The grass and the flowers and the bark of the trees. The outdoors. The freedom. The safety.

"Hear the birds." They chip around us, feeling at ease in our presence. They're not hiding from the monster in their home. They see a part of me I do not.

He leans his head down, hovering an inch away from kissing me. "Feel my breath on your lips," he murmurs. He dips his head even lower trailing his mouth across my neck. "Feel my fangs.

"See *me*, little monster. Look at my face and know it's me. I'll never hurt you."

I duck my head. *But what if I deserve to be hurt?*

Stop.

You're going to infect him.

You're dirty. A disease.

The blade wobbles at his throat, and panic hits me harder than the fear. I lift my head to check he's okay, and I find him staring at me, his heart in his eye, his life in my hands.

"I'm yours, little monster. To kill or fuck as you see fit." I can practically hear his thoughts through the calmness of his eye. He's really willing to risk dying in order to help me.

My heart twisting, I tell myself to drop the knife.

But I can't.

I need it, and he knows it.

Holding my eyes, he pushes a finger into me. Slowly. So tantalizingly slowly. When he settles to his bottom knuckle, I close my eyes on a shudder.

"Can you look at me, monster?" Not a demand like it would have been before. *"Eyes on me."*

I refuse, wanting to fight him on something...

"You're testing the limits of your cage." Maddox's words come back to me. *"You're just trying to see if you're safe. "*

"I need you to look at me," Varius says, an edge of panic to his words. "I want to take care of you, little monster. But let me do it without hurting us. Please. I need to know you see me."

Shuddering and swallowing hard, I tell myself I'm safe.

He's safe.

He'll never hurt me.

He'll never punish me.

Knowing that in my heart, I breathe out.

Open my eyes.

And I finally let Antonio go.

SEVENTY-EIGHT

HER

He curls his finger, and I clutch his shoulders, a little breath escaping me. It doesn't feel as good as the V, but I'm trying my best to give him a chance. To give *us* a chance because I'm not the only one with trauma.

I know a little of what the women did to him, but like I haven't told him everything, neither has he. I wonder if he'd still like me if he knew. Or if he'd leave.

My fingers tighten on the knife; he stills immediately. Draws back, pulling his finger out of me.

"What are you doing?" I demand, my voice shaky. I need the distraction of a poor man's V. He should leave me. I'm a fucking disease. A pedophile. Maybe I should turn the knife on myself.

"You tensed."

"So?"

"That's a withdrawal of consent," he says. "Just because you didn't say no doesn't mean you want it."

My heart twists as I stare at him. With his one eye, he sees so much. But he still can't see me. And I can't do this to him. Can't be the reason he hates himself after sleeping with me. Caring for me. He has his own trauma and grief to deal with, but he's focusing just on me when I'm not even worth it.

So I blurt out what I did with Bear. What I only did to score. Not survive. Not to get closer to Antonio so I could kill him. No. I did it just to get high.

He stares at me, but I can't look at him, hating myself and all the things I did. I know he's going to leave me now. He's going to shove me off him.

Instead, he grabs the knife from me, then pulls me into his arms.

"What are you doing?" I rasp. "I'm a monster."

"You're not a monster."

"What I did –"

"Was a weakness and a mistake. But those don't define us, Micha. You have regret over it and guilt – a monster doesn't have that. You killed him. You did what you had to to survive without actually hurting anyone. And you traded your life for a little girl. You walked into hel. You comforted the man –" His voice cracks as he thinks of his brother. "You comforted Rudy even though he traded you for her, telling him he did the right thing. The only monster you are is *mine.*"

He hauls me to his lips, bruising my mouth with the feverishness of his desire. I open for him, needing the poor man's V.

No.

Needing him.

Needing his acceptance of me. Of all my jagged pieces. Of all my worst edges.

I just need *him.*

I tug at his shirt, wanting to feel closer to him. Wanting

him inside me. Wanting us to be together like we haven't been since I was taken.

But he grabs my wrists, stopping me.

"Slow down," he says, breathing hard.

I want to tell him no. I need him inside me *now*. But I look into his eye and see his pain. His trauma. It's not just me who needs help. In my own grief, I need to make sure he's taken care of too.

"Bite me," I say.

"What?" It's a rasp, a croak of disbelief.

I crane my neck to the side. "I want to feel you in me. So we'll go slow, but I need you to bite me. Please."

I thread my fingers around the back of his head, but I don't pull him closer. I want him to choose. I want him to know he has the power to say no, unlike when he was on Antonio's boat. "Unless you don't want –"

He leans forward and presses his lips to my throat. My grip tightens in his hair. I breathe out a sigh as I tingle with anticipation. A vampire's bite releases a surge of dopamine, but all I want is him. This connection. Not a poor man's version of V. Because what's happening between us could never be replicated by those potions.

But he doesn't bite me.

Instead, he moves me off his lap. I smother my fleeting stab of disappointment. This is his choice. I will wait until he's –

My eyes widen as he lays me on the ground. He tugs off my pants, then nestles his face between my thighs. He rubs his fangs across my thigh, and I jerk beneath him.

"Is this okay?" he asks.

I tense, Bear's "good guy" behavior filling my skull.

Varius looks up at me, and I look down at him, and I tell myself I am safe. Varius isn't a good guy. He killed so many people to get me back. But I am safe with him. He will not hurt me. He will stop when I tell him to stop. When I just freeze in uncertainty.

Looking him in the eye, making sure I don't break his gaze, I nod.

But fuck, he makes it hard to hold eye contact when all I want to do is throw my head back to the sky and moan. He moves my underwear to the side, knowing I don't like to be naked these days, then spreads my pussy lips apart with his fingers.

"So beautiful," Varius murmurs, his eyes on my flushed cheeks. "So wonderfully mine."

His flashes his fangs, and I arch up a little, desperate to feel his bite. He leans down and licks me, keeping his gaze on mine. I cry out. Close my eyes for just a moment before I manage to wrench them back open.

"Good girl," he murmurs a second before he bites me.

Clenching my fists, I struggle to keep myself propped up on my elbows. He feeds from my pussy as his tongue laps at me. Dopamine and desire rush through me. My body tingles with electricity. My stomach flutters. My lips part on heavy pants. I lift my hips up as my heart sings for him.

"Fuck. *Varius*," I moan.

He pushes his fingers into me. Twisting and curling and moving them in and out, he works to get me off. I buck my hips in rhythm to him. And the whole time, he holds my gaze.

Holds my heart and soul within its depths.

"I love you," I say as I look at him through hooded eyes.

He growls back, his lips still locked on me as he feeds, but I hear the words nonetheless.

"I see you, and I still love you."

Despite being down there for ages, he doesn't manage to make me orgasm, and now my chest is growing tight again.

Because I haven't managed to do it either – not since we got back from the super yacht. All the normal tricks I used to use to chase an O don't work any more. It's like my body has fully betrayed me, and I feel so godsdamn *broken*.

"Hey," he says softly as he crawls up my body to kiss me on the lips. "What's wrong?"

"I *can't...*" I flutter a hand at my pussy. "It's not working."

"You didn't enjoy it?"

"No, I did. I just can't... *finish*." I push out the word in utter embarrassment and self-loathing, but there's no fear of rejection from him anymore. He saw the worst part of me, and he scooped me up in his arms.

He kisses me this time. "Sex is about coming –"

"I *know*," I say, feeling like utter shit. Like I'm not even a woman any more. "And it's not –"

"Let me finish. Sex is about coming, but making love is about so much more than that. I'm not doing this just to get to the end, Micha. It's the journey I want. The relearning of your body." His hand feathers down my side and squeezes my hip. "You went through something traumatic, and the body remembers. Now I just have to listen to it." He pauses as he kisses me again. "Just like I have to relearn mine."

My eyes widen. "Can you still get hard?"

"Yes, but it's harder to maintain."

My heart aches for him. Aches for us. But all he does is smile. "But we have a lifetime together to figure it out, and I will be with you every step of the way."

"I love you," I murmur as I lean up to kiss him as all my love for him rolls down my cheeks, my eyes unable to contain the sheer burst of joy inside me.

"I love you too."

"You're better than the V," I blurt out, worried he's still worried about being used. But I mean it. I might not have crested the edge and dived into oblivion, but he's given me something the V never could.

He's given me peace.
He's given me the strength to continue on.
Cupping my face in his hands, he kisses me slowly.
Exploratory.
Taking his time to enjoy the journey.
And I don't feel so broken anymore.
Because he makes me feel whole.

It takes months more before I can fall asleep with him. I was ready to try it that day he fed from me, but he's been too scared of hurting me. For the past two weeks, though, I got to wake up wrapped in his arms.

I stare into the dark of the room, waiting for the warm stretch of dawn, my thoughts running around my skull, only to keep coming back to one topic. Eventually, I turn around to look at him. He's already awake and staring at me.

I wet my lips, then whisper, "Tell me about our son."

His eye widens, but then he smiles. "He's a fighter. A bit underweight still, but neither Mother or Louise is worried about it. He laughs with his full chest." Then Varius frowns, pretending to be upset. "He cries with it too. And he makes the *stinkiest* diapers."

I look at him humorously.

"And I swear he holds in all his pee just to piss on you whenever you try to change him."

I laugh, and his smiles back.

"He's going to be a great sharpshooter," he says.

"How can you possibly tell?"

"He's got great aim," he says with pride, and I snort, then shake my head.

My smile falls a bit as I think about the questions I really want to ask. Working my throat, I look away. He doesn't push me. Just waits patiently. Then I breathe out and grab hold of my courage. "Have you named him?" I ask softly.

He grabs my hand beneath the covers and gives it a little squeeze. "I call him Nubian because I needed to call him something," he rambles, "but if you don't –"

"What does it mean?" I can feel the bittersweet emotions down our re-established bond. I know it means something special.

Something as painful as it is happy.

He stares at me, his eye so full of grief. Then he blinks and clears his throat. "It's a type of goat," he says, and my face twists with both a laugh and a cry of pain.

"You named our kid after a goat?" I ask as my chest hurts so godsdamn much over all we've lost.

"You can pick –"

"I love it," I whisper. Dayne would've loved it too. "It fits the animal theme." *Bambi. Rafiki.*

He pulls me into a hug, and I cling to him, needing the comfort of his arms. I don't want to move on from her. To make a family that doesn't have her in it.

But just because she's gone doesn't mean she's out of our lives. I will always carry her with me. As will Varius. In our tattoos and in our hearts. And in the love I give to Nubian. A little fragment of her soul because I know she would've loved him too.

I press my face against Varius' chest, and I breathe in deep, trying to ground myself in his presence. My throat fills with the urge to ask for V. My body itches with the need to drive to one of our warehouses and convince them to give me a bottle.

But I clench my teeth, and I let myself feel the pain.

The utter agony ripping my soul to pieces.

The V can't stop this. Nothing can stop it.

But time might be able to heal it if I can keep pushing through the days.

"I'm here," Varius murmurs against my hair. I tighten my

arms around him as I shudder against his chest.

He holds me until I'm ready to let go.

Drawing in a shaky breath, I pull back and say, "I want to see our son."

645

SEVENTY-NINE

HER

My heart is in my throat, beating like a hummingbird's wings. My palms are sweaty. Nausea sits hard in my belly. He isn't going to know who I am – that's a given.

But what if he cries when I hold him?

What if he turns away from me?

Worse, what if he somehow knows who I am and hates me for abandoning him? For cutting him out of me and then refusing to be his mother?

My body trembles. My feet grind to a halt, unable to take another step. Varius stops beside me, and he turns to me with a watchful eye.

"Do you want to see him tomorrow?" he asks, as he's asked me multiple times before.

But I don't want to say yes this time, like I have for the last week.

I mean, I do, but I don't. I can't. I am his mother. I want to be his mother. I don't want to run from him anymore.

But I also don't want to take another step.

I've failed him so much already.

What if I fail him as badly as I did our little girl?

I shake my head. *I can do this.*

I take another step.

And another.

And another.

Until I'm frozen outside the nursery door.

Turning on my heels, I flee.

It's been two weeks of constant attempts. Of therapy and unwavering love and patience from my husband. I'm utterly exhausted though. My heart's been beating too fast, and my thoughts have been racing even faster. I can't stop thinking I'm betraying Bambi for loving another child. And I can't stop hating myself for being a shitty, fucking mother to the child I do have. But then I hate Varius for being capable of doing what I am not. How can he love Nubian like Bambi never was? And then I hate myself even more because I know that isn't fair. Varius feels her loss just like I do. He's just coping differently; there is no right way to grieve.

Every minute, I struggle over this.

And every minute, I fight the urge to find some V.

To stop the torment raging inside of me.

It'll help.

Just one little bottle to cope.

My body trembles from the aching of the need.

I want the pain to stop.

So get it over with. Just go see him.

My throat tightens. I look at the door to his room. Varius is standing beside me, as he has been for the last two weeks, waiting patiently. Never rushing. Never showing any signs of annoyance.

"Do you want to come back tomorrow?" he murmurs.

I shake my head.

Inhale deep.

Then I reach for the door and twist it open.

My breath lies frozen in my lungs as I force my legs to move on autopilot. I walk over to the crib he's lying in. Sau stands from her chair, looking pale and hollow-cheeked. She saved our son at the risk of her own life.

"I didn't know you didn't know," she says. "I thought you knew you were pregnant. I thought Antonio would've told you. If I had –"

"It's okay," I say.

"It's not."

She gathers me in her arms, and I take the moment to hug her back. To give myself a top up of strength before I walk those few feet to see my son.

The son I tried to kill.

"I've been where you are," Sau whispers in my ear. "He will know his mother."

I tremble in her arms. Squeeze her tight, and she returns it. Then she pushes me back, holding me at arm's length. She leads me to the crib, then gives a little smile – one of encouragement. Of understanding.

Taking a deep breathe, I look down, preparing myself to hear him cry as he looks at me. A rejection that I'd deserve.

But instead, his soft brown eyes widen.

And then my little boy smiles.

EIGHTY

HER

I hold Nubian in my arms as he feeds from me for the first time. Sau is here to guide me, her skin pale, her hands trembling with constant shakes.

I see his life, and I feel Bambi's death. I experience his life goals, and I miss hers. The pain of her absence is still strong, and in the ghost of the night, I wonder if I can go into the Underworld and bring her back.

A fruitless hope.

I know this, but it doesn't stop me from imagining it.

Of bringing her home so I can raise her with our son.

But I need to focus on the present, not the past, not the missing parts of the future.

Just the present. The here and now.

Because Nubian needs me.

And so does Varius.

Besides, Dayne would kick my ass if I let his sacrifice be for nothing.

So I will be the blooming flower, like the ones Leno left behind.

I will be the cracked vase that's given a chance to be something new. An upscale project. A fix from some hippy recyclist.

And I'll be the strength Rudy believed I was when he traded me for that little girl.

I will be strong enough for Nubian.

My little daydream goat.

But I will never forget Bambi's loss. Never move on from that pain. I'll only grow accustomed to it.

And I know the craving for V will never stop. It'll claw at me in my weaker moments. It'll buckle my knees when I need to stand. Hit me while I'm down. Tempt me with its thorn-filled promise.

But I'll fight it every day for the little bundle in my arms.

I'll fight it for Varius.

And I'll fight it for me.

My name is Micha Shadow.

And I am a fucking survivor.

EPILOGUE

HIM

Three days later, I stand at the head of the table in the Shadow kitchen, having called a meeting with my twelve capos. They are all already seated, six on each side, with Khalid sitting at the other end. His girl sits in his lap, looking nervous, but then her eyes widen, and her cheeks flush. Khalid smirks as he holds a soul doll of her in his only hand, controlling it, no doubt, in ways I don't want to imagine.

I move my focus to my capos, looking them all in the eye even while knowing a few will be dead by the end of this meeting. Shawn Allen and Pitt VanBrackle most definitely. They're sexist assholes I have turned a blind eye to all this time because they got things done. But that changes today. I have been crippling this Family, our *traditions* have been crippling us, and we haven't even noticed. All this time, we could've been so much better, stronger, and more efficient with one simple change. By letting our women walk beside us instead of behind us.

I look at my wife, who stands beside me now. In front of me, even, inside my soul. She says I walked into hel for her, but wherever she is could never be hel.

And I want that for my brothers. For my Family. For our son.

So I look back at my capos and say, "For too long, we have called women 'weak.' But my wife is not weak. Nor is she a weakness. She went through months of torture, and she fought the entire time when all of you would've broken. I barely held it together in the four months I was out here without her. And when I was taken and tortured for two months, the *only* reason I did not break was because of her. Because *she* made me strong. *She* held my weaknesses, and she changed them into something more."

She looks at me, and I can feel her pain and grief through our blood bond. But though she might have attacked me and said things that struck deep enough to scar, she was still the light I clung to, the only thing that beat back the darkness. Just her presence, the need to fight and be better for *her* is what allowed me to survive all that torture.

I reach over and grab her hand, letting them all see my "weakness". My strength. If they think they can grab her to get to me, she will kick their ass. And I push through all my love to her through the bond, let her see that I mean every word I say.

She swallows, her eyes shining back with love.

"Effective today," I say as I address my men once more, "the women in this Family will be treated as equals. There will be no more breedmares to choose from. Daughters will not be taught to serve their future husbands. They will be allowed to fight alongside us and to hold rank." I look back at my wife. "And they will be allowed to lead."

I pull on my shadows right in front of her. A chair rises from them. With a smile curving her lips, she takes a seat at the head of the table. Beside me.

When she tried to lock me in the bathroom while she fought my uncle alone, he nearly killed her. When I tried to leave her at the house so I could hunt Antonio alone, he nearly killed her. So from now on, we will meet everything side by fucking side.

Together.

Stronger.

Better.

I look around at my capos. Their faces become a mixture of barely concealed outrage, confusion, wariness, and blank slates. I know this decision is going to be hard for them to accept overnight. I know women will be targeted more and treated more harshly in the shadows. But with every night comes a dawn, and if I have to drag this Family into the twenty-first century by tying strings to their fucking cocks and dragging them behind a car, then I will.

Because I have a wife who matters and who is stronger than anyone here.

And I have a son who deserves a partner to help him bear the hardships of life. Not a servant or a breeder or a second class citizen. A fucking partner.

One he can lean on for support. One who gives him council and takes care of things when he cannot. One who helps him with his struggles. One who stands beside him, against any enemy together. One who strengthens him with her mere presence. One who enhances his happiness. A true friend. A partner. Not just an interchangeable woman who spreads her legs and cleans the house.

That is the future I want for my son; that is the future his mother and I will give him.

"If anyone objects to this, speak now," I say.

For a moment, there is silence. Then Shawn Allen and Pitt VanBrackle look at each other, giving each other the courage they need because, in truth, they're nothing but cowards who like to pick on the "weak", on the women who were made weak only because we ignored them as people, not because they themselves were, and they start to speak together.

I do not care to listen to whatever shit comes out of their mouths. And neither, it seems, does the reaper because their chairs jerk back from the table. They try to stand and pull on their power, but Enoch shoves a flurry of knives into each of them, pinning them to the wall. They gasp as they hang there. Left alive just long enough to watch us eat.

"Not bad," Khalid says.

"Wait. Was that an actual compliment?" Enoch gasps as he turns to him. "I need to write this in my diary."

The remaining men look around the table nervously, not yet having adjusted to having a joking, sarcastic reaper and a serious Underboss who often carries around a kitten in order to "be more approachable." He even named the orange furball, which is a fucking menace, Relaxing. So he could say, "This is relaxing." Aleric's increasing presence in this house clearly needs to be stopped.

A job for another day. Today, is about my wife and all the women in this Family.

"Anyone else?" I ask in the thick silence.

Heads shake, saying no.

"Good." I take my seat beside my wife. "Then let's –"

I jerk my head towards the exit as one of the guards from outside crashes through the room. We all surge to our feet and start calling on our powers. Most of my men, no doubt, are expecting the Blood Fangs to have attacked or for the SCU to be finally moving in. Micha tenses, a part of her still terrified Antonio is alive.

But my face blanches as I recognize the heartbeat of the man walking casually across the living room. As he enters the kitchen, a collective gasp sounds from all.

Looking into his familiar green eyes, I murmur his name.

"Father?"

AUTHOR'S NOTE

Hello everyone!

If you've made it to the end of *Jagged Souls*, bloody hell, go make yourself a cup of tea and snuggle into bed to watch some cute penguin videos. Sorry, that was poor marketing.

Snuggle into bed and read *My Queen, My King* (the completed duet of *Death Do Us Part* and *For Better or For Worse)* for some mindless, gooey, 2-braincell read where the FMC is from a happiness-sex cult, and she brings home monsters as pets, much to the horror of her arranged husband. Lol.

But seriously, go take care of your mental health. You earned it.

Many cheers,
Miranda

PS: I talked to an actual therapist for the trauma-healing scenes to get her feedback on them, with the hope that they would help some of you. Obviously, reading isn't as good as actual therapy, but I hope it's helped at least a little. Just remember you are never to blame for what happens *to* you.

RESEARCH NOTES

There were a lot of dark holes I went down for this book. Baby farms. Forced breeding camps.

But what made me especially angry wasn't that these things simply happen in real life. The world sucks. I know that, and I know there is no depravity too low for a proportion of the human populace. But that proportion is supposed to be the minority. A few bad apples that don't paint humanity itself as a disease.

But then I learned that the prime 'hunting ground' for these camps are fucking refugee camps. And this *is* the majority of humanity's fault. Because the reason they are easy pickings –well-known fucking pickings in the area and by the governments and by the towns nearby– is because *we,* as a collective fucking whole, see them as *lesser.*

They are the people the traffickers take because they *know* they can target them, and no one will care. We have rounded them up and made them a fucking supermarket, then washed our hands of them because 'well, we didn't send them back to their war-torn country where they were raped and tortured and watched their homes burn, so they should be thankful to us'.

It is this lack of empathy that allows these camps to exist because they don't even fucking hide it. They just walk into refugee camps, take teenagers and kids away with promises of a better life, rape them until they get pregnant, take their babies to sell to adoption trafficking rings or sex rings, and then they *let them go.*

They let them fucking go because they know that even if they talk, no one will fucking care. Because they are a refugee. Because they are "lesser". And those kids, those godsdamn fucking *kids,* just go back to those camps or around it because they have nowhere else to go. No one to protect them.

And that is on us as a whole.

We might not be able to do something personally for refugees, but we can at least fight the fucking *hostility* that is shoved against them because "it's our fucking country". They are *human.*

They are fucking *human.*

When did that stop mattering?

So if you read this, and you hurt for Micha, please just share that compassion to real life people. And if you read this article and think you're okay because "it's not my country doing it" – what do you think happens when the US or the UK or one of the other countries with better resources to handle them refuse to because of the public backlash?

Nationality should not define compassion.

Thank you for coming to my rage talk.

https://www.aljazeera.com/features/2020/5/3/survivors-of-nigerias-baby-factories-share-their-stories

HONEY, DOES THIS TASTE LIKE POISON TO YOU?

He's a warmonger, remember?
That just meant he had extensive experience ravaging people.
Also a cannibal –
So he knows how to eat.
– who eats babies.
He could eat *this* babe.
There's something seriously wrong with you…
Uh, yeah – I wasn't currently getting my insides rearranged by my husband.

SPOT ANY ERRORS?

Please let me know by emailing me at:
authormirandagrant@gmail.com

WANT TO HELP ME HAVE TIME TO WRITE MORE?

Rec me in FB reader group or join my street team.

WANT TO SEE WHAT EXTRA GOODIES I HAVE IN SHOP?